# RIVERBOY

Published in 2025 by Ginninderra Press,
Melbourne, Australia
www.ginninderrapress.com.au



Typesetting and cover design by Luke Harris at Workingtype Books
Cover illustration by Pawel Lipnicki
Author photo by Letti Koutsouliotas-Ewing

ISBN: 978-1-76109-709-6 (paperback)
ISBN: 978-1-76109-710-2 (ebook)

# RIVERBOY

## Jim Ewing

# About the Author

An inveterate traveller, Jim Ewing has worked on and under oceans as a merchant seaman, fisherman and diver. A few too many other vocations include professional sportsman (Australian Rules football and boxing), journalist, psychiatric nurse, stockman, oil-rig worker, bulldozer operator, overseer (Papua New Guinea), actor, playwright, farmer...

He has had several plays produced for stage and radio, his short stories have appeared in diverse publications, and he has three published novels to his name.

When not on the wallaby in some far corner of Planet Earth, he lives in south-west Victoria.

*For two people who truly believed
in the boy they had created.*

"Written in an Australian vernacular of a past era, and perfectly titled *Riverboy*, this novelistic memoir of the 1950's and 60's flows vividly through the reader's consciousness. The omniscient narrator, with photographic skill and singing voice, presents the life of 'the boy' in a tone of tender and moving clarity. This is Jim Ewing at the top of his game."

**Carmel Bird, award-winning storyteller, essayist, editor and writing mentor.**

"Lissen cobber, rememba this,
the most important thing about
fishin' is that it ain't necessarily
about catchin' a fish."
**–Patrick Furphy-Murphy**

# Fore-ramble

Educator and wordsmith Norman Maclean wrote the wonderful, lyrical, moving, and sometimes funny *A River Runs Through It* – his only completed novel... or novella, as some would insist. Reading this decades ago, I considered whether one day I might pen something along similar (fishing) lines. His work is told from a first-person perspective. My story arrives via an observer with now only the vaguest resemblance t o the youthful character being described. Moreover, most of Australia's vast terrain stands in marked contrast to the mountainous environs of Maclean's Montana. Nor are most fish sought by Aussie anglers much like those he caught.

As in Norman Maclean's epoch however, my youthful years from 1950 onward featured small children roaming unchaperoned, allowed to make their own discoveries and mistakes: such freedom as kids seldom experience anymore. It was a time also though, when a primary school teacher could declare, 'You are *children*, not *kids*. Never use that awful word. *Kids* are baby goats!' – a pedantic chalkie, who would never, Sahara bound, hitch-hike along a dusty Algerian back-track, sit pack-on-back upon a boulder alongside a boy goatherd, and have a gambolling young animal leap up between them to butt their shoulders, insisting its ears be scratched.

But oh yes, like that lively little goat, us kids in that still Imperial Measurement System era lived largely carefree. Right into our teens, we were pretty much as innocent too... until that moment we weren't. And it is on the cusp of such a change that this narrative, appropriately, pretty much concludes.

An Australian coastal boy's story, more accurately, the boy's story in parts, the narrative which follows does indeed all but end a smidgen before his boyhood does. Most of the content is some way connected to a particular estuarine river system on the edge of a certain south-west Victorian town. The narrative never specifically identifies this place. Not that, for anyone familiar with the state of Victoria, the locality is difficult to guess. It is always however, just 'the town', whilst the central character himself, a child of post-World War Two Scottish and Irish born immigrants, remains 'the boy'.

When founded, this town's name most likely came from the Gunditjmara dialect describing the lands and aquatic systems surrounding it. The interpretation is disputed, but general acceptance is it more or less means 'Place of Many Waters'. Another, and most intriguing take however, comes via an early European settler. He claimed one Aboriginal elder assured him the local mob applied a different expression altogether to that specific district. This translated as 'Place of the Living Dead' because the location represented their idea of paradise: a far more interesting and imaginative notion.

And why not? Bordered by two rivers, this fertile area also supported creeks, a lake, swamp, magnificent beaches, shelter dunes, and a stretch of scalable sandstone cliff that gave access to kelpy reefs, with all of these water zones rich in such tucker as fish, eels, yabbies, duck, shellfish, crayfish and octopus. As for the well-vegetated habitat bordering all wetlands, this featured small edible animals and reptiles plus, attracted by both chewable greens and an opportunity for a fresh drink, wallabies, kangaroos and emus. In short, this was a setting of bounty and beauty. More idyllic spots to spend a childhood are difficult to find.

Yes, as winning environments go for growing a full healthy life, the planet throws few better dice. However, the account which follows slides in and out of this geography as it progresses from earliest consciousness until more or less terminating at that crucial point in the adolescence of most boys. But... recollection? When people review their lives, especially circa that teenage hormone tsunami, accuracy often suffers. Therefore, despite your chronicler here's years from birth to that turbid galloping testosterone period being *exactly* those of the boy depicted, an occasional slip in chronology is probably unavoidable. Otherwise though, the accuracy ought not to be much doubted.

Yet okay, memory is indeed a maze. Two people may experience the same event. Decades later one individual is hazy on detail, the other crystal clear about what transpired, only for evidence to then prove the less certain person has a far better grasp of that moment.

Another problem with a long delay to compiling past events is mortality. Most of those with whom situations, attitudes, actions, reactions, achievements, disappointments, and so forth, could have been cross-checked, tend to be deceased, to have breathed their last, or more starkly, carked. Not 'passed'. Never used, back in the day, that expression. Nor in fact, did anyone say 'back in the day'. A different time, a vastly different time. An era of uncomplicated technologies like the typewriter, a clumsy contraption from which might come the direct link to a laptop computer on which some Luddite compiles an account of one boy's early and almost strife-free life. It is why, too, this story may end up presented only in book form and not also through some dazzling visual development. Probably it belongs no more in an electronic medium than do the works of those writer greats this touchscreen world has left in its speed-of-light wake. But who knows...?

Alright though, that which follows here... Again, is its veracity absolute? As suggested, people recounting bygone emotions, revelations and situations, deceive themselves these recollections are truer than some plumbline hung in a vacuum. Infallible accuracy of accumulated memory is impossible. Simply then, what unfolds from here onward is steering a rowboat filled with childhood, a manoeuvring of it as near as possible to reliable mid-channel. However, anyone sculling with their back to a bow will find this can be a fraught task, in particular if navigating a river. This is far better achieved when overseen by a person positioned in the stern and looking forward, a keen watcher, now and again uttering words of caution...

# Riverboy

'**D**ad, you're kinda heading for the zone marker...?'
'Oh aye, yes, so Ah am. Good lad.' Scottish father's half-glance over shoulder, a harder heave on right oar to avoid large orange buoy, and soon, travelling upstream, they left the water-ski section. This new sport, how the old-time fishermen hated its Johnny-come-lately lairs! Their roaring V-8 powered speedboats, flash Brylcreem bodgies zigzagging across river in spiffy shiny wetsuits to disrupt the peace, producing fish-frightening put-'em-off-the-bite mayhem. Worse, for any anglers still of an age to also be interested in hooking up with single females, were so many good-looking bikinied sheilas getting seduced into riding those souped-up floating hot-rods.

Yet this Friday summer evening, unexpectedly the boy and his father had the river's salty seaward end to themselves. The father rowed with slow rhythmic strokes. Not that he rowed well. This the boy, although only nine years old, knew. Those days, on that river, speedboats aside there were few motorized craft. Most anglers owned classic clinker design boats propelled by oars. From infancy these men – few fishers then were not male – had been taught a blade ought to, Olympic sculler style, barely enter the surface: something not learnable in a Glasgow gutter.

Again, the boy observed his father dip far too deep. Not that their boat would have knifed through the water even had his dad won a rowing gold medal at the Melbourne Olympics. No object of beauty and sleek design that craft. Whereas a clinker's smooth Huon pine plank lines slid through a surface easy as a tailor's shears sliced fine terylene, their vessel was a three-ply hulled tub. Just the same, treasured.

A bargain-priced Christmas present from wife and mother, oh the glee when her two males collected gift-wrapped rowlocks from under last year's tinselled tree. What inelegant angles this craft had though. Backyard-built by a bricklayer, it sure showed. However, their first afloat boat, the affection would abide. And at this early stage of ownership, for both man and boy real pride attached to riding in it. In particular for the father, when at the same age as his son fatherless in a Glasgow slum, who never then could have dreamed of possessing even the crudest rowboat.

Gazing back at his boy and once more dipping oars too deep, the father smiled. The boy tried to reciprocate, in particular so as not to show how ashamed he felt of a tailor's cutter dad whose job lacked the muscular requirements of occupations done by the brave Anzac fathers of his schoolmates.

That broad Glaswegian accent didn't help. The boy, albeit Aussie born, bore traces in his own speech. As for his mother, Irish by birth but raised in a Glasgow shipbuilding suburb, hers carried an even stronger Scottish cadence than the father's. Weekly doses of Caledonian culture influenced how the boy expressed himself as well. The town's immigrant Scottish families took turns to host parties. These featured LP's by accordionist Jimmy Shand and his band, tenor Kenneth MacKellar, and nostalgic oldies such as Sir Harry Lauder. There were whiskey-fuelled haggis nights wi' neeps, Burns nights, people's birthdays and anniversaries... any reason for eightsome reels, Highland flings, and other wild knees-ups. How they sang too! Traditional songs of Scotland, full-throated and open-hearted, unlike Aussies who, despite their social extroversion, usually turned introvert at public singing.

The boy's detectable Scottish connection when speaking

though... this did at primary school lead to teasing. Smudging his writing due to being a mollydooker contributed too to ridicule. Therefore, thin-skinned and Celtic tempered, early on he'd got into a string of stoushes. This was accepted. In those days not long after the Second World War schoolyard conversation often involved exciting tales of fighting, albeit with guns not fists. Boys bragged about their dads' frontline soldiering. The boy's father also had seen active service, but mostly in an obscure place called Burma. Therefore, no dinkum Digger hero of the Kokoda Track was he, unlike apparently every one of those schoolmates' dads had been.

Then too, not only did this British Army veteran father show no interest in Anzac Day, far worse still for the boy was his refusal to discuss battlefield action. If speaking at all of his four years engaged in conflict, he talked only of the beauty of the lands and people from those far-flung jungle hills, never about any tally of dead Japanese. Worst of all, what had he returned from the war with? A collection of tropical butterflies: how unmanly!

That Caledonian heritage proved doubly detrimental too in regard to the dominant schoolyard sports of Aussie Rules football and cricket. Whereas other dads could demonstrate a stab-pass, boot a raking torpedo punt, grab a high mark, or else instruct on straight-drives, hook shots and neat leg-glances, or how to bowl late outswingers and googlies, at best the boy's father could manage a mongrel punt that shot up not quite to powerline height and came straight down. As for a cricket bat, he hardly knew which end to hold.

Indeed, an immature mind did find so many facets of this foreigner father to be detrimental – funny accent, non-participation in the famed New Guinea conflict, cluelessness as to Aussie sports. However, it was his dad's chosen career that the boy found most cringeworthy. Other male parents seemed to have he-man jobs that delivered dirty callused hands. They were carpenters, concreters, mechanics, brickies, welders, builders. Even farmer fathers drove ballsy tractors. Whereas his made clothes. Tailoring, what a sissy profession!

The river could get dangerous, fierce sou'-westers blasting between high exposed banks turning its surface scarily rough. This warm placid evening however was, as the rowing father remarked, 'One oot o' the box, eh,' and then employing another gem plucked from Aussie vernacular, 'Aye, it sure is a pearler!' A pair of splendid expressions destined to slip from the Australian lexicon... but true enough. In this moment any imperfections of nature were minimal. Only flaws in the dark green mirror surface which some nit-picker might have pointed to, were thin strands of floating shrimp-weed detached by feeding swans or else those roundels caused by salmon trout rising to take tiny baitfish. But this would about do it.

Dip... squeak... dip... squeak... raised oars re-entering water and rowlocks complaining of need to be greased. Otherwise only other audibles were water parted by bow's on-push softly rippling along boat's sides, stern's chuckling gurgle, and the father's measured breathing – in, out, in, out... coinciding with pull and returning push of oars. Yessiree, absence of other human activity, weather at its kindest, this did promise to be a pleasantest outing for hooking estuary perch. Fresh shrimp bait, rods rigged with bubble floats, and mother's cheese and Vegemite sandwiches along with hot Milo in a thermos... just the go!

For two individuals who inevitably carried superstition in their Celt blood, other favourable omens were the father ending his clothing factory workday without, as often happened, being compelled to do overtime, and that the boy had that afternoon kicked three goals to help his Blue House team win the school footy competition. At the very least therefore, this ensured positive moods dwelt in both boating anglers. Again, the father smiled at his son. This time the boy managed, via a raised thumb's okay, to display contentment rather than masked contempt.

Above water-ski zone their river's width, in the persisting Imperial measurements, was about a hundred and twenty yards, its middle depth thirty feet. Watercourse itself originated a hundred miles inland high in ancient sandstone of the Scottish-named Grampians mountains, the Great Dividing Range's tail. Fed by minor tributaries, the river then wound its way to the sea through squatter-cleared farmlands. Ironically the single patch of proper bushland it passed through was closer to the coast, a reserve occupied by the remnants of that locality's dispossessed Aboriginal group. Whole catchment area one of reliable rainfall, the flow had a healthy consistency, albeit formidable when in winter flood. As for boat travel upstream from its mouth, after five miles or so this came to an abrupt halt at a boulder barrier formed millennia before by volcanic activity.

Shallow reedbed off which father and son would anchor was now only another quarter mile ahead. There they'd cast inward searching for perch that fed along the reeds' fringe. Meanwhile, to moving boat's port side, towering cliff-like northern bank behind it, at the base of this stood at river's edge a square grey concrete pumphouse. Looking like a gun emplacement, from this structure up an almost vertical two hundred plus feet, ran grand metal pipes that conveyed brackish river water to cool turbines within an out-of-sight auxiliary power station. Alongside these pipes, and built into the rocky face, were narrow wooden steps. For a couple of years now, to fish for bream off the narrow stony strip at cliff bottom, the boy had sometimes descended these. There were three hundred and ninety steps. He always counted them.

Southern bankside to starboard was also high, but of sloping hillside covered in lush cattle pasture. Too soon dairy farming would yield to the rising tide of humanity settling in a once sleepy town. For now, however, semi-stagnation: fields going on growing grass to pass through cows as milk, urban housing growth sluggish, and the town's core citizenry continuing to cling to conservative attitudes – things that on a broader scale in Victoria itself would take many years to shift, leading even in the nineteen-eighties to a visiting English rockstar, himself pretty much washed-up, referring to Melbourne as 'a well-lit cemetery'.

Reasons this single river outing would stay with the boy all his life were several. To begin with that glass-smooth surface turned sunset-orange as their boat reached the vast reedbed. Then, with them gliding along parallel to reeds' edge and about thirty feet out from it, the boy's task was to, without a splash spooking every fish, ease a twenty-pound cylindrical lead anchor over stern and into the drink. Once done he let out ample rope while prow continued its forward momentum, and sotto voce, said, 'Right-o dad, it's over.'

Quietly enough, although of insufficient silence for his son's satisfaction, the father shipped oars inboard. After this, he deposited for'ard anchor over the bow. He too allowed a few yards of rope to run out prior to cleating this off. Thereafter, the boy's unhurried hauling-in of loose aft rope brought both lengths of hemp tight so each now entered the water at forty-five degrees: precise and perfect. 'Good job, lad,' remarked the father as the boy secured his rope to its cleat.

During his less than ten years on Earth, and river, many times the boy had done this. Less though with his father than in a clinker accompanying schoolmate Bill whose old man ran one of two riverside boat-hire businesses. As to the purpose of such exact anchoring, this prevented your craft swinging and thus causing lines to drag, baits to move. Even more importantly, epoch where anglers observed such etiquette as shutting off outboard motors to row past fellow fishers lest their scaly quarry be disturbed, sound anchoring technique indicated a boat's crew knew its stuff.

Hull gave a violent lurch – the father clumsily organising himself to sit facing inshore by placing one leg either side of his middle plank seat. The boy thought of Bill's nuggety boat-savvy sire. Balletic that small strong man's movements hardly were either, yet in any river craft he could shift from front to aft and hardly set off a ripple. Yeah, Bill's old man…? Reputation as the feistiest filthiest rover ever to have played Hampden League football. Below an oft-smashed hooter sat a toothless gob that could swallow a full lamington in one gulp: what a dad to have!

Quite a way in from where they'd anchored that high sheer bank fell away to level ground supporting a clump of mighty cypresses. The low soil these grew in spread outward to become five acres of mudflat, that part of it covered by water this shrimp-rich reedbed which stopped where the river deepened. Otherwise, to the angler pair both now facing the direction in which they'd cast, a grand expanse of open land north-eastward was gently undulant farm paddocks. Destined to one day support developments such as a vibrant university campus as well as a living graveyard of retirement homes, these too were on borrowed time.

As yet however, nothing impeded that splendid view right through to horizon over which suns and moons rose. *Whissssh… Plop!… Plop!…* close to reedbed's edge the two flicked-out bubble floaters landed well-spaced from one another. The father said, 'Aye, nice cast, son.'

'Better than yours,' thought the boy. Truthfully, for his bait had alighted right near the reeds cut-off where perch liked to patrol, whereas his dad's had fallen shorter than it ought to have. Easily corrected. Both of them using centrepin reels, if the father peeled another couple of yards of line from purring Bakelite Alvey and executed another cast… But he didn't bother.

And the rods used? Split-cane and whippy, tips hyper-sensitive to slightest touch from a fish. As yet few anglers on that river had fibreglass poles. The canes came from Vietnam. It would take a war to end that trade, and see synthetic rods – less maintenance and more durable anyway – replace them. Even towards the end of his life though, the boy would still declare, 'You can't beat the feel of playing a big 'un on a cane rod.' Especially if also equipped with a centrepin reel, one hand cupped under it to slow your fish's run.

Comfy the boat's seats were not, plain strong boards that stretched from one side of the narrow unlovely craft to its other. A small cushion placed under the bum lessened the achiness, but only by a catfish whisker. Adding to the boy's discomfort his seat almost abutted the transom, so he had to position himself sort of side-saddle, body a bit twisted, not an ideal angling posture. Still, the torso of a nine-year-old body is supple. As long as bites were being had therefore, all was bearable.

Light fading though, with this too were the boy's expectations. Ultra-calmness the problem, neither floater moving, no shift of suspended shrimp bait to entice a bite. Not that this bothered the father. His own childhood one of squalor and grime and industrial cacophony, never mind terrifying razor gangs, he murmured, 'Och, Ah almost cannae believe how beautiful this is!'

The boy thought, 'If we're not getting a bite it isn't.' As for *beautiful?* How many of his schoolmates' action-man dads would use such a woman's word? Not one!

Nevertheless, the father's beautiful now grew incrementally more so. The adjective even crept into the boy's mind. Impossible for it not to, no more than he could have prevented that full lunar rise. Inshore from their bow end, some sight alright! Early December, summer's start, therefore hardly a harvest moon. A 'blood moon' perhaps? Reddy-tangerine, ballooning clear of horizon... The dad appeared to be almost mesmerized by the spectacle. His son would not fully appreciate why, until in late retirement the father at long last opened up about copping a blast of shrapnel courtesy of a Japanese 'Betty' bomber, a slightly lessened but almost as bright phase of that heavenly satellite assisting its pilot in the dropping of his anti-personnel explosives.

Another hour, and still the waiting for a fish of any description to bite... in a protracted silence too, until finally, 'Ye know, lad,' said the father quietly, 'it's so wonderful we can sit here, neither of us feeling the need tae speak, jist enjoying one another's company. Aye, it's lovely, so lovely.'

'Lovely', another sissy word! The boy had also been thinking, but his thoughts were about how much he'd have preferred to be there alone. More so right now, seeing his father produce from his wicker tackle basket a Fosters oilcan. *Crack!* and *crack!* again, using a specially designed opener to punch two triangular holes in its top. Sounds louder than reports from a repeater rifle. How could such a fracturing of tranquillity, reckoned the boy, not frighten every fish for miles. Angrily he decided, 'We might as well just reel in and piss off!' Which is when the perch came on.

In many fish moonrise sometimes triggers a hunting hunger. Soon enough the father boated four fat perch. The boy had five, the last of real prize size. 'Bewdy, beat him!' he smiled to himself. Each perch had been brought aboard in simple fashion. No landing net needed for these teethless species, they were lifted via a thumb and forefinger pinching hold of open-mouthed bottom lip. To the father's suggestion they had enough tucker to keep a certain wife and mother happy, the boy agreed. Indeed, how his mum loved fresh perch, usually expertly grilled by herself. In the baits were reeled, then up came the anchors.

Pongy black mud washed off via back and forth swishing across water's top, onto boat's flooring the anchors got deposited. By now the moon rode high, its effect much diminished from initial rise over reedbed which had presented a gleaming golden pathway. For folk the world over that heavenly body beaming low across waters and wetlands sets in the memory bank a non-removable jewel. So too, this applied to the boy. As, slipping oars into rowlocks, his father prepared to take them home, that higher lunar angle had made the moon's pathway shorter and changed it from gold to silver, but even in this the boy was seeing pure platinum.

A sublime outing it had been, enhanced of course by catching fish. Slow rows home invite introspection. So nil words were spoken until the father had them almost halfway back to their Anglers Club jetty, when he said, 'Ah jist loved the calm way ye played that biggest perch.'

'Yeah,' thought the boy, his inner rhythm of contentment dropping a beat, 'it wasn't you who showed me how to though.'

Those veteran fishos… whiffy from tobacco and stale bait, they had taught him the basics: the way to let a large fish run, have its head, not attempt to skull-drag the creature, allow it to swim itself out until dead-beat. These grizzled roll-your-own smokers he encountered along the river's banks and jetties. Even more of them congregated on that wide wooden road bridge now coming into view as boat rounded last downstream bend.

Painted black and white, a standout under the moonlight and spanning watercourse, the bridge presented a last barrier before any craft reached river's mouth and open sea. It offered fine fishing as well, for grand bream fed on massed corals encrusting its pilings.

As for that vast ocean beyond the bridge…? The boy listened. 'It's making,' he said to himself. Tide on the rise, mounting swells and beach front dumpers were imposing a roar that all but drowned out the oars' dip and rowlocks' squeaks.

Boat left moored secure to Anglers Club jetty, homeward the fisher pair headed. Perch still needed to be scaled and gutted, but the father had to be up early for work. On by the town cemetery

– seldom a boneyard with such superb river outlooks – they drove. As they did so the boy considered how much he'd like to show that biggest perch to his sister. However, from family nest that bird, nine years his senior, had flown. Whereas the boy was nineteen-fifties born into a peaceful Australia, she'd been a wartime baby delivered amid the Blitz on Britain. Now training as a nurse in Melbourne, unguessable then that separations from this sister he loved dearly would only lengthen, and that decades later the loss of their parents would see him lose her too, completely. Funerals! How they send families large and small into states of flux. Or rather, no matter how equitable Last Wills and Testaments are, greed and dissatisfaction too often guarantee bitter outcomes.

A close to midnight homecoming, and his mother already asleep, the boy accepted his father had to get to bed. Come morning, to reduce debt on this first home of their own, he'd be off doing Saturday overtime in the town's renowned clothing factory. On the other hand, no school tomorrow, before hitting the sack the boy's chore was to clean their catch. Fishing's only catch: success means a necessary messy exercise follows, in this case scaling and gutting.

The boy, still in fishy dreamland, slept on as his father departed for the factory. Built on a disused garbage tip, its surrounds transformed into a marvellous expansive garden, another unique aspect of this business was every employee getting encouraged to own shares in it. Visionary founder, 'The Great Man', had been a World War One bugler who'd overcome shellshock but never a resultant speech impediment. In hiring a particular Scottish immigrant, he'd realized that someone who paid his way through a Glasgow night school to learn advanced cutting technique and garment design would be no ordinary rag trade practitioner. This fresh-off-a-former-troopship immigrant being also an ex-serviceman sealed the deal: 'I... buh-buh-buh believe yuh-yuh-yuh you are juh-juh-juh just the man I am lu-luh-luh looking for, uh-uh-uh Archie!'

Manager of the factory's Cutting Room department the father had become, and soon afterward, the father of an Aussie son. And so it was, with this birth, for him, and for that child's mother, and for an intermingled string of others, including that baby boy himself, a spread of memories commenced.

What is, and what is not, early memory? Through the boy's initial snatches of actual awareness would be interwoven Box Brownie photos and family anecdotes. He would not, certainly, remember being born around 8 a.m. on a rainy Friday the Thirteenth in the year 1950, or being brought home from the maternity ward by his Irish-Scots mother, nor her then thinness due to UK food rationing – she as yet to get fully nourished by abundant Aussie butter and beef and spuds.

Neither would the swaddled babe, following his short stay in the Marcus Saltau maternity wing of their damp sandstone-walled rural hospital, have a genuine imprint on his brain of an eight square yards corrugated iron shed. This was the 'Wee Hoose', a temporary rental inside which he found himself bedded down, bassinette a chipped quilted box bought from second-hand store 'Two-bob Roberts'. No hot water, non-insulated, only heating a small fumy freestanding kerosene contraption, and crapper an outdoor dunny, in years to come his Great Depression era Glasgow slum-raised mum and dad would scratch their heads in wonder at Aussies living with all mod cons whingeing about how tough they had it.

Their new arrival would have no inkling either that occupancy of this crummy tin structure on the town's eastern fringe also brought him within a couple of caber tosses of that river later to mean so much to him. Instead, it would be the next abode his family rented, a weatherboard away westward near the Showgrounds – indistinct in far background an extinct volcano – where a first true image imbedded itself in the boy's hippocampus.

'Mummy... mummy... big, big... chooks!' Now okay, the boy toddler did not remember saying this, it being recorded in family folklore. Those gargantuan animals however? These stayed saved on his cerebral hard-drive. At that two-year-old stage, sole encounters with earthbound fauna had been restricted to a white cat, a stray collie which had schmoozed itself a home, and some hens the mother purchased hoping for a steady supply of bumnuts for cake making. These incredible creatures though, were nothing like felines or canines, never mind resembling Rhode Island Reds, unless such feathered forms could be inflated to ten thousand times their size.

'Big chooks!' The circus arrived via its own special train. From railway station its accommodation caravans and those trailers bearing Big Top's canvas and other structural equipment, together with wheeled cages holding tigers and lions and monkeys and suchlike, travelled in a colourful procession to the mile distant Showgrounds... towed by, yes, elephants! And as they passed by a particular all-white weatherboard rental home, outside on its nature-strip one very small boy absorbed in playing with his toys had looked up to find himself confronted by flapping door-sized ears, a scary set of curved ivory, and multiple grey tons of huge-footed shambling saggy-bagginess. Even more mesmerizing, the lead tusker's waving trumpeting trunk: one bloody big chook alright!

Only weeks after, when that same little boy decides to go 'fishing', the journey to his special relationship with a river will begin. Except in this moment, when a second dinkum memory cements itself, the water lying before him is not a pristine stream but a green-mucky Botanical Gardens duckpond. A monocolour

Box Brownie photo shows it – stone arch footbridge and floating lilies – as something Monet might have painted. A polluted and pongy soakage though, and in that same scrapbook snap, standing by its edge is one oh-so snowy haired and clean white-shirted tot in black velvet shorts, fishing rod in his hand a spindly eucalyptus branch. Not that this perspective is what the boy will remember, his recollection the falling in, just after this shot was taken, and the dragging out covered in duck shitty sludge.

That white-painted weatherboard a block from the Showgrounds, rented family home for two more years, what else of that abode by a date-palms lined roadway would remain vivid for the boy? Definitely, as awareness grew, were first impressions of his parents, the compactness of his father, and the mother's slimness due to that war-related UK rationing, which gave the illusion she stood taller than her husband.

Other actual early images which stuck? That cherished river did not feature as yet, but in fact two rivers bordered the town. The lesser, alongside a westwards housing spread, flowed to the sea not all that far beyond the Showgrounds. Narrower and shorter than the splendid stream to the town's east, effluents from industries such as the Nestlé plant along with abattoir discharge polluted its lower reaches. Upstream however, it did run clean, and there in later years the boy would chase freshwater trout. Yet lack the other river's majesty it did. Never would it capture his heart.

That rented weatherboard though, what other capital in the boy's past incidents bank did it deposit? His first spanking ranked high! Administered by a reluctant father, after a jumping up and down on his mother's prized flowerbed, shouting, 'I'm standing on your gladdies, I'm standing on your gladdies!' Future psychologists might claim such a mild bum-smack guaranteed a child's traumatization for life. Strong suggestions could even arise the parents guilty of administering it risked imprisonment. Yet the boy, young as he was, knew he'd asked for the punishment, deserved what he got, and so copped it sweet. True, he bawled a bit and wouldn't forget, but nothing got hurt except his infant pride.

Other early mental memorabilia included that nasty old codger with a gammy leg. When the boy toddled into his front yard this narky neighbour threatened to beat him with a knobbly walking-stick. Not until fifty years later would realization come of how this fright had stuck tight, a flinching on some crowded city footpath after an elderly bloke with a crook knee gesticulated to friends via a raised cane: seeds long-dormant do sprout.

Playing with matches too, that was burned into the mind. Accompanying a same-age kid from across the street, dry grass abutting someone's wooden garage set alight. Such a thrill, fire brigade fronting up sirens blaring! Yet thereafter, chill fear, figuring what deep shit he must be in. Then such relief when older kids were suspected. After which, more fun, he and the other lad sneaking back to use their own wee circumcised hoses on the smouldering timbers. Even better, that kid's twin sister did her bit too. How strange though, she appeared to have lost her willy!

Long it would take until the boy fully appreciated the more intricate differences between females and males, raised as he was in an environment where modesty ruled. In that rented white weatherboard even its smallest resident was required to *tappity-tap* all doors before entering. As for further lasting imagery connected with that home...? The boy's by now at high school sister provided another. Boiling a large tin of peas on stove, without piercing its top she went off to her bedroom and tuned in to rock 'n roll on the radio. How Edgell-green that explosion turned their kitchen's cream ceiling!

Heat also featured in other incidents of early recall in this locality. Most homes had open fires. How frighteningly fascinating then, when their chimney caught alight – sparks, shooting flames, the shouts, the shrieks. An agile neighbour played in the town's Pipe Band. Just back from dress-rehearsal, in full Highland regalia he scaled a ladder to blanket chimney top and extinguish the blaze. A windy evening too. From then on, the boy knew what bagpipers wore under their kilts: Persil-white Y-fronts.

Then came that party at their closest neighbours. Beforehand the husband and the boy's father had ventured out onto washy reefs south of the town to 'drop-net' and get crayfish supper for the revellers. Returning soaked and bedraggled but with a hessian sack full of those crimson carapace-ed creatures – a.k.a. in future fish markets 'rock lobster' – these were deposited into a copper of boiling water, alive! Together with his pain in getting spattered by scalding droplets sent flying by wildly flapping crustaceans, the cruelty of this act seared itself into the boy's brain.

Next rental property relocation brought a move back to the town's east side. Of dark-red brick veneer, it perched lonely in a paddock atop a moderate sized hill, vehicular access an unmade and upward dirt track. This dwelling lay though, only a stone's throw from that main river and its bridge, and not a quarter mile over hummocks from pounding ocean's beach. By now the boy had turned four. Previous Christmas, Scottish rellies had sea-mailed his first fishing equipment – a cylindrical cork wound around with line, along with hooks and sinkers. The boy's father had then for himself invested in a cheap rod and reel, and together they started to frequent the river's bridge and jetties.

The family now proudly owned too, a beat-up black Vauxhall. Every so often therefore, father and son would motor over the bridge, up an ultra-long steep hill, and travel out to where a high riverside bank spilled down to a secluded rocky shore. Which of them named this spot 'The Place' would never be ascertained. But this it remained, as here the boy's line pinged straight, his cork rattlingly rotated, and he pulled in spiky flapping bream. That the father had less success soon established which angler of the two would tend to enjoy more luck.

Naturally enough, that Vauxhall's journeys weren't exclusive to fishing excursions. In time there'd even be interstate trips. To begin with however, on weekdays it conveyed the father to his clothing factory, and every Sunday the family to their Presbyterian church, following which the father, mother, sister and the boy did an up-highway run to the closest village and its bakery. Most folk with vehicles did this, to observe trays of baked loaves emerging from massive wood-fired brick kiln ovens – oh, delicious saliva-inducing aroma! Thereafter, along with drooling, soon came the chewing of crispy hot crust on the return journey, as well as in blackberry season, detours to a backcountry creek. Its sides thick with thorny green bushes, scratched arms ignored, billycans of fruit were collected for the mother's next day toil, boiling it all into jam and filling jars by the dozen. Result, an entire house redolent with tantalizing sugary fruitiness.

Yet fishing outings in that Vauxhall the boy best enjoyed... albeit not so much this particular one. Heavy rain had cut it short. Scottish father now had English vehicle fishtailing up mudded hill towards their home. Thrilling? Perhaps, but the boy wasn't too chuffed, still miffed about being compelled to cease his angling activity. Nevertheless, Vauxhall's bonnet veering one way and its boot the other, this rally driving caper began to improve his humour. Or anyway, it did until his father, jockeying steering wheel, glanced across and said, 'Ye know, son, Ah'm afraid Ah'll no be able tae take ye fishing much in the near-ish future.'

Small boys can seldom hide disappointment. Once he started school and grew less in awe of his dad, the boy's reaction to such a statement would likely have included anger too. Being only four however, all he said was, 'But why?'

'Och, we're saving for a few things, and for quite a while Ah'll need tae be working an awfi' lot o' overtime.'

Angry exactly the boy may not have been, but his personality dictated he now became peeved, and obviously.

'Ehhh, ye see though son…' continued the father in that canny way Glaswegians have of stretching a thought already decided upon. Aware of need to keep everything hunky-dory however, he then said swiftly, 'this means Ah'll make a deal wi' ye. If ye learn tae swim, ye'll be allowed tae go fishing all by yersel', okay?'

Huh…? Wow, fantastic! For the boy, in a huge sense here lay an open sesame to freedom, to independence. All it'd take was learning to dogpaddle.

Even so, mastering the dogpaddle or no, solo fishing would be, for the best part of a further year, put on the back-burner anyway. The father's 'saving for a few things' related firstly to the aspiration of owning a home. Included also though would be the covering of cost for an overseas trip allowing the mother to take their small son to visit as yet unmet rellies in the United Kingdom.

Water, water everywhere… lots more than in any river, nor for sure any of it drinkable. Bass Strait negotiated, next came the Great Australian Bight, Indian Ocean, Red Sea, Suez Canal, Mediterranean, Strait of Gibraltar, Atlantic Ocean, and finally the North Sea. Initially however, had come violent seasickness. Once *RMS* (Royal Mail Ship) *Strathmore*'s sedate drift outward from Port Melbourne's Station Pier parted all the coloured criss-crossed streamers, thereafter she had steamed on through The Heads to turn westward into that year's worst offshore winter storm.

An awful malaise is *mal de mer*. Most illnesses, there's a fair hiatus of relief following a chunder. Seasickness though – this dismal desperate wish to feed the fishes – the urgency to throw-up and its associated misery is relentless. Yet, unlike most of his fellow passengers, the boy would bear no recollection of being so badly affected. Blessed with sound sea-legs and a stomach to match, his discomfort had been brief. What sea travel did mark was the first time his mind truly opened. That voyage to Britain and back, together with its stacked events and encounters, would remain a colourful collage retrievable at will, segments such as…

*Ship's hull* separating from Princess Pier, the snapping of that red streamer held onto by a sister, then thirteen, clutching its other end, her face stricken. Scottish born and therefore known to her grandparents, and an additional fare unaffordable in any case, she'd nevertheless for the rest of her life harbour resentment about being left behind.

*Storm at sea*, and in Great Australian Bight, shared waterline cabin at night-time, floating log smashing-in their porthole, and the haring out into companionway soaked by cascading saltwater. But frightening, to a little kid? Humungous excitement!

*Smooth sailing* post-Port of Fremantle, no more brekkies accompanied by cacophony of breaking crockery together with would-be eaters turning green and fleeing topside to provide nutrition for the deep's denizens. As for meals themselves, these were served by a charming Goanese steward who, death-breath aside, possessed the warmest smile and offered consistent kindness toward a boisterous four-year-old. First human of another colour the boy had encountered, this cemented in him a fondness for, and comfort in, the company of people other than Celts and Caucasians.

*Porpoises*, performing in the ship's wake and side-wave, along with flying fish, were a fabulous introduction to sea creatures in the wild.

*Shipboard activities* included deck quoits, and also a fancy-dress ball. In this the boy, in partnership with a petite wee blonde from Adelaide called Linda whose singer brother would one day become an Aussie popstar, won first-prize as a sawn-off Turkish pasha and his pantalooned harem girl.

*Crossing the Equator* 'King Neptune' shaved people using ice-cream soap, and fit young blokes dopily belted seven shades of shite out of one another with pillows whilst astride a greasy pole roped across the liner's slopping-about swimming pool – that same watery space where, yet to master the dogpaddle and more like a drowning frog, in an opaque bubble-scape and going under for the third time, rescue would come via one in-prime recent greasy poler diving in and, taking hold of a tuft of snowy hair, dragging its small owner to safety.

*Ceylon's capital city Colombo,* and barely docked when, motherly lapse in vigilance, a king cobra got draped around boyish neck by a sneaky snake charmer. Instant crowd tossing snake-man coins, the boy's reward was his mum's horrified face. Yet following that shock came her hysterical laughter. Developed when dodging German bombs, she often had this odd response to extreme circumstances. Snakes and matriarchal mania aside, that same Ceylonese locality would instil in a now fast-filling young mind an appreciation of spicy cooking and its associated smells.

*Red Sea, and thermometer's rapidly rising mercury* brought an odour even more indelible, but of the stomach-turning sort. Cheapest below-deck accommodation meant sleeping adjacent to a hold loaded with sheepskins. Temperature topping the ton Fahrenheit... phew-spew! Companionway stink so extreme, the challenge grew to in-breathe deeply before leaving cabin and to hold this until sea air could be inhaled. Splendid training though for a future free-diver.

*Eruption of prickly heat followed by impetigo* produced a far greater challenge than reeking bales of woolly skin. Epidermal rash requiring lashings of calamine lotion had been bad enough, but the other exotic skin infection made things radically worse. Treatment by ship's doctor saw boyish backside punctured by daily penicillin injections, followed by excruciating tweezered removal of scores of scabs prior to antibiotic ointment application. A small kid, ever forget this torture? Never!

*Suez Canal*, a waterway through which, two decades later as a merchant seaman, the boy would find himself helming the last British tramp steamer, made for rich fascination – watching camel trains lope along its hot dusty embankments, every so often a rusting wartime wreck passed, and, at Port Said, peering through ship's white enamelled rust-bubbled rails while Arab bumboats afloat on the oily raw ships' sewage spoiled water way below plied their trade, goods raised up ship's side via roped baskets before their lowering holding passengers' payments.

*Gibraltar stopover* on Spain's doorstep, ashore area almost over-run by monkeys, after which came sailing on through the famous Strait out into the Atlantic Ocean, and then a swift-ish right-turn, 'to starboard' – as learned from the jovial sailors – towards the UK.

*Tilbury Docks* outside London... Crikey, such greyness, all overcast drizzly and chilly. Wasn't this supposed to be summertime? Marvellous though, the disembarking, small white deck shoes pounding down bouncing gangway to the clamour and excited shouts of porters, before being bundled into a black cab.

*Victoria Station*, about to depart north on the coal-fired *Flying Scotsman*, the boy attired to create a good first impression with his rellies, uncomfortably thick suit made insufferably worse by a prickling peaked cap plonked upon scone. Solution simple... 'Mum, it fell.' Dropped onto platform and kicked under the train's wheels. However, never a greater hate-stare than that directed at elderly doddery rail-porter when the kind man's long-handled crook retrieved detested cap, and the jabbing into scalp recommenced. The boy reckoned Jesus had it easy in comparison!

*Scotland, and Glasgow* at last. So often heard about, now here in all its sooty stone-walled slate-roof grey industrial revolution uniqueness, and the grandparents with their broth-thick gravel accents – another shamrock and thistle mix, grandmother Lizzie Irish, grandfather Jimmy Scots – both bewildered by this grandchild's broad Aussie chatter. A few evenings after arrival, following a Clydebank shipyards' Friday shift payday, grandfather weaving home along street accompanied by blootered old soldier pals, all bawling out *It's a Long Way to Tipperary*. Volunteering as a gunner in 1914 he'd survived the entire World War One carnage, fought alongside Aussies at Gallipoli and on the Western Front, got twice Mentioned in Dispatches for gallantry. If older, the boy would have worshipped 'Grandpa Jim'. However, smell of whisky and gin, along with grim visage, were intimidating – a man returned from the battlefields physically unscathed but not so psychologically. As for 'hame' during that Scottish stay, top floor of a classic four storey tenement, roof still blackened in patches from German incendiary bombs. At the foot of its stairs, playing with grandparents' gift of a gleaming red toy train, another boy, slightly older, asks a sweetly innocent, 'Can ye gi' me a wee look?' This done, away with it the young shit bolts, and a first lesson in hard Glasgow street-culture is learned.

*Irish Sea ferry crossing to Northern Ireland*, brief sojourn with another Eire/Caledonian partnering in Great Aunt Tish and Great Uncle Jock in their rural thatched cottage. Relayed tall tales Gaelic history absorbed, cross-your-heart stories about leprechauns all swallowed as absolute truth.

*Glasgow again*, for an October 1955 birthday introduction to a steaming mound of minced offal boiled in a sheep's stomach. Eaten with mashed neeps, how delicious this haggis! For dessert arrives a pink sugar-iced cake with five lit candles. Then, at month's end, comes the head saturating fun of Halloween, dunking for apples in a water-filled wooden tub, before November brings the wonder of seeing and feeling snow softly gather on the grandparents' upstairs windowsill. Soon after is the messy ordeal of farewell kisses and hugs and tears...

*Reverse journey*, same ship, same ports, similar sights, and familiar on-board activities... Only major change is that to the mother's luggage has been added a metal trunk. Among other retrieved belongings this contains a lethal weapon. Somewhat perplexing was the mother's wrath when, she and the boy visiting a cousin, a war souvenir of the father's had been used to hack wood into strips for kindling coal fire. 'Oh aye, see yon scary thingy ye'r mistreating there? *That* is going back tae Australia wi' me!' Uh-huh, Scottish in speech but a not-for-resisting Irish ire. Awed by this object, the boy, in particular its blade which, despite recent misuse, remains sharp enough for a man to shave with. Touching its edge conveyed also, no explanation necessary, the gently curving steel's murderous purpose. However, quite what to think about this mysterious 'samurai sword' the boy knew not.

Brought back to Australia by the boy were a strong sense of Celtic connection, fading impetigo scars, and an accent thicker than a clump of Scotch thistle. His tartan vowels amused adult Aussies but with him now starting school... small kids differ from wild animals only in their cruelty being deliberate: vulnerability perceived, they attack.

In fact, most primary school newcomers copped bullying. Exemptions were a few polio victims who got around on crutches or callipers. They were not just off-limits for intimidation but also intimidating examples of what might happen to someone rejecting the revolutionary Salk vaccine. Certainly, no citizen would have dared demonstrate against inoculation. Back then *antivaxcists* may have got beaten to a pulp by parents terrified of their kids succumbing to this deadly pandemic, its virus too transferrable through someone refusing an immunity needle.

Afflicted though not with polio, but instead by a Glaswegian burr when he spoke, the boy got mocked as 'Stew-pid Scotty'. In the schoolyard scraped skin and bruises ensued… until one blood-nose too many came home. That evening after tea, the man who worked as a sissy tailor produced two pairs of boxing gloves. Getting onto his knees the father demonstrated how to shape-up. Already attuned to classroom bragging about other dads' physical labours, and comparing these to his own father's scissoring profession, surprised indeed was the boy by the knowledge of pugilism displayed. Method orthodox, evasions demonstrated, punches – shoulder behind them for ultimate effect – shown rather than thrown: 'But always remember, son, yon straight left is aye ye'r best friend, along wi' his handy wee pal here, the right-cross… Boom! Okay? And really, that is all Ah need tae teach ye.'

As true as statements get. The odd rotten little sod would still pick a blue through detection of Scottish inflection, yet in schoolyards, once a targeted kid effectively defends himself, aggression lessens. Soon the boy felt much more comfortable in his own skin, albeit thin as it often was and would continue to be. Aiding his self-esteem, and actually far better for it than an ability to chuck a punch, unlike most of his classmates he could now swim.

In *RMS Strathmore*'s pool during her return journey the boy had learned proficient dogpaddling. As a consequence, and as his father had promised, out of school hours he was granted freedom to explore unaccompanied the river and its environs and to absorb the addictive atmospherics. He could also on his own exploit its main resource, fish. Never though, no matter how good the boy got at swimming, would he any time soon be permitted going solo to try that risky practice of whipping for salmon trout.

Summer and the evenings extended, after one workday the father came home to tell the boy that Brimmy and Hunty, '… two of oor Cutting Room lads', had invited them to watch this technique called 'whipping for salmon'. Done at the river's racing-out mouth, a dangerous but thrilling spectacle. While father and son perched atop a huge lump of sandstone known as The Pulpit Rock, below them, shoulder to shoulder in the natural formation's eponymous projection, this pair of young tailors pulled in one thrashing salmon trout after another while, just beneath them, a tearaway green torrent surged down channel and into the sea: one slip and maybe forever bye-bye. They used only flexible fifteen-foot canes with line of similar length tied to the ends. Feathered jigs were flicked downflow as far as they'd go, then drawn back against the current, bouncing along the surface… until, *whack*, a salmon hit.

But oh, shit-scary! Always adventurous, the boy, so inevitable when older he would have a crack at this technique. But by then, channel shallower, success would not follow. Never to be forgotten however, the simplicity of such fishing. What also registered with him, somewhat less alas, was the respect Brimmy and Hunty had for his father in insisting he take half their catch. Certain aspects of angling already the boy understood. Such deference for his dad though he couldn't yet process. Too many years it would be as well, before appropriate *satori* smacked into his consciousness.

That overseas trip though, positives as well as the odd negative resulted. Not just for the boy. Within the family's rented residence on its low hilltop existed unrest. An anxious desire by both parents to have their own home contributed. Another factor was that after rekindling so many old UK friendships, the mother had not settled satisfactorily back into rural Aussie life. She could be volatile, displaying what the passive, never obscene in speech father, would call her '...bloody Irish temper'. Other times she'd go silent. This could last a week. In a later age diagnosed as depression, in those days such phases were just 'mum's moods'.

Such a blessing then for river and bridge to be for the boy not a ten-minute strolled escape from the house, and that ability to swim allowing him to go his own way to avoid domestic unease. And then, of all the positives associated with that shipborne trip, best of all had been a welcome home present, his first proper fishing rod. A line now got cast over bridge railing instead of being dangled by hand under it. Yet in these outings to distance himself from household ructions always there'd be the return. And even if things weren't as edgy between his parents, one hormones-haywire sister of fourteen would have stoked some sort of volatile situation, she and the mother in particular often clashing.

As smart as she was sassy, the moment legality allowed, teenage daughter would depart for the Big City, seldom to return. Until then however, teen tears and tantrums prevailed. Yet perversely, an evening of rare family harmony became one of trauma for the boy. All his own doing. Small domestic group seated around dinner table, each member at peace with the other and preparing to partake of evening meal, the boy then, when served homemade vegetable soup, stubbornly refused to eat it.

Half an hour elapsed. Father and sister, soups, second courses, and desserts finished, departed table. Arms crossed and five-year-old's jaw set in determination, still the boy resisted lifting his spoon. At last, ever so casually in passing, the mother picked up the now cold bowl of vegie broth. The boy guessed, bewdy, he'd won! Smug eyes raised in triumph only saw however, the soup-bowl deposited upside-down upon his scone.

Well now, what do kids in their initial year of schooling learn first? Swear words, right? And then too, mixing with an earthy older fishing crew will also add salt to a childish vocabulary. The boy could blaspheme via some extreme expletives, and did, letting fly at his mother with every one of them.

An again reluctant father pinning him over his knee, small son copped his second ever spanking, this one far more deserved than when he'd stomped those gladdies. And yes-yes, future do-goodies would determine otherwise, but how efficiently a backside getting walloped justifiably wiped the slate clean. Decades later, grown boy and ageing mother by now living half a continent apart, would via phone have a falling-out over some trivial matter. Then, on his thirty-nineth birthday, in the post, a card. On its cover, a little kid sits with a bowl of food upended on his head, and inside, are the words, 'I may not always understand you, but I will always love you.'

Absolutely, from his very beginning, the boy had an affinity with, and love for, his mother. He did not feel anything like this towards his father, or even, despite a tremendous affection for her, his sister. Adding to mother-son bond were his ever-improving angling skills. If home from the bridge with fresh bream, should the mum be suffering one of her glums, a good catch could draw her out of it. On the other hand, able to supply splendid river tucker or not, if something caused that Irish temper to flare, beware! How capable she was, and with alarming accuracy, of throwing crockery. Yet then too, an hour later she might be displaying shamrock joy and charm in abundance: the Celtic dichotomy. G.K. Chesterton put it best – '*The great Gaels of Ireland are the men that God made mad, For all their wars are merry and all their songs are sad.*' The same went, and always will, for Ireland's women.

Travel often ameliorates the scourge of depression. Summer holidays after the boy turned six, family's too pre-loved Vauxhall packed to bursting laboured north-eastward towards a baking seven hundred miles distant Sydney. A cheap vacation to a never-before-seen city, a stay with recently arrived Scottish friends awaited. Free accommodation! The mother in good spirits, the father adopted a stoic heroic mindset: only he would drive, the entire way, never mind that recently his wife had passed her driving test. Meanwhile, for a young boy and his teen sister 'I spy with my little eye' will only go so far. Even a detour to The Dog on a Tuckerbox, plus other distractions such as fractured four-part harmonies singing *The Road to Gundagai*, relieved, only just, the trip's tedium. Then, at their Sydney endpoint, ignominy and embarrassment...

Harassed, weary father had motored into a sweltering city's centre. Yet find exit road to their friends' suburb he could not. Around and around a particular city block went jam-packed Vauxhall, to each time arrive at the same intersection. Of a wish to turn right, no such manoeuvre was permitted – and most definitely not by the beefiest sweatiest cop in New South Wales directing traffic because all lights were out of order. Again and again, came a shake of stolid law enforcer's head, large white-glove waving Vauxhall straight on... until their fourth approach.

Backseat, boy and sister dropped lower even than that very large copper's jaw. Turning haystack back and broad backside to all on-coming peak-hour traffic, hairy ham-hock forearms folded, the bloke in blue just stood and stared. Perspiration pouring down disbelieving face, this however now broke into a great grin. Both spiffy large white gloves held aloft stopped all vehicles. Next came an ostentatious pointing at intruder auto's number plate – just so every halted impatient overheated New South Wales driver comprehended its foreign origins. Vauxhall then received an almost obeisant white-gloved waving on into that illegal right turn, big cop leaning forward as flummoxed Scots driver in his overloaded British-made jalopy went by, to through the lowered front side window, say two words: 'Bloody Victorians!'

Sydney itself pretty much lived up to its residents' claims to be about the most fabulous metropolis on planet Earth. Sparkling harbour, the green and cream ferries, that famous Coat-hanger Bridge, superb beaches... and even Luna Park wasn't spoiled by the boy's chunder after a shitting-himself ride on ripper Big Dipper. Nevertheless, sightseeing and sideshow amusements aside, most of the two weeks' vacation took place in the suburban sticks with those Scottish 'New Australian' friends and their two young sons. Entire city gripped in a heatwave, out there, from shimmering sunrise to liquid red sunset, one objective prevailed: survive. In this, two things were of massive assistance, ice-cold drinks and the local Olympic sized swimming pool.

For the constantly reminiscing adults refrigerated beer and gin and tonics were the go, whilst their offspring chug-a-lugged from small classic all-glass bottles of chilled-down Coca-Cola. So hyped were the younger kids from overindulgence in hugely sugared and caffeinated beverage that the boy's sister tagged them 'Coca-Colics'. Yet even in excessive temperatures, overstimulated children also require exercise to ensure they will tire and sleep through airless oven-like nights.

A blessing then, were nearby Bankstown Baths. Now, those Scots lads couldn't yet swim, but the expert dog-paddler couldn't have been more confident. In heat to beat any sweltering smelter, upon arrival straight into main pool jumped the boy. Lane chosen a closed-off one used exclusively for serious training, seconds later he was swum into and over by a young dynamo named John who, along with his sister Ilsa, had recently attained fame during the 1956 Olympic Games as the *Konrads Kids*.

Spluttering, coughing, and comprehensively cruelled, the boy crawled out onto the pool's radiant concrete apron. Remainder of afternoon, while the four parents shared a sun-umbrella, he and the two small Scotties kept to the shallow end – until it turned too yellow as they burned too pink. His bikinied sister though, swam not a stroke. Covering herself in coconut oil, sizzling as she tanned, behind Lolita sunglasses she fielded the hungry looks of youths all demonstrating what inadequate concealment skimpy nylon Speedos gave to over-stimulated adolescent male bathers.

The joy of swimming daily in diluted urine does wear thin. Just before holiday's end the Vauxhall wended its way to Bondi Beach. Again, fools jump in... How rapidly one frantically dogpaddling boy found himself in trouble, swept outwards by a rip, while on the sand his picnicking parents and sister were oblivious to his plight. Strength waning fast, the boy began to accept that he'd either drown or be bitten in twain by a shark. Cue-in an alert Adonis lifesaver, to do what his title suggested. Preceded by a bow-wave, freestyling to the boy he surged, tossed one muscular arm around puny chest, and did an all the way towing-in to dry sand. Once there, and encircled by enthusiastic bikinied babes, the lifesaver began to grandstand, while his squirming rescuee resisted getting kissed-to-life by a bloke who hadn't shaved for five days!

Shaking free, and mortified not so much by his feeble failure at body-surfing as requiring to be rescued, without expressing even a simplest 'Thank-you,' like a wounded skunk the boy slunk away through that bevvy of bikini-clad beauties, determined to never return to Bondi, at least, not until he could swim properly. Many years it would take until he again saw that splendid beach, when during an end-of-season footy trip and staying at the Astra Hotel, he'd share those sands less with sensational babes and bronzed lifesavers than alongside neurotic young Yank riflemen on leave from serving as cannon fodder in Vietnam.

Sydney trip done and road dusted, the father returned to factory drudgery. The mother too, UK trip by ship still not fully paid for, had begun work as a cook. And where at? That riverside Old

Folks Home barely a stone's throw down from their elevated residence. For the boy though, his school holidays had another three weeks to run. Sometimes he'd fish off the bridge or swim in the river. Other times it would be a wandering over the hummocks for oceanside beachcombing. Yet mostly he'd be at home alone. Since Sydney his sister, now fully teen-focused on boys, invariably slipped away during the day, leaving her six-year-old brother to fend for himself. That this posed few problems pleased him. He discovered a facility for rustling up his own tucker, and also that solitude afforded freedom from any restrictions. Hardly could he have felt more content.

Their house's location sure contributed to that satisfaction the boy enjoyed. Yet soon enough the parents would realize their owning-own-home dream. Geez, how he wished though this property didn't have to be abandoned. It wasn't only the proximity of river and sea. Their back garden was the market type. Now that he'd sometimes cook his own nosh, how handy an access to fresh easily boiled vegies, but okay, okay, not Brussels sprouts.

Green fingers involved here in establishing this bountiful garden belonged not to the boy's parents however, but to their landlord. A shy, quiet but delightful former Yorkshire farmer, Tommy Robinson happily shared all broccoli, carrots, pumpkins, tomatoes, spuds, beets and onions that he produced. There were huge rhubarbs too, and what sweet juicy pies these made! Baked not by the boy of course, but his mother's speciality, who, in cooking at the Old Folks Home, continued to enhance a reputation for preparing quality cuisine.

But aaah, that future residential move...? Of other considerations and complications, in these sat one cat. A black stray, it had, as felines will, selected their family and schmoozed into everyone's affections. Definitely it would not want to shift either. A gifted hunter fine at dispatching mice, unfortunately the animal also relished prowling about those marram grassy sand-dunes close by the beach, its habit there to capture a snake and deposit it, not always dead, on the back door mat. Unsurprisingly, this had a most unsettling effect on a Scottish mother unused to anything remotely resembling a serpent.

Yet the home shift had to come. Two months into 1957's school year the father revealed a deal done. Substantial debt had been gone into to purchase land upon which, within a few months, a house would stand. News of their imminent relocation coincided as well with erasure of the black cat rehousing problem. One snake-taking adventure too many, it had not returned: even nine lives have their expiry date. This only added though to the boy's unhappiness about the imminent uprooting.

Nevertheless, almost inevitable debt-burdened fulfilling of the immigrant family's Great Australian Dream – to own that roof over their heads – was about to be realized. In the boy however this produced only dread, for as his father had not said where that purchased patch of dirt lay, he just assumed this to be in the town's newest housing estate far away to the north-west and miles from his wonderful world of sea and stream. But then... no. How marvellous to instead learn their future homesite sat only a half-mile off. And upon an even higher hill, this one freshly subdivided. Better still, where did its southern slope tilt down, down, down to? The boy's special river! How fast a child's emotion can swing from despair to rarest ecstasy.

Aside from new housing estates, that year the town continued to progress in other ways. Vauxhall ownership permitted not just interstate trips, and more distant fishing excursions. Car ownership also meant the recently constructed Drive-in Theatre could be attended. 'Ten bob Family Friday nights' were preferred, vehicles bursting with humanity admitted for only half a quid, and more kids emerging from their boots once the autos had drawn up alongside speaker-stand in front of towering outdoor screen. Older teenagers in hotter rods however, they parked right up the back. There, windows steaming-up during some B-movie or Cinemascope Biblical epic – films which one local wag termed 'chock-a-blockbusters' – FJ Holdens rocking from copulation became foundations for future population growth.

Not that at his tender age the boy had any inkling of such activities, but regardless of what desired entertainment motivated people to attend, very cold nights were crook for all drive-in goers. If vigorous interior actions of the young and randy guaranteed fogged-up windows and windscreens, similar conditions caused by atmospheric frigidity were not dandy for those who actually wished to view a movie. Nor were rainy nights much chop while wipers ineffectually slapped away at incessant raindrops. Yet, until TV set reception in that relatively new medium improved, outdoors cinema would continue to provide the most popular nocturnal visual pastime.

Drive-in evenings, work days, schooling, fishing... regardless of family or individual pursuits, and weatherwise whether rain and hail and gales shitty or splendid sunshine, construction of that new family abode progressed. Slower going than expected though. Their cash-in-hand builder only sawed, banged-in nails and laid bricks when parental pay-packets were opened and precious lettuce in the form of mint-green Aussie pound notes along with silver shillings connected with his callused palm. Not that such delays fazed the boy, totally content as he was to remain in rental digs so convenient to river and bridge.

Ahhh, that marvellous bridge! About two hundred yards long and around six yards in width, sealed roadway aside its construction was mostly of native hardwoods, smell that of tar and creosote and fish gut and blood... Once across it and continuing eastward up the district's longest steepest hill, beyond its crest by some miles stood towering sea-cliffs, their perpendicular faces monuments to the hundreds of lives lost when square-riggers crashed into the unscalable wave-smashed and sea-lashed bases. When older, the boy would hunt rabbits in the grand high sandy and scrubby dunes that stretched from river's mouth along the coastline to connect with those vertigo inducing clifftops. For now, however, the bridge was about as far as he ventured.

Father working constant overtime and unavailable to fish with, every chance the boy got he'd wet a line off this river-spanning structure. Yet for any angler small in stature the top railing's height of five feet presented a problem. He tended to cast over it and then position his rod through the lower railings. If a large bream took the bait there were always experienced older hands around to aid in again raising rod above top rail as well as assist getting the fish in.

Those same adult hands belonged to a mix of men – the vacationing, the skiving, the retired, the unemployed, the unemployable. All types frequented that bridge. Cold days many wore moth-eaten army greatcoats: veterans from both First and Second World Wars, some no doubt in degrees unhinged by what they'd seen and done. Warped, predatory personalities however, any of them? Paedophiles lurking behind every lamp-post near that bridge or under its shadowy ends? A later timid society would have difficulty believing that not one of those blokes ever laid a sexual finger on the boy.

What these rough diamonds did, laconically but patiently, was teach – how to tie-on hooks and which size to use for what species, and of baiting them. They demonstrated the art of accurate casting, and to which best patches along the bridge front. Basic skills in playing bigger fish were explained. Avoidance of being spiked by needle-sharp fins when handling catch too, as well as how to properly gut and scale, got demonstrated. In fact, for a still quite small child, so much angling lore had the boy stored away that when his father did begin again to occasionally join him in drowning a worm or two, the boy realized who had already become the superior fisher.

Angling is one art. Boat-building of an ocean-going craft another. Below hilltop rental property in the direction of the Old Folks Home and river, stood another house. Empty a long while but now occupied, activity was taking place in a large shed beside it. Curiosity might, along with snakes, kill cats, but seldom will it damage kids. The boy could resist no longer. Into that long shed he stuck his head, to see... magic unfolding! A crayfish boat was being crafted from keel upwards. Of full timber construction, hull planks painstakingly steamed into permanent curvature and then wooden cleated and glued in place one above the other: method traditional, a skill centuries' old. Newcomer family's patriarch a master carpenter, his two sons were acting as apprentices, the aim for with this boat the lads to become professional fishermen. The tragedy, in a way, would be that they succeeded.

Vessel finally launched and crayfishing licence obtained, those brothers would work together on the waves until disagreement meant one turned his back on the sea. The other however, in thrall to the ocean life, would skipper their boat until, in his mid-sixties, like a true pro saltwater fisho, he'd retire and take up amateur offshore angling, only for the local newspaper some months later to carry the story of his empty dingy, baited lines still out and several snapper on board, being located drifting a mile off the coast. All marine equipment neat and tidy, no sign of anything amiss except for one missing brother, the reporter called it '...another oceanic mystery, a minor *Marie Celeste*.'

Ah yes, digressions, perhaps unnecessary... Those brothers will however, still be fishing together when the boy, by then a qualified scuba diver of twenty with all the fearlessness fit masculinity bestows, reconnects with them. Asked to help salvage three deep-stuck craypots, the carrying out of this task from aboard that vessel he once watched getting constructed will bring about a first encounter with a great white shark, its close passes guaranteeing the arrival back on deck of a pale less composed individual in dripping black neoprene. And decades after this, that lost brother, 'taken by a great white' is to be one suggestion as to his disappearance.

How it all goes, the outspreading from childhood of one broad and flawed and variegated tapestry composed of others' lives and the warp and weft of life itself.


Across from this other dwelling and its long shed and emerging crayboat, opposite side of bitumen road leading to the bridge, spread that former great riverside estate with its palatial-like residence converted to serve the town's elderly. Already for a while now too, the tenacious mother's place of employment. Still paying off that trip-by-ship and also contributing financially to new family home's construction, for some years yet she'd continue there, preparing varied meals – for the demented, the toothless, the denture-ed, and others lucky enough to have both their own molars and functioning minds.

A sprawling facility, the Old Folks Home had roofs of tangerine tile and terracotta chimneys, whilst white limestone walls and spacious verandas gave it an almost British Raj inspired appearance. Surrounds were green lawns and floral gardens. Tall neatly trimmed windbreaker cypresses lined the driveways. Also, on its river frontage, stood a boatshed.

If fishing from bridge and looking upriver to the elderly's hideaway, what most fascinated the boy was that enclosed boatshed, and on its front jetty every day, an ancient man named Myers casting a line. In his nineties, an ex-professional fisherman dressed always in black coat and hat, on a mooring block he sat bent forward, known as 'The Shag on a Rock' to every river frequenter. A brilliant appellation, typically of-its-time Aussie, accurate and amusing in an era before Australians largely lost, or were compelled to forget, their inventive verbal ability. Yet, a spot-on analogy. Had a cormorant rested beside the old fellow it would have had that exact curvature, same edgy-expectant lean. Often seen to be cleaning fish too, Mr Myers. Thus, when the boy's mother asked what he might like to do when he grew up, the answer came, 'Retire and go fishing.' The mum suggested this seemed a very uninspired ambition, albeit she did allow there were worse ones.

Fishing was not the sole local recreational activity that might supplement a battler family's larder. The boy was old enough now, just, to participate in another. No shooting permitted on Sundays, one rare Saturday the father spared himself overtime toil, to suggest, 'Ah've got tae thinking, son, that it's time ye tried firing a gun tae bag ye'rself a bunny.'

The perfect era for a kid to shoot his first rabbit. Although myxomatosis had been introduced to become a cruel biological mutilator and obliterator of the 'underground mutton' population, and the Australian environment's saviour, some inland farming districts were still overrun with rabbits. Such voracious plagues meant cockies had no hesitation in allowing sensible shooters onto their lands. As the boy would learn, if not entirely appreciate, few marksmen came more conscientious or competent than his father.

Ten sunny miles were motored northward through farmlands before the Vauxhall halted, edge of a quiet backcountry gravel road. To begin with came weapon-handling wisdom: 'Never, son, must ye ever point a gun at anyone... Dinnae climb through a fence holding a loaded gun... Whoever carries the gun always walks in front, aye, ye understand?... This is ye'r safety-catch. It stays on until...' And so on.

Beside father and six-year-old son stood a fence with rusty

barbed wire running through upright rough-hewn wooden posts. Beyond this a low rise was covered in bracken and... rabbits, ninety-nine percent rabbits! They were chewing the almost indigestible vegetation down to its roots. One moving mass of twitching ears, wide eyes, hopping paws and seldom stopping jaws, along with their bobbing white tails and grey fur, an unforgettable sight right enough.

Gun placed on ground, boot planted upon second-to-bottom barbed strand, the father raised that next wire above. 'Careful noo, lad, through ye go.' The boy did as bid. Then the father, with an ease and expertise born of military training, vaulted the fence. For the shortest second this struck the boy as a very neat act for an ordinary tailor. Dwell on this though, he wouldn't, as he prepared to, for the first time, shoot. Not just discharging a firearm either, but to kill. Weapon a single-shot so-called 'pea-rifle', any fool who took the playfully named .22 lightly however, risked real injury – up to the severest one of all.

Bullet slipped into rifle's chamber and its cocking completed, the father flicked safety-catch in place before getting the boy settled on his belly behind a low boulder. Next, positioning polished wooden stock snug to his son's bony shoulder and positioning long steel barrel upon rock support, he instructed, 'Noo, see, ye must have the verra tip o' ye'r upright at the end there in the bottom of ye'r sight's Vee, alright? And then, when ye'r ready tae shoot the rabbit, ye slip yon safety off, breathe in, and then slowly breathe oot, and gently... gently mind, nae jerking... ye squeeze the trigger. Ye got that?'

The boy nodded and began to do as bid. Yet in releasing the safety-catch bewilderment arose. Beyond gunsight he perceived only a shifting block of bunnies, bunched-up certainly, but always on the move. How to get a bead on just one? The father guessed his dilemma. 'Dinnae try tae select an individual one, son. Jist fire. Ye're unlikely tae miss. Remember though, nae jerking that trigger. Jist a wee squeeeeeze.'

Squeezed... The rifle's report, short and startling, brought surprisingly small recoil. On the rabbit-infested hillside one animal lay kicking its legs prior to being smothered by shifting brothers and sisters. 'Verra good, son,' said the dad, now taking up the weapon himself. Loading and reloading in quick succession he loosed-off three rounds. That none of the rabbit trio hit moved the slightest bit after going down did settle in the boy's consciousness. What did not was that each animal had been deliberately, so accurately, head-shot.

Additional appreciation of his father's excellence as a marksman would however, come. Ejecting last spent cartridge, the dad gave his son the okay... 'Off ye go then, collect us oor Sunday dinner.' In scampering to the low rocky upslope, the boy saw rabbit hoard part before him like...? Yeah, almost how the Red Sea parted for Moses when their Sunday school attended that screening of The Ten Commandments. Something the boy wished to dwell on though? No, for how he hated being made to attend bible classes when instead he might have been given the freedom to go fishing... or shooting.

Such religious impositions were though, of zilch matter right now. Today he had become a hunter. As such, into that wee hillock's killing zone the boy ran and began to collect carcasses, his own gut-shot bunny first. In triumph he lifted its lifeless body to show his dad, before refocusing on the sun-warmed rabbits-surrounded ground. In so doing he perceived an odd movement in some surviving bracken. A shock too, for fixed upon him, and far too close, were two black-beady eyes.

The boy froze, although consciously so. He knew to stay still. However, not through advice from a father whose homeland harboured few reptiles, but via one bushie bridge angler, a retired timber cutter: 'Y'ever come across a Joe Blake, young feller, ya stop. Ya don't move, right? An' most times the bloody rotten thing'll just turn tracks an' back orf away from yer.'

Uh-huh, 'most times'… The boy's presence causing a temporary absence of bunny invaders may have been what drew this very large resident tiger snake from its fissure. Most concerning issue here was it showing no sign of retreat. Despite the boy continuing to heed that ex-timber cutter's counsel, his stillness did not come without a shouted, 'Dad, snake!'

Bullet shoved fast into gun the father hastened forward. No running though, a measured approach, stepping with care between rocks, and still ten yards away when the hissing spade-shaped scone rose high, higher, set to strike. Tiger snakes tend to be either passive or aggressive. This one was stroppy in the extreme. Instinctive aversion to humans, or simply irked through its territory's takeover by a billion bunnies? Both probably. Regardless, the boy remained rooted to the spot. Confronted by that swaying head full of deadly venom, his immobility now owed less to adherence of that former timber-cutter angler's counsel and more to sheer fear.

The father's movements too, were minimal. A slow and smooth raising of rifle to firing position, and he set himself. *Cracko!* Down went the tiger, all six tubular feet of it, writhing yes, but nevertheless lifeless, bullet gone straight through its tiny brain. A generation on, such venomous serpents would enjoy protected species status, and shooters risk a hefty fine for such an act. The nineteen-fifties saying went, 'The only good snake is a dead one,' nor was goodness ever going to be an attribute of this particular territorial tiger.

Danger over… 'Hey,' thought the boy, 'wait'll I tell the kids at school!' To all those who had Kokoda Track hero dads, he could now boast about his own father's cool shooting. Yeah, right, even if in that same war those schoolmates' fathers had fought in, his old man had instead soldiered in some place that, so far as his six-year-old's brain could ascertain, mattered stuff-all to Australia.

Indeed, and alas, not until very far into the boy's manhood would valid re-evaluation of this dad, hopeless at Aussie sports and who hadn't fought alongside those heroic Diggers he kept hearing about, take place.

But okay, fair go to the youngster too, for at this stage historical research lay way beyond his capabilities. Besides, he'd a father who refrained from revealing anything of battlefield ordeals. How could this small son know that in the face of banzai charges a British colonel had selected as his Bren operators the calmest of marksmen, blokes with the skill to drill with a single shot the oscillating head of a king tiger snake. Nor that such men would ensure the Fourteenth Army – the 'Forgotten Army' – won through in those merciless battles of India's Nagaland and Manipur and Burma's Arakan, and where during one relatively minor incident, when this time armed only with a rifle, a certain Scottish soldier would come into possession of a Japanese captain's 'samurai' sword.

Family's first ever home of their own did not reach completion until the boy had turned seven. In effect it belonged to their rapacious bank, but the parents proudly claimed it to be wholly theirs. Since displacements in Ireland and Scotland by the dastardly English, who further entrenched Celt poverty by slaughtering many landowners as well, no family forebears had possessed property. What a triumphant day then when, lifting her in a bearhug, and followed by the boy and his sister, the father bore his laughing wife through a fresh paint pongy new abode's front doorway. A marvellous moment, more so because such open displays of affection between the parents were rare.

Like many 1950's dwellings the flat roofing was of corrugated asbestos, its walls all cream brick. Located near the top of a high hill on town's eastern fringe, no other houses yet in the vicinity and therefore exposed, it stood out prominent as the nutsack on a Brahman bull. Access a steep tarmac road along its front, this continued on over hill's crest to end at the auxiliary power station fed by that riverside pumphouse. Uh-huh, and a Monty too the boy would soon be descending those cliffside steps to fish near their water's edge base.

The new home's outlook down to the north and nor'-east was of flattish farming pasture, while on a not far distant dead-flat expanse to the north-west, the district's horseracing venue, with its stables and grandstand and green track arrayed in daunting hurdles, had been established. Otherwise, away westward a half-mile beyond mile distant clothing factory, stood the town's business centre, a quadrangular cluster of banks, pubs, haberdashers, jewellers, hardware shops, grocery sellers, fruiterers, cafes, sports stores, ladies apparel purveyors, and so forth, little of it with much glitz, the older establishments tending to mustiness, with light layers of dust disturbed whenever a customer entered.

Unsurprisingly, none of this fundamentally dull hub stirred the boy's imagination. What did was his new home's southern vista, firstly its seascape. Basic primary school geography had revealed to him that beyond ocean's horizon spread nothing but heaving saltwater all the way to Antarctica. And then too, same direction, yet viewable from dwelling's rear windows, were the river estuary, its mouth, and some of the adjacent beach and dunes, as well as, closer yet and not a mile away, that terrific black and white bridge. All things nearer again in that direction however, such as boatsheds, were obscured by the broad hill's lip before this sloped away to the river.

Due south too, far end of their long narrow block and also out of sight from the new house, ran a deep railway cutting. Along this about three times per day muscled locomotives connecting to and from Melbourne. In the near future the boy would often cross these rails to, at the bottom of that downslope beyond them, get to the river's nearest boat-hire business with its large storage and repair shed, and several jetties. And sure, good fishing could be had from each jetty there, yet mateship would be the main draw to going there.

Within days of home occupation, and taking care not to crack that corrugated asbestos roof, the boy had discovered what climbing up onto it offered. Not only could he see the sheltered riverside corner supporting closest boat-hire, but also away to seaward south-west could be glimpsed the sturdy breakwater poking out into their local beach-edged bay. Not that admiring sights was the priority in that first week of residency. Interior organization and decoration took precedence, the parents insisting the boy and his sister get involved. This included steadying and shifting about a ladder while the mother dithered as to where on which wall, she ought to mount that samurai sword war trophy.

Once stuff had been stowed away and décor arrangement done though, weekends in particular then saw establishment of a garden, along with the laying of paving and a driveway. Again, to their grumbled disgruntlement, the boy and his sister found themselves allotted tasks. Nothing too testing, hers some food preparation in the kitchen, his a bit of weeding and digging and raking. For both however, simply annoying, one missing time with multiple boyfriends, the other wishing to fish.

One Saturday, asked to dig a hole, once done the boy could barely contain his short-pants scepticism and peevishness as within this he watched his mother plant an African silver tree. After all, she'd been advised the species would never grow in a salt-airy climate. 'Stupid,' the boy told himself, 'waste of time!' Who could have guessed that as a mature adult he'd cite this as an example of his mother's obstinate Celt determination, that silver tree not just surviving but thriving. By then he'd also be aware she had displayed a similar attitude after being bombed by the Luftwaffe, joining the workforce of a Glasgow armaments factory to do intricate adjustments on periscopes, gunsights and rangefinders, vowing, 'Aye well, if they bastards are going tae drop high-explosives on mah heid, Ah may as well gie them a damned good reason tae do so!'

In peacetime conflict-free Australia however, garden planning and plantings were a quiet activity. The same couldn't be said however, for the father's concreting. How aggravating the boy found that noisy churning petrol-powered cement mixer compared to angling's tranquillity! Meanwhile, shovelling and barrowing and pouring, section by finished section of driveway a perspiring father spread the grey porridge, smoothing surface as he went, constructing it from front fence to within the side-of-house garage. The boy's only contribution came from being prevailed upon to do a little preparatory raking of already levelled soil, but still, it irked him. Observing such tedious messy toil engaged him not at all. Although, okay, an odd satisfaction arose in him when, after a fortnight's hands-blistering yakka, his father's soft tailor's mitts developed manful labourer's calluses.

Far better compensation for disruption to angling activity was however, imminent. It arrived in the form of a tiny ginger kitten. Discovering this asleep on their front doormat one morning, the boy laid instant claim. Naming it 'Tiger Tim' after a comic book feline, as simply Timmy this cat would become the boy's closest companion, his first true love. As for owning a dog though, supposedly a man's and a child's best friend? For the boy canines were less engaging creatures than cats. During his lifetime, he would occasionally develop an affinity with a mutt, yet already he regarded most dogs as arse-kissers, never mind sniffers of that same region, and that if thrown a bone they were anybody's. On the other hand, a cat's *bugger you*-ness aligned more with the boy's own inclinations. Human friendship he was fine with, especially that of those veteran anglers, yet already he'd realized how comfortable he felt with his own company. And despite his youth, he somehow sensed too that if a person contentedly kept to themselves, it made for a considerable lessening of life's complications.

Despite geographical isolation in the town's underpopulated east, plus the boy's inclination to be something of a loner anyhow, school mateships were developing. Months rolling on into another summer and autumn and winter and then into a spring when he turned eight, one new mate was Thommo. Another lad into fishing, not only did they share a classroom desk, both barracked for Collingwood. That Thommo's hair was dark and the boy's blond, this Magpie black and whiteness made for an apparent ideal pairing, and at times they did after school wet a line together. However, Thommo enjoyed a closeness to his ex-Digger dad the boy could only wish he had with his own. Every opportunity Thommo got, he fished with his father, and exclusively using crab for bait, with much success. Once too often though. When again the boy found himself excluded from an angling excursion, this friendship fizzled.

Another schoolmate however, shaped as not only a more reliable river frequenting cobber, but a very convenient one. Bill, a skinny kid of tapered face who loved to laugh, belonged to the family that ran the boat-hire business closest to the boy's home – that one reached by hiking down the long slope beyond the railway cutting. And now, new house's garden established and concreting works all finished with, free once more to roam, the boy began spending every spare moment in the boat-hire's vicinity – to fish, to row, to just hang-out, with Bill.

Oh, and yesssss, to be near Bill's dad too, for what a full-on pocket-bull this macho ex-footballer father was! Round and harder than a king-size metal bin, that much knocked-about mush confirmed his reputation as the district's dirtiest footie rover ever, a nuggetty mongrel capable of KO'ing anyone. And how about that uncouth party trick of swallowing whole lamingtons in one gulp?! The boy, ever reluctant to help his own father with domestic jobs, jumped at any boat-hire related task when asked to assist. Sometimes he'd be sanding and painting an ageing clinker, at others bait-getting, braced in rowboat's bow and struggling to hold a large heavy circular hand-net dipped into shrimp-weed as Bill sculled them through a reedbed. Quickly the boy understood that Bill, rowing boats since he could walk, represented what people meant by calling someone wiry rather than skinny.

Other bait collection involved the dragging of a different net, one fifty yards in length. Bill's super-strong sawn-off sire did the actual hauling, but his son's own surprising strength in one so young sure helped. Edge of a salty lagoon, he and the boy acting as living anchors, they held onto the stationary end of stretched-out small-mesh net whilst that sturdy father clutched its runout outer section and waded in a ponderous semi-circle over sludgy submerged mudflat. Once he made his looping way back to the boys, they all then set-to hauling in before, from net's bulging middle, came the scooping into buckets of small fish called 'greyback', which Bill's cagey dad admitted, 'As bait they're next to bloody useless, but the dopey touros don't know that.'

No question, the man had a roguish streak, and such traits do get picked up by young boys... The river supported two boat-hire enterprises, of which Bill's people owned the poor cousin. Their craft were in ordinary condition, jetties they were moored to rickety, the multi-purpose weatherboard maintenance shed, albeit lengthy and spacious, unstable as well as shambolic within. The business's home, tucked in behind big shed so as to stay clear of major flood threats, was of stained white fibro cladding and rested on stilts. To describe this dwelling as of even passable appearance would have been to hugely gild one wilted lily. And then, to cap things off, how about their crapper! Along with a couple of scaly apple trees, the backyard hosted this classic dry dunny, of phone-box size, host to a redback or two. Phew, to be used as a last resort. By now the town had been mostly sewered. Some septic tank systems remained though, and yes, a few thunderbox dunnies, all serviced by one of the state's last nightmen.

In contrast that competing boat-hire establishment two hundred yards downstream represented full-on swank. Two-storied and regularly repainted in blacks and whites to match the bridge beyond, sturdy stone pillars supported its accommodation and office structure. All of its jetties and clinker boats immaculate, entire enterprise had a *palacio Venezia*-ness to it. A crusty old fellow of cranky disposition, Percy, ran the show. Afflicted by arthritis and the ravages of river-reflected sunshine, he always wore the pained expression of someone straining to produce a turd. Bill's dad, wicked missing-teethy grin fixed in his assault altered mush, invariably referred to Percy as 'Sir Fuckface.'

Predictably, the boys spoke of old Percy using that euphonious appellation bestowed by Bill's dad, which resulted in them too holding the old bloke in some contempt. Thus, one Saturday, strong westerly wind tearing upriver and sending bankside cypresses and native gumtrees and shrubbery madly tossing, they hatched a scheme to nobble Percy. Tomorrow's Sunday angling competition – the year's biggest – would require the hiring of many boats, and in relation to this Bill's rough and tumble sire had muttered his desire that the current mini-hurricane might '...blow all Sir Fuckface's spiffy bloody boats upriver and sink the bloody lot of 'em!' What then could two lively young lads feel but an irresistible urge to create mischievous mayhem?

It is a sparky adventure for any young kid just to climb out their bedroom window after dark. When on a gale-blasted night to embark on a sabotage mission, how much more this applied. Taking his father's torch from garage, the boy followed its beam to their block's end, crossed rail tracks, and hastened down pastured wind-assaulted hill to Bill's riverside place. As prearranged, the pair of junior saboteurs met in the large dilapidated shed. There, Bill selected a long sharp knife from a tool rack. 'Here ya are,' he said, and passed across this implement for severing mooring ropes.

'What're you going to use though?' asked the boy.

'Hacksaw, cos see...' A rusty one picked out, 'like, there's steel cable ties up some of them boats.'

'Not easier just to untie them all?'

'Prob'ly, but cuttin' 'em off's gunna be heaps more fun.'

A couple of river-rats, along dark blustery bankside they scuttled, and set a dozen boats adrift. Hard shoves, and assisted by that blustery wind, off they floated into the main stream: '*Hee-hee-hee-hee!*' After which two youngsters returned elated to that big maintenance shed to replace knife and hacksaw. Once inside though, deflation. Clad in pyjamas, dressing-gown, and Andy Capp hat, Bill's dad sat wrapping baits for that next day's angling comp. The lads' fright was great. Caught red-handed, no valid alibi, the young riverside vandals confessed their indiscretion to intimidating adult, this former on-field football enforcer. To which he exclaimed, 'Youz did frigging what?!'

Of feared corporal punishment however, came not even a hint. And also, how about such an esteemed adult shirking all responsibility of any link to their shady escapade...? 'Lissen youz two, yiz're gunna tell nobody about this, right?' Not a request. A dictate. Oh mate, those biceps like small medicine balls! Bill's father was not a man for any kid to ignore.

Yet nor, actually, was the boy's father, even if his not yet nine-year-old son didn't fancy conceding this. 'D'ye think Ah came doon the Clyde in a bloody wheelbarrow?' came his bristling reaction following local ABC radio's early morning bulletin about a clinker flotilla aground on the wide mudflat across river from Percy's boat-hire. This information all but coinciding with discovery of his torch lying under the boy's bedroom window confirmation enough, what made the father's ire even more menacing was he happened to be venting his spleen beneath that samurai sword.

Now, still no explanation had the boy been given in regard to that weapon's significance, however after some vacillation in regard to its effect on her overall décor, the mother had chosen to mount it right above their dining room lounge entrance door. Had the boy any knowledge of mythology he may have perceived it resembling the Sword of Damocles as, weak-kneed, he awaited his fate.

Standing before that scabbarded blade, feet planted on the floor like a prize-fighter, the father made for one quite scary sight too. Of the prank however, no more details did he pursue. Instead, the planned participation of the boy and himself in that day's grand angling competition got canned. The boy would now accompany father, mother and equally resentful and reluctant teen sister, on a family visit to church. For one young miscreant to register contrition re his dirty deed to the Big Fisherman's divine Boss? Apparently so.

As exercises to produce genuine repentance go however, 'What a waste of good fishing time!' was the boy's only thought. A lost opportunity to win prizes for rod and lining too. As for any of these religious attendances? Always they amounted to mild torture, aggravation of prickly cushioned pews to any lad clad in shorts the worst aspect, their minister's boring as batshit sermons a close second. Chances for the boy becoming even a potential believer were slight. Well, alright, except if when playing some extraordinarily large fish: 'Please Jesus, just let me land this one...?' No more using His name in vain again the deal.

Rowboat Liberation Movement escapade did result in one major prohibition. Further association with Bill was banned due to his 'bad influence'. As with attempted inculcation of Christianity within a young heathen soul, a doomed dictate. At no stage in his life would the boy accept unfair orders or impositions – a most Australian characteristic in fact, and for citizens with or without Celt bloodlines. Now nine and into his tenth year on Earth, one conspicuously blond true-blue Aussie the boy had become, all residual Scottishness fading into deep shade.

After a short while, what did fade too however, was that mateship with happy-go-lucky Bill. Parental prohibition on association with this lad whose influence, instead of being bad only ever brought pleasure, didn't cause it. Differing interests saw the drifting apart, which is how boyhood friendships usually go. Bill, developing a passion for racehorses, had got into attending the local hayburners' race day preparations and training gallops rather than involving himself with river activities. And then too, the boy's angling enthusiasm had diminished some due to another schoolmate persuading him to seriously start kicking a football.

Cubby Carroll's serial monogamist father had several ex-wives. This meant that the undersized Cubby shared his Christmases with several much older step-siblings, including the district's top sportsman, Clem 'King' Carroll. King Carroll captain-coached the Scumbaggers senior footy team, a side drawn from the comfortably well-off municipality's only slum-like quarter. This poor suburb on the south-west side had as its border mozzie-infested swampland and the town's lesser river into which the muck drained. Sullied stream also contained ponging daggy effluent overspill from the district's Woollen Mill and also blood and guts and excreta flushed out of an adjacent abattoir.

Progress and improvements impeded by these odious odorous additives, together with its low-income inhabitants, sure meant this suburb which the Scumbaggers represented was somewhat an eyesore. Yet its rugged ragged residents maintained a stubborn civic pride, an 'us against them' mentality. Among other things, this fuelled a determination to field football sides, not just Seniors but Under-14's as well.

Coaxed by his star step-brother coach, Cubby Carroll had joined the junior team. Even more diminutive than most rovers, during a schoolyard kick-to-kick Cubby had expressed keenness for the boy join him in their Saturday morning competition. The boy's father however, waxed none too pleased re his son's wish to become a young Scumbagger. To begin with, although tall for a nine-year-old the lad was one long streak of pelican shit thin. He'd be up against kids twice his weight and size. Then too, the Under-14 competition had more respectable sides. These included one representing their church – which the family were attending more frequently as the father's profile at his clothing factory rose, with religious devotion regarded as an assistance to promotion, as well as general approval. Into this consideration had also to be added that one morally impeccable boss, The Great Man, might possibly not be too chuffed about a valued employee's son taking to the field with a side chock-a-block with *scruffians*.

Indeed, to be or not to be… a Scumbagger? In thinking about his offspring playing footy alongside snotty urchins, the father did need to bear in mind himself, fatherless in Glasgow's grotty slum streets, and that he too had been a disadvantaged kid. A more valid reason to say nay was simply that down-at-heel suburb's location, town's other side, more than three miles away from the family home. And with so much weekday and Saturday overtime tying up the Vauxhall, the father figured he'd be unable to drive his lad to training, never mind to games. Which really, raised the main problem: unlike most kids of his age in that era, the boy was not a bike rider.

In fact, the boy did own a bicycle. He just wouldn't – couldn't – ride the thing. A ninth birthday present, severe self-consciousness had been the major hurdle. For a start, as steep hillsides were not great spots to master the cycling art, onto a flat area adjacent to the highway his father had taken him. There, man and husband, running alongside and holding second-hand Malvern Star upright by its seat, had tried to get his son riding. Awkward were the attempts to balance, comical his pedalling. Other kids hooning about the flat on their treadlies started to laugh and hang shit. Ridicule, the boy never could, or would ever, manage to ignore. Rosy young cheeks burning ever redder, off the bike he got, adamant, despite his dad's cajoling, that never would he mount it again.

Nevertheless, determination takes many forms. Riding a bike is one thing, kicking a footy quite another. Despite automobile transportation problem, the father found himself being swayed by his son's resolve to play footy for the Scumbaggers. Also, he reasoned that, yes, mixing with less privileged others might be beneficial to the boy. Still, what sealed the deal was a mother's promise. Obtain her driver's licence she had, but so seldom used it. Now she vowed she would provide the transport to evening practice sessions and matchdays, as well as conveying the working father back and forth. Up until this time she had simply been walking to work at the Old Folks Home. At present however, her cooking duties reduced due to some cost-cutting strategy, she reckoned she'd be able to juggle her time. Uh-huh, by canny management – something mothers tend to excel at – she declared one female taxi driver would have little trouble ferrying tyro footballer and premier tailor's cutter to and from their necessary locations. And if on occasion this meant an inability to have also prepared the family evening meal, why, 'Och, we can always buy TV dinners, aye?'

TV Dinners! For Aussie families addicted to that glittering new square box medium and unable to tear themselves away from its flickering black and white images to partake in customary table dining, swallowing TV dinners – these boiling foil-contained serves – whilst balancing them on their knees before a cathode screen, became life's most pleasing way to guts down tucker. The 'in thing' too. Slick advertising showed *everyone* doing it. In reality, sickening non-nutritious tasteless junk food, it took a year before this fact dawned on the gullible majority. Not so the boy's mum, 'Jings, whit sort o' muck is this?!', home-cooked meals, pre-prepared or otherwise, were back on the agenda quicker than someone could say, 'Mother Knows Best'.

An efficient manager of most domestic matters the mother surely was. Her single shortcoming, and increasingly, now that she'd taken to using the Vauxhall, came in dealing with the home's fourth human member, its teenage daughter and sister. '...Ah'm no running a free shuttle service, okay?' And despite the high schooler's protests about this being exactly the favour afforded to her young brother, no way would the mother budge. Therefore, friction between the family's two females always loomed.

From the boy's perspective, enjoying preferential treatment as he did, he knew this miffed his sister. But he also guessed mother's attitude had something to do with his sister, as a pulchritudinous platinum blonde in her final high school year, usually having her own transport anyway, a chilli-red hot-rod driven by Fatrat Bridgeman the town's flashiest Bodgie, a black leathers-clad delinquent with slicked-back coal-black hair and sideboards to his chin.

That a teen daughter's brazen behaviour, if drawn to his paragon boss The Great Man's attention, might reflect unfavourably on the father, also added to domestic tension. Nor, despite the boy and his sister's mutual affection, she couldn't but resent how accommodating both parents appeared to be to him compared to herself. In essence, it all guaranteed that inevitably she'd split for the big city the moment she was able.

Footy season's start now imminent, once the father granted permission to play for the Scumbaggers, typically he gave the boy every spare non-working minute he could to try an enhance his son's skills. Yet, boot an oval-shaped pill? Accustomed to a round soccer ball, abysmal were the father's efforts. What he could do though was toss a footy high into the air and encourage the boy to run, leap, spread his fingers, and grasp that spinning leather as if his life depended on it.

In another decade, a noted 'high mark' and playing the great Australian game as a professional, the boy would recognise the debt he owed to his otherwise Aussie Rules clueless father. However, right then, appreciate this run and jump and catch repetition, never mind envision future on-field glories...? 'This is so-o-o-o boring!' he kept thinking. How beaut must it be not to have such a dud dad? Incapable of launching a torpedo punt or stab-pass or drop-kick, jeez, this old man of his could not even execute an accurate mongrel roost of the footie!

If not for his father's unappreciated assistance however, the boy would have had no pre-season preparation whatsoever, because, set to attend his first ever Under-14's training session... yep, what a time for their veteran Vauxhall to break down! Until local mechanics obtained spare parts the whole family now found themselves resorting to shanks' pony to reach work and school. As for the boy maybe hiking to and from his mid-week Scumbaggers training? Impractical, distance to their ground too great.

When Saturday morning of season's first game came, having been unable to train, the boy's name was of course not on the team sheet. It hardly mattered then, that the father had been asked to once more do overtime and would miss the match. Repairs on Vauxhall completed only the preceding evening, as his mother drove the father to work prior to continuing to the footy ground, the boy glumly accepted he'd be only spectating. His single consolation was the awful weather.

In teeming rain, the father had got dropped off at the factory before, with wipers whop-whapping away at windscreen waterfall, the mother drove onward to the slummy suburb's playing patch for its junior Scumbaggers footballers. At least they could watch the match in some comfort by parking amongst the other parents' cars which encircled the sodden field. This done, the mother barely escaping getting bogged, there they waited. The boy wished his sister had wanted to come, but she had other games in mind, all to do with kissing he figured. So yuck, and anyway, so what that she wasn't there? Seeing as he would not be pulling on a boot to display his punt-kicking prowess upon that pondlike grotty field of play, it hardly mattered.

Except, hey... the young Scumbaggers were missing three players. They didn't even have a team of eighteen, never mind the luxury of two reserves. Up to Vauxhall rushed Cubby Carroll. On tip-toes, babbling in through the passenger-side window, short bubbly Cubby implored the boy, his pal, his mate, to come and get some footy gear on. The mother rolled her eyes, but nodded 'go ahead'. Alright, ripper!... Yet how was the boy to play when he hadn't brought his footy kit with him? Not that as yet he owned proper studded boots anyhow. At school they played in sandshoes.

'It don't matta,' urged Cubby, 'someb'dy'll fix ya up wif somefink.' Normally Cubby spoke very acceptable English, but that wasn't how dinkum Scumbaggers – these underprivileged products of the undereducated – talked. Around ground's puddled perimeter through the on-going rain both boys ran. About as unattractive a playing area as ever existed their approximate oval, ahead awaited a dirt-floored change shed of rusty corrugated-iron. Exclusively for the youngsters this whole woeful recreational space here. Scumbaggers senior team had its own proper arena in a more attractive part of town.

Inside shabby shed Cubby and the boy rushed. A weird and wonderful place is a country footie change-room, especially at first ever entry, and even more so if it's had no benefit of mop or broom. Strewn about were broken laces, used plasters, lumps of mud, broken studs, dried orange peels, torn apparel and other assorted crud. In awe, the boy sat on cold wooden bench slats, and waited. Someone had scampered off to scrounge up shorts and socks and boots for him. Meanwhile, he wasn't just fascinated but intrigued. His wee mate Cubby had stepped into a jockstrap. Now, the oddest of sports fashion is the jockstrap. Not only had the boy never seen one, he could not comprehend what possible purpose it would serve.

In that crowded and disgracefully kept space other observers appeared to be thinking similarly. Cubby was not just small in stature. Naked, he offered evidence contrary to what is often claimed about sawn-off males possessing prodigious endowments. Mature males standing around were probably speculating that with any luck, Cubby's chopper would become more prominent as he grew. At present however, he presented a pathetic sight. Way worse, that extra-large jockstrap had belonged to his step-brother hero 'King', of whom his moniker likely did fit in every sense. Nevertheless, if some adults were sniggering, a fully focused Cubby failed to notice. About to also play his first Under-14's game, having now scrambled into his full kit he stood stomping his boots and raring to go.

Still in his street attire meanwhile, the boy remained benched. Cubby, a dab hand at stating the bloody obvious, observed, 'Better 'urry up or yer gunna be late gettin' out there.' But a moment later came an ageing gasping supporter, hastening in, damp roll-your-own in corner of his mouth, grasping holey black and yellow socks, shorts like granny's bloomers, and rock-hard boots big enough to fit a boomer kangaroo. Too excited to be self-conscious about looking like a Disney cartoon, the boy pulled on his sieved socks, the daggy-baggy shorts and those giant boots. He then donned a tent-sized Richmond Tigers-type guernsey tossed to him. His one thought: 'Jeez, I'm a real footballer now!'

Not quite, not until that first touch of the footy... If liniment-pongy football clubrooms are intriguing pre-game places, they can also be intimidating. Supporters yell inspiration and obscenely incite violence. Players stamp their studs on concrete floor and shout and slap each other's bodies to rev themselves up, filling courage reservoirs later to be drawn from. Pre suicidal charges In the trenches of World War One, a similar atmosphere must have existed. Yet although nervous, even scared, the boy loved every alien thing happening around him.

In came the umpire. Some supporters groaned: this bastard hardly ever paid them a free-kick. Nevertheless, the bloke, there to check all boot studs for protruding nails, came across as ultra-friendly. Sussing this to be the debut game for several scrawny participants, he smiled, 'Good luck young fellas. Make sure you play fair.' Overweight, middle-aged, red-faced and already perspiring, a prime candidate for a coronary. Someone shouted, 'Ay, fer a change, give us a fair go terday Lenny, yer bloody arsehole!' The umpire just laughed, and departed.

All then went quiet as the Scumbaggers Under-14's coach readied to make his address. A teacher, podgy and pleasant with wire-rimmed glasses, Have-a-crack Jack ran the local one-room school and taught many of the players. Also, as president of the residents' Progress Association, he had a true, if a wee bit unjustified, pride in their impoverished suburb. Quite a transformation of persona when he spoke though. Mild manner fell away, demonic eyes bulged, neck veins gained prominence, face empurpled, glasses steamed-up... and what an inspirational haranguing Have-a-crack Jack gave! Driving this may have been knowledge that half these kids were too malnourished to give of their best. He had not the slightest expectation they might win.

Despite a smidgen of bewilderment, the boy aped his teammates stomping their boots. In so doing it struck him he'd never seen so many ultra-lean kids with pudding bowl haircuts. But then, no more thinking. Surrounded by shouts and hoots and hoo-ha, suddenly those borrowed seven-league boots were caught up in his side's outflowing black and yellow tide. Away through change-room doorway the motley side surged, to be met by not just applause and tooting horns but icy pelting rain and peppering hail.

Undeterred by Huey's hard wet elements smacking into them, onto muddy puddled playing field the ragtag team ran, only to be confronted by... crikey, bloody giants! The Scumbaggers had only two players about to turn fourteen. Tech College, their opponents, were all of that age, perpendicular Hawthorn stripes making them look even taller too. Destined that year to go undefeated, these elite athletes were primed to pit their pitiless selves against the club which would finish rock-bottom winless. Proof of how one-sided this match would be was but a vibrating pea in a whistle away. However, before Lenny's bounce-down, the umpire needed to find a suitable firm central spot upon which to perform this skilful act so unique to Aussie Rules football.

'Unique' also described the junior Scumbaggers oval. A sad apology for one really. Southern end's inadequate defence against wild salt winds was a patch of sickly sticklike pines age-frayed and greying. No boundary fence existed because six days per week a farmer grazed his cows on the space. Therefore, a paddock actually, with four skew-whiff posts of uneven height each end, and in front of them a ten-yard square of sloppy black mud. As for the ground's centre area, its gluepot ooze emitted such an evil miasma that lads with asthma had to steer clear of it.

Umpire Lenny had to, of course, give this middle cricket pitch a miss as his bouncing point. But in selecting another spot he needed to also be cautious. Mudhole centre aside, because playing field doubled as grazing land, in banging the Sherrin or Ross Faulkner down to get game underway he had to avoid planting it in a fresh cowpat. In fact, a disgrace, the entire surface, covered as it was more in bovine excreta, thistles, nettles, capeweed, and boggy black gunk, than grass.

Regardless, a game would be played. Named as a half-back flanker, perhaps fortunately the boy remained unaware of this field position being also euphemistic rhyming slang for chronic onanists. But at that stage of life masturbation wasn't in his vocabulary either… Up went the toss. Down along with the persisting rain came spinning coin. Uh-oh, a bad start, the Scumbaggers would be kicking against the wind. Squelching to his position, the boy found his head reached only to his opponent's gold and brown striped chest. They shook hands, the older boy crushingly. Yep, a bully, just like all his teammates.

At least the rain temporarily lessened. To timekeeper's madly ringing bell and car horn tooting, a shrill blast of whistle and umpire Lenny deposited ball onto terra-not-so-firma. Yet a decent bounce. Tech College ruckman tapped ball to their rover, who hand-passed it to a winger, who punted it high to towering centre-half forward who took a skyscraper mark before wheeling into an arc and parking a stab-pass right into the bread basket of their leading full-forward. Without pause this show-pony jerk booted a goal. Ten seconds it had taken. The signs were not favourable. Again, it began to bucket down, even more icily than before. And not only was the boy's guernsey awfully loose, but sleeveless.

By three-quarter time the score, in ceaseless downpour, stood at 29 goals 19 behinds to zero. Jeez, how much more might Tech have booted in dry conditions? And try as he might, the shivery boy had not won a kick. Not that most other Scumbaggers were getting any either, Cubby included. As second rover he was in the play plenty too. One lad only bucked the team's pathetic performance. Smaggs, their captain, what a player! Small and nuggetty, bowl-cut's black fringe falling over eyes, long sleeves reefed up to elbows, how he bored in and under those perilous packs. Without Smaggs they'd have been sixty goals down.

Not until well into the final quarter did the boy get his big chance. Once more his gumtree-tall opponent had the ball, but thanks to the on-going wet and a boot slipping on sloppy cowpat, this towering tool took a fall. Down like a lopped bluegum he came. Onto a Scotch thistle too! This further distraction meant the yelping big yob took a long moment to regain his feet before sprinting toward goal. Hesitation enough however, allowing the boy to grab the back of that brown and gold jumper. Slippery ground, the size-sixteen borrowed boots... towed along as if on skis, he held on. *Pweeee!* Umpire Lenny's whistle blew. 'Holding the ball!' he called.

The boy had earned his first free-kick. Grabbing soapy ball off his peeved opponent, he heard car horns blaring crazily. Acclaim! The feeling of being a prince – a sensation to reoccur right through his senior playing days whenever plucking a 'spekky' from the skies or booting a 'major'. Captivated by fishing he'd been. In that instant though, he became enthralled by football.

Meantime, their game continued. The boy's grubbed kick was easily cleared by the Tech back-pocket, after which, with one minute to go, as if there hadn't been ignominy enough, the opposition ruckman tapped ball to his rover who as usual handpassed to a winger who this time however, booted it to the centre-half back who bulleted it to the fullback, who roosted it through the Scumbaggers goal: if their opponents stayed scoreless, apparently Tech received no percentage boost. Full-time bell then tolled. For whom? Well, for both the euphoric 253 points winners and the doom and gloomy single point losers.

Oh well, at least hot showers awaited, yeah? Um well, they

would have had the struggling club been able to afford its gas bill. Nonetheless, despite a cold-water cascade providing shite icing to one stale and mouldy cake, the boy felt a firm sense of achievement: first competitive game played, he now belonged to a real footy team.

How much the boy had been looking forward to this Tuesday evening after Saturday's game. Even better, following this, his first dinkum Under-14's training session, came the once-a-month 'pie night'. Unfortunately, buckshee meat pies meant half-starved kids who would never pull on a footy boot turned up, something which a few regular Scumbaggers players took exception to. The boy found himself targeted as, '...another bludger just frontin' fer the fuckin' free tucker!' Accuser their lard overloaded ruckman, a useless blimp incapable of getting a kick in a Fitzroy brawl, he did nevertheless possess an effective line of invective.

In minimal fairness to this rotund ratbag, the boy did look nothing like Saturday's second-hand Sadie who'd played on their halfback-flank. Tonight, he actually looked like a footballer. Not only did he have on shorts which fitted and weren't also useful as a windsock, but his parents had bought him new boots that, even if of moulded plastic and not leather, looked pretty spiffy. Along with these they'd forked out for a classic Collingwood training jumper. Alas though, those black and white stripes afforded no armour against accusative arrows. Tears were nearing, until Smaggs the Brave stepped in. 'Leave that kid alone, Froggy, or I'll friggin' drop yer. He played in our backline on Sat'dy, an' 'e wuz one of our bloody best too!'

Oh, what a lovely pie night lie! But from then on, the boy would idolize Smaggs. Yes, ah yes, the gallant gifted Smaggs... from a broken and stony-broke home, that year to win their junior league's best and fairest medal, as well as captain the Victorian Country Schoolboys side. This pride of the Scumbaggers would be approached by several VFL sides too. Yet before the big-bucks era, little more than prestige came from playing in the Big Time. Poverty ensured that, by assisting his hapless cash-strapped family through taking up an apprenticeship in the armed services, Smaggs would slide into obscurity. He'd be crippled in Vietnam, and never kick a football again.

Smaggs or no Smaggs though, Scumbaggers Under-14's were abysmal easy-beats. For another four years they'd continue getting flogged, until that season the boy and many of his teammates were nearing thirteen, when suddenly no longer undersized, they'd win their opening game by ten goals, to walk off their grotty ground in elated disbelief but also aware of how much bigger they'd grown and now belonged to a team to be reckoned with. Until then however, the Scumbaggers single formidable aspect involved a posse of perfervid adult supporters.

Such prodigious expectorators this uncouth coterie embodied! Every perceived poor umpiring decision induced projections of phlegm. Nor did they just send the air green with excessive spit, they turned it blasphemy-blue too. And indecent vocabularies are all too transferrable to pint-sized players. Soon kids little higher than the umpy's kneecap were questioning both his judgement and parentage, sparing no obscenity in so doing either. Inevitably, the boy joined in, even if he didn't see how one faulty call by the umpire could make for a thirty goals difference on the scoreboard.

By that mid-season the Under-14 competition's controllers were considering a Scumbaggers ban. The father too, conscious his son's association with feral behaviour and blaspheming could come to the notice of his morally upright and ultra-Christian boss, readied to pull plug on the boy playing. Yet then, at a meeting of all parents and players, teacher-coach Have-a-crack Jack had his very impressive say. From that day onward, on and off field, swearing by young Scumbaggers went the way of the dinosaurs. By this oratory too, Have-a-crack Jack may unwittingly have also been laying the foundation for a later career as a state politician.

Every footy season has its end. After the boy's initial one, fishing again ruled. This September school week finished, home he'd come intent on wetting a line instead of getting footy gear ready prior to booting a ball the following morning. Indeed, chasing bream he had on his mind as he entered an empty family abode. In finding this space vacated there was nothing unusual. Clothing factory didn't close down until five p.m., the mother often found herself delayed by extra food preparation at the Old Folks Home, and as for one boyfriend besotted sister...? Once high school classes ended, usually she was a no-show for a couple of hours. Yet today, a note lay on the kitchen table: 'Sorry kids, dad and I have had to hurry off to Melbourne for the weekend.' It went on to say that, factory having opened a city centre retail store, the father was required to personally advise its fitters.

Did his dad's increasing indispensability to The Great Man occur to the boy though? Not a jot. Yet, still short of turning ten, that the penny did not plummet in regard to his father's capabilities was understandable enough. As for the note, its only bit to give the boy cause for pause was a line entrusting his sister with brother-care duties. Child carelessness, reckoned the boy, might be more accurate. Confirmed by, on his bedroom pillow, another note. In this were instructions from one teen sister high schooler that he heat and eat a Cornish pastie she'd placed in the oven, and, '...see you later, Sis XXX.'

Ahhh, so she actually had been home. Seeing a splendid opportunity for a two-day escape though, she'd grabbed a change of clothes, and scarpered. Heh, that ever-wilder sister! The boy hadn't a clue about what hot hormones pinging around inside a well-developing body might lead to, but he readily accepted that all weekend she'd be partying with her dodgy Bodgie pseudo-Elvis boyfriend Fatrat Bridgeman. 'Yeah, probably spending most of her time jiving at the Palais,' he reckoned.

So, there it was, forty-eight hours fending for himself. Any worries, did he care…? A fair while now often looking after himself anyhow, the boy's only thought was, 'Bewdy!' Ahead, all those unsupervised unrestricted hours spendable in catching fish – starting immediately. To mark footy season's end, a pre-birthday gift had been one lacquered beautifully tapered cane rod. Love at first sight best described his reaction. Taking this and other necessary angling accoutrements from the garage, off down block and over rail track and on down paddock to the river he hiked. Heading for the bridge? No, those closest boat-hire jetties.

Riverside cypresses passed through, once on the flat bankside disappointment dented enthusiasm. Of those jetties, the boy had a favourite. But, bugger, it was occupied. Except, hang on…? To his delight he recognised the angler to be Bill's mum. Sat on a canvas chair at that jetty's L-shaped end she had two lines out. Always a welcoming woman, the boy knew there'd be no hassle with invading her space. As for her son Bill, previously the boy's good mate, no way would he be about. That interest in hayburners had so developed, Bill now spent all his spare time with jockeys and strappers at the town's trackside stables, on course to himself eventually own successful stayers, one a runner-up in the Melbourne Cup.

Who the boy did also expect to see though was Bill's nuggety wee he-man dad. But when he asked after that redgum tough ex-rover, 'Aw, he's away at Killarney Beach pumping spew worms,' explained Bill's mum, 'so we can add more variety to our bait supply.' A handsome rather than beautiful woman almost a foot taller than her stocky spouse, this represented her idea of being the one currently running their boat-hire – something to be done none too seriously. 'I'm better at finding fish than fielding phone calls,' she grinned. A fine angler too, therefore very true. The boy gave thought here to the contrast with his own mother who refused to go within cooee of stinky baits and wrinkled her nose if an uncleaned bream got popped into her pristine sink. Although, okay, superbly cook any fish his mum could, yet get her to place one paltry pilchard on a hook and actually catch one herself? Unimaginable!

Bill's ma however, few male anglers could match. Those were the days too when some gruff veteran fisho could growl, 'Women've got no bloody right to be on our river!' Now alright, this might well have had association with a perceived right of standing in a boat's bow and flopping out the 'old fella' to urinate overside... a sight at which Bill's no-frills mum would not even have blinked. However, yes, this lady? Not just the only female the boy had so far met who enjoyed fishing, but rare were the masculine piscators who scored such impressive results. No right to be on a river? Bill's mum *belonged* on one!

'Help yourself,' she said, referring to her bait packet of green shrimp.

This done, the boy positioned himself alongside her, cast out, and began to chat. Some anglers do resent close intrusion, but he knew Bill's quiet-natured mum would not object. Instead, she readily answered all questions. And there was another thing. Fishos can be secretive, clamming up about which species are biting, who's caught that week and on what, and where, but she disclosed all such info without hesitation.

Already their river's foremost female angler had landed ten good fish. Her creel dangling over jetty's side held a mix of bream, mullet, salmon, and trevally. However, what most captured the boy's interest was she herself – her elegant casting, the retrieval almost dainty, dextrous impalement of multiple shrimp on hook, the effortless re-depositing of that bait into stream, then the gentle placement of rod flat on jetty planks whilst pulling out a little slack line. And something else too... 'You don't use a sinker?' he noticed.

'Most natural way to present your bait. Fish feels no weight.'

'Ah, right...?' The boy, employing a running sinker rig, twigged an implied recommendation. Today though, any hope of this? Nope, for meteorological circumstances were about to intervene. Rumble of thunder came as if from nowhere. Air had gone still, the river glassy, those rings of rising fish which happen when the barometer plummets were suddenly everywhere. Above the angling pair cumulonimbus cloud accumulated.

'Hmmm, time to give it away,' said Bill's mum.

'Not me,' responded the boy. Like, quit without catching a single fish? To make a longer cast, hurriedly he peeled line off his centrepin until... it jammed.

'Ooh, you've got an over-run... here, let me sort that out for you.'

Those sensitive fingers and savviness would have released fankled monofilament in a jiffy, yet, 'Aw, she'll be right,' the boy reassured her.

'You might be sorry...?' Bill's mum tossed across an empty spud bag hanging on the jetty's back railing. 'Maybe this'll stop you from getting too wet,' she smiled, 'but if it gets really bad don't stay out here, alright? Especially if there's lightning.'

After her departure lightning did arrive too. Massive flashes though, not forked, so little danger. Rain became the real pain in the bum. Like a Jersey cow pissing on a rock, down it gushed. Spud bag provided but briefest protection. Nevertheless, soaked-through boy fished on, figuring not only that he couldn't get any wetter but because the fish were stirring. Any tick of the clock he'd hook something. Had Bill's mum been a smothering one she'd have reappeared, called him inside out of the elements. Yet she knew it is usually better that the young decide for themselves, and hopefully also, learn from their mistakes.

In rejecting help to free his reel's stuck line, the boy's own line of, 'Aw, she'll be right,' was right too, for the shortest second of his centrepin's scream. Then, jammed by that overrun, it ceased to, and along with precious new cane rod, off jetty it shot and into river leaving the bubble-trail of an outwards speeding torpedo. Sopping-wet and stunned, the boy stared toward the waterway's middle to where whatever had grabbed his bait had headed. A sobbing sorry-looking mess, he then fronted Bill's mum to spill the news of his loss. 'A bloody big kingy pulled my rod in,' he blubbered, believing a mulloway – in that district also called a kingfish or 'kingy' – had done the awful deed.

'Oh, that's a bugger,' came the response, 'Wet bum and no fish, eh?'

To make so light of his tragedy? This vexed the already upset boy no end. However, swallow one bitter fait accompli pill he had to, as well as accept that the thin sympathy given's justification. He had declined this wise woman's offer. She'd have prevented what occurs when a weighty fish hits and a reel cannot run. Instead, he'd responded with that casual throwaway Aussie phrase, 'Aw, she'll be right.' He now appreciated how problematic this could prove to be. A few years further on he'd come to understand that its utterance can even be fatal.

At the not quite so new anymore house high on hill, lying all alone in bed mourning for one lost treasured rod made for a miserable sleepless night. Had there been a sister around she may have commiserated and comforted. The mother certainly so had she been home. But no, parents in Melbourne, sibling focused on making whoopee with her Bodgie beau. Yet for the boy direr circumstances loomed. That earlier soaking brought, by two a.m., a fever. Heavy sweats alternated with shiver-shaking worse than a cocker spaniel crapping razor-blades. When early Sunday afternoon the sister finally fronted, she discovered a brother with his internal system turning inferno. Not that she looked too-flash herself, having apparently spent a month in a tumble drier. As for offering sympathy either for yanked-in fishing rod or feverish illness? 'Say one word to the oldies about me staying out and I'll murder you!' she promised.

Not that, as well the boy knew, his sister would ever harm him. Despite parental favouritism often falling his way, strong mutual love persisted. She bore too, that caring nature of the born nurse she'd soon become. Quickly therefore, her tenderness prevailed... together with panic. How to make her young brother recover before evening when their folks returned from the big smoke? Might an elixir of some sort fix him? Rummaging through drawers and cabinets she found a half pint bottle of herbal medicine. Ingredients uncertain, sourced in Ireland by their mother on that overseas trip from which the sister had been excluded. At least its handwritten label stated, 'For medicinal purposes only'.

Now delirious, the boy accepted a solid sip. Table-spooned down his cakehole, oooogh, putrid! Caught in his throat and lungs too. Once stowed in belly though, ooh yes, a growing glow, spreading through his innards. Feverish face croaked, 'Sis, can I have some more?'

Not until late on the following Monday arvo did the mother see her comatose child at last awake. Seated at his bedside she gasped, 'Oh, God, thank-ye, thank-ye!' and in a rush of mixed emotions applied a crushing hug. Yet the boy, even before opening his eyes, how great he felt. Giddily light-headed, sure, but fully free of the awful flu-like lurgy. Off went his mum to phone clothing factory and tell the father their beloved son appeared to be none the worse for his nurse-to-be sister administering a massive overdose of the mega-potent Paddy moonshine 'poteen'.

Never would the boy hear more overjoying news: Bill's dad had rung Tuesday to say that, dipping big shrimp net in the weed-bed across from his jetties, he had brought up the rod and its jammed centrepin reel. He'd also *almost* caught the culprit. Not a mulloway but a huge bream, he said, however '...the bloody line broke at the hook just as I went to lift it into the boat.'

The boy did detect a tantalizing aroma of bream fillet frying as he collected his beloved cane rod, but the expression, 'Lying sod!' never entered his relieved skull. Still, shitty outcomes do sometimes arrive for tellers of porky pies. Dragging nets is strenuous exercise. Soon after, a healthy fish diet didn't prevent Bill's squat tough-rough dad being hospitalized with a heart-attack. Actually, like many middle-aged men in that era, heavy smoking more than hard yakka contributed to his coronary problem. Back then too, a crook ticker usually meant sitting upon an armchair in a dressing-gown and slippers, continuing to puff on a Rothmans or Craven "A", and awaiting death. Pharmaceuticals to boost buggered cardiac systems and keep humans sparky and active far beyond when they ought to have carked were yet to come on the market.

Shortly after that special cane rod's return, and with the boy now turned ten, a shoal of salmon trout entered the river. Saturday morning, bearing same treasured fishing pole, downhill toward his favourite watercourse trotted the boy. Taking not cross-train-track route though, but via road — all the quicker to get to the bridge and into the thick of those fish. Turning left at bottom of hill from his home he began to jog faster. Longer strides took him on flat bitumen to beneath rail bridge from where he speeded up even more when the roadway tilted thirty degrees for a couple of hundred yards to not level out until both boat-hire businesses were on his left and the cemetery to his right. Then, at sharp bend ahead where Anglers Club building invited demolition by some runaway truck, he headed off-road along a riverside shortcut.

A minute later the Old Folks Home was being skirted. Had this been a workday, his mum would have been in there engaged with her part-time cooking job. Ah, but ha, a free and easy mid-spring post footy season Saturday this, no work for her today, no school for him. Other lads may have had better lives but as yet he'd never met them. On along riverside's dirt path the boy hastened, past the oldies facility's boatshed. Alas, no more did 'the shag on a rock' adorn its jetty, for ancient angler Mr Myers had finally fallen off his Earthly perch.

Eyes now fixed on the bridge, the boy saw along this, anglers of all sizes and ages standing shoulder-to-shoulder and hip-to-hip, while lumpy salmon trout around two-thirds of a pound were jerked up over its top railing and deposited flapping onto roadway. Pounced upon, fishy existences then ended by having throats snapped open at their gill openings – tasting better if 'bled out'. A swift despatch, but humane...? Debatable. Just the same, none of those bridge fishers had fronted there to engage in animal rights.

Catching methods employed varied. Yonks to go yet until the ubiquitous 'plastics' showed up, some anglers cast metal lures or feather jigs. The majority however, used bait, trolled or fished under a float. For catching salmon trout, the boy favoured the floating bait method. Albeit when madly feeding a species that bit on almost anything, what floaters offered was both an anticipatory and visual kick. At a fish's touch the wee red and white bubble chosen for use this day would first twitch, and then bobble, before plunging, its colours rocketing out of sight. After this, hook set, rod would bend mightily as gallant fighting salmon got skull-dragged in before, if the angler got lucky, it tangled a dozen other lines. But yes, such congested fishing. A lad better not foul some narky old fisho's line: 'cast straight or get castrated' almost the case!

Everywhere, as the boy stepped onto the bridge, were animated tête-a-têtes between piscatorial assassins disentangling monofilament, a task complicated through fat salmon trout frantically flapping in the centre of their birds-nested lines. Yet, despite myriad personalities and differing ages and temperaments, few fishers exhibited testiness. Knowing that once the mess got sorted there were countless fish still to be caught clearly contributed to equanimity.

Into a freshly vacated pozzie slipped the boy. So thick was the shoal below, soon he had his bagful. Too soon, for what terrific fun! Still, to fish on via 'catch and release'? Nobody yet did this. In preparing to depart though he noticed that on sandy bank, bridge's river-mouth side, a collection of kids had encircled one raggedy adult. Whatever the reason, nothing sinister in it. The youngsters were all happily excited.

Bearing his catch and fishing gear the boy clambered down escarpment beside where roadway connected to bridge, joined the gathering, and encountered his first genuine swagman. One of the very last too. This wanderer had asked these kids for a few fish. In return he'd demonstrate how to cook salmon trout bush-style over the campfire he had set. And not just that, he'd share the result with them. Come the Twenty-first century, an unshaven and unwashed bloke, clothes unravelling, boots holey-soled, would risk arrest for vagrancy, and further charges of indecent intent toward minors. Here, the swaggie readied to provide a group of unaffected rural children with not just a precious memory but practical survival instruction.

Of those kids who'd gathered, all except one were male. Pauline most certainly was not. From an outlying farm, she attended the same primary school class as the boy. Had she, he wondered, been fishing too? Perhaps. Pauline did excel at sports. From afar he'd admired her netball skill in the schoolground's asphalt quadrangle. Although yet to get much interested in girls, as Pauline ran, leapt, stopped, propped, and put ball after ball in netted hoop, her slim blonde blue-eyed freckled prettiness stirred something within him. Should he ever want to include a girl in his activities, he knew who should top the list. However right now, when Pauline saw him and smiled, the boy blushed and turned his attention to the swagman.

Where bridge abutted riverbank afforded a dry nook, and there the swaggie had his bedroll stashed. Misshapen Digger's hat a strong hint of former soldiering, whiskery chin added more hard-lived years than the man must have actually clocked up. No matter, for to children any adult over thirty is just plain *old*. What the plucky bloke surely possessed was kindness, as well as a dexterity for preparing bush tucker: 'Y'see kids, when yiz clean yer salmon...' demonstrated, leaving head on, and during scaling and gutting not slicing all the way to its vent. This meant that into the intact orifice then went a thin green length of coastal wattle, to emerge through the fish's gob. Both ends of wattle rod were then settled onto forked sticks stuck into sand at either end of compact campfire.

Ring of rapt kids soaking-in his savvy patter, the swaggie slowly rotated the trout. The tales he meanwhile regaled that young audience with were funny ones of far-flung trails. How could the boy intuit that nearly twenty years on, steamy jungle banks of another river, the mighty Amazon, and more or less an adventuring swagman himself, he'd roast fresh-caught catfish in the way being demonstrated here?

But crikey, the time! Expected home for lunch, the boy knew he had to get going. His mother's oven slow-roasted beef, together with rich gravy and crisp Yorkshire pudding, could not but top semi-cooked salmon trout, no matter how unique that experience. Yet the boy did appreciate departure meant a further missing out, of fun. Some adults had fronted with sausages and sauces and paper plates: an impromptu picnic about to commence. That smiling swaggie had scored a long-neck beer too. Hmmm, bugger! A moment's hesitation, a staying of departing feet... Bangers and bush tucker trout, or his mother's superb preparation? Nuh, a no-brainer, mum's cooking won hands down.

In leaving behind those bush-grilled snags and scorched salmon trout though, and especially the swaggie himself, the boy couldn't but still somewhat kick himself. Homeward trek continuing on by the Old Folks Home, he booted his own bum too for not speaking with Pauline. She hadn't been fishing, just observing, as he'd seen her return to the bridge and re-join her angler-farmer father. How simple to have sidled up to her dad and, one fisherman to another, discussed catching salmon, and thereby at school have a valid reason to approach Pauline, and... Yeah, if he'd had sufficient courage, as well as enough interest? 'No, this is best,' he decided – a stressless stroll away.

Not that this hike itself didn't challenge. Late morning and very warm, his fish-heavy hessian bag wouldn't lighten any once the road steepened. At this point he'd reached the cemetery's south-east extremity, its high stone wall. Uh-huh, their burg's only boneyard, often referred to by townsfolk as its 'dead centre', and yeah, disturbingly convenient to that aged care establishment where so many decrepit souls drew their last breaths too. Had that sandstone block wall sourced from now disused district quarries not occluded the tombs' view, what a superb up-river one it offered, had the recumbent residents have been able to appreciate it.

Quite a different sight, and a daunting one, once cemetery corner got rounded though was that steep-rising road ahead crowned by railway bridge. Ever heavier and smellier bag of salmon draped over shoulder, cane rod and reel seemingly weightier too, by now the boy had begun to freely perspire. Should he detour, instead climb the steep sloping paddock, take some shade under a tree on the way? No, almost midday, and road route the fastest for getting home before mum's roast burnt.

Nevertheless, that strip of macadam ahead, how abrupt its upness. And after that got topped, soon after came the even steeper street climb to reach their house. Relishing such exercise, the boy was not, when life, as it does do, dished up a nicest of surprises. Drawing in beside him was a capacious royal-blue Buick. Stranger danger? On the contrary, the whole district knew this vehicle. Familiar to everyone too, when Yank gas-guzzler's automatic driver-side window lowered, was the amiable pink face this revealed. As for The Great Man's stutter, legacy of his World War One shell-shock, all and sundry were aware of this as well, and respectful of the impediment. 'H-h-h-hello thuh-thuh-there, y-y-young...' He said the boy's name. Memory phenomenal, at his famous annual Christmas Party in the factory's gardens and presenting gifts, he could do this with almost every child of his many hundred employees. 'Uuuuh, duh-d-d-d-did yuh-yuh-yuh-you g-g-g-get any fish?'

'I sure did, Mister Jones!' Proudly for his father's boss, the boy shook the bloodied stinky salmon-packed hessian bag.

'Ah-um, it's a luh-luh-luh-long walk yuh-yuh-yuh-you've got ahead...' The Great Man knew where most of his employees lived too. 'C-c-c-c-come on, I'll-uh g-g-g-give yuh-yuh-yuh-you a lift.'

Naturally, The Great Man was attired in the required finest tailored suit of his company's making. Only then however did the boy notice several other immaculate suits inside the Buick. Of these so-well-dressed jokers, three in the back seat were emphatically urged to shift over and permit this fish-whiffy urchin to join them. Visiting bigwigs being given a sightseeing tour, an Asian and European mix, all were in Australia to study the clothing factory's – and The Great Man's – progressive methods.

Easing inside blue-ducoed limousine, the boy felt a bit awed, particularly by those bemused Asian faces. The only two Orientals he knew of in town belonged to a couple running the solitary Chinese restaurant. As marvellous company founder/owner/ managing director himself popped the boy's cane rod semi-upright in through a downed rear window, all these foreigners' thoughts may have been worth bottling. But they'd have included what an unusual and wonderful human being this Great Man was.

Yet what the boy's mother thought – on her knees weeding along front fence when big blue Buick whispered onto the nature-strip – was very guessable, if non-printable in those days of heavy censorship. Roasting beef put on low, she'd slipped out to do a lick of gardening. Among things she might have now been thinking was how she'd wished to wash those reeking clothes her son had on, but he, insisting this would bring bad angling luck, had nipped out the door before she could collar him.

Graciously The Great Man declined abashed mother and son's offer of some fresh but uncleaned salmon trout for his supper. In time, by then a recipient of a knighthood, he would lie within those same high sandstone cemetery walls outside which he'd stopped to give the boy a lift. That blue Buick one of his few extravagances, his grave would be unpretentious. Instead of dying mega-rich he'd have given away most of his wealth to charities and the Arts. As for the remarkable rag trade business built through his own acumen and tenacity and compelling personality, too soon after his demise, mismanagement, economic circumstances, and the decisions of politicians, would send it down the gurgler, and with this, Australia-wide, thousands of people's livelihoods.

That clothing factory, and the dynamic gentleman who founded it... Occasionally the town spawned elite sportspeople who lent it some renown, but its true fame came from garment production. Nor would any district have a finer citizen than the trousers, skirts and suits-making business's founder, affectionately known as 'FJ', career begun as that war traumatized former bugler blowing high-notes to attract buyers to his horse-drawn hawker's wagon.

When finally, he'd got his bank-financed clothing works built, The Great Man had incurred further debt by endeavouring to make it attractive for those toiling under its roof. There were clean working conditions, fair wages, and a canteen featuring chef-cooked foods at affordable prices. Employees were also encouraged to be shareholders. As for its disused garbage dump location, the factory's surrounds underwent transformation into a lavish garden where breaks for coffee and cake and cigarettes and gossip could be taken in an uplifting environment. Even its name, 'Pleasant Hill', was aimed at instilling quiet pride in each worker.

And yet... at working day's end every employee, from downright dills to the most skilled, could barely wait to leave. Home-time hooter sounding, out exit doors they spilled, pounding downslope from the elevated edifice – an indication The Great Man's forward thinking hadn't quite succeeded. If in charge of family car, the boy's mother would join a line of autos at the factory's front waiting to pick up its released inmates. If the boy accompanied her, after hooter's blast he found that oncoming flood of stampeding humanity... *thud-thud-thud-thud-thud...* unnerving. This apparent desperation to escape inculcated in him a determination never to become one of that work-force. Moreover, even belonging to its hierarchy didn't much seem to lessen the unbearableness. Managing the Cutting Room his father may have been, and once human tsunami had passed, as befitted his position, at a dignified stroll he would show up. But never could he disguise his gladness to be vacating the premises.

Only one employee showed no changed emotion on departure, an always on foot ever-smiling chap named Tucker. 'Och, ye never see Ronnie onything but happy!' the father exclaimed in some wonder one wet post work evening when they'd offered the bloke a lift, but with a 'thanks but no thanks' wave, on he had walked – an ebullient marcher actually, arms swinging in military fashion, invariably whistling. The father surmised such contentment could only stem from never owning a car. A correct guess. When this exuberant pedestrian eventually purchased his first auto, how he changed! Repayments, registration, repairs and running costs ensured Ronnie Tucker never marched or whistled ever again.

A few other dwellings had begun to be built on the hill and in its vicinity, and even a motel was being constructed at its base. The family's own home still stood alone though, albeit another solid repayment largely clearing bank debt meant the father's work week tended to often again end on Fridays. Saturday overtime now a rarity, quality fishing time with only son had come back onto his agenda. Even better for both, another piscatorial partner had been found, as fine an angler as ever existed. Best of all for the boy, by this time able to swim impressive freestyle, he could accompany his father and their new friend in the risky exercise of fishing turbulent freshwater upriver runs.

Owner of a small general store situated on the highway midway between the family's hill perched home and clothing factory, Old Ron opened his door before dawn and shut after dark. The father, one of Australia's maybe ninety-five percent citizenry who smoked, one evening stopped by the store to buy a packet of 'coffin nails', and the two men had got talking about fishing. From this had come Old Ron's promise of an outing to demonstrate how to catch brown, a.k.a. English, trout when the main river's upper reaches were in flood.

How old would Old Ron have been? Not sixty, yet a hard life had aged him, once working several jobs to cover the medical expenses for a dangerously ill wife. His fissured face was swarthy too, with thick-lips and broad-nose suggesting Aboriginal or Islander ancestry. Yet in those days, should community bigots have any such suspicion, an individual's daily existence could be made very uncomfortable. Therefore, people often kept a Koori connection hidden, and this may have applied to Old Ron.

Whatever his background, a gentle soul, and one overspilling with wisdom, never more did the latter come to the fore than a week after heavy rains fell in the Grampians mountains catchment. One of his adult sons minding the store, in his delivery van Old Ron drove the father and the boy some miles out of town to a stone bridge, upriver from which a series of freshwater pools were separated by shallow rocky stretches known, when floodwater gushed over them, as 'runs'.

After parking and negotiating a barbed boundary fence, the two men and the boy were, step by precarious step on slippery grassy river edge slope, making their way alongside rushing and churning waterway. All the while Old Ron explained... pointing out why, where river flow passed low and calm, trout would lie under certain overhanging bank-side bushes to eat particular insects which fell from them, as well as clarifying how in the present moderate flood, this spot was worth a try, and that other not – more inviting in appearance maybe, but supporting submerged, if non-obvious, snags, and better left alone. Many veteran fishos had by now passed on advice to the boy, but it was Old Ron who'd really teach him, along with his father, the finer techniques of angling, and true appreciation of that wetting-a-line pastime.

An inundated islet, its hardy tea-trees juddering in the discoloured debris-bearing current, curtailed some flood-flow. Before water-force again cojoined into a down-rush of rapids, in this islet's lee slowly whirled anti-clockwise an eddy. Nimble as Timmy the cat springing at a starling, onto an out-jutted in-river boulder hopped Old Ron, whippy split-cane rod used as a counter balance. Once stabilized, he shook loose his silver lure – the only sort of spoon to use, he said, in such brown water. Then, turning to the father and his lad standing on green-grassed sharp angled bank, he told them exactly where twixt coffee-coloured rock-dotted rapid and the islet's back-end his 'wonder wobbler' would land.

Not a long cast, but inch perfect, jerkily deliberate retrieval of lure accompanied by commentary, '... and so y'see, by flicking it into that placid patch behind those big rocks, I might just... Ha!' Thin flexible rod bent like wheat stalk in a hurricane. Speckled back of a large thrashing brown trout showed, before the fish swirled, dived, and then, shooting upward, its shaking head raised clear of the water, threw the lure. To his two spectators Old Ron just laughed, 'Oooh, good luck to him, eh. Wasn't he a beauty?'

The boy had by now seen many big fish hooked and lost. None ever escaped without bereft angler involved cursing the air blue. Here he saw something new: gracious, even amused, acceptance of a fighting fish's right to thwart its stalker. Over time he and his father would be privileged to watch Old Ron play many fish of prize size, delight in their fight, and land most. Should they not be bagged however, 'He's gone,' was about the strongest expression this splendid man ever uttered.


Persistence of those mountain rains kiboshed further fishing of runs. River, so swollen all rapids disappeared, transformed into one vast fast-moving muddy mass. Nonetheless, away downstream this had not stopped a rowing four's training session. Launching from a concrete ramp between the two boat-hire establishments, recreational river users of that time never wore lifejackets, most certainly not sporting scullers. When their shell went side-on too close to bridge and the surge drove them into a piling, splitting their flimsy craft in half, these blokes were, in an aptly coloured river, truly right up Shit Creek.

In normal times the river emptied into sea via that narrow rock channel where Brimmy and Hunty had whipped for salmon. To counter sand build-up and blockage, long ago this stretch had been dynamited through solid reef at an angle of thirty degrees south-west. The natural mouth however went straight out. Massive flood, surging away all barrier sand before it, had restored this, making an opening three hundred yards across. Swept out through it went one sculler, to drown. His three stronger-swimming mates managed to reach shore beside the river end's 'Danger Board' or they too would have suffered the same fate.

Dining-table mealtime that day, 'Aye,' sighed the father, 'Ah heard that poor bugger tried tae swim against the current, and that's nae different tae getting caught in a rip, which ye've always got tae swim across tae get oot of.'

'Not that,' thought the boy, 'you'd have a clue.' He wasn't in a great headspace anyway, those racing floodwaters kiboshing all prospects of catching fish from river's fresh or salt sections. Yet his opinion was close enough correct. When swimming his father only breast-stroked. In summer at main beach the old man's attempts to bodysurf were cringeworthy. His swimming style resembled a sodden sinking sponge. Further hindering his buoyancy was that very odd habit of wearing, not togs, but ankle-length slacks, the reason for which the boy couldn't fathom. Not that he gave this a lot of thought, or in fact, of actually never having seen his father's bare legs, the norm within their family home being one of absolute modesty and non-nudity.

In regard to his father's ignorance of oceans and active motions therein, as always, the boy kept all disparaging sentiments to himself. Not that conversation at family meal times often flowed anyhow. Of late though, further curtailing animated talk had been that just three diners occupied the table. Teen sister had cleared out to begin nursing at Melbourne's Austin Hospital, taking all that disruptive restless hormones-fuelled feistiness with her. The boy wasn't quite sure why, but he missed the tension his sister had contributed.

Summers and swimming! That was *the* time on their coast, and the older a kid grew the better it got. Contributing to ebullience which came with heaps of sun were the preceding gales and rain and hail prevailing mid-year. So wild were district winds, not only during winter but its equinoctial blast-throughs too, that the joke went folk bred thereabouts were recognisable because they always walked at an angle of forty-five degrees. However, those summers which followed woeful winters? Oh yes, they were glorious!

The boy would remember them as almost endless. Perhaps in that epoch they were longer too? Swimming began early October, at the Blue Hole, a deepish dune-sided backwater on the sanded-up river mouth's eastern side. Drier months bringing no sand removal floods, a bar always separated this spot from the main outflow, providing a placid kids-safe water space. And a very blue pool it was indeed... until temperatures rose. These triggered another rising, of blanket weed off the bottom. Greenness and a strong pong then took over and most swimming shifted to the main surf beach.

Admittedly this ocean beach's reputation for secure swimming would soon enough take a hefty hit when a huge-bodied lifesaver only just survived after losing half his torso to an even larger shark. Otherwise, a clean curve of sand stretching from the fishing boats protecting concrete breakwater eastward to main river's mouth, it offered minimal dangers and mild body-surfing – board riding an activity yet to catch on. Sun was the one real hazard. Skin cancers? Those days nobody worried. Hundred and ten Fahrenheit in the shade, kids were told, 'Off you go, get sunburnt, and then peeling will reveal a healthy tan!', thus laying the foundation for skin clinic specialists to later make oodles of motza removing basal and squamous carcinomas. As for metastasising melanomas... well, bad luck, huh?

Single person on those sands who may have been seen to be seeking some sun protection was the father. Yes, always when swimming he wore those light full-length slacks. Some contrast, this covered-up pale-skinned Scotsman offered to all those bronzed Anzac examples of beach manhood strutting about in their bathers like muscly lyrebirds. As for the burning and peeling boy, he just tried to ignore this further example of his old man's embarrassing peculiarities, and hope none of his schoolmates would see and comment. Otherwise though, yep, barely did he give a thought to never even seeing his dad in shorts, let alone swim trunks.

If coastal summers had extra specialness, the cooler short Easter breaks were not far behind in what they offered. Nothing to do with religion, it all involved travelling to some inland location. This early April, final fling of benign days before winter's harshness and footy season's start, destination was the Grampian Ranges. Ever assimilating herself into Australian ways, the mother had joined the Country Women's Association. As a bonus came a cheap rent CWA weekender up by those same mountains from which the boy's favourite river emerged. Father, mother and son would go there for the four-day religious break. 'Aye, and we'll tow the boat up too,' announced the family patriarch. Old Ron had given him some good oil about an alpine lake stocked with rainbow trout.

Except for when a negligent truckie ignored a give-way sign and almost cut boat and borrowed trailer in half, a smooth journey. Mini-convoy actually, for Vauxhall and boat-trailer were tailed by an elegant old Daimler conveying two Austrian friends. Franz and Elsa were a generation older than the boy's parents. They would share the weekender and, as non-anglers, join in bushland hiking when lines were not being wetted.

Sparsely furnished flimsy wooden cottage settled into, urbane Franz and Elsa were left to their orchestral LP's and European literature, while off upward motored the family threesome. To reach elevated lake would take time, a winding steep half-hour drive. 'Aye, Ah'm hoping the brakes are sound on oor poor auld bus when we're journeying doon again,' muttered the father. At that testing road's end though, gee, what a reward! Did a more picturesque lake exist in all Victoria? Over a thousand feet up, and under bluest skies, they'd arrived at a bowl of purest water set in untouched native bush.

Once out on this most beautiful lake's surface, its pureness posed a problem: too clear. Mother in boat's bow, and father and son taking turns at oars, they'd rowed to an island, anchored off it, and cast out juicy scrub worms which wriggled under quill floaters. Sizeable rainbow trout did every so often swirl yet not even a nibble came. Place a newspaper on the bottom twenty feet under keel and Jack Hill the blind miner could've read it! Such aquatic clarity put any chance of hooking a rainbow at about Buckley's. One person only aboard waxed content, the relaxed non-angling mother, settled in bow and reading a book. Albeit seldom did she accompany her fisho males, simply she'd no wish to miss being on this lake.

Too guessable though, was that the mother would grow bored. In a small boat, hints about wanting to go ashore can only be ignored for so long. When a frustrated female finally adds an, 'Ah'm awfi desperate for a pee too!' plea, it does need to be acted on. Yet, never mind that not a single rainbow had even sniffed at the baits, miffed the boy was.

'But mum, we might get a bite any tick now,' he protested. Actually, not without reason. Day drawing on, and water darkening, that mirror surface reflecting bush mountain surrounds had also started to stir more with feeding trout, and hunger can turn a fish incautious. However, one numb-bummed and full-bladdered mum, her Irish blood-pressure rising, insisted, 'In, okay? Nae delay!' The father, aware further resistance meant a barney and perhaps an adverse mood-swing, told the boy to reel in and up anchor.

Only the father rowed. Perched in boat's stern, to himself the boy fumed, 'Just when they were about to bloody come on!' His father wasn't much less piqued. Vigorously plying the oars, he had them streaking along. This brought to the boy a thought that his dad's rowing technique had greatly improved. Yep, fairly flying. Why not then, toss out and tow a lure? On a ten bob per week lay-by, the father had paid-off a Mitchell spinning reel, an instrument far handier to troll with than a basic centrepin. Biting through the monofilament above his father's quill floater, the boy adroitly applied Old Ron's clinch knot tying technique to clip-on a swivel attached to gold wonder wobbler. This he cast far outward into their wake before releasing further line as he settled rod's butt on middle rowing seat, its tip sticking out over the stern...

*TWANG!* So fast did the Mitchell run, it sang like an insane giant mosquito. A swift lifting of rod set treble-hooks firmer into a five pounder which, with a spectacular leap, attempted to shake lure free. Secretly, the boy gave thanks his dad had the reel's tension set loose. He had neglected to check. Reel unable to release, either a snapped line or, more likely, one trout rod and brand-new Mitchell shooting straight into the lake's depths would have resulted.

But wow, that magnificent hooked rainbow! Way back in the wake, leap after leap after leap, a revisiting of scenes from The Old Man and the Sea movie the boy had seen at a recent Liberty Theatre screening. Meanwhile the father, after at hook-up ceasing to row, shipped oars and with bated breath waited, landing net at the ready. Even the mother was engaged, forgetting her bursting bladder, and, 'Careful, son, careful, careful...' engrossed in an activity she knew bugger-all about and normally cared even less for.

Eventually however, played out in a way Old Ron had instructed him, the boy guided a spent stunningly coloured rainbow trout floating on its side in toward the boat. Once netted and boated though, 'Och, poor wee thing,' muttered the mother, 'sae pretty too.' Feminine finger stroked vivid red stripe running nose to tail along shining silver-scaled side as the fish lay gasping on boat's floor. 'D'ye no think, son,' she smiled, 'ye should put it back?'

The boy stared, incredulous. Forego photographic proof of catch, never mind the opportunity to show and brag to Franz and Elsa? And what about the fine dining to be had, this fish affording an opportunity for his mum to demonstrate her cheffing skills? Nope, prize rainbow went into the bag, no argument. And those future catch and release angling trends? At this day's end, only receding further and further over that alpine lake water and those native bushed mountain crests they were.

Franz and Elsa knew the boy expected fulsome praise. In their sumptuous strudel accents, quite a fuss they made too about his splendid rainbow trout... two refugee Jews, whose own rainbow had a much darker end. Of their family members – all of whom had pooled resources to enable this delightful couple to escape the Nazis – every one of them had been exterminated. Elsa, heavy-bodied and sweet natured, spoke five European languages. Slight statured Franz had an accountancy business and always dressed dapper, white spats included.

Franz even wore a bowtie climbing mountains! He had a polka-dot one on the morning following their superb grilled trout supper. Both couples and the boy were two hours up a narrow rocky track leading to the Grampians' highest peak, and both women had dropped back to do what ladies prefer to accomplish under concealment. Not so men and boys, and trackside they likewise released some pressure. Also trickling nearby was a small waterfall. Tripping off low cliff it became a wee creek that crossed the path before chuckling on down through gorse and bottle brush and stringybarks into a valley where it became the beginnings of the boy's favourite river.

Sun high, native bees buzzed in the warmth. 'I am here thinking, Errrrchie,' said Franz with his heavy Austrian inflection, 'vy is it zat ve are not also availing ourselves of havink a vash?'

'Oh aye, that's a braw notion, Franz,' responded the father.

Both men unbuttoned their shirts. Already the boy had his T-shirt off as he set-to, scooping water over bony ribs and under armpits. At the sight of Franz' bared belly though, he stopped as if shot. Nor did that ugly zigzag disfiguration escape the father's attention. Unlike his son however, he could guess its cause.

Responding to the father's specific gesture at his gastric region, 'Ach, vas shell splinter,' explained Franz, 'at Verdun.' Cupped hands raising water, the World War One survivor took a sip. He dabbed his face and neck. 'And you, Errrrchie,' he said, 'how vas it with you? Any vounds?'

The father, hesitating, glanced at the boy. He then shrugged and raised high a roomy leg of trousers he himself had made at the factory. Revealed were horrendous puckered scars behind his lower thigh, knee, and calf.

'Ach zo, a shell found you as vell?'

'Nae, anti-personnel bomb.' The father let trouser leg drop before the boy got any closer.

'Dad, can I see properly?'

'It isnae necessary, son, okay?'

Seldom did the father speak with such stony adamance. When he did, the boy knew not to pursue whatever the issue. At least he'd discovered why his dad never wore shorts, never mind swimming trunks, and always entered the sea clad in those daggy slacks. Understandable? Perhaps, but it crossed the boy's mind that few of those Kokoda Track hero dads of his schoolmates would have a wound like that, and how great it'd be if he could drag his own in for a 'show and tell'. Explained too though, to some degree, was that oddity of never even in their home seeing his father's legs bare, where before the boy had put this down to a puritanical Presbyterian atmosphere ensuring nakedness just did not happen.

Dwell on this curious situation of strict modesty however, the boy wasn't likely to do. Yet his dad's horribly scarred leg...? That knowledge was sunk away, to be raised almost too many years hence, when appreciation existed that such medals of the flesh counted for far more than a row of metal ones on any chest. The irony attached to Franz's battlefield legacy would also be retained. That this ageing gentleman, having faithfully served his Kaiser, could well have been, as were many former German soldiers of Jewish origin, murdered by the Nazis…? The boy now had an awareness of the absolute ridiculousness of war and blind ideology.

In buttoning on his shirt, Franz frowned slightly and said, 'Errrrchie, just now, something it is occurring to me… you know vat is the date today?'

'Aye, April twelfth. Why?'

Animated chat from the approaching women filtering through bushland cover, Franz, shirt buttoning not yet completed, patted those scars on his chalk-white tummy, to say, 'This very day is zee anniversary of zis gift here, my French souvenir.'

Many drams would be downed in the CWA cottage that evening.

The beauty of that Grampians lake demanded another visit. The boy had begun another football season, but one team had dropped from the Under-14 competition. This created a bye, and therefore the chance just before winter proper's onset, of a long-weekend away for the Queen's Birthday. Not that this marked Elizabeth Regina's anniversary of Earthbound arrival, or that it had a clear connection to any other monarch. But hey, Australians still dutifully stood for the British national anthem. And anyhow, what Aussie would, for any reason, knock back a holiday?

As Franz and Elsa were already holidaying, away on a European walking tour, this time only the parents and their youngster went. Nor would they stay at the CWA abode. Instead, they'd kip in a small square tent at the high catchment itself. Last trip, the father had noted a gumtrees-surrounded public camping ground and figured it far better to base themselves in that alpine bushland instead of daily towing boat up and down around hairpin mountain bends. A free campsite too, so that sat splendidly with Scottish sensibilities.

Despite the natural gorgeousness and isolation however, that too clean pristine body of water again did not yield many trout. Two only of modest size were boated in three days. Yet to a slum-raised father, his work hours all inside a factory, this mattered not. 'Communing with nature,' he called all angling, to catch fish never his priority. On the other hand, that young man the boy was growing into, he did wax impatient when bites weren't forthcoming.

Just the same, some of the father's attitude transferred. Indelible for the boy were those moments of thin surface mist over undisturbed waters at golden sunrise as they rowed out to cast pre-brekky lines. And later re-entering campsite to the blended aroma of eucalyptus smoke and bumnuts and bacon and beans fried over an open fire by one – this time staying in tent – mother, that would stay with him always as well, along with recalling those cheeky kookaburras forever set to swoop and snatch a crisp rasher out of the blackened frypan.

Unconscious memory also stored away that habit of his father's when, upon rising from sleep, he'd quit their simple square tent to stand and, with slow deep breaths, all but drink in the eucalyptus-saturated air. Maybe the son appreciated his dad's gratitude at enacting something impossible in the polluted industrial city of his youth, and maybe he didn't, but indeed, this life-embracing act was not for erasure.

As for the mother's mornings, apart from brekky preparation, a wee bush stroll and plenty of reading did her fine. Interest to again accompany her two males boating and angling she hadn't. Yet, far removed also from her slum childhood, relaxed contentment sure kept her darker silent moods at bay. And should a touch of glumness come, some kookaburra's laughter through that gum-scented atmosphere could always draw a chuckle, even about herself.

Essentially then, another happy alpine lake time. Never however, to be repeated. National Park Authority, that most egregious intractable of state departments, realized what pleasure ordinary punters derived by camping free amid aromatic gumtrees beside a mountain catchment. Soon a substantial fee applied. But then, in a typical strange act of bastardry, they chose to forego all revenue and just ban everyone from pitching a tent in 'their' park.

The general public's attitude when this prohibition became law, had been a standard one, an apathetic, 'Aw well, who cares...?' But well, the boy sure cared. His parents too, and other battling families who'd loved the no-cost freedom of pitching a tent in that exquisite tranquil invigorating environment. However, what could they do either? Nothing but move on. The boy managed to rationalize, 'Anyhow, the fishing's better back home.' Just the same, very true too, for that year large catches were being had from the river. Although later in life he would stew over mongrel bureaucratic acts like that camping ban, young fast-moving minds can soon forget vexations if distracted, particularly by something such as Old Ron saying that he'd got onto a new miracle bait called 'clickers'.

Crustaceous creatures, also called 'pink nippers', these pale soft-bodied yabbies lived under the sand in shallow seawater. A thrusting-in of stainless-steel pump into wet beach, along with considerable physical effort, reached and extracted them. According to the good angling oil, clickers' impact on bream catch had been profound. But were these wondrous claims only a further fishos' furphy? Similar tales had passed the boy's ears. He had learned to be sceptical. Nor had Old Ron himself yet tried this so-called super-bait.

Came that Sunday morning after one of Old Ron's sons had obtained for him a bucketful of fresh clickers. Moment of truth imminent, how hopeful the boy felt, made even better by his father's decision that, to test the miraculous claims re these baits, church-going and sermons about divine miracles could be foregone. Also aiding the boy's upbeat mood was the football of the day before. His Scumbaggers had copped their standard shellacking, but he'd been named 'best player' and as such scored a ten-shilling note which, for additional good luck, sat stashed deep in his pants pocket.

Old Ron's boat was being used. A graceful vintage white clinker with blue gunnel, it had a five horsepower Seagull outboard too, which just on dawn propelled them upriver, the boy in bows, his father mid-boat, Old Ron steering. Destination was a wide coral bottomed section of stream known as 'the Bay of Biscay'. Ten thousand days from then the boy would, as a merchant seaman, cross that actual turbulent body of water off France and Spain after which this river feature had rather imaginatively been named. Today, as Old Ron cut his engine and they drifted in to it, hardly a ripple disturbed their local 'Biscay'. Only sporadic bird calls from the cliffs on its south side broke the silence... temporarily at least.

A plethora of promises to expect lively action they'd heard. In anticipation of this only one rod each had been brought. Nevertheless, in the boy resided a mix of hope and doubt as out went the three clicker baits. Wait didn't last even until rods were put down. Three terrified tenors in sync, all centrepin reels screamed. Lines criss-crossed and tangled, the fish full of force and fight. Yet finally, on the clinker's floorboards, and thanks to clickers, lay a trio of black bream, all two-pounders, proof as to the irresistibility of this revolutionary bait.

A short angling sortie therefore, for only an hour later, creel filled with fish, up came the anchors and homeward they prepared to motor. Once at the Angler's Club jetty, more time would pass cleaning their bream than it had taken to catch them. A glorious morning's fishing could be tarnished by one thing only, the outboard's refusal to start.

Those bloody British-made Seagulls, how notoriously temperamental they were! Predominance of oars a thing of the past, ever more boating anglers used outboards. However, more reliable makes yet to dominate the market, on their river the norm remained some blaspheming rowing-homeward angler scowling back at and towing a useless silver Seagull. Yes, knuckles barked and shoulder strained from repeated wrenching of start chord, oar-power returning him to jetty, tilted upward in the stern of his boat would sit one silent alloy lump of diabolical Pommy marine engineering which, having powered him miles upriver, was playing dead for complete return trip ahead.

Three non-churchgoing Sunday anglers should perhaps then, have expected their prayers for a purring Seagull to go unanswered. Pull after unresponsive pull Old Ron's outboard went on behaving like so many of its shonky brothers. And so... to rowing, father and son each plying an oar. In the stern their older companion, elbow resting on useless outboard and rolling own ciggies, instead of directing invective at his Seagull, sat smiling and smokily reviewing their catch. Such a calming influence allowed the boy to derive real pleasure from interaction of sculling with his dad, this man in whom too often he continued to see only inadequacy.

'Hey, this is really fun!' laughed the boy aloud. A smidgen competitive as well though, the father knowing every so often he needed to cease rowing lest they go in a complete circle, and a young son conceding this tailor dad had more strength than often he credited him with.

Post that first clickers experience, Old Ron's classic clinker became the boat of angling choice. However, the boy fished less in it than did his father. The men began to, after work on Wednesdays, and regardless of weather, go out together on the river until midnight, each outing improving the father's piscatorial ability. Until life's adverse vicissitudes and work pressures prevented it, the pair would fish together for many years. Only away from the river and the blue and white clinker did the two men and the boy all continue to fish together.

Each year arrived the first of September's trout season opening. In this, as a unit, the two senior anglers and the junior were solidly involved. Now, ample trout stock did swim about in both local rivers. To these, as the mother did point out, went the town's sensible anglers at season's start. But no, reckoned the male trio, they were more imaginative and ambitious than that. Largely Old Ron's doing actually. Long troutless months at an end, he'd instigate an excursion to some inland lake. Planning had military precision. Essentials of satisfying rations to feed the participants along with effective hook and line weaponry to capture their wily adversaries were assembled. Precedence however, went to obtaining proper ammunition – the bait.

Designated principal scrub wormer, after school in the week before trout opening the boy dug all over that pastured riverside hill below their home. Another full footy season now behind him, bigger and exuding energy, he went at it hard, targeting those roots of bracken which were the large fat scarlet worms favoured refuge. However, the accessing their other prime lake bait witchetty grubs, that involved true grown-man yakka.

On a soldier settler cobber's uncleared bushland property, the father and Old Ron worked in tandem to axe down standing gumtrees, the bark of these marked by tell-tale chewing from cockatoos. Did it register with the boy that for a man who usually handled only tailor's shears, his old man exhibited a pretty handy technique when handling a heavy cast-iron blade? Possibly. His concentration centred far more on what came next.

Once felled trees were split open, nifty young fingers were required to winkle out the big greasy wood-munching grubs. All up, a win-win-win enterprise: fine exercise for the men, a tasty snack or two for the boy – how neat to bite off the head and swallow a juicy tasty witchetty! – and as well, the soldier settler got more of his block cleared for farming, little knowing that far into the future global warming fears would see it all replanted in native trees.

Scrub worms and witchetty grubs aplenty they had collected though, for a single day's fishing enough to last six months, and so away through trout opening's early a.m. pitch darkness motored the father and boy in their now almost vintage Vauxhall, off to pick up Old Ron... 'Dad, did you put the bait in the boot?'

'Och nae, Ah left that up tae you, son.'

'Oh... shit?'

'Aye, that would be right... or it would hae been had ye no remembered. Well done, lad!'

A U-turn, uphill run done in the blackness back onto their nature-strip. Quietly on foot so as not to wake sleeping mother, father then accompanied son along driveway to collect all those worms and witchetties from within garage. After which, the boy making to return to car... 'Ah, but see the noo son, when ye've forgotten something, it's aye awfi' bad luck tae turn straight back withoot stopping and counting tae ten.' And so, not until numbers were recited and father's Celt superstitiousness satisfied, did bait make it into vehicle's boot. Nor did the boy give a thought to his dad's whimsical irrationality, because he'd inherited it too.

Ten minutes later two senior anglers and their junior partner were on dark open highway, destination one low-lying lake situated within an extinct volcano. Reputed to provide the world's fastest trout growth, of late monster fish had been seen feeding there. Arrival still well short of sunrise showed they'd hardly be alone. Word about those huge trout out, Vauxhall had four hundred other parked cars for company.

Along lake's otherwise black shoreline flickered scores of campfires. Gear and bait and victuals gathered, angler trio got their gumboots in motion, and the trudge around crater lake's waterside commenced. Surrounding heights as protection against a now rising wind, from calmest pocket of shore passed came the *whissssh-whissssh-whissssh* of active fly fishers. The boy could just make out human shapes wearing waders standing up to their crown jewels in water, casting and casting and casting...

'Posers!' remarked Old Ron with a snort, 'Wasting their time in any case, until it gets light.' Yet telling the boy that in his younger days, okay, he had tried this arty-farty angling, and allowing it took skill and provided fair physical exercise too. What he couldn't abide though was the snobbery of many who practiced it. 'Look down their noses at what they call meat fishers, but we catch ten times as many as they ever will, eh?'

Knew a bit about snobs too, did Old Ron. And a valid right to dislike them he had. Once a champion single-sculls rower, on Lake Wendouree he'd beaten every other Aussie oarsman contending for the 1936 Berlin Olympics. Yet in those days a lowly baker, his rivals all private school and university educated professionals, the Rowing Association had sent some squattocracy blueblood to Germany and shunted one young Ballarat bread-maker into sporting obscurity. Not a man who hated, Old Ron, but the bitterness from such unfairness would stay with him until his dying day.

After going by a hundred bait anglers with their lines already out, a vacant patch of bank arrived at, hooks were worked into witchetties and 'scrubbies', and outward went long casts. After this a further yard of slack line peeled off reels got looped around empty beer cans: an early warning system, a tipping over indicating fish's picking up of bait. Then came the toey wait until first light, ears alert to clink of a falling tin. Meanwhile, in that coldest pre-sunrise hour, dry sticks were gathered, and soon another fire got added to that flickering red necklace adorning entire lake. To only provide warmth though? Oh no, for quickly a fry-up of snags was on the go, and tea brewing in a billy.

Yet come daylight's arrival, what a shock! Just as well they had brought that stock of bangers to eat. Almost certainly fish would not be on the menu. Ringing the lake at its highwater mark lay lifeless rainbow trout. Up to ten pounds, and of fine condition, but yep, all were dead as doornails. However, just as Old Ron suggested to the father, 'Perhaps we ought to try for healthier waters somewhere else, Arch?' an angler further along did hook a good one, played it awhile, and landed his fish.

Right, the lake wasn't a total dud. So, stay they did, all day. Yet of those hundreds of lines in the water offering flies, lures and baits, only a handful caught surviving rainbows. Of the boy, his father and Old Ron, not a single bite did they get between them. In time scientists would ascertain the likely cause of this fish die-off to be algae-based contamination. Whatever the reason, always the boy would recall that trout opening as one of his life's few great disappointments.

Late afternoon, fishless trio moping off toward lakeside carpark, the boy considered how dismally his father's count-to-ten bad luck avoidance had failed. Just as superstitiously though, he blamed himself – that forgetting the bait had jinxed them too. When they reached the Vauxhall, the father, maybe similarly contemplating their dud result, sighed, 'Aye, it would seem we were aboot a week too late, eh?' and gently ruffled his son's hair.

Down on his Jonah self anyway, but also averse to any display of male-to-male affection, the boy pulled his head away.

Old Ron seldom missed much. Placing just as gentle a touch on the boy's shoulder, he said, 'That's fishing y'know. If we always caught them, wouldn't that be boring?' When the boy nodded, he added, 'But your dad's dead right, a week ago here, and we'd have been hauling them in hand over fist.'

Over a decade and a half later the boy would experience staunch but less subtle support of his father than that given by Old Ron. In his too-cocky late-twenties, toiling on a Scottish oil rig but taking weekend leave, at a party thrown by family friends in Glasgow he'd run into granite-hard backing for his old man from pre-war pals. In fact, he'd cop a verbal arse-kicking, delivered by these men of tough experience and iron integrity who held a miles' higher opinion of their cobber than, judging by his son's disrespectful utterances, did this crummy young Aussie they were meeting.

As for Old Ron's path in the future, and the boy's later contact with him… Excessive overseas travels done, but as yet to resettle permanently in his home district, nostalgia will nevertheless bring about several sporadic returns to favourite boyhood haunts along the river such as those jetties once owned by Bill's family or the bridge. One winter's night he'll be trying his luck on the latter. Through bone-freezer air will arrive the sound of line peeled from a centrepin reel, invalidating assumption of having the bridge all to himself, and after deciding, 'I might as well go and see if this bloke's getting any,' still well short of this other angler, that fluid casting and easy retrieval of line by the cigarette-smoke-shrouded figure is going to tell him it can only be Old Ron.

For quite a while they will talk, this marvellous most decent man – by now indeed old. He'll reveal that although he isn't ready to quit life, tertiary cancers are giving him no choice. Not complaining, just reckoning he had worked hard enough to deserve a few extra years to enjoy his fishing. And yet, optimistic too. Huge 'uncatchable' brown trout occupied the broad – and by this time non-polluted – lower stretches of the town's other river, and he had a theory to catch one…

A week later, fast as a barracuda through a herring shoal, word will fly around their local fishing fraternity about Old Ron, found dead on that secondary stream's grassy bank, classic split-cane rod in one hand, landing net in other, and settled within this an enormous brown trout: what a way for that grandest of anglers to go!

In the Anglers Club rooms old photographs showed sturdy men posing alongside huge mulloway. All had been landed in the town's main river. No more though, were such giants caught, nor many smaller ones either. Rare reports, seldom substantiated, spoke of monumental struggles with a 'kingy', but usually the angler lost it – another 'one that got away'. That everyone fished with light line for bream contributed to this lack of success, but on the angling grapevine mulloway developed an aura of non-capturability: 'Lou, I'm tellin' yer, there wuz this joker last week, 'e hooks inter one an' lets it run till his three hun'red yards a line about runs out, then he pulls anchor, rows after it, but then away she tears again, right down and out the bloody mouth an' straight for friggin' Tasmania! Poor bastard never looked like stoppin' it.'

As to why so few mulloway entered the river anymore, some anglers believed they baulked at swimming over that blasted-out rock channel, for in earlier times they crossed only an open sandy mouth. Yet this just beginning summer, arrive once more they did. In big numbers too, following a large shoal of whitebait into river, and sending that theory re aversion to the rock channel down the gurgler. Real cause for mulloway paucity, beach netting of them in South Australia, had recently been banned. What a season then, for catching these game fish, awaited. Anglers therefore began to use slightly heavier gear. Yet mulloway still bore that bogeyfish reputation. Uncertain anglers remained beaten the moment they hooked one.

Did such doubt trouble the boy however? Fresh whitebait netted from straight beside the Anglers Club jetty, still powered only by oars, upriver he and his father ventured in their now beginning to wear-out boat. At a growth stage of really filling out physically, the lad rowed.

'Where d'ye suppose we should...' began his father.

'Reedbed opposite the pumphouse,' responded the boy, interested not at all in hearing the question in full.

'Och, aye, well maybe, Ah suppose...?'

The father's lack of enthusiasm drew a scowl. Okay, the boy knew most mulloway were being hooked further up nearer the Bay of Biscay, yet he had this feeling... Besides, his arms were tiring. He wanted a chance to quit sculling without being seen to be running-out-of-puff stuffed.

Boat positioned parallel to shrimp-weed alongside its drop-off, down went the anchors. Soon 2/0 Mustad hooks adorned with whitebait and attached to twelve-pound breaking strain monofilament – light enough to catch bream but with mulloway in mind – hit the water. Centrepin reels in use were bigger too, six inches across. Hardly had the boy placed rod athwart boat alongside rowing seat, its butt resting on gunnel behind him than it whipped towards the bow and almost disappeared over-side. Only just, he snatched hold of the cane, its screaming greased-up reel very close to smoking.

'Christ, son, a mulloway – let him run... aye, aye...let him run!' cried the father, excited for his offspring, and in standing up, threatening to capsize the boat.

The boy thought, 'What the hell d'you think I'm doing? Bloody sit down!' But, lip buttoned, he continued to allow the fish its upriver run along the weeds' edge. Once people regularly began to hook them, strategies for successful 'kingy' capture varied. Some were accurate, some dubious. Advice that, until fish slowed, the angler should not reef rod back to set hook, was sound.

Otherwise, powerful creature going full-steam, line just snapped like fine string. Yet, hook not set but the mulloway turning to swim swiftly back, a manic winding of reel was required to keep tension on fish before it spat the hook... hence that upgrade to six-inch centrepins enabling far quicker monofilament retrieval.

Textbook therefore, the boy's playing of his mulloway... until its U-turn! Now, despite frantically rotating reel handles, feel the weight of that charging-back fish he could not. Such trepidation, of any second line going slack and finding himself a member of the my-mulloway-got-away club. Aaahhh, ha, but not yet! The fish slowing, he caught up with it. Determined to permit no more slack line and also to further imbed hook, the boy hauled hard on his cane and kept this heavy pressure on. Racing thoughts centred on one thing: once this formidable species he craved to capture had been landed, how lagging in the successful fisho stakes this would leave his father, and... *Snap!* Clean as a rifle shot, line broken, fish gone. The boy didn't know whether to weep or scream.

A long moment of graveyard silence ended when tentatively the father, too well knowing his offspring's touchiness, ventured, 'Ehhh, d'ye no think that... perhaps, um... ye put too much pressure on him, son?' Reaction to this observation, the boy's blazing glare, saw the father say no more, and to wish, despite being absolutely right, that he hadn't spoken.

This single mulloway failure though, true to Celt superstitiousness, seemed to put a mozz on both of them. Many moons would pass over that river, and several more 'kingies' in the next three or four years be hooked and lost by each, before first the boy, and then the father, bagged his breakthrough mulloway. The real pity would lie in each doing it separately, and neither sharing in the other's actual triumph at the time of catching.

By now the famous tumultuous Nineteen-Sixties had been entered, but for some years yet rural Victorian backwaters would remain to a large extent placid shallow changed-resistant pools. Locally, the one exception was at the clothing factory where The Great Man's constant forward-thinking kept him ahead of his competitors.

Still, the boy too had broadening interests. Although sometimes near obsessed with fishing, as his physical and mental development continued, he did find other things into which he might direct his energies. Footy of course, he was already into, and throughout the warmer months beach cricket along with swimming – white zinc cream now often plastered on young noses but with proper sunscreen protection still not considered. When it came to additional kids' activities though, winter or summer there were also those fads which came and went.

Town's eastwards housing creep had seen establishment of the boy's primary school as the district's newest, which maybe aided in its students fast embracing some craze or other – hopscotch, hula hoops, yo-yo's, paper planes to fling and ping down locker-sided corridors or, if game enough, behind teacher's back fired across the classroom... and even in schoolyard letting fly with rubber-band powered shanghais that propelled fence staples, until their headmaster kiboshed this when some kid copped one in the eye, partially blinding him.

As well, monumental games of marbles would start, a score of kids rolling their alleys into a ring gouged in playground soil. What a coup to then eliminate entire mass of small coloured glass balls via 'eye-dropping' your tombowler from a standing height, and to then pocket the lot! The boy's super-size tombowler had been unearthed at the unattended town tip site by his mother as she rummaged amongst the junk. Her occasional 'rake-the-midden' habit, developed after discovering a talent for restoring antique curios, saw such items once cleaned and repaired, on-sold to boost her housekeeping allowance.

That huge tombowler though was a keeper for the boy. And use it, and devastatingly, he did. How satisfying to stroll homeward post-school rattling pockets stacked with cats-eyes. Uh-huh, king of the ring! Dead right, for a solitary day, top shite. Next lunchtime along had come a skilful kid employing a deadly tor. A knobbly ultra-hard pale-green marble got out of an old-fashioned bottle for which it had acted as a stopper, not only did it take out all the boy's cats-eyes and his prize tombowler, but also guaranteed evaporation of any lasting passion for this marbles lark... not that he wasn't set to embrace whatever next fad got introduced.

As for schooling itself, arithmetic barely interested, and even reading and writing not much. Drawing he didn't mind, but only to sport would the boy truly devote himself. Why not too? All able-bodied pupils had been used as slave labour to construct their own playing oval. After shifting tons of soil by shovelling and raking and barrowing they were certainly entitled to use it. So yeah, 'Gimme footy and cricket anytime!' reckoned the boy. Rounders, a form of softball using a small flat bat, he got into as well.

Ah, and then there was British Bulldog. This could get brutal. Done at lunchtimes, a few kids would stand in the oval's middle to be rushed by a mass of stampeding brats. Runners brought down then stayed to face the next on-rushing wave of boyhood... and so on and on, until only one lad was left to charge from one set of goalposts towards the other through a mob of salivating evil bloodthirsty young tossers. A bummer to be that last runner. Cruising for a bruising this individual would be. A test of mettle too, however.

This single character who'd be pursued by the rest usually came from the bigger kids' brigade, to which the boy, by now one sturdy blond fifth grader, belonged. When his day to become a potentially maimed Lone Ranger came, he felt ready. Not that misgiving didn't arise as he gazed at the daunting taunting tribe of knobbly-kneed thuggery awaiting him. But then, biting on his silver bullet, upon shanks' pony at full gallop he sprinted toward them. Momentum meant some gave way, but soon they were on him. Down the boy went, piled onto by a score of shorts-clad lads with rock-hard boots and bony knees and bayonet elbows and clawing fingers. Pinned under this pyramid of pulsating flesh, to his amazement he then saw, right above his face, that of a guffawing Mulgrew.

Now, Mulgrew, otherwise known as 'Stoolie', was a despised dobber. Several times he had caused the boy and others grief with teachers. A protected species though, father a prominent lawyer. School staff were always seeing to his well-being. Shithouse rat cunning too this dingo. No-one had ever caught him one-out to give him a proper pummelling. However here, right now, what an opportunity! Irresistible... *almost*. Yet if an arm could just be freed...?

So okay, so tempting. But, 'Nah, no, better not,' decided the boy. Well, until Stoolie lobbed a gobbie of green mucus into his mush. Incensed, yet ever more pinned-down, the boy could form a fist but not let it rip. Though, oh wait a minute, head he could move. Not only had a father from Scotland's toughest slums done some instruction in rudimentary pugilism when his son was younger, he'd also taught a handy wee move known as the 'Glasgow Kiss', a most effective but decidedly non-affectionate gesture.

Unmissable, Stoolie's schnoz. His howl instigated an unfolding of that pernicious mountain of vicious pre-pubescence. From pupil pile emerged the boy, his own face covered in the mashed-nosed Stoolie Mulgrew's blood as well as that same such delightful young mongrel's expectorant. Upon extrication however, off to the Headmaster's Office he found himself marched, six cuts of heavy cane across outstretched hand pending. Yet, worth it, simply to give their school rat a strong message? 'You bloody bet!' thought the boy.

Straight afterward, kneading and massaging bruised mitt, as headmaster returned cane to its cupboard, the boy reckoned he still agreed with his own sentiments re that retaliation… but only just. Amelioration of pain came though, via that same main educational cog which had administered punishment. A fair-minded old fellow their head teacher. Carrying a gammy leg from First World War service he did not relish his role as chief corporal punisher. On the brink of breaking into a grin, he winked, 'Not bad though, lad, extremely efficient. Just in future, be more sensible when and where you defend yourself.'

Certainly, the headmaster knew of Stoolie Mulgrew's ways. Not that, it simply being his slimy nature, even a badly battered nose would stop Stoolie from continuing to dob others in. Nor did that headbutt's justifiability prevent legal eagle parent Richard Francis Mulgrew S.C. sending the boy's father a threatening document. Even if litigation-wise the matter went no further, go down well domestically this did not, in particular with the family's senior feminine member. More her husband though than one hot-blooded son copped the maternal wrath: 'Imagine, you demonstrating tae oor boy…' Uh-huh, that unsubtle art derived from Glaswegian street-stoushes! However, once her feelings were vented and her two males left alone together, the boy fielded a wee pinch of reassurance from his dad. Grinning, he reciprocated. Sometimes, yes, this father and this son did connect.

The British Bulldog incident unfortunately precipitated, for a time, another of the mother's slides into silence. However, despite a treading-on-eggshells ambience in the family home, the boy figured he preferred the stony quiet of this to that shrill racket emanating from a house near their hill's base. Town growing, and ever more new homes getting built in the vicinity, this piece of domestic weatherboard wreckage had however been trucked in. It belonged to an ever-expanding family called Dawkins.

Former farmhouse, rough removal had sent its walls all wonky. Interior was likely a disaster zone too, for within it thirteen unruly kids ranging from a ten-year-old to ankle-biters provoked in an apparently almost perpetually pregnant Mrs Dolly Dawkins, fits of screaming. Shrieking really. Abattoir pigs having their throats cut were more sedate.

Doubtless Mrs Dawkins also suffered from depression, but of a much more severe sort than did the boy's mother. Endless domestic drudgery and over-production of babies sure did not help the poor woman's condition. On the other hand, that family's potent sire Douggie Dawkins…? A milder mouse of a man would be hard to find. A good foot shorter than his wife, he spoke in whispers. Nevertheless, his genius at reproductivity was exceeded by his mastery of technological equipment. He could repair just about any electrical item. Almost overnight a mini-Matterhorn of junk containing wiring circuitry had grown to dominate the transported home's backyard.

Those child tearaways infesting shaky home's internal space though, what a strange mob to behold! All thirteen exophthalmic and box-headed, they were obvious targets for schoolyard cruelty. Tagged 'The Dorks' by some sixth-grade wagster, one teary wee Dawkins lad, queried about the flatness of his scone, blubbered it was because his mum hit him over the head with a frying-pan, which unfortunately, might well have been true.

Fortunately, avenues of escape from the domestic racket going on downhill were plenty. Fishing of course was foremost, as well as five days per week fifth-grade stage schooling – less welcome usually, though that depended on the subject. But then again, matinée movies provided quite another diversion. Saturday mornings, and footy season finished, angling often took place, sure, yet during those arvos which followed, 'the pictures' had precedence.

Town boasted two Yank-inspired theatres, the Capitol and the Liberty. A grander structure of two stories, the former edifice, of additional interest for all kids who attended it was a titillating Adam and Eve mural, albeit that for eager small boys, strategic spoiler fig leaves foiled their curiosity. The Liberty on the other hand, its main attraction wasn't celluloid images but an external treat, that tasty tucker to be had a few yards downstreet… if a kid could afford the product. This family-run business claimed to make the *World's Best Hamburgers*. As to the veracity of this? Few locals had ever travelled globally, so no-one ever questioned it.

Both these theatres though, a magical and captivating atmosphere they did offer within. From the moment lights dimmed and every twit in attendance automatically stood for the British national anthem featuring a po-faced Queen with her bottom parked upon some sedated gelding, another world had been entered. First entertainment would be a black and white newsreel accompanied by a commentary of considerable gravitas. After this, on flickered vintage serials presenting ludicrous escapes from the previous week's cliff-hanger finishes. A string of cartoons usually followed that. Thereafter, should the feature film be some schmaltzy love-story, the rolling of its frames always provoked Jaffa-rolling down aisles and cat-calls every time its luminous stars pashed on-screen. A torch-flashing attendant bawling 'SHUUUUDUP!' at his raucous brat audience only furthered the fun.

Yet nothing cinematic or the usher's live pantomime performance topped that major attraction of those matinées. This was the swapping of comics. Pre-screening, at interval, and once lights went up and the show ended, in foyer and on sidewalk outside children paired off facing one another, each holding a stack of comic books. The smaller War Picture Libraries sat atop larger publications offering The Phantom and Batman and cartoon characters' capers. Individually flipped by one kid, the other perused: 'Readit, readit, readit... *haven't* readit!' – at which the never scrutinized comic would adroitly be plucked out by the holder and handed across. Once stack had been gone through, this process reversed.

The heroics of war were a dubious attraction for the boy. He prized combat stuff. British editions, better drawn, more realistic, and slightly less jingoistic than their USA counterparts, were preferred. However, that the battlefield bullshit from both sides of the Atlantic was awfully thick, escaped him. What he did notice though was that no stories set in the steaming muddy conflict zones of Burma and North Eastern India ever featured.

Now, if silver screen entertainment for local audiences began with them rising to silently laud Liz Number Two on her nodding nag, flesh and blood horses often captured public attention in that district too. Punting-mad Australia a horseracing nation, featuring foremost here, naturally enough, was the Melbourne Cup. Even in school all study came to a halt while this got broadcast over loudspeakers. Gambling addiction never then an issue, pupils and teachers alike held sweeps. Occasionally enterprising kids even acted as SP bookies.

Yet their town did host its own thoroughbred races, a public holiday granted for the gruelling Grand Annual Steeplechase. For a close-up view of this – hindrance by health and safety rules non-existent – the boy and other kids would position themselves on fence near the final hurdle to absorb not only that wondrous scary thunder of hooves, but to learn obscure obscenities as the jockeys, jostling for position in their run to the judges, yelled and snarled at one another.

Had the boy remained close mates with Bill, seeing as his old pal now spent all his spare time on Sport of Kings activities and stable-hand duties, he could have got even nearer the action. However, although enjoying the spectacle, the boy had scant interest in actual hayburners and their human close connections. In fact, if within touching distance of horses, they unnerved him. Only in adulthood, when a Riverina footy club's 'guaranteed job' turned out to be that of a stockman, would he learn to ride, develop an affinity with one special Arab mare, and learn to appreciate these superb equine animals.

Oh, but riding of a vastly different manner though, suddenly became all the go. Somehow this developed on the far undeveloped side of that same high hill the family home stood upon. Its steep north-western slope ended abruptly at a huge boxthorn bush, which in turn formed a barrier to one famous highway bend known as 'Battarbee's Corner', the landmark where lead cyclists in the annual race from Melbourne often made their winning moves. Still, a kid could end up a loser thereabouts too. On a bike, no, but mounted upon a grass sled. If in hurtling down that incline they were unable to avoid zooming into that spikey boxthorn at its base, severe puncturing often resulted!

A difficult to miss hazard too. Sooner or later most sledders ended up getting spiked. Grazes and bruises were common also, albeit surprisingly few broken bones. Helicopter parents a rarity, and dads little inclined to curb their kids fun and daring, within home garages were built sleds along lines and designs of those used in snowfields. And greasing runners' undersides with animal fat to make them go faster, potential disaster was never an issue.

Despite his non-carpentering trade, to his son's astonishment one tailor father proved quite adept at woodwork. Unfortunately, the timber scrounged from clothing factory's maintenance shop was narrow in width and thickness. This made for a fast but low-to-ground vehicle, which, in the kids' Butchers Picnics, proved to be problematic. In these, everyone positioned line abreast before all made a madcap downhill dash, if edging in front the boy had every chance of winning, yet should he veer off course, and a high-sided sled fly onto and over him...? Ha, but come on, such additional risk was simply an almost indispensable fillip to the sensation of speed and the danger of boxthorn impalement!

A simple, thrilling sport. What a shame that it too would soon enough become taboo, children made to cease grass sledding, cocooned as they started to be by a cottonwool society. Not that, anyhow, those Battarbee's Corner sledding derbies had any chance of longevity. The hill's continuing subdivision into building blocks could not but kill off such activity. As for that famous Princes Highway corner itself, its title came from the family name of accomplished artist Rex who'd taught renowned bush brushman Albert Namatjira the basics of painting... something else for later re-examination, future town councillors wondering if they ought to still express pride in this association?

A sled though, for a while, this the boy rode. What he still did not ride was a certain pushbike gathering dust and propped in back of the home garage. That self-consciousness block of his meant too that, except for a double amputee or two, he had to be the only local kid older than seven who couldn't handle a bicycle. Until anyway, just on dark one evening...

Walking homeward from fishing, roadside nature-strip of that steep hill leading up from the cemetery toward railway bridge, to its side in the half-light lay some kid's abandoned two-wheeler. The boy surprised himself by thinking, 'Why not, nobody's around?' Uh-huh, what possessed him to try he'd never quite explain. An inspired instant nevertheless. Absence of eyes belonging to possible mockers had to have been the major contributor.

Angling gear set aside, onto borrowed bicycle the boy jumped – a faster and faster rolling downhill, accompanied by rising fright when he realized the bloody thing had fixed pedals! Ever-quicker these rotated too, and yet… 'Hey,' he gee-ed himself, 'I'm upright, I'm staying upright!', seconds before metal steed ended this thrill ride by spilling him arse over head at hill's bottom beside the cemetery side-gate.

Despite post-prang limping home, knee torn out of jeans and a few inches of skin off one shin, minimal pain felt. Fishing gear stowed in garage, the boy then dusted-off and de-cobwebbed his discarded Malvern Star, and pumped up its tyres. Now, like every other able-bodied kid in town, he could ride a bike!

Ability to pedal a two-wheeler proven, oddly enough the boy still preferred walking. He always would. Even in later years when hitch-hiking around the planet, if a ride couldn't be hitched, onward he'd wander. But had the boy, back then, paused to contemplate this trait, he'd have twigged inheritance from his genes. One of his grandmothers deserved 'monumental walker' recognition. This was his dad's mother, a tiny Scotswoman four feet eight in her brown stockings, who would clock-up impressive pedestrian mileage well into her nineties.

In the past year both of the boy's widowed grandmothers had migrated to Australia, albeit they'd chosen to live independently rather than become fixtures in the family household. Tiny Scottish Gran occupied a musty mildewy boarding-house single room, tall Irish Gran an airy apartment. The boy preferred the company of his mum's lively mother. She told earthy tales from Shamrock Land and loved to wickedly spill cringeworthy family secrets. On the other hand, 'Wee Gran' was a simple Glaswegian lady with few wants and limited conversation. In her early twenties, husband already dead, she'd become a washerwoman to survive. Had the boy now joined in those lengthy walks of hers, a bond might have evolved. Yet few lads with boundless energy are going to develop strong attachment to a small slow-moving grandmother who speaks sparingly, and of trite matters never likely to engage him.

Of far more interest to the boy was the ambivalent relationship between his mother and hers. In contrast to stumbling conversations twixt the father and Wee Gran and constipated sentences of sheer banality, here Irish blood simmered alongside a glimmer of glee, and the subjects raised were broad. Conversely, the little old Scottish lady had but two real interests, which she combined. Walking took her to and from her other love, in her Glaswegian burr 'the picturrres'.

Uh-huh, heavy rain, hard wind, solid hail, or in fine sunshine, off Wee Gran would toddle to current films showing at the Capitol or the Liberty, and even in the most horrendous weather, always refusing to accept a lift from the father. This addiction to a 'braw walk' caused her 'ain son' embarrassment. Anxiety too, for what if wagging tongues got in The Great Man's ear re a certain Cutting Room manager's cruelty to his old mum? And here as well, it would take the boy a long time to realize that while a person's parent still lives, regardless of that offspring's age, seldom will simplicity apply when they are trying to be a dutiful son or daughter.

That young Aussie son of a Scottish father though, dutiful, him…? Normally the boy usually didn't hang around home long enough to be that. Even less so now that, having at last learned to ride a bike, and by this stage in 1961's primary school year confidence growing apace with bodily sturdiness, his independence had undergone an upward spike, and more distant localities were being accessed.

Not all destinations however are bicycle friendly. Railroad tracks make for bumpy riding and buggered tyres. They are damned dangerous too if a train hammers through. This particular morning therefore, the boy would set off along the railway cutting on foot, fishing rod in hand or over shoulder, hiking to the power station prior to climbing down those multiple hundred so-steep steps to riverside pumphouse. In readying to go he could hear his mother's own water consumption contraption pumping, clothes being laundered. A washday Monday, but no school due to teacher shortage from a minor flu epidemic – Bewdy to that!

Cylindrical Simpson washing machine already had several Persil-white sheets hanging on the Hills Hoist noticed the boy as he gathered his angling doodads. However, if the mother had her clothes-cleaning chore to do before going off to prepare those old folks' lunches, the boy also had a pre-piscatorial foodie task. Feline cuisine needed to be dished out. Back veranda, Timmy rubbing against his calves, he spooned tucker into the cat's bowl – 'gourmet sardines'. 'Ooh yeah, ripper,' he thought, 'I'll keep a few for berley!'

Yet in filching from Timmy whilst feeding him, an awareness of weather honed by regular outdoor activities also kicked in. In standing on their crazy-stone patterned open rear veranda, the boy detected a wind shift from westerly to due south. Flapping sheets then drew his attention beyond them to a column of charcoal smoke rising over distant rooftops. 'Shit!' he realized, before diving inside and shouting, 'Mum, the wind's gone on-shore!'

Mother's restricted view through small laundry window was enough to show those cleanest of white sheets making like sails in freshening southerly, and also to their right that billowing oncoming black plume. 'Och, Lord, the eight o'clock passenger freight!' she cried, fleeing outside skirts flying, followed fast by the boy. In semi-panic and semi-joy, they gathered the sheets, rushing them inside right before steam engine's voluminous sooty black emission encroached up backyard, engulfed, and then passed over the house. 'Jings, how close was that!' laughed the mother, giving her offspring a cuddle for his alertness.

To be sure, this Scots-Irish mum had her ups and downs, but affection she never lacked. They re-hung the sheets, and then off the boy went to wet his line, river's edge, down beside that power station pumphouse.

Rail tracks were designed by some ratbag to make them awkward for walking along. Never are sleepers neat-spaced for easy pacing. The broken rock packing is uneven and painful underfoot too. Yet any trespassing pedestrian choosing to use a slick rail itself to progress tightrope-style risks a sprained ankle. Ergo, in uneven steps, sleeper by sleeper between the twin iron lines, hiked the boy. Next scheduled train midday, safe enough, although rogue freights had to be considered. Now and again single replacement locomotives belted through too.

By these early Sixties, diesels did run on this route but coal-fired steam engines remained its monarchs. From town's long passenger platform until it passed that auxiliary power station the line inclined upward. Rainy days, piston arms jerking as drive wheels slipped then gripped, heavy-loaded freights made hard work of tackling that last quarter-mile to the top. Going slowly as they passed this section, faces of driver and coal shoveler rutilant from boiler's open fire-door, if the boy happened to be standing trackside they'd wave. Sometimes a whistle blast was delivered too. These heaviest trains were also handy for flattening pennies placed on the rails.

This morning though, the boy had not the broadening of coins on his mind but bream. Leaving rail-line behind he swung open power station's access gate into a paddock across which a foot track led to the pumphouse steps. Cliff's edge reached, he then commenced downward climb. Staggered in uniform stages, the narrow wooden steps were otherwise almost precipitous. Affixed to rockface by steel spikes they descended parallel to those impressive rising iron river water-sucking pipes which serviced the power plant's generators.

The boy wondered if at the steps' bottom company awaited. Auxiliary power station functioned more or less automatically but it did have two watchmen who alternated on day and night shifts. Both approaching pension age, one had a crook ticker. Of shambling gait and grey pallor, this shaky bloke shuffled to work in all weathers, his steps short but quick as he huffed and puffed upward past the boy's house, and upon reaching his workplace, went no further. The other elderly fella however, he drove a rusty-trusty Morris Minor to his electricity generating employment space, and for exercise didn't at all mind climbing down to the riverside.

What the boy's father called 'a romancer' – his polite way of saying 'bullshit artist' – for an impressionable kid this ageing watchman was a verbal gold mine. Spilling from his lips came far-fetched tales of man-eater sharks finding their way into the river, gargantuan ocean-based stingrays and squid that swallowed little kids whole, wrecked galleons bearing bullion... He spun stories about horse-racing swindles, of Chinese junks sailing in to disgorge hundreds of illegal immigrants at the breakwater, and nor did he hold back on hair-raising adventures concerning himself, some even, maybe, containing a kernel of truth.

Level of pumphouse's flat concrete roof reached, the rising smell of ready-rubbed tobacco burning in a rollie told the boy that indeed there'd be a witness to his fishing. Yep, there the watchman stood, leaning against building's grey wall. Dressed as always – hobnailed boots, bib-n'-brace overalls, and a red moth-eaten paratrooper's beret, albeit one thing he never claimed was to be an ex-soldier. Via a stream of exhaled nicotine smoke he offered, 'G'day there, youngsta. Wot yer gunna fish fer?'

'Bream, Mr Eassom.'

'Usin'?'

'Same as I usually do here, crabs,' said the boy.

'Go ahead, I'll watch yer get 'em.' An individual allergic to hard work.

Not that crabbing was arduous, only hard on the hands as it amounted to turning over coral-coated rocks along the narrow strip of river's edge poking out from cliff's base. By placing thumb and forefinger across crabs' backs, the small angry crustaceans could be picked up without a hunter getting nipped. Popped into rusted tin they'd then do scratchy sideways laps around its base.

This morning, capturing a half-dozen took only until the watchman's ciggy expired. However, after this, instead of embarking upon some implausible entertaining yarn as he observed piscatorial proceedings, he pinched thin stained rollie stub out and dropped it into his bib 'n brace top pocket. 'Scuse I, youngsta,' he apologised, 'but a man's gotta go phone-in a coupla bets.' And with this, he departed arduously upward.

Aaah yep, mobile telephones? Impossible to even imagine them back then. The watchman needed to climb all that so-so-so steep way up those doglegging three hundred and ninety steps to get to a public phone outside the power station and from there connect with his SP bookie or TAB account or some accommodating mate, or however else he intended to put a few quid on a galloper or pacer or dishlicker.

Momentarily the boy felt his sudden solitude, but soon figured he wasn't too sorry to be missing the usual feast of far-fetched fabulism. He had serious fishing to do here. Reward for warning his mother about the train smoke had been not just a promise of a scrumptious rhubarb pie as that night's dessert, but also French fries getting made '...tae go wi' all thae bream ye'll be bringing hame.'

Great expectations then, which crab bait might well help fulfill. Bigger fish did tend to take a crustacean, tiddlers leave it alone. Slower going, yes, but often it paid off. Best not to be a crab though, or for the angler to have much of a conscience or compassion. Bait presentation involved first twisting off the nippers before removing all legs on one side, the theory being bream grab a crab at its most vulnerable spot. After this, through eye on crab's leggy side went the hook, its point then worked out of opposite eye on the legless side – a practice to produce a plethora of protests from appalled animal liberationists, had they existed in that era.

Baiting done, outward under a running sinker sailed first unfortunate wee creature, and rod got placed flat on a couple of poking-above-surface rocks. A twenty-minute wait, but then rod's tip buried in the water and reel screamed. Ever-faster turning handles blurred before, following a game fight, into and onto coral and limestone bank came a bream of two pounds. A short while more and another was landed. Great, tonight's main course taken care of! Just as well too. Thereafter all fish action died.

For a while the boy amused himself by skimming flat yonnies across calm river, counting the skips… 'Onetwothreefour fivesixseveneightnine!' But then, enough. What else to do? Take a gander inside the pumphouse? More often than not the pumps weren't in use, today no different. Blockhouse-like square structure had an internal pool twenty feet deep into which dipped the three pipes all a foot and a half in diameter designed to convey river substance up cliff and across to power station's turbines as coolant. To allow steady replenishment of its reservoir the pumphouse's frontage to stream had low concrete gates. What the boy hadn't known was these permitted not only a fresh through-flow but also allowed entry to fish.

Structure's open frontage had by its outer closest corner a small chest-high wall over which its internal pool and pipes could be observed. Forearms resting upon this, and chin on them, closing his eyes awhile the boy daydreamed – what bliss these riverside environs gave. But when once again he consciously looked into pumphouse pool, 'Jesus!', he nearly shat. Staring at him, barely sub-surface only a few feet away, almost imperceptibly swaying tail and wafting fins presenting an impression of hovering, lazed the world's biggest black bream! Seven, eight pounds…? No, more. Side-on to the boy, one great glazed obsidian opal of an eye encircled in washed-out gold fixed upon him, the fish gazed without fear, curious… if anything. Water of triple-filtered clarity, magnificent creature's every feature stood out, its grand blue nose, those parting and closing lips of similar hue, shilling-sized dark-silver scales, and the gently waving greyish tail and pectoral fins.

Once over his shock the boy took practical stock. Ambition took over. Imagine the fame claiming both Anglers Club cup for season's biggest bream *and* a possible world record! Ever so slowly he lowered himself behind the outer small wall and backed away. A rush followed, to cane rod, a reeling in, and removal of sinker to employ the technique of Bill's mother – using only a hook and no weight. Fresh crab selected, a soft-shelled one. With this put on, back to pumphouse's front crept the boy, and keeping low, peeped in.

Fish had shifted, moved into far shadow deep down to feed on corals along artificial pool's back wall. 'Good, he's hungry,' thought the boy. Resist a yummy soft crab it shouldn't. Then, remembering too his berley of Timmy's sardines, in were tossed a small crushed mittful of these to further whet king bream's appetite. Only after this came the flicked presentation of weightless bait. Cast restricted by structure's side wall and nearest vertical suction pipe, crab nevertheless plopped into a promising spot, rod got propped at an angle upon concrete gate's top, and the boy dropped out of sight to wait.

And wait he did, waited, waited, waited. Not impatient, optimistic. Yet realistic also. No black bream could reach such a size without astounding canniness and caution. Chuck in a truckload of luck too. But crikey, so bloody big! 'Can a bream grow to ten pounds?' wondered the boy, spreading a little mayonnaise on his earlier estimated weight. Hooo-eeee! Except, okay, water did magnify. Regardless though, for this species, what an enormous...

Scream, the reel did not. It steamed as it shrieked! Forked lightning too, moves slower than did the boy. Lunging, he grasped his severely bowed rod. Yet, same moment, the reel stopped, and instead of feeling a great fish fighting... snagged! Massive bream, so strong, so savvy, had charged straight around one of the three big suction pipes. Done two loops of it as well. Dinner-plate side now flashed as, again and again, the fish jerked mightily, trying to break line, until... *Snap!*... away it dived bullet-swift, and escaping through same opening under concrete gate through which it had entered, shot back out into the river's middle.

Knees still shaky from excitement, the boy approached home. Barely could he wait to relate his tale. To the mother, folding those now dry sheets before leaving for her midday cooking job, the details were blurted. But, disbelieved! 'Oh aye,' she smiled, 'anither one that got away, eh?' Then, on evening, when the father got home from work... 'Och, Ah'm sure it was aye big, son, but d'ye no ken bream dinnae grow tae onything like that size.'

To have his piscatorial knowledge questioned needled the boy nearly as much as suggestions he was maybe even lying. Because porky pies he did not tell, there his real anger lay. Other faults, sure, he admitted to. Fib though, no, this he never did. Could it have been of any use whatsoever to know that in a rich and varied existence awaiting him, two things would continue to infuriate: receiving ridicule, and being branded a bullshitter by some drongo with all the life experience of a hermit crab? Probably not.

But indeed, as in time the boy was to learn, journeys into

remotest locations and associated anecdote accumulation, when served as verbal dinner-party fodder to the unimaginative, will not only draw sceptical sniggers but also see the storyteller realize that, unless with similarly inclined and experienced companions, the true traveller ought to just keep his or her gob clam-like.

This evening's sceptical indoors ambience more than enough for him however, severe his huff, outside hustled the boy. In a geraniums filled garden-bed Timmy was stalking skinks. Picking up his ginger tom the boy sat under a half-grown almond tree and, patting cat, divulged dark feelings about parents with no capacity for faith in their offspring's veracity. Ah, such wonders loud purring can bring about too. Once placed into a cooler headspace by his pet's sympathetic reassurance, the boy resolved, sans corroborative witnesses, to never again speak of losing a large fish. After this he related that morning's happenings to Timmy. The cat, pleasingly, appeared to hang on every word, even if the only one which really interested him was 'bream'.

Hmmm, cats? Intolerant and insouciant and independent they may be, but they are non-judgemental. By now the boy had come around to accepting he had never been going to land that huge bream anyway – its line-snapping strength, all those snaggy options available within the pumphouse… He therefore put it to Timmy, 'What do you reckon then puss, good luck to our fish?' The cat purred its agreement. As for any possibility that king bream might later be caught by his master in the open river? Once hook in that wily lunker's mouth rusted away, odds it'd again take anyone's bait were wafer slim. Just the same, some other mighty cousins lived in those salt waters. Land one of these, the boy promised Timmy, he would do… 'Yeah, mate, we'll show them!'

Meanwhile, at least that nice-sized pair had been bagged prior to the bumper bream busting free, and two aromas were beginning to mingle – frying fish and chips along with baking rhubarb pie. The boy reckoned, alright, one doubting mother could be forgiven. His disbelieving dad though, probably not.

River, Anglers Club jetty, start of another summer, pink Saturday dawn, attack on fish imminent... Yet upon bream, no. Single special still-to-be-landed mulloway occupied an eleven-year-old mind. At first light the boy had set off like a footslogger, armed to the teeth with four rods. Rather than in a clumsy fashion rope quartet of canes along bar of his bike, he'd instead bound them together and hiked on down to one ever-shoddier ply-hulled boat, their banged together by one shite non-shipwright house-builder vessel.

So yes, after spooning a bowl of cold sugared Weetbix into himself, to block's end he had headed the boy, then across familiar rail-line, and onto that long paddock slope leading to nearer boat-hire jetties. In so doing, mid-point of grassy hill he had passed a broad circle burnt into its green pasture, and within this a scattering of blackened innersprings. How massive the bonfire which, after dark a month back, blazed there! Effigy of a long-deceased Pommy political activist propped atop it, and around flaming perimeter kids of all ages and adults detonating crackers and igniting skyrockets and Roman candles and Catherine wheels... merriment and shock and awe absolute. Culmination of many months' preparation, tree limbs, broken furniture, mattresses, old fence palings, cardboard boxes, threadbare tyres, all were chucked on to build this pyre: anything flammable and available to make one wee combustible mountain.

In helping to construct the enormous cone for torching the boy had reunited briefly with Bill, whose rugged wombat-bodied old man organised it all. Such planning! Prime target too, of course and unfortunately, for future banning by a timid society concerned by men and women making like reckless children again, and all the while letting their own kids handle explosives as if they too were adults, with everyone thrilling to setting off their own fireworks. Like crikey, how about copping that night sky turned into star showers, the blasting of countless objects to bits with thrupenny bungers! As for a few burns and some deafness from hurled crackers and premature detonations... hey, no worries at all!

Such had been the boy's recollections as he inserted key into Anglers Club jetty's end-shed door, entered its fishing rods and other angling odds and sods adorned space, crossed its bare planking floor, and emerged into expanding dawn with the river and neat array of moored boats before him. Reaching their own tub, drawing stern rope in tight, he half-hitched it to mooring post, and then bucket in hand clambered into the listing boat. These days perpetually leaking, it always needed to be bailed. Beginning to do this, he once more recalled how fantastic that last Guy Fawkes Night had been, *the* ripper moment a letting-off of monster mortar rocket by Bill's dad, that former rough and robust ex-rover, since his heart trouble now ailing and frailer, but still such a motivator. Unlike his own dad. 'Och, Ah've heard enough explosions,' he'd said, opting not to attend the bonfire.

'Bloody typical!' thought the boy, tipping another half-bucket of scummy water over the gunnel. Together with fireworks memories, subliminally this morning he had been enjoying that cosy superiority brought on by rising before both the sun and every other local except their milko and his cart-pulling draft horse. But recall of his father's no-show for the bonfire pyrotechnics brought him down, inducing a sort of emotional damp squib-ness.

Yeah, and today another no-show. Supposed to be going after mulloway together, specific aim for each to again try breaking his duck and landing one, last night the father had cancelled, all because the factory received an urgent request from some venerated Outback cattleman. Mail-order suit required to be sent to his remote property, only one master tailor possessed sufficient expertise to entrust speedily cutting that garment, The Great Man apologising, 'Su-su-su-sorry Archie, bu-bu-bu-but it's t-t-t-top priority!'

Done over the weekend it had to be, and as in previous instances the boy could have felt pride in his father being so valued. Instead, he bridled. After all, not only had he caught them fresh salmon trout for bait, but also cycled way inland on a back lane to obtain a chunk of fresh roadkill kangaroo. Salmon and roo containing oodles of blood, this oozing scent made the chance of mulloway cruising onto a hook high.

Indeed, all that bait-getting effort, and then the father reneging, this had resulted in the mightily irked boy's four cane rods burden: so much bait, if he had to fish solo, he'd use not only his own fishing poles but two of his old man's. Total overkill though, and he knew it. What if, as did sometimes happen, a mulloway school came through to hit every line almost simultaneously? No-one else in boat to slide wide landing-net under even one weighty fish and heave its thrashing body aboard, meanwhile other rods being wrenched left, right, and very likely over the side...? Inviting disaster alright.

He then considered his solitary situation, and even if only hooking one big mulloway, the strain of holding long cane in one hand whilst attempting to get fish's heavy heaving body netted, how would he manage that without achieving a complete stuff up...? For peace of mind, decided the boy most emphatically, none of this ought to be given further thought.

Their failing boat sufficiently bailed, multiple rods and mega bait supply and gear got aboard, slipping both mooring ropes, the boy pushed leaky craft out past the tethered line of immaculately maintained other boats, and drifted into the river proper. Sun just tipping horizon, a light already warmish down-river breeze raised surface ripples. Oars slipped into rowlocks, in starting to scull upriver the boy surveyed their humble vessel. Uh-huh, not ageing well. Rot affecting its gunnels, three-ply hull now wore a few glued and screwed on patches. That seepage along keel would keep his feet wet and himself sporadically bailing as well. 'Okay, I've had fun in you,' he thought. Even with his dad sometimes too. But never a pretty object anyway, the boat's days sure had become numbered.

Zephyr an easterly – *When the wind is in the east the fish bite least* – would this old pearl of wisdom apply, wondered the boy. With any luck, no. Despite possible handicap of having to single-handedly haul in and capture that first ever mulloway, optimism had begun to ride high. And why not? Geez, what a piscatorial arsenal he had at his disposal – ace baits, and four... *four*... sturdy fishing poles! In fact, ought he to have brought even more? Anglers always accumulate too much gear. As well as this quartet of Indian canes lying bunched with their tapered ends projecting over the stern, father and son now also had several lighter trout poles arranged along garage's wall racks. Add to these, reels, lures, traces, and all other manner of angling paraphernalia, and they could almost have opened a fishermen's warehouse!

But no, this morning's quadrupling of opportunity to bag a mulloway was plenty. As for a single angler using four rods at once? No restrictions then existed on the number of lines an angler might have in the river. Some boats had so many rods sticking out they resembled bloody porcupines!

Right on sun's complete rise, over went the anchors, boat lying in against shrimp-weed just out from the Mile Post. That exact distance from the mouth, this modest landmark of a faded white pole stood stuck upright in dry bankside mud. A productive pozzie in front of it, parts of the bottom supported coral encrusted limestone reef – excellent fish habitat. The possibility of capturing that first mulloway, the boy told himself, could hardly be better. All the more by using such splendid baits. Out, one after another, they went, two hooks holding salmon and two with roo.

Hardly a better chance for mister mulloway, eh? An hour, and two, and then three went by. Save for those lines bowing in a risen breeze nothing moved. That bloody easterly! The old 'fish biting least' take seemed to be right on the money. 'But why?' asked the boy, directing this at a drifting-by cormorant. Equally puzzled to be asked, the bird ducked away under sparkling surface. Certainly, a corker morning. Complain about the weather at least, the boy could not. However, uncooperative mulloway, that was another kettle of fish. Sure-fire scent of salmon and roo chunks spread along the bottom, perfect running- out tide, but not one ravenous 'kingie' making its way upstream following bait-trail for its date with destiny? Simply, this could not be. Thus, all but convinced of inevitable action, the boy lay athwart the boat. Rowing plank seat his bed, gumboots resting on one gunnel, sun-hatted head on the other, he dozed awhile, and then went out to it…

My, how high into sky's powder-blue had Earth's solar furnace climbed by the time the boy awoke and again sat up. Beams of sunlight now slanted sharp-angled as they speared into the river deeps. Cheap wind-up wristwatch indicating ten minutes to eleven produced creeping pessimism. Jeez, five hours without a touch! 'Okay, that's about it,' decided the boy. On the hour, further fishing would be given a miss.

*Tick, tick, tick, tick, tick, tick, tick…* Big hand hit twelve. 'Right, bugger it!' thought the boy gruffly, grumpily. He grabbed a-hold of the furthest rod. Yet, although inclined to reel in hastily, some time ago Old Ron had suggested the wisdom of slow closure to an angling outing: 'You just never know. It only takes one bite to make a blank day successful.'

Gradually then, each untouched hook got wound in and de-baited, and one by one, rods were diligently laid to rest along boat's side, for too right, an angler just never knew when that overdue hit might come. This, always, was fishing, and perhaps its most addictive aspect, although usually the piscatorial procrastinator is simply wasting his or her time.

Only that cherished first-owned cane now remained in action. Further fishing minutes would ensue however, through need to bail out current ankle-deep leakage before homeward row commenced. And bailing taking place, vacillation in complete cessation of angling was seen to be vindicated. 'We're in!' whispered the boy to his twitching cane as centrepin's slack eased outward. Rod reached for, line's momentum accelerated, zipped taut, end eyelet buried in drink, and the reel purred – no scream however, fish moving off in an unhurried manner.

The boy guessed a biggish lump of roo to be the reason behind this sluggishness. Not swallowed, only mouthed. 'Should've given him more slack,' he thought. Too late now. That mollydooker left hand of his gripping cane, right mitt clamped upon reel handles to stop their anti-clockwise rotation, hard back he reefed the rod, laying into this so-long-awaited mulloway... or kingfish or kingie or jewfish, or whatever the hell else anyone wished to call it.

Hook set, an imposing force affected cane's end, dragging it downward. Bewdy, a fair weight sure enough! Allowing reel to run once again, the boy cupped hand under it to control fish's initial bullocking charge. Such power! Yeah, couldn't be anything but a mulloway. Having by now 'done' a few, the boy reckoned he knew. Lose this one though? No bloody way! Patience and extreme caution ought, this day, to finally see his first-ever of this forever sought-after species pulled in and boated. Rock his father too, wouldn't it. That'd teach the old man a lesson about choosing work over fishing.

Meanwhile, run an expected considerable distance, this fish oddly did not. It had got to doing short, deep, dogging pulls.

The boy figured he'd either hooked a midsize mulloway without much grunt or more likely a 'soapie', beneath breeding age and so named due to being at a soft-fleshed stage. 'Doesn't matter,' he reasoned, for in future they'd be bigger. What mattered was putting an end to losing them, of breaking his mulloway duck, and being able to brag about bagging one.

Tiring now, and high sun spotlighting those depths, upward and in toward boat's side without further massive fight moved the fish. Yes, its impressive head gulping on a gob stoppered by chunk of red roo meat, up it cruised. Except... Jesus, the disappointment! 'Shit on it,' sighed the boy, 'it's a bloody bream.' A splendid specimen, okay. Yet a mulloway it was not. And the objective of this whole outing? To capture that strong long-bodied so long longed-for kingie. Instead, another frigging bream, of which he'd caught so many, and so often.

However, but hmmm, hang on...? Just another bream? Actually, quite a fish this was. Nor had it yet been brought aboard, a fact emphasised by the bream abruptly wrenching around and strongly diving away, again deep. Anxiety increased now, the boy weighing up just what landing this bream might mean. He stayed calm though, kept his head while allowing the fish its. More nerve-wracking runs followed. In the end however, up the bream drifted, thoroughly stuffed, to turn tiredly onto its wide sun-splashed side. Only then, the silver scales flashing as guided landing-net glided under it, did the boy derive proper appreciation of this consolation prize's size. This confirmed it might be much more than simply second-rate compensation.

Rapid rise of net deposited catch onto boat's sloshy floor. Bream gasping its last lying there by his gumboots, 'Got to be four pounds, at least,' the boy assured himself. How satisfying the sound of this estimate too, rather than a metric assessment of 'under two kilograms'. Once that pending system for Aussie lengths, weights, and currency got introduced, how dismal the reduction in so much, especially fish dimensions. Whatever the measure however, as had dawned on the boy during his playing of the splendid bream, no Anglers Club member that season had weighed-in one anywhere near the four-pound mark… and hey, the Biggest Bream, not the Biggest Mulloway, won that coveted VFL Premiership-size silver cup at the end-of-year presentation!

Duly presented to the boy too, at the Anglers Club annual get-together, was that grand perpetual solid silver trophy. The odd aside of 'arsey young bastard' could be overheard, but so what? And helped immensely when a never prouder father fired him an, 'Och, they're only jealous, son. Ye aye beat they tossers fair and square.' Another rare bit of bonding, yes, and the boy felt chuffed for them both. No junior angler had ever before, or as it so happened, ever would again, win that Heaviest Bream for the Year ornament. In the years ahead some rotten bludger would 'borrow' the Norm Kennedy Cup and never return it. Not before however, on its list of recipients, had also appeared the dad's name, as they became the only father and son Heaviest Bream winners.

In adulthood, when hitch-hiking through Africa, the boy would collect mail at Australia's embassy in Lagos. Upon opening the single letter awaiting him he'd find in it a newspaper clipping of his old man gripping that same splendid dual-handled silver trophy. Won with a massive bream of nearly five pounds. And caught where? Off the bridge! As so often though, and by this stage a regret to both, no dinkum get-together celebration could be spent, only a congratulatory postcard sent.

The singular full-on celebration for the Scots is Hogmanay. This seeing-in a fresh year produces excess, of dancing, singing, laughter and traditional food consumption – albeit usually not haggis. And then there's the massive chugalugging of booze. To kick out old 1961 and kick-in a new 1962 the boy's parents were hosting the local Celtic diaspora. Closer to puberty but still sexually benighted, for the boy these notable shenanigans provided interesting visual enlightenment. Bagpipe and accordion tunes roaring out of a ramped-up radiogram, seated on lounge carpet he gazed up at dancing couples. Swirling before wide young eyes were twirling women, skirts billowing, and on astonishing show stockings, suspenders and French knickers... 'Wow and woo-eeee!'.

Whatever else the very green boy's overstimulated brain may have exclaimed, his floor-level POV mostly provided an appreciation that some ladies' bottoms were way wider and wobblier than others. These were the lively images too that he'd take away on that year's family holiday road trip. Post the January First party, father and mother and son would motor four hundred miles to Adelaide, the determination to depart on that same day something which may perhaps have been better thought through.

Awakening late that New Year's morning neither parent harboured any enthusiasm to tidy-up – the mother, coming down from previous night's high spirits, a bit blues-hit, the father still stung from imbibing Highland spirits. Therefore, despite all the Caledonian celebratory detritus scattered and splattered everywhere and house resembling Sauchiehall Street after a direct hit from the Luftwaffe, all cleaning received a huge miss. At least before departing mid-afternoon, the sole clear-headed member of that traveller trio, in bidding goodbye to his cat, remembered to leave out tins of feline food so non-holidaying friends could feed Timmy.

These trips here, there and everywhere though...? Stunned from Scottish partying or no, such travels were the parents' greatest pleasures, never to be quelled until that final fatal excursion they undertook. And sure, best of all, road journeys tended to palliate any depression afflicting the mother. Ergo, harmony generally filled the forging-ahead automobile's interior. Alas though, this day emotions were not on stable foundations due to those Hogmanay celebrations. Even vehicular interior being superior to their former falling-apart Vauxhall didn't much help. Faithful old black ducoed bus had been traded-in for a lettuce-green Torque-flite Valiant. Okay, second-hand too, this new family chariot, yet compared to the British chariot's basic design, far swisher.

Without a doubt the father was wishing he'd waited a further day to get underway. After-midnight Scotch slammers meant that had breathalysers existed, still half-hammered he'd have been caught three sporrans over the legal alcohol limit. Warm day, no air-con either... the boy could smell his sire's overproof exudation. Then again, continuing semi-inebriation had the benefit of keeping crushing hangover at bay. To motor on well into the night the father's intention, by consuming plenty of water he hoped to limit his suffering. Another solo chauffeuring effort too, the mother loathing to drive after dark. Travel plan sat as, that somewhere around Tailem Bend, after a wee kip in back seat had by the dad, on then into Adelaide early he'd pilot them, to beat the traffic and city's Hades heat.

As for the father's drink-driving... sometimes reasons exist to exceed even that customary Hogmanay compulsion to get pleasurably blootered. The Scots have ample traditions. One biggee concerns that initial individual who turns up at your door after *Auld Lang Syne* has been sung. This character has a particular name...

Party's midnight bringing and ringing-in just done, '*Ding-dong!*' and when the father answered their doorbell, on coir outside mat and holding a large roughly wrapped paper parcel stood extra-large framed Robert MacShae, a.k.a. 'Barge-arse Bobby'. Gob fixed in a gargantuan grin, his shift as a wardsman at the hospital just finished, in brrrroad Aberrrrdonian he bawled, 'Happy New Yearrrr tae ye, Arch!', and guffawing, thrust out his gift. 'Aye, and here's ye'r firrrrst foot!' Not that, as the parcel unravelled in the father's hands, yon severed lower human leg within it stayed long in his grasp. Dropped onto door-frame, the inside flooring there was fortunately of polished wood. While amputated portion of limb found its way into an outside bin, the mother's swiftly applied mop removed all bloodied smears.

Oh, och aye, the 'first foot' is what Scots term that bold earliest caller who crosses a home's threshold following Hogmanay's midnight chimes. Fair-haired though, this person must not be, for the Celts ken a year's bad luck will follow. No worries however, Barge-arse Bobby's mane was blacker than a coal sack. Nevertheless, his blackest of black humour, the father had to force himself to find funny. Any other time such a surgically removed limb would have been tossed into hospital's boiler-room furnace. As macabre jokes go, though, a cracker, even if it did take the father two overflowing single-malts to recompose himself and shake off his shock through laughter. Barge-arse Bobby on the other hand was reckoned to be shock-proof. A former frontline Scots Guards sergeant, the other party-goers maintained such a gory prank had to be all water off a duck's back to him. The boy overheard comments about heaps of blood and guts action this larger-than-life bloke had seen. It must have been far, far more, he felt sure, than had his own dad's experience in what... a minor Burma skirmish or two?


'Daunting' might well have described another former British Armed Forces sergeant who happened to own the Adelaide home to which the Victorian trio were going. Not that Big Tom Godden carried a gun during World War Two. His armament had been a truncheon. An ex-military policeman, albeit of disarming amiability, limestone ashlar shoulders nonetheless suggested 'not a man to be messed with'. From Somerset, he and his wife and three kids had migrated to Oz aboard former troopship *S.S. Georgic* which also brought the boy's parents and sister.

Of this South Australian vacation, to the boy's mind four things would adhere. First up came the teenage Godden kids' intolerance of a pre-pubescent being lumped onto them. Adelaide's heat seared itself into his brain too, that Sydney summer a few years back like mild springtime compared to Croweater capital's egg-fryer pavements. And then there were those two further 'unforgettables' which, all beaches being situated so far away from the Goddens' suburb set the stage for. One involved a plump plunging neckline, and the other a plummeting body – his own.

Only the city's main public swimming-pool could provide daytime relief, albeit scant, from those tar-melting temperatures endured by the plebs in Adelaide's northern suburbs. Prevailed upon to take the boy with them, the three teens – Sandra, a freckles-afflicted redheaded of sixteen, and her year younger twin brothers Alfie and Ralphie – made no pretence that once poolside, while they joined their *pimplesome* peers, their pest guest would be on his own. Sandra's attitude disappointed most. A secret smoker, 'Listen boychild, don't you dare say anything!' and so super-cool that, despite sweltering temperature she risked freezing to death, but smitten with her the boy. Still sexually in his shell, a confusion of feelings assailed him. Two bulging freckly boobs about popping out of a cutaway pink bikini top were huge contributors to his southern discomfort.

Yet, aloneness something that never threw him, the boy could cop a social chop-out. He'd find some other kind of amusement. And so, deserted at that pool complex so comprehensively overcrowded in sunburnt swimmers and splashers, up into a shimmering sky he gazed – and up, and up, and up... This aquatic centre's dive tower, what height might it be, eighty feet, a hundred? There were several levels. A magnet, the boy drawn to it like an iron filing. Ascent of steep steel steps commenced.

An Olympic-size pool layout actually wasn't a new experience to the boy. Not only had he been mown down in Bankstown's baths by John Konrads, the previous month, to great fanfare, one had opened in their own town. Compulsory primary schoolers' participation on initial ice-cube mornings, although dreaded, had led the lad to real proficiency in freestyling. Ever stronger too, now into his twelfth year, he'd quickly taken to diving too, executing quite a few off the ten-foot springboard. Granted, there'd been one back-dive where an overdone flip landed him plank-flat on his stomach. Crikey, a true waterboarding torture if ever there was one, excruciating sting bringing a tonsils-tearing scream, though released of course underwater so nobody twigged.

That gutser belly-whacker aside however, few qualms did the boy have about spearing-in head-first from quite a height. On his way to swim in the Blue Hole too, he'd now sometimes do twenty-foot dives off the apex of the bridge's arch. Therefore, yep, high-diving induced near enough to no fear, meaning years later during his merchant seaman stint, there'd be a hefty collect on their chief Engineer's bet about lacking the bottle to spring off another bridge, of dizzying height, their ocean-going freighter's. He'd even, when bumming about Mexico, go perilously close to taking Acapulco's diarrhoea inducing plunge!

Indeed, occasional blood-rush moments of madness, whether high-diving or otherwise engaged, were to reoccur throughout the boy's life. As for this Adelaide occasion, maybe it was just as well for one high-dive-happy Victorian schoolboy that his tummy plums were still more than a year off properly dropping from enlargement, and therefore wouldn't be left bobbing on the surface when he rocketed into the dive-pool's depths. What a vertiginous drop he'd now taken his toes to the brink of! Down he stared, down, down, down. Fully developed or not, did he have, he wondered, sufficient testes to pass this test?

Now fair enough, climbing dive tower to its very top had not been on. No-one was doing that. However, a few game kids around his own age were up here in the blistering desert-born breeze, leaping off this second highest platform. Over its edge, again, he peered. Height seventy, eighty feet...? He knew only that the deep purpose-built pool below looked smaller than a blue postage stamp. Sheeee-it!

'So ay, ya gunna jump?' grinned a weedy gap-toothed kid.

'No, I'll dive,' replied the boy without thinking.

Gappy teeth kid gaped, 'Really? Geez mate, you're bloody mad!'

Perhaps to some degree. Playing hero though, the boy certainly wasn't. Dive he knew how to do. Off that springboard back home, once only had he chosen to jump. Resultant awful shooting of water up a nose he'd neglected to hold had sent his sinuses haywire. Therefore, dive here he would... if able to so will himself. Yet, once positioned with ends of all toes over platform's edge, how easy it turned out. No leap, simply by leaning, tilting, and letting himself go.

Nothing fancy either, no swallow-dive. Body rigid from the second that he became a human dart, in plummeting the boy thought through his drill: 'Arms straight out, hands one atop the other, feet together, tuck head in between shoulders, and on entry, angle the palms upward...' ensuring a curving return to surface. Otherwise, if stuffing up and spearing straight into pool's concrete bottom? Might as well say, 'G'day quadriplegia!'

*SPLOOSH!* Close enough to a seven-out-of-ten entry, then like a cork, up he popped, unscathed. First thought, 'Perfect dive!' His second, 'What'll Big Tom's kids have to say about me now, hey?' Aw yeah, Sandra in particular!

And just possibly those three teens may have been suitably impressed, had they witnessed the feat and not been horsing around with their pals. The boy found himself disbelieved by the twins, and simply dismissed by Sandra. When he protested, she contested, 'Alright then, let's see you do it again.' Even with Victoria Cross winners though, a day's courage can be used up in one go.

Tail between his legs but determined not to be unjustly labelled a bullshitter, the boy later tried insisting to the adults he'd done that bowels-loosening plunge. They wouldn't believe him either. All he got was an invitation from the two mature males to join them in a neighbourhood wander, something about to provide a bonus standout for the demoralized boy's Adelaide stay.

In that evening's diminished heat, the father and Big Tom along with the boy and the Godden family's Alsatian Rex, began their stroll around the still radiant suburban block. Now, too many mutts get called 'Rex', but this dominant dog deserved his name. A gargantuan animal, yet also possessed of Big Tom's gentleness… unless a cat shat on his passive sensibilities, which a large Persian pussy just might do. Overheated by its excess fur, and dusk temperature remaining around ninety Fahrenheit, this thoroughly ill-humoured feline sat on its front fence's baking-hot bricks. Rather than offer Rex a conciliatory meow, it rose, arched its back, and hissed.

Instantly two men and a boy were missing one dog. Off after one fleeing Persian bolted Rex, into that neighbourhood house's wilted garden before terrified cat and enormous dog then tore in through front door left wide-open to invite any hint of breeze from miles-distant sea. Crashes, yells, growls, yowls, but mostly human howls of rage, erupted from the weatherboard dwelling's interior. Big Tom and the boy's father wide-eyed one another. Both then looked to the boy. Enriched with a mix of laughter and alarm, 'Coom on, we're off!' came Tom's pure Pom directive.

Quite a sprint homeward in that lingering heat! Nor was it until the mothers were cooking in an oven-like kitchen, the teen trio in a back bedroom under ceiling fan listening to Johnny O'Keefe, and the two men and the boy well settled into cold beers and one ice-cubed lemon squash that, in the fading daylight, poor Rex limped in dragging his hind leg: one very sorry for himself canine.

'Oooh, look at you,' cooed Big Tom, 'Coom 'ere boy, coom 'ere.' The Alsatian hobbled across, planted furry jaw on his master's knee, and sad-eyed him. Big Tom leaned slowly forward, to then remark, 'Cats!' Up jumped Rex, ears pricked, and gave a sharp ecstatic bark. Big Tom's broad hand delivered a playful cuff to one furred ear. 'Go on, you booger, noothing blooody wrong with you a tasty bone won't fix.' This being a Sunday, the wives' food preparation a traditional English roast haunch of beef adding further Fahrenheit degrees to home's already heated interior, a big bone with a bit of meat left on it was the very object Rex could look forward to.

High-diving takes many forms. Only a week after return from Adelaide, the spectacle of a far hairier dive than that done in South Australia had been scheduled at the local airfield. An air-show, main attraction was to be a solo parachute jump. In those pre-skydiving days a novelty, preparation for demonstration primitive too, this involved the parachutist clambering onto wing of a Tiger Moth and holding onto one of its struts to await take-off.

The mother had chosen to stay home hoovering carpets over ogling sky and risking a cricked neck. Just father and son motored the seven miles out to the flat grassy local airstrip. There they joined several thousand other gawkers to see Tiger Moth with its clinging-on daredevil taxi out, turn into stiff wind, begin its revving run, rise into the air, and then in a series of upward circles, climb to around a thousand feet. There it levelled off.

'Ah'm nay at all sure this guy is high enough?' observed the father more or less to himself.

As he did tend to do, the boy thought, 'Jeez dad, how would you know?'

Well, to begin with one of the father's wartime pals had been a paratrooper. Not that he'd ever mentioned this. Nor had he spoken of witnessing in Burma some unfortunate pilot 'hit the silk' at inadequate altitude. As for the Tiger Moth's height, it had stayed low so the jumper could easily be seen. After waving down to the crowd, the bloke let go of wing strut. Yet instead of executing a controlled body-glide prior to ripcord pull, the parachutist tumbled, continuing this head over heels plunge until a couple of hundred feet from terra firma when a white nylon tail started to trail behind him.

Too late! A quarter mile across from gasping spectators, as is said in skydive circles, the poor bugger 'creamed'. Actually, he bounced, most bones in body broken, and then lay spread on the airstrip dead as a shotgunned swallow. People rushed forward. The boy managed just one step. 'No,' was all the father said, an insistent hand upon youthful shoulder not to be resisted.

As the pair drove home the boy sat stonily silent. Other schoolmates were at that air-show. Once classes resumed, they'd be squawking about racing over and copping a close-up gawk at that carked parachutist. The boy on the other hand had got to perceive only a dun-coloured lump lying inert on manicured aerodrome grass. Not until the Valiant had climbed hill and passed into their driveway and the father shut off its engine, did he say, 'Son, during the war Ah saw a Spittie pilot bale-oot from aboot that same height, and his chute didnae open either. We had tae retrieve his body. It wasnae pretty.'

Craving further war gore detail, the boy heard no more – as with other brief occasionally alluded to connections of his father to that 1939-45 conflict, never mind that samurai sword, none was to be forthcoming either. An incident to instil deep dread however, that jumper's death, nor a name to be forgotten, the parachutist's: O'Brien. Only when the boy reached his tearaway twenties would he resolve to exorcise this psychological demon by making, at a safer five thousand feet over that same airstrip, a couple of static-line jumps.

Start of February... Father long since returned to work in the clothing factory, mother engaged again in cooking full-time for the Aged Care facility, back to school went the boy. Ahead lay his final year of primary education, in a system influenced by such anglophiles as Sir Robert Menzies PM, far too English in its focus and approach. First southern Australian summer week back though, as so often happened, the delayed heatwave hit. Air-conditioning in the boy's state school classroom amounted to one tiny electric fan whispering sweet nothings at fifty perspiring pupils and one elderly sweaty cantankerous male teacher. As academic attitudes evolved, masculine educators would become scarcer than chooks' teeth in junior educational systems. However then, from grade four upward, men tended to take charge of classes.

One crusty character right enough the boy's new sixth-grade teacher Sammy Smith, a bony and bespectacled sixty-something and severe of aspect. Yet he had a nice sense of humour. Ability to draw cackles from his class would enable him to develop in them an appreciation of poetry. A smart start was selecting 'The Man From Ironbark'. Numbed young bums fidgeted less over the wittier rhymes of Paterson, or of Henry Lawson, than when subjected to sugary stuff penned by what one kid heard his father call 'poofy Pommy poets', a term all boy pupils then took up.

Certainly though, not a bad old stick was Sammy. He only turned prickly when dipping-nib-in-ink pupils messed up their pages. Because writing involved an ink-well, cack-handers such as the boy were disadvantaged. Sentences by those who were right-handed dried behind moving pens. Mollydookers were apt to drag sleeves across their wet script. Avoidance trick was to cock pen hand and keep left elbow resting above the fresh inking. But should a leftie scribbler become lax...

*Cracko!* Sammy's weighty ruler whacked across the boy's left knuckles. Flexing hand in pain, salty drops formed on his forehead from furnacelike classroom and which had accumulated in both eyebrows, fell... *plip, plip* ...onto his notebook. Jesus, the chances of producing a pristine page in this Hades atmosphere? 'Buckleys and none, old son!' he might have told himself. Like, why even try? As Sammy returned to his chair, down emphatically onto desk top went primitive steel-nibbed pen. If copping another belt from ruler, or even cuts of the strap or cane, so be it. Obstinately, up the boy looked, and yep, he had Sammy's direct attention.

Journeyman teacher removed tortoiseshell frame spectacles, mopped own brow with a handkerchief, and observed sternly, 'Uh-huh, Mister Messy, a bent penny then, for your thoughts?'

Every boy and girl present ceased their composition. All eyes went to the boy. Gee, as if this heat hadn't already reddened his cheeks! 'I'm... I'm thinking I'd rather be fishing, sir,' he responded, not wholly untruthfully.

'And I...?' replied Sammy, a smile breaking across haggard dial, 'I am thinking I'd rather be drinking a very big cold beer.' Then seriously he said, 'But lad, we've all got to keep trying our best here,' before addressing the rest of the class, asking, 'haven't we students?' Which at best, brought unenthusiastic agreement. Chuckling, the veteran chalkie spoke again to the boy, 'Y'know, coincidentally, in regard to your fishing reference, staffroom at lunchtime, someone mentioned a huge shoal of trevally came into that river of yours this morning.' Sammy knew his students well, in particular the boy.

Fast as Fangio, a cycling home the second that final school bell rang it was. Rod and reel grabbed, some buggering about trying to find one particular item, then back onto bike the boy jumped for another swift trip, this time to bridge. But bugger, already fishers crammed its length. A mixed bag, some adults, others kids even more motivated than the boy. Hearing about the trevally shoal, from various schools these young smarties had got their arses out of afternoon classes, and wagged. All up, this show of so many hopefuls provided an excellent example of the angling bush telegraph's efficiency. This the boy had expected, and why he'd aimed to get there quickly. But there'd been that frustrating delay – 'Where'd I put my bloody sherry cork?' – searching about the garage.

Not that sherry corks were more efficient floaters than others, however when trevally found their way into the river, the white plastic tops made them popular with fishos. Gleaming voracious fighters, trevally were also called 'silver bream'. They hit like the Lone Ranger's bullets of that same colour. And when they did, in using a sherry cork, when this shot six feet underwater, a bridge vantage point let its shiny whiteness be seen tearing down, aiding judgement of when to hit into the streamlined fish.

As for acquiring these white-crowned corks, winos reclining on pub pavements and in parks were a popular source. The boy's however, had come via his mum, who liked to serve her lady friends sweet sherry. Timmy had been the cause however, of today's hold-up in locating it. Typical cat, appreciating cork's viability as a toy, he had at some stage cuffed it under the lawnmower. Yeah, that quarter hour taken to find the thing had allowed just enough time, it seemed, to stuff any chance of scoring a spare pozzie along the bridge railing.

Near-bridge's middle the boy stopped to watch trevally after trevally hoiked out of the water. Oh, the impatience of needing to wait until some git with a bagful quit. Although... ha, unnecessary! He sussed a spot to be got. Amid close-packed casting line of haulers-in were two lads still in their Christian

Brothers College uniforms, so a fair bet they were waggers. And of innocuous scholarly appearance too, the boy reckoned it unlikely any resistance would be received if he squeezed in between them... which proved to be true.

Bridge angling often went like this anyway. If fish aplenty were on offer, live and let live applied, give-way acceptance. Be fishers Catholic or Protestant, white or black or brindle, a fine rod-and-lining egalitarianism usually prevailed, almost a kind of fisherfolk United Nations atmosphere. No Nikita Khrushchev banging his shoe or gumboots here. Today especially, fun to the fore, and manic action, simply jammed together jokers swinging flashing trevally up and over the rail one after another after another...

Get into a feeding frenzy, do trevally, bite on anything edible. Not huge though, these that had ventured into the river. Few weighed much over a pound. Most were just pan-size legal length. Although, crikey, didn't they go! Such fighters, flying along sub-surface flipped over on their silver sides. With otherwise a dorsal blue-hue, lovely fish to look at. But when hooked, sure enough, they put one hell of a strain on rod and arms of any younger angler. Cut pilchard the boy's chosen bait. By the time this ran out a score of fish were stashed in that sugar-bag he'd brought. What sport! Ecstatic stuff. 'Will I keep going?' he thought. As backup bait, ugly parasitic grubs occupied every trevally's throat. Stuck on a hook, the fish readily took these. But no, he'd enough to clean already. Off bridge and down onto river-edge sand the boy went. While he scaled and gutted it occurred to him that a few trevally ending up in Sammy Smith's chalk-whitey hands might ensure a fair hiatus before any more pain came from knuckle bone zone ruler strikes.

Summer still not done, farm tanks running low for want of rain, and sweaty sixth grade lessons an on-going pain in the freckle, at recesses the main pastime of runs and wickets play at schoolyard cricket continued too. Once his secondary education started the boy would get into proper Saturday Colts competition – something else to eat into angling excursions. At present though, and footy season still two months away, as in so many summers before, weekends were devoted to obtaining fresh bait and the pursuit of fish. To this end, on a sunny February arvo Saturday otherwise ideal for straight-driving a Kookaburra pill using a Grey Nichols bat, catching crickets and not a cricket ball was occupying the boy's interest.

A minor annoyance concerned his father's involvement, albeit necessarily so, to drive them to what might be called the 'cricket ground'. In the dry spell an area of sun-browned dairy cow pasture, technique for gathering the zippy insects involved flipping over dry cowpats. Once lifted, wow, how fast those crickets dispersed to vanish into dry tufted grass or down cracks in the soil. Not that the father caught many. The insects appeared to be too quick for him.

That cutting cloth in substandard lighting might have damaged a Depression era apprentice's eyesight didn't occur to the boy. But actually, he didn't really resent doing the lion's share of capturing anyhow. Fun it was, mitt flipping down to trap these fleeing wee black creatures, nimble fingers seeking to pin and pick them up. Yet his dad doing no more than holding a large jar and capping it once a cricket got deposited therein… yeah, okay, it did niggle a bit. 'As usual I'm doing all the work!' he thought. But alright, yep… no chauffeur conveying them into the countryside, no fishing with crickets for perch.

Those very fish, off they motored to find the very minute sufficient chirping live baits were caught. Spot chosen lay in the main river's brackish region some miles from its mouth, a wide deep quiet stretch of water above a rock barrier that blocked upstream travelling boats from entering it. There, on a warm windless day such as this, as sun's effect diminished, riverside insect activity would only increase. Famished fish ought to then fin about set to pounce on any lively bait flicked out. Yes, an ideal situation awaited. Nevertheless, as sometimes happened, the boy couldn't shake a frisson of miffed-ness.

Even when on the unmade lane that led to what they called simply 'The Hole', and permitted the novelty of driving their Valiant, a bit of shittiness stuck to the boy's liver. No valid reason for it, other than perhaps inheriting a sliver of his mother's predisposition to get the blues. Even when the father, alighting to open clanky planking gate which they'd drive on through to a hilltop with commanding view of the river, offered, 'So long as ye'll no steer us on doon intae the drink, hows aboot ye drive us all the way up, eh?' the boy found it difficult to display how chuffed this made him. Then, when Dobbin the retired Clydesdale trotted over to inspect gate's closure, and the father laughed about the horse's '...incrrrredible farrrrrrting', the boy only felt irritation – all these years in Australia and still ridiculously rolling his 'R's'!

As seen from grassy hill's apex, in roughly an 'L' shape The Hole stretched maybe four hundred yards in length and eighty wide. At each end of it were barriers of broken stone out of which grew bullrushes, spiky reeds, and clumps of tea-tree. Yet even in driest seasons these allowed some flow to trickle on through. In flood of course, a different story. The river flew over the whole caboodle. Normal flow though was sedate. Ocean king-tides pushing upriver could infiltrate the lower section of blocking rocks and provide salt to mix with otherwise rain-pure content. This permitted the support of both freshwater and saline inclined scaly swimmers.

The father's plan this evening was for togetherness. They'd cast at The Hole's upriver end, having made their way out onto its broken rock 'island' via stepping stones to where estuary perch might be caught by perching on a large flat rock with ribbons of water running by each side of it. Technique concerned flicking a shot-weighted cricket into a feeding spot where, in soft swirls and gentle curving ripples, downstream through-flow commingled with the expanse of still water.

In the boy however, that skein of sourness persisted. Despite wanting it to be otherwise, and aware that really, his feelings had little or nothing to do with his father, he found himself saying, 'Dad, if you don't mind, I'll chase redfin instead of perch.'

The parental dismay was palpable. The boy too, harboured unhappiness. He really did want to join his dad, but hoping his own disappointment in himself didn't show, he turned and moved away. A degree of cutting off nose to spite face here too, because insects flying or crawling out of the rich native foliation behind that flat rock in islet's middle made all water in the near vicinity of it mightily fish-friendly. Even more significantly, trophy-sized perch had been landed there. Yet for the boy, not to be. He could not shake his negativity.

Away along steep-sloped bankside he went, intent on casting out over a narrow patch of reeds and weed where previously he had caught good redfin. Uh-huh, redfin, or freshwater 'English perch', for although allowing some salty inflow, that igneous barrier downstream also restricted this sufficiently to let The Hole support such species, making for a splendid habitat that suited brown and rainbow trout as well. All these fish were inclined to take a cricket too. Reminding himself of this, the boy's mindset shifted brighter.

As for estuary perch habitat, although The Hole's upper-end top layer was quite drinkable, this presented no problem for them. Unless their aquatic environs anywhere happened to become polluted, other water qualities didn't seem to affect them, and certainly not when quantity of salinity might be lacking. Fresh or brackish or salty conditions, perch thrived. The river's other major saltwater species, bream, had adapted to The Hole too, however they needed to stay deep where at least a smidgen of sodium chloride always existed.

Redfin, trout, estuary perch, bream... every one of these species would swallow a cricket. In preparing to more or less dangle this angling bait before one or another of them, the boy could feel that lid continuing to lift on his blues-ish spirits. Prior to a wriggling half-wrecked black cricket being flicked toward fishy jaws however, lead shot needed to be held between teeth and, via careful bite, crimped onto monofilament just above number 6 suicide hook. This done, impalement of jumpy insect effected next, the wet-fly caster's method followed – long toss on ultra-light line, unfortunate cricket allowed to sink, before very, very, very slow retrieval. If no hit, re-cast.

As ever with live-baiting, self-debate re ethics required curbing. Besides, whether taken by a fish or sustaining entry of barbed steel through its middle, things never were going to end well for the cricket. Nevertheless, totally insensitive to his skewered baits the boy was not. Conscience at times tweaked, and on an Eastern wind a whispered tenet of Buddhism entering his ear, he might think, 'What if reincarnation's real?' And hey, piscatorial impalers made to come back as a cricket or worm or witchetty grub or shrimp or clicker or crab, to themselves be stabbed...?' Shudder! As for Christianity's compassion, some peccadillo occasionally still saw him pay penance through being forced to undergo the tortures of Presbyterian Sunday school and church, and so religious based regret too could intrude. Like, oooh and crikey, what if Huey and Jesus were dinkum? How unfavourably they'd view using Mustad and suicide hooks in the torture-murder of helpless wee creatures.

Really though, first cricket sailing outward, the boy's concerns re his live-bait's fate were at best fleeting. Adroit the cast, retrieval ultra-slow, then casting again and even more slooooowly reeeetrieeeving, on he persisted, method as taught to him by Old Ron. Very satisfying it is too, to make long casts with a light bait or lure.

In fact, so much did this quasi-fly fishing technique appeal that soon the boy would make his own ultra-whippy rod, tie a few wet and dry flies, and give actual artyfarty fishing a try on their lesser but better trout-stocked river. Yet an overrated and under-productive pursuit he'd find this. To start with, narrow stream heavy in bankside vegetation, to do those impressive fluid ever-lengthening casts smartarse exponents of this supposedly superior practice employed? Almost impossible to nail without his artificial flies catching more trees than trout! Yet so much effort for so few fish, that would be the real killer. Fishing brings many benefits, but to the boy one of these needed to be food. Era when workers' wages remained constrained – even for managers in major clothing factories – what most counted to him was contributing to the family larder.

Casting of black cricket into The Hole continuing, the boy also kept an eye on that Cutting Room manager and father fisher two hundred yards distant. Rock barrier's middle and camouflaged by tea-trees, squatting on prominent flat rock, he too employed the wet-fly method as demonstrated by... 'Yeah, Old Ron...?' thought the boy, reflecting that despite their splendid friend still going out on the river with his dad, these days the veteran angler seemed less keen. 'But he's so good at it. How could he lose interest in fishing?' he wondered. Just the same, in persisting with his fruitless casting, the boy accepted a diminished interest in angling might be fair enough if too often your efforts went this unrewarded. An hour now and nary a touch. Along with sun, his enthusiasm was lowering.

That over on the rock islet the father had fared no better didn't, as at times in the past it may have, make for any boost to the boy's pleasure level either. Both of them had expected action. He really was hoping his dad would catch... just not as many as him. Yet, two beaut baits out, but not a single touch? They might as well give it the Big A, eh? Quitting first though wasn't the boy's way.

However, it would only take his old man to shout across, 'Whit d'ye think son, pack it in?'

A shout came too, the 'Oi!!!!' anything but negative though. Yet low-pitched so as not to scare other fish or spook the one already hooked. Whatever his dad had on, impressively bowed that sensitive split-cane rod he'd brought surely was. Substantial weight and power there alright, reel's purr audible over river's murmur – the quarry, presumably a large perch, running deep.

With interest the boy studied his father's approach to playing this fish. Not standing up but staying in squat position, over-cautious perhaps in allowing fish its head, but otherwise a carbon copy of Old Ron who so loved playing a good specimen he'd prolong its fight even if this risked the hook working loose. Heh, yeah, and if Old Ron sometimes made a meal of working a big 'un, his dad had to be turning this into a smorgasbord. What sort of surprised the boy was in finding all his thoughts about this were positive.

Impressive, definitely, was the father's calmness. Nor did this self-control alter when, raising one hand, he beckoned to the boy. No urgency, but certainly insistence. The boy understood – 'He needs me to help him net it.' But he knew as well that, had he been catching too, probably he'd pretend he didn't see his dad's wave of wanting assistance. Nevertheless, not this day. Dropping rod, along bevelled riverbank the boy set off at an in-leaning lope. Then, boulder barrier reached, outward he began to rock-hop. Weed-slick stones, thick upright reeds and bullrushes, tangled tea-trees... done quick this couldn't be.

When finally, the boy broke from last tea-tree and creeper entanglement, there the father stood, his back to the river, delicate split-cane rod in hand, line gone slack, and looking directly at his son as if the lad had committed a criminal act. How bad the boy felt. Had he risked a broken ankle, could he have got there quicker, slid landing net under the fish before it broke free? Guiltily he said, 'You lost it?'

'Och, well... not quite,' replied the father. Small smirk spread into smile. His focus transferred to a patch of spiky reeds sprouting from the dry silt surrounding nearest tea-tree. And lying in the reeds' midst...

'Dad, shit, that is the biggest perch I've ever seen!' exclaimed the boy.

At this, the father's overjoyed appearance signified how much more than landing any trophy fish it meant to see his son's core display of absolute awe rather than, as the boy had too often shown, a hint of envy.

True to the boy's nature however, soon enough after that huge perch's capture, ambivalence arose. Weighing-in on Anglers Club jetty scales at an ounce under six pounds, and therefore perfect for filleting, no such notion crossed the father's mind as he prepared to clean his catch. 'This is really weird,' thought the boy, for at the riverside cleaning table his father had produced not a fishing knife but an old pair of tailor's shears. With these he snipped-off fins, employed one blade to scale it, and finally gutted his perch by scissoring open its stomach as he might cut a length of cloth. Thanks indeed the boy gave that no other anglers were around to see this, albeit for the father he was only applying his unique skills for a practical task.

Next evening, as the boy cautiously picked his way through a portion of that six-pounder oven-baked whole by his mother, he thought how much easier eating a boneless fillet would have been. Therefore, when the prize perch had its revenge and a bone lodged in his father's throat, requiring a drive to hospital Casualty for its extraction, the boy's attitude to his dad bagging that big fish had swung one hundred and eighty degrees: that stuck bone served his old man right for a failure to practice basic filleting.

Nevertheless, next Anglers Club presentation night, when the father won Heaviest Perch for the Year, the boy would again feel that same kind of pride-filled glow and happiness which had grown within him out on The Hole's rocky tea-tree green islet. And although through the years ahead such favourable sentiment might dim, even now and again almost extinguish, always there'd be a rekindling, until much, much later, would arrive that moment of true affection properly catching alight, when for son and father it became near enough to an eternal flame.

Appendicitis, when it hits suddenly, is no joke. Nor, for a boy going on twelve, is having his genitalia shaved prior to that useless bit of lower gut, the appendix, getting cut out. And considering the absence of hair down thereabouts, the boy couldn't see much point to this shaving procedure anyhow. He didn't twig either what that cold silver dessert spoon, brought along on a tray with safety-razor, brush and soap, had to do with proceedings. Oh yes, still a most innocent kid. Just the same, there were these… stirrings.

In love he fell, plunged actually, with two of the trainee nurses assigned to care for him. Nicki and Vicki were trim-slim brunette twins with trendy short hair and cheeky humour in an era when teenage Nightingales learned on the job and academic qualifications hadn't taken precedence over aptitude. Nurses then were prevailed upon too to do the most distasteful shitty tasks, as well as engage in such delicate routines as shaving lower torso territories. These poor angels were also required, without aid of purpose-built equipment, to lift and shift weighty patients, hence countless later cases of 'nurses back'.

As for the starched nursing uniforms – regulation accessories to these appeared to be suspender belts and nylon stockings. For the increasingly interested in things feminine boy, Nicki and Vicki needing to bend as they remade adjacent beds and tucked in 'hospital corners' furthered a young lad's education re certain wonders of the female form and associated undergarments. By the time he left hospital he had a fair inkling as to the purpose of, PRN, that cold silver spoon.

Once back home recuperating and straining at the bit to once more hit river with rod and line, the boy sustained himself by reconjuring images of nurses busily bedmaking. For male youngsters in that virtually pornography-free era, captivating glimpses of active ladies' lingerie was often as far as titillating revelation went. But oh-yes-oh-yes, in the boy stirrings there were alright!

Mealtime, and the family had colourful company – or as might be said in an era far ahead, 'company of colour'. The father had brought two fine fellows about his own age to dine. Not all that unusual this, but that one was a coal-black Senegalese and the other a tawny turbaned Indian made it a little more so. Both ran clothing factories in their own countries and were in Australia to study the local garment manufacturer's renowned system and enlightened approach to its employees. The Great Man had decided they ought also to be treated to Aussie cuisine home-cooked by one Irish-Scots mum who by now, via her Old Folks Home cooking, had a very favourable reputation as a chef.

Here then, were these exotic men at their kitchen table, with the boy, determined not to stare, and unaware of other reasons for his father being asked to play host. The mother, maybe trying to find some middle ground, had prepared, not specifically Australian fare but instead spicy crispy Cantonese chook. In this decision she'd been fortunate. Many Sikhs are vegetarian, but not this one, and most Senegalese love getting stuck into any tucker!

Attacking their food with delight this manly pair sure were. Yet the boy did detect in his mother a discomfort, her fawning over-politeness to these articulate blokes almost as if she suspected they hadn't long descended from the trees. The reason was only because with her Glasgow upbringing, *RMS Strathmore*'s Goanese steward had so far been the only non-white she'd ever got to know. And now here were two human hues, one midnight black, the other river-flood brown. Some nervousness on her part was fair enough.

The father on the other hand, looked more relaxed than the boy had ever seen him. Carefree in conversation, his broad 'Glasgae' brogue engaged seamlessly with the Senegalese's heavy Frog-inflected English and the Sikh's melodious rich-curry tones. Each man having a dram in hand definitely enhanced the chatter too. All down to The Great Man though. His own policy to hire anyone regardless of education or origin or skin colour or disability or intellectual impairment, had seen him not only hire a Scotsman to manage his Cutting Room, but to soon conclude that his new employee was the most non-judgemental and non-racist person he'd ever encountered. In this, how much faster on uptake re his master tailor was the boss than that of the man's son.

The Great Man would continue to ensure that when foreign businessmen visited, the father acted as his ambassador. A pity then really it was, that when the three men excused themselves to shift onto front veranda for a private post-prandial chat, the boy had no idea of the boss's high regard for his dad. Nor, until when well into retirement the father at last verbally opened his wartime storage, would the boy learn that in Burma not only had his dad fought alongside African askaris, but he owed his survival to the cool turbaned head of a hot-blooded Sikh tank commander named Nand Singh. That veranda get-together amounted to a wee conflab between three old soldiers.

And then too, had some former Jewish ex-serviceman been included in their get-together, the father's non-bigotry would almost certainly have extended to him as well, due firstly to the ethnicity of that refugee tailor in Glasgow who'd hired a raw apprentice to provide his working life's start, but also because in that rag trade had been made many other Jewish mates involved in aspects of the same caper. Besides, outside of work were friends such as Franz and Elsa. Yet the father did draw a line at Zionism. Of this he'd say, 'Aye, unfortunately Ah'm afraid it's nae mair than jist anither form of fascism.' However, in keeping with his favourite expression, 'There are three sides tae every story – yours, the ither fella's, and the truth,' he had also advised his son to some day visit the Holy Land and make up his own mind regarding that particular ideology... which in his late twenties the boy would.

Onward advanced 1962, and into winter footy season when, after three years of being the Under-14 easy-beats, the young Scumbaggers, now sturdier pre-teenagers, kicked off on a winning streak. They still couldn't overcome the older bigger-bodied and better resourced Tech and CBC sides, but suddenly they had confidence in one another. And how brilliant for any team's morale that is! The boy too had a break-out year. Presentation night inside the Drive-in Theatre's café prior to first feature film, he won the club's Third Best and Fairest trophy.

Alas, all players weren't at that season's breakup. Cubby had needed to ditch Aussie Rules for the brutal stampede of Rugby League due to his family moving to Sydney. Another absentee was Steely. Surname of Steele, this lad had turned up at training out of the blue. About all anyone knew about him was he had a bad stutter. Kids being kids, too soon Steely got mocked as 'Missssttter Sssssstttteele!' In this mimicry, the boy did not join. Contact with The Great Man and his speech impediment meant he knew better... or he should have.

The boy's refusal to ridicule meant Steely trusted him, didn't quit the footy club, and they became not just teammates but real mates. Steely wasn't very skilled though, and one wet night of match practice, as the boy bent to pick up a slippery loose ball, Steely clumsily threw his boot at it. Missing leather, he collected the boy's fingers. Anger and pain overcoming him, the boy swung about to snarl, 'You ssssstupid bbbbbastard Ssssstttteele!' Steely left training that night and never came back. Never either, would the boy forget the hurt in that kid's eyes. He'd forever retain the shame of causing it.

How would the father, had he known of that episode with Steely, have reacted? The boy guessed that despite his dad's inclination toward pacifism, at the very least he'd have got his arse kicked, and hard. As for his mother, there he *knew*. If aware he'd delivered such a cruel retort, her Irish ire exploding, a torrent of razor-sharp words would have been fired, one stinging totally deserved verbal slap. A physical one wouldn't have been out of the question either.

Yet sport is replete with heat-of-battle reactions, oratorial and physical. It happens, always has, always will. The important thing is the retaliator, if over-reacting, learns thereafter to keep his or her own emotions under control, and their opponent's feelings in mind. Do such situations arise when fishing however? Seldom. When it comes to angling, peace usually rules.

This particular just post-footy season Saturday violence lay only in the surging silty flying-by springtime floodwater. In light rain several miles above The Hole, father and son had been flicking silver wonder wobblers into river's surging runs seeking trout. Nor had they got a single hit, and the rain-slippery banks made it a dangerous exercise. Whippy rod in hand, balancing on a smooth sometimes splashed boulder, the father enquired, 'Whit d'ye think, son... Ah ken Ron wouldnae fish in such conditions as this?'

Definitely Old Ron wouldn't now, the age and stage reached where rock-hopping around on rainy days over slick terrain beside rushing runs had passed him by.

'Okay dad,' agreed the boy, 'let's give it away.' Sure, for they weren't looking like jagging a brown or a rainbow anyhow.

As the father reeled in and reattached wobbler's treble-hooks to an eyelet, he ventured, 'Feel like driving on oot tae take a look at the Falls afore we go on hame?'

No worries there, thought the boy. River running a banker, the Falls would provide quite a spectacle. It also meant a delay getting home, and he had a fair idea that once they did, a prevailing upon to mow the lawn would result, a fate equating to one pet hate when he might instead be grabbing a heavier bream cane and heading on down to the bridge to bag a couple.

The Valiant took less than ten minutes to reach the Falls' carpark. In solid drizzle father and son walked to a vantage point. Even if just a toilet flush compared to Rhodesia's fabulous Victoria Falls which the boy would one day witness during arduous African travels, these roaring tons of brown water flung over a forty-foot drop were nevertheless spectacular.

Another spectacle occurring was the recurring upriver migration of elvers. Annual, but unusually early, the first few wee eels had begun to, like tenacious baby snakes, wriggle and weave and slime their way up the rocky heights at either side of the cascade. If able to stay out of the beaks of birds and jaws of fish, they'd determinedly make their way into the river's upper reaches and grow into large fat greasy serpentine creatures before retracing their journey back out into the ocean and swimming more than two thousand miles along its bottom to breed in the Coral Sea: another of nature's astounding phenomena.

Errant elver worming up a weedy rock found itself picked it up by the boy. He let it slide around his rain-wet palm. The watching father observed, 'Och, whit a journey they make, thae wee fellas, frae yon tropical waters tae here, and then tae years later, go all that way back again...' His gaze wandered away upriver. 'The natural world, eh? Whit a mysterious lovely inexplicable thing it is.'

'Lovely... inexplicable?' repeated the boy in his head. Such sissified language he could do without, even if no-one else was around to hear it.

However, peering through the misty rain his dad had kept on looking upriver above those tumbling Falls. 'Hie,' he said, 'is that no some guy fishing up there… come on son, ye'r eyesight's aye a lot better than mine?'

The boy confirmed that they indeed had distant company, someone who did appear to be wetting a line too. What else then could they do but go and see if the bloke might be getting better results than they'd had further down the same river? Bankside uneven, sometimes slick grassed, often muddy and rock dotted, they made their slow way along it. A chain before reaching the fisher they appreciated him to be no ordinary angler. A traditional one though. A blackfellow.

Presumably from the Aboriginal Reserve some miles further upstream, for a rod the bloke had a thin whippy green eucalyptus sapling. About eight feet of line tied to its tip ended at a single worm on a hook under an echidna quill floater. His angling attire was comprised of a battered homburg hat, ragged Richmond football jumper, patched dungarees held up with bind-a-twine, and old footie boots in sockless feet. A cut in half spud bag, its strap also of bind-a-twine, hung across his back.

Noticing the pair's approach, the Koori gave them a grin. Had it not been so friendly it would have been dead scary – top front teeth missing, just two incisors showing. 'G'day boss,' he said to the father.

'Archie,' replied the father, extending his hand.

The Koori shook it. 'Mick.'

'Aye, good man. So, ehhh, ye doing ony good?'

'Aw, got a couple I s'pose.' Affirmation hardly necessary, firm flapping taking place inside that spud sack.

The boy, a mite intimidated in meeting his first ever Aboriginal, but reassured by the rapport twixt his dad and the man, asked, 'Can I have a look?'

'Course yer can,' cackled the Koori, and lifting bind-a-twine strap over his homburg dropped bagged catch at the boy's feet.

In the boy delved. 'Geez, dad, they're huge!'

There were three browns, all around the four to five pounds – as the father too now saw. 'And this is how ye're getting them, aye?' he enquired, 'Just by flicking oot ye'r floater and then walking doonstream along...'

'Don't f'get the worm.'

'Aye, wi' just a single worm under it, hoddin' ontae ye're pole as ye walk?'

'Yair mate, keepin' pace with yer slower flow there 'long the edge.'

'Well Ah'll be buggered.'

'Yiz're Scotties, ay?' asked the Koori.

'Me? Aye. But the lad no, he's pure Aussie.'

'Not many pure Aussies left, mate... Got a bit a Scottie in me meself. My mob's all MacLeans.'


Back at their Valiant the father released boot's catch, and into it the boy put that trout gifted to them – the Koori's biggest – into his own catch-bag. 'That was nice of him, hey dad, giving us a fish?'

The father agreed. 'Ye know, he and his people aroond here... dirt poor so they are, but Ah hear most of them'll aye gi' ye the shirts aff their backs.'

'Yeah,' smiled the boy, 'Mick didn't look too rich?'

'They've been given an awfi' rough deal, son, the poor auld Abos.' – the remark compassionate, an accepted Aussie colloquialism of those days which the father had absorbed, and no disrespect or disparagement whatsoever intended.

On the drive home, future possibilities were discussed of finding out how they might visit the Aboriginal Reserve, look up Mick, and perhaps even give him a decent fishing rod, albeit he hardly needed one. For whatever reason or reasons however, it would never happen, and that novel interracial interaction beside flooded river, drift off into the boy's memory like the trickle of a clean summer streamlet.

Another presentation night, this was for primary school year's end. Twelve by two months now, the boy had received one minor prize, for art. To his parents, 'He has the brains to go far,' was straight-shooter educator Sammy Smith's assessment, 'but good luck getting him to knuckle down and study!' Spot-on, for little else but ball sports and fishing caught his pupil's interest. Yet how fate sees that life's cards fall haphazardly. When Grade 6 teacher Sammy moved on to other family groups, nipping in to collar the boy's mum and dad hustled Grade 4's chalkie blowhard Davy 'Doughnut' Jones.

Gut of ten-poisoned-pups, a Welshman hardly taller than a dwarf but ego huger than Uluru, what a boaster! His own poster-boy, Davy Doughnut loved bragging to pupils about his attributes: a big kid himself who never properly grew up. These claimed qualities included a gift to predict society's future innovations, and the superbness of his singing. Granted, hailing from Wales, like most leek-eaters he could hold a note. Otherwise, the bloke was the type of total goat primary teaching sometimes produces, a licence to lord it over little kids too ignorant and cowed to question their crap the prime contributor.

Braggadocio aside, Davy Doughnut also prided himself on an ability to steer students into apt occupations. And in those days parents did tend to respect whatever a teacher had to say. 'You see this expressive artwork of his here?' came the sonorous melodic Aberystwyth pronouncement. Stubby finger tapped passable crayon drawing of the bridge and river mouth. 'Architecture is what your boyo ought to be going into, you see,' went on the tumescent tosspot, 'for a grand ability with the pencil he indubitably has. Therefore, your laddie must, *must* you know, go to a Technical College!'

Alright, the boy could draw. Deft left hand could keenly transpose sights seen onto paper. However, a different fish-filled kettle is applying straight lines to symmetrical designs in Technical College draughting class. Less than one academic week into 1963 a certain new secondary school student had found this out. Already tech drawing class bored him witless. In this year that he'd turn thirteen, here he stewed, knowing a massive mistake had been made. Never should his parents have listened to Davy Doughnut Jones.

Neither did high-summer commencement of schooling help. Pencilled side-elevations and plan perspectives reacted poorly to sweat. An antiquated uninsulated space, their tech drawing space had a low furnace intensity. The same went for all classrooms in this whole dilapidated learning ghetto known as 'The Annex'. Until recently a disused high school on the town's western fringe, wooden-walls and corrugated iron roofs made it at that time of year a slow-oven. Too many kids wishing to enter practical trades, pupil spill-over had caused relocation of Tech School's lower forms to this unsuitable collection of crappy classrooms where the only positive on summer sizzle days might be if a sea breeze filtered through weatherboards cracked from warpage or damaged by termites. By mid-year though, these same defects ensured Siberian winter conditions.

On this baking day, unfortunately for those junior students within, the tech drawing room was slightly newer than most. Therefore, its walls less exposed to extreme weather or voracious insects, these admitted not a hint of sea freshened air. Jesus, what a sweatbox! 'Slovenly work,' growled Shitey Whiteside, their draughting teacher, his shirt all but pouring perspiration as his aggravated eye examined the boy's abysmally drawn effort. 'Come on, up here!'

Uh-huh, not just smudging left-handedness but sheer disinterest contributing to his substandard pencilling, the boy collected his first dose of enthusiastically wielded secondary education leather. Anyone speculating on what professions he might at that moment have been giving consideration to ultimately entering, the betting would be London to a brick that architecture was not included.

The Annex enjoyed no popularity with any of its young occupants. It wasn't just the disjointed joint's discomfort. Chock-a-block classrooms for technical drawing, basic science, social studies, and rudimentary English doubled as incubators for discontent among students undergoing a surge of testosterone. Only young males and their ripening plums occupied its desks. Girls were totally absent. As it now stood, this local technical college system segregated by sex its early teens. The majority of female scholars aiming for domestic and secretarial work anyway, even those few wishing to enter the sciences attended the town centre's main school.

Indeed, in that awful western edge gulag Annex only one member of the fairer sex could be found. Helen Chaffee was nineteen, straight from teachers' college, took art classes, and went eye-poppingly braless. She also wore what some Form 2 kid called 'Gosford skirts'. The unworldly boy didn't quite get the meaning, only that they were excitingly short, with their art teacher simply a sweetie following the then fashion trends. Yet for her to be in close confines to hormones-haywire lads deprived of mixing with girl students their own age...? Not the healthiest situation. Barely was there a lad not in love with The Annex's art instructing chalkie. Nicknamed by some imaginative junior larrikin 'Miss Passionfruits', this fast became just 'Pash'.

Fair enough though, even if thin-plated, silver linings almost always exist. Firmest at The Annex, of course, centred on that mini-skirted art mistress, which many an involuntary swelling verified. But after two weeks of being at the complex, the boy began to develop a broader focus. His secondary school's intense concentration on sport caught his interest, in the still-frying February weather particularly so its Under-15 Tech Colts cricket side's activities. Russ Mac the deputy headmaster and former Sheffield Shield wicketkeeper who coached this team soon noticed a tall slim blond lad batting and bowling at their practice nets, and detected a promising all-rounder.

Now, no worries, the boy had a tendency to resent authority. Russ Mac however, instantly he didn't just like but respected. That made two secondary teaching connections he now felt good about... three perhaps, if Helen Chaffee's twin principal assets were also counted. Or did that bring the amount to four? Maths and addition never would be his strong point.

As for Russ Mac being an ex-wicketkeeper, most glovemen have a reputation for terrier-ism. They tend to be small, feisty and yappy. Shortish Russ Mac was, but together with wire-rimmed spectacles required for the eye damage which ended his cricket career, he always wore a smile. Bore too an aura of positivity, and had he chucked his chalk away he'd have made a fine professional coach. Easily he enticed the boy to join his Tech Colts. From then on therefore, except for seasonal breaks between footy and the white flannel game, Saturday morning fishing had got the gong.

Besides, 'only nongs go fishing,' many of the boy's classmates would reckon. At and around that age of thirteen, uninformed opinions are pretty much uniform, and they knew what was cool. Bait-whiffy fingers definitely did not cut it, even if this did discourage picking your nose! As for the height of cool in this surfie stomp zeitgeist, i.e., to be a blond lair... okay, well, a show-off the boy was not. However, very fair hair got him halfway there, something which could not be said for the three Aboriginal kids who attended The Annex.

After Mick, that trout fisho met above the Falls, this trio of lads were just the boy's second contact with Kooris. One of them, Clarrie, attended his class, and no-one aspired to surfiehood more than Clarrie. This resulted in him one weekend pouring peroxide into his mass of curly charcoal locks and at Monday school assembly sporting the first-ever tangerine Afro.

These three kids came from that reserve located – conveniently for many of the town's conservative community – over ten miles outside the municipal boundary beside the boy's favourite river. In getting to know them better, he pulled on heavy boxing gloves and sparred with them in the school shelter shed. Despite those basic pugilism moves his dad had taught him, the boy fast realized the limitations of his fisticuff skills. The Koori mitts were quicker, footwork and evasive skills slicker. Fortunately, they already counted him as a cobber and so didn't take too much advantage. Yeah, a laughing and joshing happy-go-lucky trio these kids were... to only, in those rolling-on years ahead, one by one die too young. But until then, post school days, whenever the boy might run into any of them, mates they would all remain.

Cricket though, the Koori kids did not play. Footy was their go. Therefore, a whites-wearing whitefellas-only first game for Tech Colts Under-15's the boy found himself playing. Batting at first wicket down, too soon he strode to the crease. 'Trudged' perhaps better described his gait, for a fearsome fast attack he'd be facing. Its spearhead Kenny N, the district's sporting schoolboy champion, would soon choose a footy career over cricket, and become one of Geelong's greatest half-forwards. Now he was only a rangy six-footer with bumfluff and pimples who bowled quick as lightning.

Fifth delivery of Kenny N's opening eight-ball over had sent their opening batter's middle-stump cartwheeling. The boy had three balls to face. Two came through, almost unseeable, rocketing by to miss both bat and stumps. Eighth delivery then thudded into his pads. He'd have been LBW had the ball not somehow kissed a thinnest willow edge. Instantly his batting partner called him through to steal a quick single, getting himself to the non-striker's end and signalling that although he might be gutless, he was no fool.

'Over!' called the umpire, mega-thick glasses giving him a huge prehistoric frog-ness.

The boy, oblivious to his batting partner's strategy, felt pretty chuffed. First-ever competition run scored, he'd heard Russ Mac shouting encouragement. Heady stuff. Bradmanesque, he raised his bat before again settling over it to take strike for the day's second over. Tapping bat on the crease, the boy got around to looking up. Green mown grass in distance supported a white-clad monster with red hair and saliva dripping from its incisors. More alarming, adolescent psychopath and sadist and hater of all batsmen Spud Hall had already started bolting in to bowl.

The bouncer luckily didn't climb to head height or it may have been hospital where the boy woke up, if indeed he ever did. Instead, the delivery cracked into collar-bone. What dropped quicker, cricket bat or teardrops? The boy's lachrymose vision showed a cackling Spud Hall and his sniggering teammates... all bar one. Jogging over from his fielding position in the gully, junior uber sportsman Kenny N asked, 'You alright, son?' And when, numbly, the boy nodded, his chest received a reassuring rub from the young superstar, and into his ear was whispered, 'Don't let the bastard scare ya.' Yes, a youthful champion sportsman, but more importantly a champion adult human being in the making.

As for not letting Spud-the-bastard scare him, easier advised than done. Nevertheless, drying eyes and again facing up, to his surprise the boy felt less spooked than angry. Not that Spud's next bouncer wouldn't have fractured his skull had he not somehow got a madly swung bat in the way. But... be buggered if it didn't race to the square-leg boundary for four! And what applause from Russ Mac! From his teammates too. That all three stumps got flattened next ball didn't matter. Nothing is better for a kid's id than the realization he possesses ticker. Not that this stopped the boy wondering whether he might prefer sitting on a jetty observing a bobbing floater rather than watching some carrot-topped maniac galloping in to attempt sporting homicide.

How sports oriented though, that whole town, cricket and footy its dominant codes... Yet between that more sedate one where red leather balls whacked into willow and the manic other of booting inflated leather, came those mid-spring and autumn breaks. The boy had stored away his gentlemanly game's white boots, but before studded black ones were laced on to participate in Aussie Rules thuggery, an April getaway would take place. Reports of mind-boggling trout catches in the Snowy Mountains had, like snow melt, trickled down to the coast where resilient Jesus's final days were about to see both tech school and clothing factory take holiday breaks.

Towards faraway alpine lake in their Valiant beetled the wee family three of inveterate travellers, two males determined to massacre fish, the female member armed with excellent romance and mystery novels and resigned to, most-times, reside in tented confines.

Ah, and hey, that tent... roped in a zipped pack to zooming vehicle's roof-rack, loaned by The Great Man as a thank-you to the father for ensuring the previous year's massive order for

Commonwealth Games athlete uniforms had got completed on time, it amounted to a canvas cottage. In having four separate compartments this luxury tent most importantly provided privacy for a hyper-modest mother never seen even in lingerie. Not that the boy desired any such observational opportunity. However, along with his boosted testosterone, curiosity re the female form sure was increasing. Certainly, he would have welcomed more enlightenment than that provided by those anatomically inaccurate artworks behind The Annex's toilet doors. In fact, so puritanical an attitude did his mother exhibit that solid did the odds seem to be he'd been found in a cabbage patch. And about babies entering the world conventionally, he remained very hazy on that.

Upon roof-rack alongside the tent went three large eskies 'for bringing back fish'. Aaah, there's nothing like overconfidence! Expectations were however, of making it to a trout fishing mecca and a killer-diller catch. Therefore, as the Valiant ventured ever closer to reputed Great Dividing Range angling El Dorado, fish capture and not female associated mysteries had precedence in the boy's thoughts. Plenty think time the drive provided too, for it took almost a whole night and half a day to reach the mountains and ascend to Lake Eucumbene. Once more, impressive powers of endurance the father exhibited. Yet if his son appreciated this, he forgot it the moment one magical basin lake surrounded by snow-lined alpine ridges appeared.

Not another human in sight either. An open grassed patch close to the water sufficed fine for a campsite. Exhilaration soon gave way to impatience though, as like, geez, how complicated could it be to erect a tent? Well alright, if French designed, plenty. Not just the boy felt frustrated. 'Och, even bloody Einstein couldnae work this thing oot,' grumbled the father, supreme his ability to cut intricate clothing patterns but peculiar multi-dimensional tent assemblage not his forte.

Urgency attached too. Breeze that blew down off the whitened heights had quite an edge to it. Once sun departed sky-blue day, sub-zero night awaited. Now true enough, in most tents freezing temperatures present problems anyway, but not with this swank shelter. Insulated, it also had a nifty gas heater. All irrelevant though if it didn't get erected.

The boy ran his elementary technical drawing studies eye over spread-out paraphernalia, to suggest, 'How about we try...?' Attaching this section to that, he reckoned. Attempted. An abysmal failure.

'Uh, but see, wait on the noo?' puzzled the mother, 'Whit aboot if ye put yon longest pole o'er here, tae there? And then see, that ither pole there, should it no go intae...?'

Of course, what would a woman know? Which permitted father and son to share one of their rare completely in-tune moments. But just to humour her... Shortly afterwards two males were sharing a different reaction when the mother's intuition proved to be dead right. Restricted since her World War Two work in opportunities to use her intelligence, she'd one of those brains which allows a cerebral stepping back from the complex to arrive at simple resolutions. Usually, this gift only got a run when she would set-to repairing those occasional tip-salvaged objects such as an antique clock she'd once got ticking again. Now though, husband and son convinced she'd fluked this raising of their swish blue-gold tent to its full splendour, her reward was desertion.

Off hared the angler pair in search of fabulous fabled alpine fishing. Not that this fazed the mother. Clad in warm woollens, an Agatha Christie whodunnit for company, contentedly she curled up inside her cosy canvas palace. But indeed, so capable, yet never to have enough opportunities for accomplishing what she might have. Did she strive though, for something monumental to mark her life? Not her way. Well, not quite.

Right around the time she and the father would retire to

Queensland's Gold Coast, there'd be an amusing yet revealing incident. A lovely apartment with Pacific Ocean outlook purchased, she'd nevertheless get her fully grown son to climb the scaffolding of another under-construction high-rise, anxious to know if its penthouse offered a better panorama than that of the spacious flat they already had – might it be a better purchase? A precarious ascent and descent will then see that big son of hers testily question why the hell she wasn't happy with her new just-bought abode. And the explanation? 'Och, all mah life Ah've jist needed tae have a rainbow on the horizon tae set mah sights on.' She didn't necessarily have to achieve. The unquenchable requirement was to aspire.

But oh, Lake Eucumbene! Already an angling by-word for taking rainbow and brown trout of almost unbelievable sizes and quantities. An artificial body of water associated with the Hydro-Electric Scheme, its existence had drowned the original Adaminaby township. However, except with the ex-residents of 'Old Adaminaby' these never-before-seen piscine catches by far compensated for that. What an incentive to give Snowies' angling a shot were those outdoors magazines bulging with photos of cheesy-jawed jokers holding trophy fish! And that week prior to the family coming up to Australia's main mountain range, how driven had been the boy in his bait-getting! Manic as a man gripped with gold fever, such digging-up of that paddock sloping down to his river he'd done, grubbing out enough scrub worms to last all Easter no matter how many of these already legendary lake lunkers were bagged. Yep, all splendid then, so long as the fish decided to cooperate.

Shit, even a nibble would do! Rewarded by a superb view – those snow-capped ridges, the stands and stretches of alpine gums, clear pure body of water itself – but zero trout. Two fruitless hours later, disillusioned fishers returned to camp. It got worse. Their formerly vacant site had attracted company. Not far from blue-gold French luxury canvas perched a humble khaki pup tent, beside it one chunky orange Dodge ute, with alongside this a blazing wood fire. And who should be warming her rear-end by the cheery flames and having a friendly natter with two grizzled individuals but one wife and mother.

Of the two newcomers, one fellow looked quite a bit older than the other. Despite the alpine frigidity both blokes wore sleeveless jerseys. Arms large muscled, sinews prominent – hard workers and hardmen. Also, as it turned out, a father and son, they were underground miners from Wollongong. And though it be coal they dug, their info was solid gold. 'Place called Providence Portal is where all them big fish are,' the older miner told them.

'Yair, that's for sure,' concurred the son, nodding, and tangled red hair shedding a black dandruff of coal-dust. 'Foreman on our shift wuz 'ere last week, see. 'Reckoned go there cos them fish're all headin' upriver ter spawn.'

Coal specks flecked the greyer chap's scone thatch too. That morning straight after work-cage emerged from the Earth's bowels they'd hit the road. Lake mighty icy, no tubbing until they got back home either. Be ripe at night sleeping inside that shared pup tent! But at least they'd come prepared, with heavy sleeping-bags and that great Aussie supplementary warmer, Bundaberg rum.

Already these knockabout characters had poured the father a large mugful. More a Scotch drinker, but nevertheless a Scot, 'Slangivo-o-o-or!' toasted he, employing the Gaelic emphasis. Chucked it back in one go too. More than any other of his father's achievements, this impressed the boy no end.

Not just him either. 'Aw, that couldn'ta even touched the sides, Scotty,' grinned the greying miner, 'Yer better 'ave another.'

Duly poured.

'Arch...?' cautioned the mother.

Too late, the father now well and truly had a taste for Bundy.

Next morning, heavy lay the father's head. Nor are tents, even one with separate rooms, soundproof to snorings of the sozzled. Result, as they prepared to breakfast, one miffed missus and a sleepy son seated at a flimsy camping table alongside vacantly gazing vacationing tailor in a state of substantial hangover. Bundy aftermath keeping his father in low gear, the boy waxed toey, acute his impatience to get to this Promised Land of Providence Portal. Yet until the dad's alcohol wracked body received palliative care via a fare of baked beans and greasy bacon and eggs liberally splashed in Worcestershire sauce, with plate's leftover state to finally be mopped up by fried bread popped into gob, they weren't going anywhere.

Alcohol's affects or not, mountain air does put an edge on any appetite. Despite restiveness, once the boy tasted his mother's cooked tucker he relaxed. Besides, no point rushing. Their coal miner guides were themselves far from sparrow fart starters this morning. Only now, whilst tentatively assembling angling gear, were they brewing extra-strong coffee to counter their own unsteady heads.

If over-generousness in dispensing Bundy rum as well as imbibing it had meant a dubious morning reward of cranial thumping, for the miners a grand payoff awaited. Leading the lake-skirting two vehicle fish-seeking convoy in their Dodge, and just like the seedy Scotsman piloting Valiant behind them, they could not have but been buoyed upon arrival at Providence Portal.

'Oh aye,' exclaimed the father, stopping beside the coalminers' ute and focusing fractured rubies eyeballs on his boy, 'this does look promising!'

A sight that unfortunately the mother, left to her book and other tucker preparation activities, would not experience. A real pity, for pretty it was. Exposed though. Backdropped by mountains, remnant river entered reservoir here. Most importantly however, this allowed all resident trout to swim upstream and do as nature intended them to. And as the father had observed, it did appear to be a spot likely to produce a positive result.

Both pairs of anglers alighted from their combustion engine chariots. The miners had intended to be straight bait fishers, but wrongly assumed that lakeside worms were readily diggable. What the day before they discovered was the hard turf held none. Which turned out well, for the boy's overdone spadework back home meant his scrubbies could be shared just as freely as Bundaberg rum. The largesse of Wollongongers therefore got repaid.

In-feeding river entered Lake Eucumbene by flowing across a silted flat. A small delta in fact, fringed by spindly trees, icy rising breeze now clipping the area meant this would not be a particularly fishers-friendly day. Yet no way might any adversity prevent those scrub worm baits from sailing outward. One by one, done, followed by propping of rods upon forked sticks. Angler quartet then awaited confirmation this location equated to a piscatorial paradise. Verification came quick. One after another flexible rod bowed, and reels ran. Hooked heavy-bodied trout hit the top, thrashed and splashed and surged, got played out, and, to elated whoops, were scooped into landing nets.

Convincing the boy to stop catching these ripper fish presented one of the day's only two problems. The other, to some extent, was cleaning all the rainbows and browns captured and kept. In prime condition, the cream of their species, taken from squeaky-clean snows-fed waters how they gleamed! Once gutted and scaled, into eskies they were packed and stowed alongside rods and gear.

Both vehicles now set for departure, the father, perusing their picture postcard surroundings, sighed, 'Aye, how exquisitely beautiful this scenery is. It's jist... gorrrrgeous!'

Oh no! On colossally came the boy's inward cringe in awaiting a rough-tough coal miner response to such sissified sentiments.

Yet, nothing...? Not even a non-committal grunt or gravelly cough, never mind an alpha male fart.

'You're spot-on there, Scotty,' agreed the older miner.

'My bloody oath y'are!' enthused his son.

The boy stayed schtum. Dodge and Valiant got motoring, mining pair soon detouring to New Adaminaby where the drowned original town's displaced inhabitants were re-housed. There they'd pick up bags of pub ice for preserving current catch and of all that to come in the next two days before they were on their way back to Wollongong whilst their Victorian pals headed southward. Uh-huh, and neither party to ever see each other again: ships that pass, be it either on breathtaking lake or open sea. Such is travel, and so goes vacationing.

Campsite arrival saw the mother put her Agatha Christie aside and emerge from tent. Shown, inside the Valiant's raised boot, that whacking great stack of trout, and her males awaiting amazed praise, 'Oh aye,' she po-faced, 'Ah suppose it's fish Ah'm expected tae be frying the nicht, eh?' She did have this near compulsion to display minimal delight, albeit a twinkling in those Irish eyes often gave her away.

Easter holiday over, for once the boy looked forward to resuming at The Annex. Most classmates might reckon fishing uncool, yet they could not but be gobsmacked by photos of that massive catch, much of it by now distributed among the grandmas and family friends, with the grandest rainbow trout going to The Great Man as his deluxe blue-gold tent was returned.

However, entering The Annex's grounds the boy found not lads exchanging banter and bullshit about Easter antics, but a sharing of shock. Bunty was dead! A terrifically likeable kid off a dairy farm, popular with everyone, over Easter when helping his dad to spread feed for the cows he'd been seated on their tractor's mudguard. His father had cautioned him to shift to a safer pozzie, but Bunty had replied, 'Aw, she'll be right, dad.' – his last words. Tractor lurching into a hidden bog, Bunty dislodged, huge-tyred wheel had rolled over him.

At assembly that morning, Russ Mac copped the unenviable job of addressing all students. Meaning well, half-way through he lost both his way a bit, and the boys too, by emphasising the perils of a 'she'll-be-right' attitude. Despite Russ Mac's popularity, and the truth of what he said, absorb his warning that junior Tech group, including the boy, refused to do. Agreement afterward adjudged their deputy-head disrespectful to Bunty... they can be odd over-sensitive animals, adolescent lads.

The boy found himself sorely missing Bunty. Of late they'd begun sitting together in the class of Schmoo Schmidt, geography teacher and Stawell Gift runner-up, and by now the third chalkie the boy decided he liked. Schmoo had taken to calling them 'our two Snowballs'. As both had put on an upward growth spurt, they were quite twin-like blond string-beans. Similar sense of humour too. Bunty would have grown into one of those typical lean laconic Aussie cow-cockies, and the boy had expected them to become best mates.

Something the boy so wanted was a best mate. The majority of other lads appeared to enjoy one. The growing up in houses with few or no neighbours hindered this aspiration. At primary school there'd been a few pals, Bill and Cubby the closest. Yet a truly inseparable one? Legendary footballer Ted Whitten, when asked why his premiership team were so successful, had answered, 'Because we stick together like shit to a blanket!' In other words, they were all absolute best mates. The boy coveted meeting a reliable cobber who felt as close to him as that.

Of course, also always sought after at school was acceptance by the in-kids. Everybody wished to be invited into that cosy freshly adolescent pimpled cluster surrounding these few who used hip American slang and quipped witticisms picked up from older brothers always glued to witless-Yank-TV-shows. Yet a funny thing... in adulthood these same with-it wiseguy classmates would lead lives less scintillating than those of retarded gnats, whilst many kids who had craved their company went on to lead adventuresome ones, and when decades later again running into these beige former apparently charismatic characters, they'd be left wondering, 'How did I ever reckon there was anything special about you?'

Following Bunty's funeral that bleak school week's wintry mood matched the early arrival of this same season. Those rains and chill winds which hammered in were set to not much let up until the emergence of September's wattle blossoms. Asphalted assembly area's poor placement worsened the situation. Wide-open to prevailing sou'-westerly gales, its only positive aspect was students got to stand with their backs to all rain and hail. Any teacher speaking to them had to yell into an icy tempest. More odious for that poor chalkie, the nearby abattoir right in wind's path sent its rending facility's stomach-turning stink down their throats.

Nevertheless, that assembly space's positioning could be reckoned almost impeccable compared to the abominably situated canteen. A wonky draughty plank shed hardly bigger than a bush dunny, this stood in conspicuous isolation on the westernmost asphalt edge. Behind it a grassed slope angled to a flat stretch of ground bounded by tea-tree hedge where at recess, in crazy congestion, hundreds of kids played kick-to-kick footy. That canteen itself however? A spot to linger least. Its continued existence resisting all hurricane winds seemed almost inexplicable, a near miracle. Possibly those wide gaps in its rear boards lessened the impact of unnerving Beaufort Scale blasts whaling into it and thus prevented its non-demolition?

A frighteningly shiver-ish stage that canteen did provide

though for the volunteer mothers to perform their tucker supplying duties. In such Antarctic conditions these dedicated dears braved not just death from their café den caving-in. Risked also were strained varicose veins, blown chilblains, bleeding piles and frostbitten extremities. How cold too were those pies they supplied – aside anyhow from the first few out of the tiny food warmer provided by the Department of Education. 'Under-resourced schools' a latter-day complaint, concerned folk raising this issue would be incapable of imagining the adversities experience by both servers and served at The Annex tuckshop in 1963. As for nutritious foods? Fatty meat pies, along with pasties and sausage rolls and sugar-saturated apple charlottes, that was pretty much the students' lot.

No argument, when compared to those learning at the town's central main Tech complex, poor cousins they sure were at that separate shite-hole Annex. Paucity of resources and class congestion caused instructor stress, and ergo, the dishing out of excess corporal punishment. Maxie Matthews even copped six cuts of near lethal leather when, stuffing up a sawcut during woodwork, he uttered a mild, 'Damn!' Such a soft expletive, but it sent their usually meek mannered ex-tradie teacher freakily murder-mental. At least Maxie recovered. Their unhinged carpentry chalkie got sent to the local nuthouse.

Meanwhile, the boy and his schoolmates, by attending practical classes in not just woodwork but sheet metal, fitting and turning, simple draughtsmanship, and suchlike, except for 'keep your gob shut around touchy teachers', what else were they learning? Well, for those slower on the up-take and blue-collar bound, plenty. Brighter students on the other hand – the boy marginally among these – assessed their educations as being only fractionally furthered, if at all. Not until constructing his own first home would the boy reconsider this opinion. Able to measure square, saw and chisel with accuracy, to join timber corners, easily hammer in four-inch nails, affix roofing and guttering, and to solder as well as lay copper plumbing, he'd issue a, 'Thanks fellas,' to those tradie-chalkies who drilled such skills into him. He'd even think with some fondness of that bloke who went insane and almost maimed Maxie Matthews.

Yet alright, developing abilities useable in his future aside, plus occasional sporting participation against other schools, what else might a now pimple-faced First Former at this third-rate facility have to look forward to? The bi-annual school social perhaps? 'Girls, mate. Girls!' Huey Almighty, what excitement among The Annex's sex-segregated youth as they anticipated dancing with those mysterious owners of freshly mounding chests. As to other hidden parts of the female anatomy, to four-fifths of The Annex's First formers, with at that time even the written word subject to rigorous censorship, most guesses they'd venture were well wide of any accurate mark.

Social night, main school's aircraft-hanger-like hall, to the boy's delight who should he find himself holding onto in the *Pride of Erin* but Pauline. Yes, she the scintillating netballer who he'd shyly fancied during primary education, and crossed paths with that day of the salmon trout shoal at the bridge, here they were dancing together while teachers manned exit doors ensuring no couple slipped outside for any hanky-panky.

Chemistry developed rapidly. Shallow opinions were shared. 'Gee,' he thought, 'she's really pretty!' Almost as tall too, but now curvier than just six months ago, even if in the crush of prancing pupils one shithead had whispered, 'Carpenter's dream, china.' Well, who cared? Small breasts didn't cancel out Pauline being just about the best looker in the place.

Clock encroaching on witching hour saw a race to arrange external dating. The sour reality was Form One's two genders would not mix again until school year's completion. Had nerves not tongue-tied him the boy may have been one of those to succeed in cracking it for a rapid reuniting. Alas, growing up girl-less in the town's isolated east, now in single-sex education to its west, at his best when conversing with a teen female he was not. Sure, he'd managed to chat with Pauline about everyday happenings. To lay-on some lovey-dovey stuff however...? Nuh, a brain block.

After playing *Hokeypokey* a fourth time the geriatric band began to pack up. As if from long distance the boy heard Pauline saying, '...it doesn't matter anyway, our farm's twenty miles out so it would all be too difficult.' Not quite. Alright, a forty-mile round-trip on his bike that might have been, and on mainly gravel roads, but plainly the boy could have managed. Besides, Pauline, fit netballer that she was, how about her riding her own bike to meet him halfway? Even better, for then they'd be alone too, maybe by some warm secluded haystack...

But no, and lacking in motorized transport, agreeing with Pauline on the impracticality of pursuing any sort of romance, this left an emotion similar to excitedly lighting a skyrocket on a wet night only to find it a fizzer. Any enduring affection would be restricted to, once in blue moon, waves at and from a passing back-country bound school bus. For sure, some kind of sensual spark had been struck in both. But for the boy, so far as female company went, together with even the remotest familiarity of their topography, he'd be stuck in the dark for another couple of years. The single bright aspect to foregoing marathon cycling for romantic weekend entanglement was, at least, that no severe cutting into angling outings would result.

Saturday, November 23, 1963, and another run of salmon trout had come into the river. Yet imbedding this date in the boy's thirteen-year-old head would not be that quick catch of fish off the bridge he intended to get prior to nipping away to play Colts cricket. Instead, it was a stifled scream followed by a thud that came from the short hallway inside family home's front door.

Working-class people used telephones sparingly. Calls were expensive. So, when a phone rang it got answered. A future where folk considered incoming calls an intrusion and ignored them by switching off and slipping portable mobile devices away into their pockets? Unimaginable! Therefore, that morning, the father once more earning weekend overtime dollars, and the mother fixing her angler cricketer son scrambled eggs, when that heavy black Bakelite telephone in their foyer shrilled, hastily she'd quit the kitchen, instructing as she went, 'Stir thae pot anither minute, aye, and then take it aff the hot plate. Ah'll no be long.'

Moving fast, the boy found his mother sobbing and distraught and, phone fallen from her hand, collapsed on the foyer's floor rug. Accident at the factory and his dad badly injured...? If considering this first thought which came to mind – heartfelt concern for his father – would this have surprised him? Perhaps hirsuteness wasn't all that grew with puberty. As he attempted to help her up, 'Mum, what is it?' asked the boy.

Tears streaming, the mother managed, 'They... they've murdered President Kennedy!'

Pausing his Cutting Room weekend overtime, the father had rung through about this Friday, Texas time, shooting. Few Aussies of that era would not remember where they were when learning of JFK's assassination, for how the Western world adored this bloke. Later generations might be ignorant that during something called 'the Cuban Missile Crisis', had Kennedy not possessed the intestinal fortitude to resist his Military's lust for a pre-emptive strike, all civilization may well have vanished under a mushroom cloud. Revisionist historians would denigrate his name and guarantee he'd be the last U.S. president most people ever again fully put their faith in, but never would the boy's mother fall out of love with John F. Kennedy. Trying to dry her eyes, she told the boy, 'Awa ye go, son. Go and... dae yer fishing. Ah'll be okay.'

The boy did as she bid, albeit seeing how severely mauled already by the black dog this had left his mother, and aware those were probably the last words he'd hear from her for at least a week.

A few weeks after JFK's chips were cashed, something else kind of died. Due to their segregated schooling the boy had managed to continue, what even at best stretch had to be called a tenuous romance, with Pauline – chanced glances from a distance, those passing bus window waves, and there'd been sneaky hands-holding at a couple of school sports days too. Hey, they'd even kissed! But okay, only once, and sprung by one of her teachers, so briefly as nearly not to have. Then, however, had come the end-of-year social. Admitting she'd met a neighbouring dairy farming lad, a CBC attendee, Pauline vowed that, 'When we're older, if he wants to marry me, I'll turn.'

Into what, a frog-kissing princess? But nah, no worries, the boy well knew of those polarizing moves when a Protestant bride married a Roman Catholic, and vice versa. However, Pauline at thirteen harbouring matrimonial hopes, this the boy couldn't fathom. Such a notion couldn't have been further from his mind. As for changing religions in order to legally live with someone? Really, he didn't get that either. Both his parents had explained the practice to him, their own upbringings long familiarizing them with sectarian bigotry. Yet neither exhibited any religious prejudices. Correctly, they expected their son not to either.

Pauline falling for this other kid would not therefore, turn the boy anti-Catholic. As for her ditching him implanting mistrust in females? Well, could he even claim Pauline had been his girlfriend? Tomorrow he'd simply go fishing and forget he'd ever met her. Just the same, when picked up from the dance by his parents, and sitting in the Valiant's back seat, as they drove home the boy felt very alone.

Very last hurrah of that '63 school year turned out to be a 'Fathers and Sons Night'. Attended by eager boys all hopeful of scoring an eyeful of saucy slides, and to hear revelatory depictions regarding naughty sports, here they were perched on plastic chairs alongside uncomfortable dads who'd never got around to mentioning the evils of masturbation to their offspring, let alone explaining foreplayful fumblings and the ins and outs of fornication. Yet the talk, conducted by their Tech's toothy uncomfortably smiling geek chaplain, ultimately left everyone, fathers included, exiting the assembly hall wondering what chickens and eggs and flowers and bees had to do with the price of mushrooms on the Chinese fish market. Not even as a word, had 'sex' been heard.

Xmas and New Year had passed. There'd been the usual Hogmanay party to welcome in 1964, fortunately including no post-midnight arrival of any severed leg with a 'first foot' attached. For once, this main holiday period would not see an extended road trip. Trouser sales were booming. Demand for quality strides with extraordinary resistance to wear and tear was through the roof, and The Great Man had asked his staff to take only a short vacation break. Father and son did, late on New Year's Day, take their ever-leakier boat out on the river to try their luck, but had none. After this, the boy saw his loyal employee dad return to factory toil.

Not that, still, the boy wished to spend heaps of time with his old man. Less so probably. At thirteen, more physical recreational activities were appealing to him, as well as girls now never being positioned far behind in his mind either. What at this juncture he most passionately wanted to embrace however, was the ocean. In particular skindiving had caught his interest. That coincidentally, if done without a wetsuit in Antarctic-chill waters this acted as a terrific repressor of erotic urges, probably wasn't going to be detrimental either. Indeed, a shorts and T-shirt only clad trial and error learning it would be. Not solo though. Also involved were two lads from the rival high school.

Snappa and Titch were larrikins. They'd been in the boy's class at primary school. There they'd been fringe friends though, not mates. Yet bumping into them again on a summer lunchtime at Dutch Tony's fish and chip shop...? The teenage transition stage does see attitudes change. Former pals fall away, new ones emerge. Out on the sidewalk, chatting as they chomped on crispy vinegared and salted chips, casual chiaking had transformed into a fond bond.

They were opposites, this pair. Snappa, a habitual drooler when enthused, sat on the fattish side, whilst his ever-giggling straw-thin cobber Titch got about in a permanent slouch. Between drools and giggles, they persuaded the boy he ought to try something they were already into, freediving. It wasn't just new adventuring to be done that swung it for the boy. How good did the promise to immediately spear fish underwater instead of acquiring them via the usual protracted hook and line method sound? Only grouse!

One hour tinkering in garage all it took – rake head sawn off, long wooden handle then having tight-wired to one end of it twin barbed prongs, and to its other end a rubber loop of bicycle tyre tube, and *voilâ*, a crude 'Hawaiian sling' hand-spear appeared. After this, mask and snorkel and fins bought day before for a few bob in the Salvos op shop dropped into backpack, off the boy cycled to rendezvous with Snappa and Titch at Thunder Point.

Thunder Point! As apt names go, never a better one. Sound it gave off like the rumble of heavy guns. A bare headland situated south-west of town, monster Southern Ocean swells surged in to smack against its cliffs – *Boom!* Base of these a perilous place to even stand, the waters just out from them were normally an insane spot to skin-dive. But not always. Snappa and Titch had picked their day. Wind a balmy northerly, sea a blue pancake, for anyone getting in their first ever dive, only perfect.

Ideal though just up to a point. When into placid sea the flippered, masked, homemade-spear-toting trio jumped, oooh-eeee, bloody freezing! In an instant three sets of fresh adolescent testicles nestled under armpits: 'Faaaaaark!!!' Along with the crow's call, through snorkels issued plenty of other expletives. Once accustomed to the cold however, outward they finned, each towing a roped-to-waist float-bag. The trio's tyro diver was awestruck. To the boy a new sensation, a wonderworld! Columns of kelp rose from far below, sprouting from a diversely coloured seaweed garden and multi-hued reef. As for fish, deeper swam morwong and sweep and some ponderous unpalatable 'kelpies', in midwater salmon schooled, whilst inches below surface cruised an unhurried shoal of garfish.

Absorbed and enthralled, the boy floated awhile almost inert. By now a strong swimmer though, he reckoned that once he did start submerging, he'd take to snorkelling's simple techniques like a lively fish dropped into a water-filled barrel. Meanwhile, Snappa wasn't holding back. His own Hawaiian sling primed, down he dived to make the first kill. *Thoonk!* – a fat sweep, excellent eating. Even better, the sweep's death didn't spook its companions. In fact, its struggles and blood-spill attracted more. These fish were obviously unaccustomed to anyone spearing them. Ergo, began a massacre. Nor, impaling sweep at will, did the three juvenile assassins give any thought to blood scent and vibratory dying perhaps attracting some huge great white predator with an insatiable appetite.

Many silver-bodies dangled from floats before shivers superseded the thrill of sub-marine killing. Snappa, treading water and removing snorkel mouthpiece, suggested, 'How about we try and get a cray before we get too cold?' Inward towards shallower reef they finned. However, without a further word, Titch their thinnest sea-hunter, deciding ice had started to form in his backbone, swam on in to towel-off and get dressed.

No worries, one less diver, all the more crays for two, eh? Also, to be killed by spear. Conservation regulations permitting only capture by hand lay far into the future. Down to a tight ledge glided the boy. Poking head into dark horizontal crevice, mightiest fright blighted his day. Across mask's tempered glass spread a suckered tentacle. Shit and crikey, shades of *Twenty Thousand Leagues Under the Sea* – a giant bloody squid! Spluttering and coughing-up salt swill he hit the top. It took until he'd gulped a fair bit of air before he got wise to underwater magnification, and that the creature had been no more than a small octopus. Relieved that Snappa seemed not to have seen his panic, again the boy duck-dived, returning to squeezy ledge for another squiz. That smart wee ocky had however, scarpered.

Ever chillier but still relaxed, on his lungful of air the boy stayed down. Kicking over to a larger ledge, in he peered, and... Wow, there, solid legs spread as it gripped on, lay a red carapace-ed bull cray. What a beauty! Positioned way back, but quite reachable by spear. Yet not now. Urgently required was another breath. Up he came.

Snappa had just done the same. 'Seen anything?'

Taking snorkel from gob, 'Yeah, a ripper,' responded the boy.

'Really? Where?'

'Ledge behind that big knob of rock.'

Down tore Snappa, to seconds later fin upward, big cray impaled on the end of his spear. From there uncontrollable shivers prevailed, and both boys terminated their diving.

A few more times that summer the intrepid young teen diver trio would jump into the briny together. And yet for the boy that magic of freediving diminished, and finally he dropped out. Not that his interest in the underwater world lessened. At eighteen he would read a book by Jacques Cousteau, buy a set of ex-Korean War commando 'Porpoise' tanks, jump off breakwater's end, and by the time shore had been swum to, have taught himself to scuba dive – in later financially leaner years a skill enabling a smidgen non-legal acquisition of abalone to fund building of his own first home. However, now dive-wise he had ceased to accompany his two pals. Why?

As their first outing revealed, Snappa possessed an irrational competitiveness. Not that the boy lacked similar drive, but Snappa continuing to swipe crays and fish from under his nose spoiled the seafood gathering fun, never mind causing one inherited Celt fuse to shorten – soon blood in the water might not just be coming from speared fish. As for Titch, that initial dive day, deserting the way he had without a word? Were oceanic difficulties to later be encountered, he'd have an itch to ditch his mates. A nice lad, no worries, yet with a tiny ticker and scant sense of responsibility. The boy appreciated what great enjoyment could be had with both of these lively guys, and therefore fully cut ties to them he wouldn't. But keep diving together, no.

Something else too, contributed to this splitting from Snappa and Titch. One day, that pair otherwise occupied, the boy had discovered the immense joy of free-diving alone. Just the underwater glories and him. It sent his mind on sublime walkabout. Amid fabulous flights of fancy, he also became conscious that fish, if not being speared, let a diver get close. They'd surround, become ocean brothers. On the other hand, diving in his mates' company, always it turned into a slaughter.

The ease of spearing sweep tweaked the boy's conscience as well. Curious creatures, in they'd fin toward human intruder, and then to get a better look, turn side-on to – *whop!* – cop the chop. Not that he'd ever stop taking fish, for what delisho tucker they provided. Better though, to rod and line them, allowing also a fair chance for escape. But settled, his future diving would usually be solo, with rarely a scaly swimmer speared. Crays and abalone though? There'd be zero compunction gathering those ocean edibles.

Still unbagged by either the father or his son was a mulloway. Leaves falling, days shortening, seas roughening, diving gear mothballed, the boy's leisure energy went back into river pursuits, with one pressing quest – to land that first 'kingy'. April's standard hiatus twixt cricket and football having again arrived, and so no obligation to bowl a Kookaburra or roost a Sherrin, this he decided must be it: the hunt for that mulloway was on.

Easter too, but with no inland excursion chasing trout planned, indeed full focus could centre on the river estuary. Not that this year a trip in pursuit of browns or rainbows had been possible. As the boy chose to see it, his father had shirked parental piscatorial duty by choosing to take only the Holy Saturday and Sunday off work. Along with a skeleton staff – and against union rules – he'd even be beavering away on Good Friday! Due to an enormous orders' backlog they'd be toiling on the Easter Monday too. So, almost unavoidable. Try telling that to the boy though.

Then again, something else had lengthened the odds of a father-son fish together at the end of any week. Two truths were that the old man did enjoy his gargle, and that he had got into a phenomenon known as the 'six o'clock swill' – something at its most enthusiastic post-work every Friday evening.

But, ah well, tis an ill-wind that will blow nobody any good. The boy had no sporting obligations on the Easter Saturday, and therefore could sleep that complete day if he desired to. So, bewdy, he'd fish an all-nighter on the Friday. These long hours would be put in on the bridge. Fishing a complete night in their boat wasn't on anymore. Built as it had been with non-marine plywood, it had become so dilapidated with rot that an occupant angler dozing off at midnight and failing to bail might wake to the alarming situation of sitting on the river's bottom. Besides which, on the bridge an angler's legs could get a proper stretch.

Around mid-afternoon that holy day Friday, two cane rods tied to bike sticking out behind it like the tail of a red-bellied stinger, off toward bridge the boy down-hilled. In his backpack, together with spare tackle, were several thick sandwiches and a large thermos of soup courtesy of his mum. There'd been no getting away however, without her asking, 'Why're ye going the noo though? It's no even three o'clock...?' Explanation: 'meat' anglers often find it harder to find fresh fare for their hooks than to catch actual fish, and he had plenty of bait gathering to do before, on evening, beginning to try and score a mulloway.Once at bridge, bike parked to one end, the boy ventured onto the river's sandy downstream side. Under lumps of washed-in kelp he began capturing creamy coloured sandfleas, with which small salmon trout could be hooked. Easily enough done, getting the tiny fat jumpers, and popping them into a sealable jar. After this, back on bridge, the boy clambered through railings beside its arch to sit on a small flat platform projecting from the main structure. Next, threaded onto a wee hook beneath quill floater, sandfleas were flicked out. Yet jagging smallish fish to cut into chunky sections of mulloway tucker wasn't easy. Young salmon were scarce. On the other hand, this thin supply of baitfish might also be a favourable sign. When hungry mulloway are in their vicinity, small fish seldom hang around.

Not until twilight were sufficient small salmon bagged. From platform, the boy climbed back onto bridge proper, and soon, *plop* and *plop*, two chopped chunks of salmon on 3/0 long-shank hooks landed in the drink a fair distance out from the arch. Onto rail alongside were then leaned the canes with their big centrepins. Off each of these reels the boy peeled a yard and a half of line. Bulky bait, such slack ought to let a swimming-off mulloway gulp it down without feeling any resistance.

Right, ripper, mulloway lines in water accomplished. High time now to take cover. In the shallows of that broad lengthy mudbank across from Sir Fuckface's boatshed where clinkers unhitched by a couple of young ratbags had once gone aground, scores of black swans spent each day feeding. At sundown, bellies filled with shrimp-weed roots, running feet slapping surface and wings flapping, en masse they'd take off to overnight upon more sheltered waters... a ritual which this minute they were enacting. Approaching from a few hundred yards upriver, and rising to a set height before levelling out, bridge anglers watching them were left with similar emotions to unfortunate footsloggers stuck under an enemy squadron's bombing run.

Eyes to sky, the boy reckoned these feathered buggers did it deliberately too. Always they withheld their poo until just short of bridge line. The shower of shite then let loose straddled their target and hit any exposed human. A smart reason then, to fish beside the arch. While other anglers swore and ducked, by pressing against the higher sheltering structure the boy could delight in this splendid coordinated unleashing of wet guano. Once the swan bombers passed, he returned to his rods.

Light well on the fade now, the boy wondered if his father would drop by later. This being Good Friday, and all pubs ostensibly closed, still did not mean when the dad and his reduced Cutting Room crew knocked off working their holiday overtime that they'd miss their usual weekly swill. Because their particular rubbidy was also favoured by the coppers, it had an open back door – and until well after-hours too – to both clothing factory employees and the local constabulary. Besides this there was always an option for a piss-up at the Army Reserve shed by the foreshore. One way or the other, it could be that later-on this night a fairly pickled old man might steer their Valiant by to see if any bites were being had. However, should he do so there'd be no stopping to try his own luck. Instead, heading home, he'd get stuck into a mum-cooked feed awaiting him in the oven, and thereafter, thoroughly tuckered out, tuck himself up in bed.

The boy well enough understood that his overworked dad had every entitlement to these unwinding, if habit-forming, Friday imbibing sessions. Growing competition from cheap overseas garment makers had hugely upped production pressure at the factory. Plus, anyway, most overtime monies went straight toward erasing the bank's final loan. So yes, a few shillings spent to suck on a schooner and de-stress along with fellow under-the-pump workmates struck the boy as fair enough. His mother however, felt otherwise. Nevertheless, although mightily non-chuffed at these weekly sousings, always she had wholesome food awaiting one tipsy husband upon his homecoming, even if sometimes days of huffy wifely silence did follow. Yeah, work pressures equating to marriage pressure, but luckily The Great Man's canny revamped marketing strategies would by mid-year greatly ease all related work and domestic crises.

On the bridge, the boy in mulling such things over, might also have appreciated there might be other factors contributing to an ex-serviceman belatedly beginning to routinely overindulge in grog. But he didn't. Another aspect to a Friday evening did occur to him however: that any angler operating from this river-spanning roadway would never be without company. Blokes from more laid-back jobs, and not stress-driven to attack liquid amber, turned up in numbers to fish late into the night. Sometimes they'd do all-nighters as well. No worries though, reckoned the boy, for the bridge afforded space aplenty, and should the action be dull later on he'd have others to yarn with.

In the half-light, his attention turned from such friendly competition to the cane rod tips. Even a diminutive dip might mean imminent action. Old-timers had said mulloway didn't always straight-off do tearaway runs. At times, all slack taken out gradually, they'd sit on the bait, rod slowly bow but then rise, yet line remain taut… 'Now see, young fella,' they'd say, 'if this happens, give the bugger a few more feet of slack ter let 'im get yer bait right down 'is neck.'

With ten p.m. came two definites. First, the father must have had a bonzer Easter booze-up with his work crew and would now not cruise by in the Valiant. Second, and ripper, mulloway were around! Right on dark two fishos further along had got runs: sharp and fast, baits dropped, not taking it properly. The boy had noted though that these jokers fished with no slack. Meanwhile, full night-time now, he lit a small kerosene lamp and placed it between both rods. From each reel he then peeled off a further foot of monofilament. Lamp's glow would show any loose line starting to snake out.

Eleven p.m. and still not a sausage. Otherwise, a spectacular night – stars a sparkly dandelion shower fixed in the heavens, wind barely a whisper, absolute peace. Although how soon before a few drink-driver hoons came tearing through burning rubber and octane? Beware, all north side of bridge anglers had to be, of these idiots out to scare. A quick shift of selves and rods hard against the railing might be required to avoid bodily and fishing gear damage. Yeah, and where were the cops at such times? Dead right, chug-a-lugging free beer at that legally shut to general public, illegally open pub!

Not that safe fishing couldn't be had at any time on the bridge. A railed-off walkway ran along its full downstream length. Alas, catches there were, for whatever reasons, far fewer than on the upstream north side. Actually, an oddity this discrepancy in fish take, for as one veteran fisho had once observed to the boy: 'Y'know, every single fish what comes into this river or goes out of it has ter pass under our bridge.'

The all-quiet continued: no souped-up Holdens yet smouldering across bridge bitumen, no reels smoking either. The boy figured he'd wander to the arch's other side for a jaw with his nearest fellow fisher, ask had he detected any piscine activity.

Should a run come while absent from his rods, centrepin's loud ratchet would bring him racing back within seconds – yep, set to get that long coveted tearaway mulloway landed. Uh-huh, oh yeah...? Another angling lesson pending here.

Meanwhile, closest angler being approached hadn't arrived until after dark. Bridge itself non-lit, and streetlamps near each end offering but slight illumination, nonetheless when he ignited a cigarette via his lighter, the boy recognised him as a tank-bodied plumber with whom he'd spoken a few times. Pleasantries were exchanged. Such regulars knew the boy's angling ability and didn't patronize him. In this regard winning that heaviest bream trophy had sure helped. But even the most respected fishing folk stuff-up.

'Doing any good?' asked the boy.

'Yair-nah,' shrugged the plumber, 'not a touch so far.' Heavy-ish gear, clear his quarry was also mulloway. He knew how to catch them too. Usually a spew worm user, he'd nevertheless gained fame the previous year, pictured in local paper cradling a forty-pounder taken off the bridge on a live mullet. 'And you,' he asked the boy, 'any luck?'

'No, but they're about. Blokes down the town-end had runs before you came.'

'Yair, told me when I come past 'em.' As often applied on that bridge – nil secrets, every angler in the same boat of permanent anchorage, scant advantage in non-disclosure of fish activity. 'That's what's got me out here near the middle, see,' continued the hefty plumber, 'cos them kingies, early on they come through that there channel where them blokes are, but they got this circuit, them fish. Takes 'em up to the old fogies boatshed...' A drag taken on his nine-out-of-ten-doctors-recommended menthol fag. 'Then yair...' A healthy cough, 'they work out to the mudflat, till round midnight they scrounge back along the bottom an' pass under the arch here see, an' that's when you an' me can expect...'

Off it tore, the boy's nearer centrepin. Into an instant sprint, but the reel stopped. 'Shit, he's dropped it!' he thought, still running. But no, rod rocking on top rail like a tightrope walker's balancing pole, another inch and it'd be over and into drink – so rapid the mulloway's run, as reel spun line had overrun and looped the monofilament over one handle. The boy grabbed teetering cane. Same instant the twelve-pound line parted.

Retrieving limp monofilament, the boy saw the break had come at his hook's eyelet. Misery and buggery! Again, that longed-for mulloway, lost. And again, Jesus, the hollow pain of it! By kerosene lamplight another Mustad hook got tied on. Be no more deserting rods to go chatting, irrespective of how dull further fishing got. Move before dawn from his pozzie by arch's east side he would not. Missing that mulloway had but one positive aspect to it. The fish had come through well before midnight. Early. More must follow later, right? As Normie Rowe would sing in a couple more years, *it ain't necessarily so.*

Daylight's hint above that huge hill to bridge's east altered the boy's mind from glum to forlorn. Not once since losing that mulloway pre-midnight had either of his rods dipped or a loose eyelet even slightly rattled. Only movement had been of anglers. One by one they'd left unrewarded, that big plumber included. Of course, as always with fishing, in their stead were arriving the pre-sunrise triers. One joker, car parked near bridge's eastern end and headlights shut off, and on his way to flick out a lure for estuary perch, asked in passing, 'Any action?'

'Not a thing.'

'Been at it long?'

'What time is it?' enquired the watch-less boy.

'Just short of four a.m.'

'Um... about eleven hours then.'

'Fuck me, you're keen!' chuckled the bloke. But then, 'Ay, ay... you've got a touch there.'

Enough dawn, just, made visible cane's slow downward bow

and then its gradual resumption to straight. Kero lamp's glow showed line retaining a tightness: fish still there. With care the boy drew more monofilament off centrepin, and then waited. With breath baited? Far more as if inside him a banquet of hope and anticipation had been laid out. The perch chaser though, felt no such tension. 'Arrr, bloody thing's dropped it,' decided he, going on his way.

Five minutes elapsed. Figuring the guy was likely right, the boy picked up his cane to reel in and check bait. Yet then he leaned on top railing, peeled off more slack, let the line sit across his forefinger. He did this less through canniness than sleepiness. In semi-dreamworld, he figured once daylight brought definition to that Old Folks' Home boatshed over on dark western bank, pack up and piss off time it would be. Bloody oath, onto bike and off home, for a whole day in bed filled with shitty dreams about buggering-up another chance to break his mulloway duck.

Stinging finger later running blood because, half-asleep, the sensation of slack line's gradual take-up didn't register, would be irrelevant. Mulloway, in as dopey a space as the boy, had lain for almost quarter of an hour mouthing the piece of cut-trout until, finally feeling the hook, speed-of-light acceleration resulted. Almost as quick, youthful alertness reasserted. Not fast enough however to prevent piano-wire-tight line deeply slitting forefinger as it zipped out. Yet, pain? Intoxication only, from the fish's sheer power.

Straining forearm raised cane higher, permitting its pliant tip to lessen pressure on line. Meantime, cupping hand under whirring reel to curb fish's progress brought a numb thumb, bashed by a whizzing handle. But no worries. 'What a huge-un... run, you bloody beauty, run!' urged the boy, letting it do just that, directly upriver.

Running, running, running too, came the other anglers, attracted by centrepin's ratchet racket. With them arrived the usual mixed-bag of advice. Some sage, 'You're doing just fine, son. Keep letting him go,' and some plain stupid, 'Clamp the reel, clamp the reel... you're gunna run outa line!'

Heaps of monofilament still on his reel, as best he could the boy shut out this human cacophony. He'd played big fish before. Alright, not one this size, but he knew his stuff, enough anyhow not to attempt to stop a still-charging fish weighing twice your line's breaking strain. Not until his mulloway slowed way down, did he then clamp reel, heave back on rod, and set hook. He reefed again to make certain it had embedded. And just as well. Turning fast, back towards bridge raced the fish. Impossible to crank centrepin quick enough to keep up. 'Why didn't I switch to frigging spinning reels?!' thought the boy, half-panicked, winding feverishly. Allow such a fish slack line, and if lip-hooked or barb stuck in hard part of gob, short odds then on a dislodged hook and the quarry lost. A prayer whispered this mulloway had it well down its gullet.

Actual praying the boy had begun to do too. Hooking a huge fish turns many an atheist angler religious. Meanwhile the assembled successors to Saint Peter continued to offer uneven slices of advice: 'Someone chuck a big chunk-a bitumen in the water, scare the bastard away from swimmin' under the arch!' 'Nah, don't worry, they hardly never go right under the bridge.' 'Bullshit, course they frigging do! Ow'd yer think they go upriver?' 'Yiz'll be fine, young fella, just catch up with that fucken slack.'

The boy brought his line taut just as the fish veered. Fortunately, after careering parallel to the bridge front, once more it tore off upriver. Further mad rushes followed, and line retrievals. Each time however, these runs shortened, the mulloway tiring. After a whirlpool-like surface swirling crazy-wild enough to turn any angler's nerves raw, on top of the water, finally, it lay side-up, exhausted, played out, scales argent in torchlight directed by several fishos. 'Christ, that's a twenty-pounder!' exclaimed one.

Not quite, but for a river fish, large alright for a species that at sea grew to over a hundred pounds. The boy tried to steady shaking knees, for still positioned in bridge's middle, he'd yet to get it to shore.

To being accurate, the mulloway required beaching. Due to bridge's height no one tried to lift a weighty fish. What took place was what the boy's father, once he also began to catch mulloway off the bridge, would call, 'The march of glory.' Angler, rod near bowed double, had to drag the surfaced and struggling creature along bridge's length, obliging any other fishers alongside to reel-in their lines before he reached them, after which they'd join the white-knuckled walk shoreward in an atmosphere of barracking and anxiety and merry bullshit until the hooked mulloway or huge bream or perch got drawn out of river and onto the bankside sand.

Yet plenty could go wrong. Leaning over top rail and starting to tow his fish, this the boy too well knew. Hook might dislodge, fish bite through line, or if monofilament had frayed on coral, a sudden convulsion or jerk could break it. Mishap this time though, if granted reasonable luck on crabbing trek along bridge deck's hundred yards to its end? 'No way Huey... pleeeeease!'

Heart-in-mouth prayers answered. Thumping and flapping on sand lay the mulloway. All atremble, the boy hared down bridge-end embankment, shoved fingers – including that painful slit one – into the grand fish's gills, and spot-lit by those torches, in triumph hefted his trophy for all gawkers lined along the railings above to admire. And applause he got, albeit some a smidgen lukewarm. Jealousy is part of angling territory. Also, when it's a kid outdoing veteran fishos, they usually don't overdo the lauding.

Jubilant and relieved in equal parts, the boy continued to hold up his struggling fish. In doing this, that first time ever strange special smell of a fresh-caught mulloway entered his nostrils, an odour so distinct as never to be forgotten.

Shaken awake to find one splendid and smelly mulloway waved before his bloodshot eyes, a somewhat seedy from Good Friday pub fill-up father nevertheless evinced none of the bridge anglers' ambivalence. Such delight he displayed, diluted only by not having been there to share in his son's first 'kingie'. A bite of brekky along with strong coffee, and then father and son were off in the Valiant, prized fish weighing what turned out to be 17lbs 10oz lying in its boot, and the boy, on reflection, definitely wishing his old man had witnessed the actual catch.

Yet they were together now, enjoying one of their, of late, ever-rarer father-son sharings. All the same, deep down in the boy snuggled smugness in being one-up on his still mulloway-less old man. As for sleep deprivation in the successful angler, continuing filled – in fact overspilling – with adrenaline, he wasn't for bedding down any time soon. Entering his teens meant he'd exchanged cocoas for coffees too. His mother, even she adequately impressed with his magnificent fish, had made a triple-strength cappuccino to sustain him as he did the rounds with it. Visits would include to the two grandmothers who'd later receive juicy cutlets, and to every known family friend. Never mind how unseasonably warm this autumn morning grew either, that splendid first-ever mulloway in Valiant's boot had to be proudly displayed. The priority stop-off straight off though? Where else but at Old Ron's place!

In an academic sense this 1964 Form Two year for the boy wore dismally on. Football-wise however, enjoyable! For several reasons, including convenience of training and wishing to test himself against tougher opponents, he'd quit the Scumbaggers to join the Under-17 Tech side. Improvement in his skills and confidence on the footy field had been profound.

As for non-sporting and non-academic interests, stimulating developments on a broader scale had begun to be taken notice of. For example, the biggest national event that year would be the 'Fab Four', the Beatles, winging in to tour Oz and ensuring most teenage Aussie males became considerably hairier.

Change came in the weather too. A severe early winter set in, with its standard frigid sou'-westerlies and horizontal rains. The Annex's exposed uninsulated isolation saw a bear-with-sore-headedness develop amongst both students and teaching staff. Inadequate funding ruled out any form of heating other than that from overcrowded classrooms' bodies, combined with ripe farts. But oh, moody adolescent scholars gone sour and uncommunicative, foul-tempered teachers swearing under their breaths...? Toxic atmosphere meant any innocent remark by a student had better not be misconstrued.

Of all days, this last one before a longed-for two-week holiday break, something the boy said sure got taken the wrong way. W-a-a-a-y too much. Copping 'six of the best' for insolence struck him – whilst being struck – as grossly unfair. If for some deed deserving of a walloping, okay, he copped his whacks sweet. Yet this transgression? Simply, that on their grassy playing flat down behind the clapped-out canteen, he'd pointed out to physical education teacher 'Tracksuit Joe' that their run-up for high-jump practice – something the boy excelled at – seemed too soggy to use safely. No way had this valid suggestion warranted a flogging.

Tracksuit Joe could lay it on too. A middle-aged Czech refugee and former Olympic gymnast, iron biceps upped the oomph of his strap deployment. For the boy, disappointment went with discomfort. Joe had joined that very short list of teachers he liked. Oddly too, the bloke seldom acted unjustly. Everyone though, has bad-hair days. Now and again all The Annex's stressed teaching staff had theirs. Perhaps Joe and his missus had quarrelled that morning? Or did this uncharacteristic testiness relate to pending male menopause? Then again, could financial woes have arisen from that private gymnasium he'd constructed beside town's outlying psychiatric hospital where their ex-woodwork teacher was now a patient, and in which Joe might become one too, the way he was behaving here?

Not that the boy was actually puzzling over such possibilities. Determined to show resilience in front of his shocked silent classmates, he took the final leather cut, pushed pained mitts into his pockets, and now re-joined the group beside Clarrie.

'How'd yer go?' whispered Clarrie.

'Yeah, no... I'm okay I suppose,' mumbled the boy.

'Over nothin' too, ay? If he done that ter me I'd bloody job 'im.'

A true chance too, considering Clarrie's pugilistic ability. He'd want to avoid the be-muscled Joe getting hold of his throat though.

As it turned out, the boys would all get the last laugh, albeit stifled. Done with meting out punishment, pent-up ire expired via making the boy's mitts red-swollen and throbbing, Joe tossed heavy leather strap aside to announce he'd demonstrate the soundness of their high-jump's approaches. A flex, a stretch, controlled release of flatulence, and in towards low bar he loped, planted take-off foot, and slipped fair on his track-suited arse.

Cycling home after that final class of term, handlebars-holding palms still smarted. The boy considered how miserably so far this year's schooling had gone. Thank Huey for a vacation hiatus! Not that there'd be no school-related activity. Tech Under-17's training and playing would continue. As for leaving the Scumbaggers...? He had loved his seasons with those wrong-side-of-tracks teammates, few who were not delightful rough diamonds. Yet football savviness improves only if playing at a higher level. Also, how handy to simply start lively training straight after stultifying classes ended! Ah, and then there was Schmoo Schmidt.

Their thoroughly likeable geography chalkie and accomplished professional runner doubled as footy coach. And not just this. In an era that favoured articulate inspirational tough speech, Schmoo's oratory was legendary. When he spoke, kids listened. If occasionally he hurt some over-sensitive lad's feelings, too bad. Confidence instilled in the majority outweighed upsetting a minority. Acned misfits transformed into fully focused young men. Abilities were elevated for not just sport, but to navigate life.

Onward, homeward, the boy continued to pedal. For the moment forgetting bruised hands, he smiled. Yeah, Schmoo's sensational pre-match addresses...? Sometimes they could be too inspirational. Only his second game with the Under-17's, the boy had been selected as back-pocket to mind the resting ruckmen. Opponents an up-country side consisting mainly of cumbersome cow-cockies' sons, recent growth spurt made him marginally tall enough for his task, but muscle development had yet to catch up. The kid to be minded was a monster, three years older, four inches higher, seven stone heavier, uglier than a busted bum. Instead of exchanging handshakes, he belted an elbow into the boy's thin gut. He then did it twice more. Yet what had Schmoo Schmidt said, knowing this mob's rough-house tactics? 'Not one backward step, fellas, not one backward step! Line in the sand, fellas, line in the sand!'

Downfield had come the ball. Another back-thrust elbow, then into a pack had charged that monstrous resting ruckman – trailed by the boy. Over bent the lumbering adversary. *Biff!* went the boy's neat uppercut. Sideways toppled the giant, clutching an eye, bawling like one of his farm's bull-calves being castrated. Emitting a flood of tears and snot too. 'That's fixed you!' the boy's thought. David must have felt similarly when he poleaxed

Goliath. But Goliath stayed down, permanently paid-out. Never would the boy forget, shortly afterwards, hearing the roughhouse ruck's equally ugly old man, 'Number ten, Tom, that's him!', right before daylight disappeared.

A vicious back-swung punch as the massive mongrel ran past, consciousness regained whilst held up between Schmoo and some parent acting as their trainer. Nose badly broken, blood streaming out of it onto boots… Comprehensive concussion? Conclusively! But come off the field? Not in those days. 'You alright?' had asked his teacher-coach, wiping the boy's crunched bloodied schnoz with a towel. Only one response possible to that, a dazed nod. 'Good! Now listen, son,' cooed Schmoo, 'it took guts for you to have a go at that big bastard… guts and frigging stupidity.' Uh-huh, their coach did have this black-humour side to him. 'So right, get back into it, and for the rest of the game, for Christsake, just play the ball.'

As he pedalled, still contemplating the on-field assault, the boy began that usual awful uphill stretch to home, dismounted halfway, and eventually wheeled Malvern Star onto driveway. In doing so he continued to recall the remainder of that match played in a mental fog. From this he'd only emerged late in the last quarter when taking an overhead mark. Otherwise, participation in the game had all been on animal instinct. Yet, for himself a precedent set. In future, fear of getting hurt would never see him back down from anyone. Regardless of their size, or even weaponry. Over the years some stoushes would be won, a few lost. However, no cringing in retreat meant he'd always be able to live with himself. As for 'turning the other cheek', that was for the meek, and Christians, and cowards.

Bike had been put away in garage. Right, bewdy, holiday time! A far from restful one though. Together with footy training runs and actual games during this next fortnight, there'd be attendance at weight-lifting sessions. Following that KO, Schmoo had insisted the school's rudimentary gym needed to be utilized and iron pumped to add beef to a too-lean frame.

Yet these commitments aside, other school connections could be forgotten and there'd be ample leisure days. 'So, what else,' the boy put it to himself, 'can I get up to?' Well okay, occasional domestic chores would get chucked his way – lawn mowing, washing dishes, a bit of vacuuming, maybe painting window frames, and the most onerous and alarming of all, gripping the extended T-handle of an uncontrollable electric-powered contraption as it careered across kitchen lino or down polished floorboard hall, heavy triangular head holding three circular choir buffers going at 1000 RPM, and throwing its operator around like a bull seal ragdolling a conger eel!

Still, seldom taking more than an hour, these tedious tasks were mainly just the parents testing his willingness to apply himself, and even the buffeting buffering had a small element of fun to it. Opening garage's back door and stepping onto house's rear veranda the boy gave thought to which classmates might be knocked around with during this break. But hmmm, a couple who could have been grouse to hang out with were holidaying interstate? 'Aw well, being on my Pat Malone won't hurt,' he decided. Yeah, hardly, for solitary activity never a bother, he always had his good old standby, fishing, as a leisure-time option anyway. Nevertheless, tossing in a line every day, given the waterways' present state?

Heavy rains had sent both the town's bookending rivers into flood. Main one's saltwater stretch, definitely be no mulloway to chase. All would have shot through out to sea to avoid fatal muddying of gills. Sure enough, bream could be got by using a heavy sinker and dropping a bait into the rushing current's deep sections, yet scant sport did anyone get from simply skull-dragging fish up from the bottom. As for those upriver runs, no, they were running stunning unfishable bankers.

Okay, so how about plucking a trout out of the other river's freshwaters, trying his luck in the back-eddy of a flooding pool? Maybe, maybe...? But mostly, in both rivers but that one in particular, with those surging brown downflows came eels. Yuuuch, no bloody chance would he chase after these snakelike slimies, reckoned the boy. Horrible writhing objects to deal with, he hated handling them. Nor did even thinking about eels make him the least bit peckish, even if in himself, he now detected a sudden hunger.

Nipping in through house's rear door, the boy aimed to make himself a sandwich, cheese and baked beans and tuna its filling... but anything really, except jellied eel! A not at all unusual fending for himself of course. At this time in the afternoon often his mother would have been home, cooking job at Old Folks Home done for the day. However, eyes on some pricey domestic item for future purchase, she had ditched her old job for a better paying doctor's receptionist position. As for the father perhaps being around, not only would he be stuck working further hours at the factory, this was, after all, a Friday. Factory's end of day hooter, it'd be, 'Shelve those shears, get into the beers!'

When alone in the home like this too, occasionally the boy missed his sister. Now a fully qualified nurse, rare indeed was it that she'd return from Melbourne. As he opened the fridge, his narrow capacity for analysis centred on her. When not these days caring for paraplegics at the Austin Hospital, parental chat reported the apparent enjoyment of a whirlwind social life. Included were three broken engagements to separate suitors. The boy's limited sphere of experience did not let him appreciate that pre the later Swinging Sixties years, at this time a ring on the female finger permitted boudoir behaviour otherwise frowned upon by a wowser society.

These fiancés, none of whom the family had met, were guaranteed however to capture a young adolescent's imagination.

Reputedly they were a shady Greek nightclub singer who crooned his last syllable supporting a knife stuck between his ribs, some Hungarian who'd stolen an aircraft to escape Russian oppression, and a world- ranked Italian middleweight boxer. The boy vaguely wondered whether his sister went with these fascinating extreme-action-men as a reaction to also perceiving their father as a bland non-action man?

Anyway, her business, eh? Someday maybe he'd ask her.

The boy set-to making his tuna-based sandwich. Tin-opener a manual one, in operating it he again became aware of the sensitivity in his hands from that leather tenderizing Tracksuit Joe had given them. Amusingly though, this brought back thoughts of eels – how great it'd be to drop a bloody big ultra-slimy one down the back of Joe's tracksuit!

Chunky sanger got together, munching on this the boy returned to garage. Moping around among scattered tools and junk, once more he pondered what, during this school break, he might get up to. Whatever happened though, for sure, not even the sheerest boredom would force him to go catching eels.

'Geez, frigging bloody bastard eels!' he thought. Oh, very right, like them even one little bit the boy did not. Nor, as in this instance, either thought-wise or aloud, did he much cuss hard – to employ the 'magic word' – though as with most young teens such self-restraint would soon enough disintegrate. But as for eels? Having slimed into his mind, for now they weren't leaving. The rotten things, if taking a bait, always swallowed your hook, necessitating much mucky mucking about to despatch them prior to re-rigging greasy with slime line.

The boy's thoughts now brought in his father, to be entwined in these greasily coiling considerations. Almost incomprehensibly, his dad loved tucking into boiled eel! What the son ought to have twigged was a connection to Great Depression survival by his widowed grandmother, eels one of few nutritional fresh foods she could afford to buy off a Glasgow slum street barrow. But Aussie-caught eels, put to bubbling on a stove? House thereafter stunk for days. Last time this took place – after the boy acceded to his sire's expressed desire he bring an eel home – had come the mother's whispered wish, 'Jings, son, promise me ye'll nae ever bring anither o' thae ugly reeking overgrown slugs hame again!'

Dead easy then, absolutely, to resist fishing in eel infested waters. The boy's immediate problem was how to stop these be-slimed creatures from writhing up through cerebellum canal into his scone? 'Come on,' he put it to himself, 'concentrate on something else. What *are* you going to do during these holidays?' Bugger! So, okay, the eels had tailed away, but in their place had imposed themselves more notions of chores his folks might propose – mopping floors, hanging washing, clearing roof gutters, gardening that entailed strenuous pulling of stubborn weeds when energies might have been going into things far more pleasurable... Every one of these tedious tasks had to be, if possible, avoided: lazing days, not slavery, the vacation to be aimed for.

As laidback leisure goes however, no creature does it better, makes time to take things easier, than a cat. Timmy, a feline needing zero patting to purr, now brought his emphatic '*Rrrrr-rrrr-rrrr...*' into the garage. Standard tail-in-air greeting, but sniffing too, at that tuna sanger. Piece of fishy crust broken-off, the boy passed it down. Morsel in mouth, the ginger tom beelined for a corner and began its licking and chewing. Watching his cat, an object propped in that same corner provided the boy with a way he'd be able to fill in one day at least of his school vacation. A pursuit less messy than eeling, but a blood and gutsy one nevertheless.

Where Timmy had taken his tucker, right by him leaned the .22 pea-rifle. Cobwebby, barrel rust-flecked, and unused by the father for some years, the boy hadn't much been interested in taking up shooting. However, in those early outings when rabbits were in plague proportions he had been well instructed in weapons etiquette, and had no qualms about handling a gun. So, bingo, why not go and bag a feast of bunny!?

Timmy rubbed against the boy's calves as firearm received its check of not being loaded. Although almost certainly it wouldn't be, a father's emphasis on shooting's golden rule had been well remembered. 'Now, where's the gun oil?' thought the boy. Once located, rifle would undergo a thorough cleaning.

Wintry Monday of those term holidays, both parents had been waved goodbye. Off to their respective work places, but not before, 'Yes mum, alright, alright, don't nag. I'll do the bl...'

'Dinnae ye dare swear!'

'... the dishes, okay?'

Quick and inadequate compliance carried out at kitchen sink, after this the boy hastened into garage. Sliding well-oiled .22 rifle into a spud bag, he bound it to his bike's bar, pocketed some bullets, and readied to ride off to where an underage shooter could fire away with near impunity. So long as he stayed well clear of habitation and shot sparingly in pinging a few furry feral foods, there'd be little chance some nosy joker with nothing better to do would dob him in to the plods in blue.

As for mentioning this intention of hunting to his father, not asking means you never get told 'No.' To arrive back after bagging some bunnies might bring a mild scolding, but by providing tucker for family larder this sneaky shoot would otherwise be let go through to the 'keeper. An admonition to choose carefully when and where he shot might be delivered too, yet the boy reckoned today he'd do just this. By going coastal a good safe distance east of any houses, today's strong cold westerly wind would also carry gunshot sounds away from this closest habitation.

About to mount bike, the boy found Timmy again at his feet. In a reverberating figure-of-eight the cat schmoozed around his jeans' legs. 'What d'you reckon Tim, rabbit kidneys for dinner?' he grinned. Purring puss licked his chops. A smart animal. And definitely, there still being no kids that the boy had connected with in this now developing immediate neighbourhood, the ginger tom remained his closest mate thereabouts. Albeit admittedly the cat vanished from his mind whenever those subdivision pegs across the way brought thoughts of more new homes going up. The boy would imagine, running about outside of these, the bare legs of such frisky jejune objects as ever more frequently now occupied his teen attention.

Dear oh dear, that segregated schooling at The Annex...? How it contributed to the boy seeing females around his own age as a delightful natural phenomena, but one also cloaked in mystery. So envious he felt of classmates who lived in well-populated communities where, if these jokers could be believed, precocious girls gaily played not just physicians and hospital handmaidens but got into activities which went 'lots further'... whatever that entailed?

No replaying in scone risqué schoolboy repartee here however. Rabbit hunting his sole focus, pedalling, pedalling, downhill at speed, went the boy. He'd donned a heavy polo-neck jumper and his woollen Magpies beanie. This going at pace would warm him further. Fast over-leaning hard left around home hill's bottom corner taken, and beyond this the railway overpass sped under, flashing pedals now accessed the next long downward section. Thereafter came familiar passing of boatsheds to one side and cemetery the other, then a zipping by Anglers Club building, the skirting around Old Folks Home, and a crossing of bridge. Once across river, after steering into a right-hander toward the Blue Hole, next though arrived a new environment, with a rutted track to the east being taken.

Unmade dirt thoroughfare, no more than twin ruts made by car wheels, crossed rough pastured farmland, going by a disused barn where every Sunday one select local football team, and every off-duty copper – plus a couple who were not – drank their way through an eighteen-gallon keg. By now the commotion of breakers crunching on a still out of sight ocean beach was audible, and shortly after, as track petered out, pushbike became pushed. Up abruptly rising paddock, as if drawn by the sound of those crashing waves, progressed Malvern Star and its dismounted rider. Of anyone else there was no sign, this chosen shooting zone's million-dollar ocean view homes and environmental despoilment many years away yet. Instead, the high farmland ended in huge empty dunes which fell away to beach sands – a spot that, except for surf-fishermen, few punters ever frequented. Gee, but the outlook southward from that drop-away! An unimpeded ocean panorama, whilst off to the east began miles of colossal cliff that included a massive sea-cave.

Quite a position for palatial homes it sure presented – once such marine vistas became fashionable, which as yet they were not. That most coastal inhabitants still tended to eschew ocean views may well have been a hangover from earlier immigrant settler attitudes. More than enough of heaving seas and seasickness experienced, they usually chose to build their homes well away from anywhere with even a glimpse of waves.

History adhered too, as well the boy appreciated, to those towering cliffs further along. In rugged terrain back from these lay scattered graves containing the remains of sailors and hapless passengers whose square-riggers had come to grief when blown in and bashed to pieces against sheer near unscalable rockfaces two and three hundred feet high. No direct thought though, gave the boy to this as, leaning bike against a weathered post-and-rail fence, a re-check as to total absence of company took place. Aloneness verified, rifle then got unbagged and bullet got slid into its breech: one young teen hunter, set to shoot underground mutton.

Fast achieved. Not sixty paces taken across low tussocks along sandy ridge top – *Pee-ow!* – right on the button, one furry mammal lying prostrate. When jogged over to however, a myxo victim, eyes diseased and long beyond seeing – a bunny gunned out of its misery at least. After this, continuing on, the boy encountered increasing marram grass and fern and low tea-tree and berry-bush along with other scrubby cover, but ran into no more rabbits. Ooowf, how cold though! Despite sunshine, heart-of-winter wind had veered more on-shore, buffeting in as if blasted directly from Antarctica's snows and ice.

A smart move then, to have worn heavy pullover and beanie. Yet obtain additional warmth by walking more briskly? Not when toting a gun in rough country – another early boyhood instruction from his father which had managed to sink in. 'I'll give it another half hour,' decided the boy. After that, if killable rabbits were still a no-show, he'd target an empty beer can and, after drilling that, hightail it for home and some hot soup. Too bad for Timmy. Tinned sardines and not fresh bunny kidneys the cat'd be eating that night.

As with fisherfolk though, gun hunters just never know… Softly to himself, 'Yes!' murmured the boy. In a low foliated glen between two buffalo-grassed sandy rises, movement. In a patch of fern, up-popped scone with, belonging to it, one pair of very long ears. Giant rabbit? 'Hey,' he realized, 'it's a hare!' No hesitation. Headshot too. Animal dropped stone-dead on the spot. In the hurrying downward to where deceased hare lay, a thought slipped by that such effective accuracy would have impressed another skilled marksman in the family. Animal's size surprised, five times that of a full-grown bunny. 'Yeah, they're from the deer family,' the young gunman reminded himself. Also, that they were therefore, very edible. Bewdy, and Timmy would do far better out of this result as well.

Right, first things first. At the very least an edible deceased beast must be gutted. Skinning could be done later. Yet running pocket-knife up hare's furry belly brought further surprises, to begin with the streaming blood mass this released. Then the spilled entrails started to move, three foetuses contained therein. From fully stoked, the boy went to feeling like shit. In fact, this moment would result in him almost being done with guns. In future, only if hard-pressed for tucker, or to despatch feral species predating native wildlife, might he drill an animal. Also, the abruptness of shooting felt similar to spearing fish – too immediate, summary execution.  True, rod and lining took piscine lives as well, yet this amounted to death at a reasonable distance, with a reprieve possible through equipment failure or fish's savviness or angler's stuff-up.

Now though, one totally lifeless hare, one very messy carcass... Holding gutted dripping-red animal upside-down by its hind legs, the boy bore it to rise's buffalo grassed crest and gazed far down to the waves-pounded sands. 'Could always climb down there and wash it?' he thought. He may well have done so too were it not for a phenomenal distraction as sensational as any that coast ever provided.

Sightline from deserted beach straying outward over inshore breakers, the boy stood gobsmacked. Just beyond furthest curling swell, casually cruising parallel to shoreline, were a gargantuan whale and its infant. Subsequent generations of locals would be told, sold a furphy in fact, that only when the act of commercial whaling ceased did these gentle giants return to this marine nursery. Instead, despite dwindling in numbers, never had some not stopped at this special krill-filled spot. As if in salute, the mama raised a huge fluke before whopping it down to flay spray across the choppy wind-lashed waves.

One long week it had taken two adults and one young teenager to finally chew through that massive pot of Irish stewed hare chunks. Such energy and expertise the mother sunk into making it from the hacked-up animal and what seemed like half a ton of *praties*. The boy reckoned it the highlight of his school holiday. From there though, how the next 1964 months fairly flew. Once through to September's customary trout opening excitement, of course preceded by excessive youthful bait-getting, what followed as usual too was disappointment. The intrepid anglers three – the boy, his father, and, though so rarely now, Old Ron – had embarked for yet another fishing mecca lake in the flat country just short of the Grampians, only to again endure a no-take outing. Not that, in listening to Old Ron yarn, it made for anything other than a memorable day.

No enjoyment whatsoever is to be had however, in a football grand final loss. Especially a close defeat. For those participating on the playing field, that is even worse. The second last Saturday that same September, by a point in their season decider, down went Tech Under-17's. More confident now since weight training gain of a smidgen additional muscle, the boy had played quite well. Yet that mattered not. At any level, losing a grand final devastates, and perhaps only a groom failing to perform on his wedding night might feel gloomier. For the boy, this defeat experienced just weeks short of him turning fourteen, never again did he want to know that hollow runner-up feeling and the bitter taste this left in his mouth.

A brief break to get over that lost footy season decider, then came tossing a coin to see who'd bat. Slate cleaned, cricket again commencing... Play once more for Tech Colts the boy did. Yet before the celebrations of a fresh year in which he'd turn fifteen began, already his heart no more lay in the flannelled fools' game. Batting and bowling, fair enough, so long as the crease was occupied a good while or arm got rolled over plenty of times. But hanging around in a sun-baked outfield awaiting catches that seldom came, or sitting sore arsed until the chance arrived to bat only to lose your middle stump first ball...? Footy always offered further chances to make up for mistakes, clean-bowled in cricket none.

Nevertheless, for some seasons still the boy would continue with cricket, even play in representative games for their local association. However not long before getting that key-to-the-adult-world door, one stinking-hot day in the field too many, he'd give the game away, and let footy be his remaining ball sport. Otherwise recreationally, a strong interest would of course be retained in fishing. He'd return enthusiastically to free-diving too, and other lesser sports sometimes take his fancy. Standing out in full-sun summer heat frying like a saveloy in batter though, nah, he was done with that!

If the boy felt no longer fully committed to cricket, even less did Form Three studies engage him when in 1965 schooling at The Annex recommenced. Increasingly drawn to the written and spoken word, except for English classes most subjects bored him excreta-less. Not that at the Tech completing composition ever stretched the brain of any student with an IQ exceeding 70 either. Ability to spell your surname correctly all but ensured the assessment 'excellent'.

Yet okay, thanks to Helen 'Pash' Chaffee's presence, attending Art classes was no chore either. Besides, a reasonable facility with pencil and crayon and brush the boy did have. What a mini-disaster then, when Pash and her mini-skirts departed to take up a post at the main school. Nor did this promotion prompt commotion and consternation only amongst her youthful now female teacherless pupils. Left bereft also were a couple of single male chalkies who'd trail after Pash the way Labrador puppies follow a towed pork chop. Then, worse again for any besotted male, juvenile or mature, next thing they knew Pash had on a wedding ring. Central school's veteran maths teacher, suffering from terminal cancer and a bulging bank balance, had calculated this as his time to attain spiritual purity by making an income-poor woman monetarily secure.

So yep and uh-huh and all things considered, not the greatest year unfolding here: Pash a May bride, school increasingly tedious, any fishing done not particularly productive in either rivers or lakes. Then even footy season turned out to be only an okay year personally and teamwise. As for their two school socials…? What a washout! No amorous interest attracted at all from that intriguingly curvaceous species the boy, albeit becoming a smidgen more educated re their configurations courtesy of schoolyard circulated Playboy editions, continued to be largely in the dark about.

Preoccupation with female structure ruptured the purity of the boy's angling endeavours too, when he – less often now – went. Definitely, his interest in the piscatorial had undergone diminishment. Whereas in dreamy younger days he'd while away his time by watching stream drift by and clouds above do similarly, along with observing antics of the water environment's animal life, surging hormones and emerging adolescent pimples increasingly distracted him from absorbing innocent nature's aesthetics.

So yes, it should have been 'thank goodness for football', and its effect of rechannelling energy and focus. But uh-huh, overall, a far from stellar season had. Eventually Tech Under-17's bowed out in the first semi-final, and badly. A less wrenching ordeal than blowing previous year's Grannie, true, but nevertheless, opportunity wasted. Footy-wise even worse though, those hero-worshipped Magpies had hardly done much better, underperforming much of the season before blowing the VFL preliminary final.

When the sports jocks a kid idolizes are playing patchily, might it affect his own on-field form? Indeed, crash-hot in ball-getting that season the boy had not been. Presentation night saw no trophy come his way. At least though, neither did he win that Best

Clubman booby prize. Yet under-performance can have an upside. Going home empty-handed, the boy resolved that the following year he'd put in a dinkum effort – pre-season hard running and bigger weights, and more skills practiced to turn him into a well-rounded player. And for very good reason. Despite restricted life experience, absolute awareness he had that in a rural setting, shining academic achievements guaranteed steady employment far less than excellence on the footy field. Moreover, if he sussed little else, the boy did understand his path to adulthood did not include a destination marked 'university'.

If, to the boy anyhow, most subjects taught were a waste of time, then hey, what about this for a joke? Final term exams scraped through, he now found himself stuck twiddling his thumbs in the stagnant chemistry classroom. At academic year's near close all The Annex teachers ceased doing what they'd been trained for. Students were left to idle away final schooldays playing chess or chequers upon desktops, or else playing with themselves beneath them. And even the most pleasurable of these pastimes will soon enough lose its gloss.

How fortuitous then, that shoal of large salmon trout showing up at the Breakwater, and continuing to hang around. A get-out-of-school-jailhouse card had arrived. Provided students showed proof of doing part-time work – kids off dairy farms helping to milk for example – worthless final non-learning weeks were avoidable. Despite dubiousness as to his offspring's professional fishing bona fides, the father acceded to copious pleas and agreed to sign an appropriate note. Bewdy, and an unaccustomed feeling of unlimited affection towards 'good old dad' too! Once his pro fisherman statues got accepted, out of crummy Annex and home to rig up heaviest tackle to catch jack salmon went the boy.

Good vibes his father's way the boy sent during all that initial casting-into-sea from long Breakwater's end day. Not only because of the sheer escapism this release from school gave either. A productive enterprise, over a dozen hefty salmon lay in the spud bag he'd brought along. As this first stint as a professional fisherman – there'd be more later in life – drew to a close, the boy's satisfaction increased upon hearing the factory's hooter. Soon he'd be picked up, driven home, and then jump under a hot shower. Wow, and how looking forward he was to that!

Fish the boy had caught, but much wet weather had caught him. Rain had threatened when, before work, father had driven son down with all his gear to the Breakwater – that pier of concrete and timber and giant boulders poking out into their town's surf-beach bay. An hour later heavy showers had begun. One happy day it'd been, sure, hauling in a hefty fish each time the shoal's long circuit from beach to back reef took them past his stoutest cane rod and medium-sized side-cast reel and salted pilchard presentation, but what joy too, reckoned the boy, there'd be in leaving. Yeah, he was bloody freezing! Just the same, that early rain did see him having the place all to himself, meaning he couldn't over-complain.

An open space though, the long dual level Breakwater with its lower roadway side and narrower elevated seaward wall. No shelter could be had therefore, except to ineffectually press against that higher wall, so the boy's overalls were now soaked through. Salty spray cascading overhead and over him whenever heavy swells whumped into that sheer-sided seawall had only added discomfort. Nevertheless, he had bagged all those salmon! There'd be dinkum moolah made from this ostensibly iffy fishing venture, sold for three bob a pound to Dutch Tony who made fishcakes from the strong-tasting species.

As for the Breakwater itself, it did exactly that. A solid straight-line structure with that high backwall and its eroded lower roadway, moored in its lee bobbed several cray and shark boats perfectly protected from those monstrous Southern Ocean combers. From looking at these, the boy glancing back along puddled lower section. More rain appeared imminent, but, 'Ah, terrific!' he saw his father approaching. In gumboots, sensible given the inclement present and the scattered pools of water lying about.

Upon discovering one only son had become a money-earning angler, the father offered congratulations, before insisting, 'Och, Ah'll aye carry these tae the car for ye.' And he bearing the fish, off they set along Breakwater back towards the Valiant. In doing this, they followed train lines laid from a time of far deeper harbour when locomotives came to collect coastal steamer cargoes. The rails also ran by a rusted leeside ladder.

Just as ladder was passed, to its top, one after the other, clambered two genuine professional fishermen. Gargantuan men, day's sea toil on their sharker done, they'd climbed from a dingy used for ferrying duties to their main boat. The first up of these huge humans addressed the father, 'Ay, yer don't wanna go wearin' them poofter farm boots round 'ere, mate.' Not satisfied with this bit of slinging-off, the fat-on-muscle twenty stoner turned to his unshaven companion. 'Whaddayareckon? Aveterbe a shirt-lifter wouldn' e, Brick?' The offsider, undoubtably nicknamed for being thick as one as well as his red-coloured hair, let out a laugh both harsh and challenging.

The father hesitated. Face reddened. He glanced a moment at these antagonists. Yet then, saying nothing, he took the boy by an arm and resumed momentum towards the end carpark. There'd be no doing, as the boy so craved him to, of taking a proper crack back at those shit-stirrer dills – a swift one-two, *whack-whack*, belting both of them into the drink... From being so chuffed in the presence of his dad, once again the boy felt shame.

Aaah, the pitfalls of youthful observation and perception... or more accurately, lack thereof. The fishermen's sudden sullen silence hadn't registered with the boy, nor their stony expressions as if indeed impacted by a swift left-right combination. In those eyes of that smaller bloke in gumboots at whom their ridiculing smartarse remarks had been directed, they'd seen potential murder, an unspoken, 'Ah wouldnae advise ye tae continue attempting tae humiliate and intimidate me in front of mah boy.' In Glasgow's back streets, implication of pending severe *molocation* is often the most effective retaliation.

The Breakwater salmon were long gone, and hare-killer pea-rifle, again unused, re-gathered cobwebs and dust and rust in the garage. Hogmanay had just passed, the father's initial hangover of 1966 not quite. Evening, January the First, family threesome tucked into a mutton curry. Previous Sunday the mother had planned roast lamb for Aussie friends, the Carneys. By this time almost twenty years in Australia and copious cooking assignments behind her, oddly never had she roasted a lamb. Enquiring of these guests-to-be what to ask the butcher for, Kevin the hubby advised 'two-tooth'. Then, when after departing oven, their roast fare ate tougher than an old boot, Kevin Carney had wryly declared, 'Letty, next time make sure your sheep had its *first* two teeth and not its *last* two when those bludgers slaughtered it.'

Didn't those butchers cop a verbal lashing too, from a Gaelic tongue far sharper edged than their boning knives! After that though, a case of waste not, want not. Neither the Scots nor the Irish are great ones for chucking out tucker. The mother's hand-cranked mincer had transformed unchewable roast into a ripper curry. Easy to eat as well in front of the telly, glued as they were to the Edinburgh Military Tattoo's hullabaloo. However, two distinct types of cuisine were being consumed, two mild serves and a single flaming chilli one. The father's curry, he'd insisted, needed to set his palate on fire. The mother's response, a bland,

'Oh aye, nae worries,' revealed not the devilment behind her eyes. Prepared had been a separate Hogmanay hangover-expunging serve of extreeeeeeme piquancy!

Studying his sweating steaming father shovelling in that furnace curry, and despite such pronouncements as, 'Och, my God, love, this is marrrrvelous!', the boy remained sceptical genuine enjoyment, or even efficacy in purging Scotch whisky malaise, applied. That nostalgia attached to the super-hot dish he did appreciate – some association with Indian forces the father had served alongside in that Burma kerfuffle. But of deeper motivations for someone subjecting themselves to internal cactus spike torture...? As might have been said by those rock 'n rollers the boy was now into, he didn't 'dig' it.

Ha, yeah, that Britbeat! The Beatles, Rolling Stones, Gerry and the Pacemakers... Yet despite embracing the Rock and Blues scenes, never would the boy lose his love for traditional Scottish music. As he continued watching those massed tartan bands crossing their telly screen, in front of it Timmy the cat lay curled up on a rug. To the skirl of pipes and the drums' paradiddle, the cat let out a low yowl. So well did this blend with the bagpipes, the mother quipped, 'Och, Timmy's no able tae help himself frae joining in.' They all laughed, the father half-choking on a chilli, until... the animal went rigid from a seizure. Stretched stiff as a board, Timmy bid goodbye to his ninth life.

Through open lounge-room window came strains of a single bagpipe, the Edinburgh Castle battlement's Lone Piper. Beneath garden's almond tree the boy finished burying his best mate. Always there, Timmy, for confidential disclosures, gambols in the garden, and above all else, affection. Inconsolable, the boy... his tears wouldn't stop. Not a kid to cry either, that soup-over-scone incident in small boyhood and its aftermath spanking the last time his eyes had really gushed. Nor, once he took care of his feline friend, would he cry again until middle-age when a dry tear-well once more filled to overspill following the fatality to both his parents.

After placing garden flowers on that small fresh mound of earth covering Timmy, on foot the boy made for his river. No fishing equipment taken. He needed just to walk out onto a jetty, and to sit.

Life does chuck up its tragedies vast to almost imperceptible. Far outweighing these speed bumps are, for the lucky majority, plenty of middling-to-good days. Even those less lucky folk will crack a fair number. And now and again, then come those brilliant ones. For the boy in his fifteenth year, nearing end of his summer break before commencing Fourth Form, ahead lay a wonderful nine days at Bawley Point in New South Wales. They'd be indelible, pure magic.

Deemed to be fine on his own for a long train trip, the robust boy, enough bumfluff on his face now that he'd scored an electric razor at Christmas, arrived at Sydney's Central Station. Amid surging platform passengers and porters, he was met by his father's rag trade pal Reg, in whose spacious Humber they'd motor to the southern New South Wales coast. A tall raw-boned Pom of patrician appearance, Reg's bent-at-reflex-angle nose lent him a striking resemblance to the Duke of Wellington. To give the boy a different experience, albeit including familiar fishing elements, he had offered to take time off as manager of a textile mill from which the father selected much of his factory's cloth.

A jovial fellow was Reg. It belied his World War Two ordeals as a ship's engineer on runs across the Atlantic and to Murmansk surviving U-boat wolf-packs and air attacks. Yet very much a bloke of great good nature and ready wit, his deliberately light-hearted accounts of wartime naval actions were terrific travel entertainment. The boy didn't twig that this trip had been planned as a calculated step in preparing him for manhood. Nor that he could have wanted for a better mentor than Reg, although some of those more risqué quips made were passing right over his ongoingly quite innocent scone.

Bitumen left behind, scrubby bush bashing down a sandy track began. As Humber bumped along bound for the scattered shacks of tiny untrendy Bawley Point, Reg gave an account of being bombed by a long-range Luftwaffe Condor. Stoked listening to this, the boy couldn't prevent himself once more regretting how boring in comparison his own father's war had been. He said as much to Reg. A sideways glance and a contemplative stroking of that classically broken nose, preceded, 'Remind me, when we get to the guesthouse, to fish out a book for you.' Which the boy was okay about. Only though if it did, in fact, concern fishing. Otherwise, bloody books? He'd had enough of reading fusty irrelevant guff at school!

Bawley Guesthouse's eccentric proprietors might well have been straight out of a witty novel. A weird pair, and perfect fit for their wonky veranda-surrounded wooden building itself, Andy and Mavis were time-worn but never forlorn. Pear-shaped she got about in grubby floral shifts and geisha-like makeup of white powdered face and cherry-red lipstick, whilst he went barefoot in shorts, half the bum out of them, and no underdaks. Reg and the handful of other guests seemed to ignore all their idiosyncrasies.

The boy simply found this whole strange bush backwater intoxicating. And this was before encountering Natasha, who'd be far more so. Meanwhile though, Reg located that silverfish-gnawed book from guesthouse's dilapidated library. As the boy had guessed, it concerned World War Two's Burma campaign. However, in his dusty and musty-smelling single room of small bed and smaller window and curtains hanging in threads, read right through *Burma 1941-45* he did. A non-engrossing account though: prose turgid, no photos... only snippet to stay with him a remark by some Supreme Commander named Mountbatten, stating a certain stoush amounted to 'Britain's Thermopylae'. But like, hey, a classic history reference? Tech studies never touched any of that ancient Greek garbage.

Away, therefore, the book was put, and all but blind to fearsome Burma battles and their backgrounds the boy remained. To everything else thereabouts though, how wide were his eyes! Top spot belonged to accompanying Reg onto cleanest beach bookended by cunjevoi covered rocky points. On the littoral zone of wave-licked sand, a stink-bag of fish-heads would be swished across backwash to entice shoelace-length worms into raising their hungry heads. Grasped with wool-bound pliers, these were with great care hand-dug intact out of the wet white grains. Thereafter, hooks baited with cut-up worm got cast into sparkling surf to catch the silveriest of bream and whiting.

How much more exciting too, although a bonus barely needed, when whilst playing a fighting fish on long whippy rod, arrived at low level two-seater RAN Fireflies, Griffin engines r oaring, trainee Navy pilots zooming through to beat-up both beach and peaceful wee Bawley Point!

For days things went thus, fishing and barnstorming Fireflies, together with gentlemanly if occasionally ribald mentoring from Reg. Sun-bathing was done too, along with body-surfing. But then... Natasha! The teen daughter of an upmarket Sydney couple, their top-of-the-range Ford Fairlane had brought them for a brief stay. And with this young maiden's materializing, what a sudden odd disinterest in fishing the boy developed. Instead, he found a fondness for playing volleyball, badminton, table-tennis, flicking a frisbee... any activity which could be done with Natasha in which she leaped, pranced, stretched, and paused in all manner of radiant poses, especially those which caused her to bend.

Fifteen also, but an advanced fifteen, well Natasha knew her effect on adoring adolescent males. A brunette with shortish hair, she had a lovely tan and a captivating laugh which splendidly showcased her pearly-perfect thousand-dollar teeth. Along with this, tight Double Bay boutique shorts emphasised ideal sporting gluteals. Best of all however were her hand-embroidered scoop-necked T-shirts. Whenever Natasha stooped to pick up ball or shuttlecock or plastic frisbee, revealed was that despite reaching an age and stage where she ought to have, she wore no bra. For the boy, a new and enthralling experience. How far in his mesmerised mind, in an instant, had angling with Reg distanced itself? Far, far further than he'd ever dreamed he might cast a line.

Still, if Natasha's platinum-heeled parents had not got around to buying her a pricey brassiere, other awareness they did have. No distance would they stray when their daughter and the boy were engaged in sports play. Yet, despite his naivety, the boy had some perception. He sussed that stare at Natasha's natural wares he shouldn't. Instead, he needed to restrict intrigued ogling to sneaky peeks. How captivating though, a lively female's brief but real exposures, compared to those shared perusals with classmates of Playboy bunnies! As for Natasha, she pretended blissful unconsciousness of those stolen glances.

Uh-huh, that daily play, and him in thin nylon bathers too... Concentrate the boy had to on his frisbee tossing technique, to prevent full extent of his fascination with Natasha being apparent. However, what in his greenness he had not got to contemplating was anything of an advanced amorous nature. To perhaps actually be invited to touch those two wondrous wobbly upper objects was about the length to which his aspirations extended. He did though reckon, definitely, that him instigating a kiss wouldn't be an unreasonable ambition. To achieve this therefore, almost on nightfall...

Bream in batter supper done with, and relaxing in squeaky single bed surveying cobwebbed and mildewed ceiling, the boy geed himself up that he *must, just must,* invite Natasha into his pinch-shoulder room. What did his feelings equate to? Watching a gradual taking up of his slack line by what he knew to be a huge fish? Well, somewhat. But this was miles more exciting. Might the pretext of showing Natasha something like his latest Angler's Monthly, convince her to join him here in seclusion?

From noisy narrow bed, out onto Bawley Guesthouse's lengthy veranda ventured the boy. Ah, brilliant! No more than a Teddy Whitten flick-pass away, stationed in a hammock, lolled the object of his infatuation. Neither normally vigilant parent in the vicinity either. Bewdy, Natasha could easily be approached, albeit gingerly, 'Um, Tash... I was wondering...?'

But oh, so casually, cut off. 'Go away. My parents say you're too common and I am not to play with you ever again.'

The rebuff rocked him. Snobbery did exist in their home community but it was disguised. Besides, even most of the town's better-off were almost borderline battlers in those days of restrained wages. He tried, 'But I...?' to say more, before turning on heel and making a red-cheeked retreat.

Not that Natasha's rejection much mattered. With next morning's woodstove cooked brekky of bacon and bumnuts eaten, she and her Bellevue Hill parents were in their Fairlane and fairly tearing back to Sydney. Just the same, for the thwarted boy, actual sensual awakening had dawned. Something not lost, of course, on world-wise Reg. Taking his somewhat crestfallen young charge aside he counselled, 'Remember, there are always more fish in the sea...' before reeling him back onto an angling tack as they resumed breaming and hooking whiting together from the beach during their final Bawley Point days.

What a stay it had been though, this first extended time away from his own folks. And for confidence-building, what is better than proximity to a sagacious adult who's prepared to feign his young companion has approximate equality? Indeed, it's unbeatable. Deliver many solid learnings then, this single

Bawley Point sojourn did. For one pubescent lad, the realization that a youth with a rod in his hand may not necessarily be fishing, perhaps stood as the most significant.

Back home and unpacking, the boy discovered beneath unwashed underwear, a square object. That knocked-about copy of *Burma 1941-45* had been snuck into his suitcase by the well-meaning Reg. But why? He'd already read the book... although alright, lightly scanned it be more accurate. Gathering all soiled clothes, he started for the laundry. His mother would be fully justified to tell him, 'Hie, ye can dae all thae filthy claes yersel'!' but she'd say no such thing. On the way to get his washing done he also took the Burma book, handing it to a settee-seated cigarette-in-hand father as he went by him, and shrugging, 'This is pretty grotty dad, but maybe you'll want to put it in our library or something?'

Glancing at the war tome's front, and then at its back cover, the father rose and crossed dining-room lounge. In wedging the work into a shelf alongside publications and pictorials mostly on Scotland, he enquired, 'Aye, and where'd ye get this?'

'Reg gave it to me.'

The father just nodded.

'Er, dad, where's... um... Thermopylis?'

'Thermopylae,' corrected the father, resuming his settee-ing and smoking. 'It's an obscure wee place in Greece.'.

The boy waited. No further information came. 'Yeah, I thought so,' he muttered, and giving not a glance either to the samurai sword affixed above door into their kitchen, he continued on through toward the laundry beyond.

For some days after returning home a strange restlessness prevailed. This the boy attributed correctly to Natasha, her persistence in nightly visiting his padded pillow dreams. Yet within a week these engagements faded, and reinstated to his consciousness was angling – of a sort he sought to do again. That thrill of reeling in those silver clean-gilled bream onto Bawley Point's whitest sands remained sharp. Why not then, do similar here? It would mean using full-on surf-fishing gear though, for local beach conditions were too heavy for those flexible 'tailor' rods Reg favoured. A dinkum crack at surf angling on the wide-open Victorian coast required a heavyweight 12-foot cane.

With his father's assistance – via cash rather than in rod-making – all necessary items were purchased: 'Aye, a verra early birthday gift for ye, okay?' Scottish extravagance requires a reason. Included were a gaff, large star sinkers, hooks and swivels, strong line, a grand wood-turned Alvey side-caster, and of course, that stout cane of imposing length, along with eyelets and stainless-steel reel attachment fitting. The boy's challenge was to transform the latter items into a true instrument for poling big fish out of a heavy sea.

Instructional publication on rod-making by veteran angler Athel D'Ombrain borrowed from library, did the trick. A formidable fish catching tool got fashioned. Tremendous weight transference required to cast it, on the balance of probabilities more hernias would be produced than fantastic catches. Nevertheless, lacquered and adorned with all shiny white porcelain eyelets and gleaming fittings, impressive it looked.

Common knowledge was that local surf fishing required not only muscle but plenty of patience. Seldom were catches plentiful, if at all. But the reward could also be substantial. Gummy and school shark might be hooked, or mulloway, big snapper and jack salmon taken… Sometimes even tearaway yellowtail hit baits. Unlike at Bawley Point though, rarely did a bream get hauled out of the southern surf. As for that much-needed patience? This applied not only to awaiting sporadic bites. Until sea turned placid, pointless to go. Heavy swells generated by distant deep-south gales prevailed. It took a high weather front's humidity to settle the surface. Heavy rain helped too, a strong northerly even more so.

Just such a north wind blew this late summer afternoon. Untried king of rods tied along his bike's bar and sticking wa-a-a-a-y out behind it, off the boy set to try his luck in the salty surf. Freewheeling downhill, he willed that some sort of sea species would cooperate and end up on his plate that night. He also detected smoke coating his nostrils. Bushfire!... but alright, not close, a reminder instead of from whence today's northerly emanated. The Grampians, location of their glorious mountain lake and floating boat fishing for trout, were ablaze, and that quaint valley hamlet containing the CWA cottage under threat. Tinder-dry Victoria in March, one careless match all it took.

Yeah, rural wildfires...? Rail bridge ridden under and river in sight, into the boy's mind shuffled Danny O'Callaghan, demented Irishman, rummager in town's main street garbage bins. Sent silly by a motorbike accident that cracked his skull like an eggshell, Danny went around shouting, 'Bloooody Austraaalia, great cooontry for dryin' clothes and bushfires an' feck-all else!'

Approaching cemetery bend near the Anglers Clubhouse now, the boy thought also of their old boat beside the jetty beyond. At its moorings and in absolute disuse, those sub-standard materials used in construction had finally stopped holding it together, and there it lay, listing, half-sunk and irreparable. Briefly, as he pedalled on, with him rode a mix of regret and nice nostalgia. Then anticipation of which fish types might grab his ocean baits took over. As for his destination here? After crossing river via the bridge, he'd beeline for that seldom frequented beach off which those whales had been observed the day he shot his hare.

The great down-sloping dunes' ridge top arrived at, bike dropped and untried lengthy surf-rod untied, and then, further burdened by backpack loaded with tackle and bait, descent commenced on a soft-sand slightly winding foot and animal track. Through spiky marram grass, an ever so steep two hundred feet took the boy downward to reach seaweeded beach. Then it struck him what one hell of a climb back up it'd be. Geez, and if he caught a bagful?! Heh, hey, bonzer problem to have, eh? Did look promising too. Swell slight, between two sandbars covered white from light breakers, a deep hole of turquoise water awaited.

Footy shorts worn on this venture for convenience in wading out, teen resilience would see the always icy ocean water all but ignored. Rod end bouncing from weight of a dangling four-ounce star sinker and two 4/0 hooks baited with pilchards, on grainy pudding sand, and legs slapped by small incoming waves, the boy barefooted outward to thigh depth. From there, twisting big Alvey side-caster forty-five degrees for free release, he hauled back, and with this heaviest of home-made surf canes, heaved. 'Jesus!' Only luck prevented a rupture. Some contrast to casting a tailor rod at Bawley Point. However, sinker sailed far out. So, a satisfactory start. All seemed to bode well.

Alas, by evening's arrival... fishless! An expanding appreciation of surf-fishing's drawbacks the only dubious positive. That it represented a feast or famine exercise with usually the latter applying had been known. But apparent also was that persistent sou'-easters, as had blown the full week before, gave sea an east to west sweep that forever shifted quite heavy sinker from left to right. This, plus that drifting kelp kept fouling the line, necessitated constant re-casts, each of which stressed and twisted internal organs.

Another half-hour, and darkness encroaching, on were coming the sea-lice to reduce fat pilchards to just useless head and skeleton baits. Shit and double shite! 'Last cast,' the boy told himself. Once more the arduous task, over-long cane not getting any lighter. Big wooden Alvey added weight too. Outward soared star sinker and baits. A backtrack up sloping beach before sore arms rammed rod butt into sand... and this accomplished, the boy positioned himself alongside rod. Yeah, easier than standing and holding pole upright with its end stuck in his angler belt's cup. He kept however, a finger in contact with the strong line.

Okay, so no fish. Otherwise, an all-fine feeling though, right? Sky a deepening orange, still warm, evening star showing... uhhh, oooh, hey, hang on, finger detected a 'pick-pick-pick'. Very light, yet not necessarily a tiddler. Cautious snapper or salmon perhaps? Surf-fishing threw up plenty of possibilities. In day's final dimming any one of these marine denizens may have been playing with that bait.

When abruptly the thing took off, the boy reckoned he'd hooked a submarine! Heavy cane bent like wet spaghetti. Crikey, the bulk of this hulking creature! Not that it was expending a mass of energy, taking place only an inexorable slow-paced charge straight toward Tasmania... which may have been where whatever it happened to be ended up. Once all run out, the twenty-four-pound breaking strain monofilament snapped easy as cotton. Hooked had been possibly some sort of shark, but more probably an enormous bull-headed black stingray.

By now night had enveloped, 'Bugger!' thought the boy – so much effort and nothing to show for it except one rotten unproductive surf-rod too heavy for comfortable use by anyone short of the current Mister Universe. And what awaited? Bearing this and burdensome backpack, in complete darkness, up that testing loose sandy climb. In footy shorts too, pricked by marram grass during the groping upward. But to look on the bright side, unencumbered by weight of fish at least. Um, but er, hang on...?

Bloody right, on warm nights such as this tiger snakes sometimes coiled upon just such sandy tracks awaiting prey. If not gone already, the gloss sure was falling off this surf-fishing caper. Fortunately, as warily he climbed, the boy came face to fang with no stroppy serpents, and once at dune top resolved to do further fishing in the surf. A couple of times he'd catch too, snapper and a gummy shark. Yet in general Murphy's Law applied to angling on southern beaches: something would stuff it up. In comparison, river fishing was simpler and usually productive. More seductive too. Sweet whisper of stream trumped a constant roar of breakers. Heavy long cane surf-rod would in time, like the pea-rifle, find itself confined to the garage.

Pea-rifle would however, feature in one final incident. The father, deciding that of late he and the boy had done very few sire and son bonding outings, midweek made a surprise early return home from work. Smiling as he came in through the front door, he suggested, 'So, son, whit would ye say aboot you and me going oot tae get oorselves a fish *and* a bunny?' Leaving the boy to consider his proposal, he made for the toilet where, at workday's end, he liked to sit awhile, catch up on that morning's newspaper, and savour a cigarette.

Mother as yet not in from current doctor's receptionist job, the boy made himself a basic baked beans sanger. He didn't feel particularly eager to engage in a fishing and shooting foray with his old man, but nor was he opposed to the idea. Where might they go, though? Definitely this couldn't involve their now cactus boat. Hell, how about that last time some while ago when they'd gone out in the collapsing craft? A sieve-like leaking, more bailing out than hook baiting, anchored over from the power station pumphouse, and the fish in full non-cooperation mode, and absence of angling action seeing father attempt to extract talk from silent son – as difficult this, as for Doc Kirkham last month prising out one of the lad's holed upper molars... oh, that gloomy dentist's surgery with its antiquated pedal drill and ether anaesthetic!

The boy thought some more about that final shared outing in their disintegrating boat – how he'd wished his father to axe trying to coax conversation from him when he just didn't feel like talking. Sure enough, the old man had in the end simply sat and observed the river environs. His standard 'communing with nature'. No worries there. The boy felt contented to do this too, studying clouds and birds passing in flight or floating by before them feeding upon the water – cormorants, pelicans, musk ducks, dab chicks... That day there'd been moorhens as well, over in those shallows a little upriver from the pumphouse and its steep-rising pipes.

'Ahhh, right, ri-i-i-i-ght!' twigged the boy. That gaggle of moorhens had been gathered below one extremely steep section of embankment. All but a cliff, but in places narrow ridges held enough soil to support grasses and tenacious shrubbery on which fed sure-footed rabbits. This, he guessed, would be the area where his father planned to suggest they'd go with rod and rifle.

Spot on! Once the dad had, in a pall of wispy nicotine medication, emerged from his meditation space within internal privy, it was of this very location that the father spoke. '... and ye ken, son, it occurred tae me that nae-one has ever wet a line at the bottom of yon climb, so we carry oor rods doon, and on oor way, we shoot a couple o' bunnies too. Whit d'ye say, eh? Be a lovely wee shared adventure.'

There he went again, that sissy expression, 'lovely'! The boy swung negative. What he ought to say was that he'd prefer to stay home and watch *Rawhide* on the telly. However, but only just, his father's keenness swayed him. He sussed too that to decline might find a repercussion in his dad deciding his only son could go out and mow that bloody lawn, nature-strip included. 'Alright,' he said, suppressing a sigh, 'I suppose.'

'Ye dinnae need tae be so enthusiastic,' remarked the father who, when niggled, had ample capability to be sarcastic.

'No, no, really, let's go!' bucked-up the boy, not wishing to be a killjoy. Besides, taking the gun along? A bit different that, so this might actually be fun. Although... 'Dad, it's really steep there y'know?' he hedged.

'Oh aye, okay, so maybe too dangerous for you then, eh?' Full well the father appreciated this growing son's development into an individual disinclined to baulk at a challenge.

'I was thinking more about your knees?' partially fibbed the boy, 'Not too flash, are they?'

'Och, if they could stand up tae week-long jungle patrols, they'll dae fine  on sae minor a short climb.'

Clueless as to Burma's rugged topography, the boy thought airily, 'Yeah, but you're talking about strolling around on flat land,' prompting him to almost say aloud, 'But this is going to be really, *really* steep?' The old man did, definitely, every so often moan about unsteady legs too. What age was he now? Almost fifty – frigging ancient! A near-perpendicular eighty degrees that couple of hundred feet or higher of riverside had to be. Up and down this on dodgy knees...? Oh well, it was the old fella's funeral.

Doctor employer stuck with a patient backload, the mother had yet to get home when, toting implements designed for both hook and bullet, father and son set off together. Down their long block, then along rail track past power station they hiked, cut across paddock toward cliff lip drop-off to pumphouse, but thereafter, clambering over those metal cooling pipes, with care made their way further upriver along bevelled scrubby scarily high embankment's top.

At the point picked for descent, gun at the ready, over they peeped, only to see every bunny speed into cover. Who'd have thought the second they caught sight of two human hunters peering down at them the furry fare sought wouldn't instead wave 'G'day' with their paws? Nevertheless, not an auspicious beginning. It could even have brought a notion that this bream and bunnies getting expedition might be mozzed and ought to be aborted. But no. 'Och, we'll tak the gun doon wi' us,' decided the father, 'An incautious one might jist stick its head oot later?'

A couple of hours after that very iffy cliffiness had been negotiated and the precarious descent achieved, perhaps predictably every juicy bait which was cast into that virgin angling territory had sat out there untouched. They still did so right until very last light. As always, eh, that anticipation a fish *must* come along meant darkness arrived before they packed up. Had either of them thought ahead though and brought a torch? As for the rifle being put to use, some animals are dumber than others. These rabbits weren't, and stayed hidden away. The weapon would have been far better left up on the heights. But yes, hindsight's a great thing.

As he had after that surf-fishing episode, the boy found himself ascending more or less by feel. This time tiger snakes weren't a possible problem, only an infinitely more testing climb. Complicating this further he'd been entrusted to be their gun-bearer. The father held all four rods they'd brought, bound together in a bundle.

A matter of individual climber feeling and finding his own way, underfoot the ultra-steep slope offered a combination of rock and soft unstable soil. At first, even though hindered by firearm gripped in one hand, the sports-fit boy negotiated the going without much difficulty, and his dad's 'D'ye need a hand, son?' offers of assistance were annoying. Adamantly he'd respond he was fine. True too, until about a hundred and fifty feet above river. Here difficulties began. A particularly perpendicular section, it also had alarming friability.

As above by some distance now and unaware of his son's problem, the father pressed on, the boy dug in with fingernails and peered almost straight up. He was just able to make out his dad's shape, its uniformity of movement suggesting scant trouble in scaling the treacherous face. Had the boy ever been sufficiently interested to enquire, he may have learned that wartime patrols in Burma at times involved ascending monsoon-muddy mountains so abruptly upward that only jungle covering stopped the monkeys falling off them! Furthermore, a bit dodgy the father's knees might be, but on his feet all day at the factory, his leg muscles were still in fine climbing condition.

Without warning a clump of earth and aggregate supporting the boy's boots gave way, followed by a crashing-bashing mini-avalanche. From an already reached embankment top the father shouted in alarm, 'Son!...? Son, are ye okay?'

Pressed with chest against slope, and hoping desperately that the stem of this shrub he'd grasped had its roots deep in a fissure of rock, upward into the blackness the boy responded, 'She's right, dad. No worries!' Which he definitely was not. Saying this too, resurrected the dread thought of his schoolmate Bunty being dead a moment after he'd said much the same thing. Although were the boy to fall, a direct plummet it wouldn't be, with death unlikely. Plenty bouncing before he hit the bottom though, so broken bones were emphatically on the cards.

'Dinnae move, son, Ah'm on mah way back doon,' came the already descending father's steady reassurance. How fast he came too, and with such certainty. Reaching the boy and supporting him with one hand, with his other he half-hitched a length of chord to the .22's barrel and then chord's other end to its stock. Next, slinging the weapon over his back, he apologised, 'Sorry son, Ah should hae done that in the first place.' After this, instructing his less sure-footed offspring to cling to his belt, he returned both of them to the riverside height's crest.

Sitting safe in the darkness, both recovered their breath. The father brushed away dirt from around rifle's bolt and trigger. 'Ye did verra well, son, tae keep hold o' this,' he said, 'Ah thought one o' they crashes was oor gun landing on they rocks doon there.' An affectionate elbow tickled the boy's ribs. 'Aye, a good soldier never loses his weapon. Who knows, maybe ye've a future in the SAS?'

That remark about the SAS had been a joke, but as their homeward trek commenced, it did remind the boy he'd still no idea what avenues to pursue so far as careers went. Earlier that month, his father, concerned about too cruisy son's lack of direction, had forked out a couple of hundred precious bucks to a visiting vocational guidance counsellor – an extensive interview ending with the filling out of a questionnaire including a plethora of possible professions, and the boy ticking the box 'explorer'. As the careers advisor later suggested to both father and son, 'There isn't much call for explorers anymore.'

This the boy accepted. He was only being honest.

'Sae alright, whit d'ye ken might actually be the best profession fur him tae tak a crack at then?' asked the father.

'Well,' had smiled the man blandly, 'all I can say is he has the ability to be anything he wishes.'

An apoplectic father's purple forehead looked in danger of exploding. 'Whit, Ah've paid ye mah week's wages fur you tae tell me something Ah already bloody-well know?!!!' Without another word, or making a move toward that mangling he clearly had in mind for this bludger, he'd hustled his son outside. Interview's dud outcome somewhat irrelevant to him, what really hurt was the wasted hit to one Scottish pocket. Yet blame the boy his father had not. And since then, until the SAS remark, he hadn't looked like mentioning possible post-school job options.

Most importantly, no push had there been to consider that unmanly profession of tailoring. Nevertheless, as now he continued to accompany his father across unlit paddock towards power station and rail track, the boy couldn't but concede that an action-man his dad sure had been on that dark unstable near-sheer riverside. So, fair dues to him. But the boy, go so far as to perceive in this old man of his, an enduring bona fide cool competence? Scant chance. However, and not for the first time, he did puzzle why, in a Scottish shipbuilding city where confident men took on muscular jobs like riveting and welding and ironworking, his dad had chosen a soft profession cutting clothes?

gain here, the father's reticence to disclose, be it about war or simply youthful hardship, contributed to the boy's lack of understanding. Not until in Gold Coast retirement will his dad finally throw light on a fatherless Great Depression era kid seeking to fill the Glasgow Herald's solitary job vacancy: 'Apprentice tailor wanted'. Over a couple of Highland single malt drams, to his grown son he'll speak of a sooty city's queue of desperate boys a block and a half long. For just one position! In revealing this episode, also expressed will be his continued perplexity as to why feisty suit-maker Andy MacRobb – the former Polish refugee Abraham Mandelbaum, not five feet tall in his socks – had singled him out, vowing, 'Errrrchie, my boy, I em knowink thet it is for you alone God vants to be havink zis job!'

And only then, in that Palm Beach apartment's armchair comfort, when the father expands on those circumstances prior to his hiring by 'Wee MacRobb', will the obvious dawn as to why he got the job. Yet not to the dad. Instead, visiting son, finally of an age to fully cherish his old man, will explain, 'But dad, don't you see…?' – that as a diminutive urchin at last reaching queue's front, when a young thug twice his size tries to bully him aside, the exquisite precision with which smaller lad's forehead delivers concussive contusion to one suddenly putty-nosed aggressor, is witnessed through the window by his potential employer.

'Och, funny how that's never occurred tae me?' the father will say in wonder, as the son goes on to surmise that Wee MacRobb, his own share of bullying endured due to small stature and racial status, wouldn't have failed either, to appreciate that headbutt's accuracy and steadiness of execution – qualities essential in a master tailor and cutter.

That night after their cliffside drama though, as father and fifteen-year-old offspring departed paddock beside power station to proceed along dark railway cutting, those Glasgow Depression-era circumstances were only another secret which would stay under the radar far too long. This present incident though, their almost disastrous fishing-shooting venture...? Just a terrific outcome! A mutual understanding, which even if short-lived, relaxed that stiffness which too often applied to their father-son relationship.

As the steel tracks and cross ties were followed homeward, from out of the darkness an adult arm wrapped around young shoulder, and a haggis-rich voice said, 'Noo, lad, Ah dinnae have tae tell ye...?'

'She's apples, dad,' responded the boy with a laugh, 'I know, not a word about any of this to mum.'

The longed-for minor miracle was pending – the sending of all The Annex students to newly constructed Tech complex in the town's north. Week leading up to Easter, 'Prepare to move!' they were told. Even better, humungously better, this facility had been built right alongside the High School. 'Bewdy,' reckoned the stroppiest classmates, 'we'll get inta heapsa fights!' whereas the boy, albeit not averse to indulging in an occasional blue, preferred to focus on a different opportunity. Finally, and daily, he would be in close proximity to girls!

Once transition happened, those Tech roughnecks who perceived the high school lads as fairies soon found their belligerence markedly diminishing. Of the poncy aesthetes, other side of that low fence separating both student groups, some revealed themselves to be handy exponents in the art of fisticuffs. Nevertheless, high schoolers were more inclined to be likeable larrikins than brawlers, preferring to joke with someone rather than poke them in the hooter, or to have them belt you with a roundhouse right. And among their best joshers? Two were none other than Snappa and Titch!

A mateship reconnected. Lunchtimes the boy would lean on the fence yacking to this chiacking pair whilst distractedly gazing in rapture at the pulchritudinous pedestrian parade passing behind them. His profound ignorance of physical female territory and its associated intricacies hugely amused Snappa and Titch. Despite themselves not yet completing that raunchiest rite of passage, regular interaction with these delicious butterflies breaking out of their chrysalis girlhoods meant, compared to the boy, the pair had an adequate idea of feminine topography and how they'd go about navigating that territory when the opportunity arose for full exploration.

Before this, and far more importantly, for Snappa and Titch their co-ed situation provided a natural mingling with girls. With the boy and his cobbers, their new Tech education space remained largely unchanged from The Annex. Aside from a tiny senior student clutch of serious scientific-minded chicks, they remained in a females-free zone. Therefore, for those such as the boy with limited opportunity outside of school to interact with girls, these tantalizing teen femmes on the fence's opposite side were as exotic and untouchable as caged animals in a zoo. To the boy they were in fact, as alien as had been that king bream inside the pumphouse. Yes, a sight so gobsmacking, yet at the same time a fish frustratingly uncatchable.

Soon though, the boy began to accompany Snappa and Titch after school. Walking their bikes homeward across adjacent parkland and football ovals space, their post classroom study of heavenly bodies had nothing to do with rudimentary astronomy. The high school's two shortest mini-skirts belonged to 'Dinger' Bell and 'Popsy' Thompson. In later times, the boys' activity may have been termed sexual harassment. But were three fifteen-year-old males wheeling Malvern Stars as they trailed after this pair of micro-uniformed beauties to be blamed when these girls kept stopping to cast back flirtatious smiles? Not that Dinger and Popsy were as yet seriously interested in more than being admired. Things at this stage weren't likely to progress further than ogling, eyelash fluttering, giggles and puerile jokiness.

Indeed, in Australia's rural areas during the early nineteen-sixties, take-up of a specific pharmaceutical advance had been slow. Like most of their sister students, no way were these girls tempted to, as the saying then went, 'go all the way'. Pre freely available oral contraceptives, a teen female's greatest fear was of disgracing herself and her family through falling pregnant. Hypocrisy, of course, ruled. Mass murderers were held in higher regard than some unfortunate unwed up-the-duff lass, yet the lad who 'did the deed' and planted his seed, he'd earned himself The Golden Manhood medal.

Not that the boy enjoyed anything like a position to compete for this accolade. His naivete in anything to do with horizontal sports was so far little improved by again associating with Snappa and Titch either. Sure, they sounded savvy when speculating about this fascinating activity, but they too were far from crystal on essential procedures. All up, it amounted to three fertile-minded teenage mates still theoretically fumbling in the dark.

As had eventuated when they skin-dived together, mateship with Snappa and Titch once more faded. Those mini-skirted flirters Dinger and Popsy became, for the boy, too much of an un-scratchable itch. Increasingly he opted to ride straight home across the park rather than stroll beside his more ogling-addicted, mates, and should he have no homework to complete, slip down to the jetties or bridge and jag a bream or two. Nevertheless, at school lunchtimes across that dividing fence, he still jawed with Snappa and Titch. Yet, here too that personality divide between them again became apparent.

Mutual on-going interest in girls they shared. However, what a contrast their chosen sports. Barely could the boy believe it. The highschooler pair had begun to play hockey! Fair dinkum, you had to wear a dress to participate in that, right? For the boy, real ball games could only be cricket or footy – the latter activity another reason, with winter approaching, to see less of these two mates anyhow. Commitment to Tech Under-17 training straight after last class three times per week would restrict opportunity for loitering to follow long legs and short skirts. Yeah, and it reduced those times available to bag a few bream too.

And regarding those river bream... they were now also in schools, gathered together prior to spawning, making them easier to find and catch on relaxing non-sporting Sundays. But aaah, angling wasn't quite the same, lines out as always, but picturing under that surface fish with fins wafting this way and that, movements seductive as a fan-dancer's, or the way the breeze teased at hems of twin mini-mini-skirts belonging to two teen highschooler babes.

The adorable Dinger and Popsy, for the boy how unignorable they were, even when hooking into a good-sized bream! But in them directly, lay another factor in the boy's cooled closeness to Snappa and Titch. Together with those mesmerizing legs and tantalizing feminine torsos, came danger in the form of two burly brawling truck-driver fathers! What if either girl took umbrage at some innocent remark made in jest? Hey, a bloke already risked injury enough on the footy field! Nah, his high school mates were welcome to their titillation. He was opting out.

Yeah, aside from roosting a Sherrin, leisure-time focus would be re-concentrated on angling. At least, in contrast to the possibility of getting punched-out by some gal's irate papa, casting a line contributed to the expectancy of a lengthy existence – suicidal acts of some dingbat rock-fishers excepted. As ace racehorse trainer Bart Cummings liked to say, 'One day spent fishing adds another to the rest of your life!' By centring his mind on pursuit of fish, the boy figured those other destabilizing micro-mini-skirted visions of Dinger and Popsy would be eradicated from it.

In the family home's hallway hung a framed poem *'Out Fishin'*. A homily of sorts, it included the line '*...His thoughts are mostly good and clean, Out fishin...'* True too, for the angling majority – except that is, when nothing is biting. One fishing spot which did exist though, where despite long waits between touches absolute tranquillity of thoughts undisturbed by leggy girls could be had, lay in depositing a bait in that smaller stream west of town.


A relief it was to no longer have an obligation to do anything religious on a Sunday. Both parents, albeit they never said it, were probably agnostic anyway. Certainly, without a painful mishap in the home, Jesus hardly got a mention, and except on Christmas Eve all of the family's church-going had stopped. Significantly, the father appreciated how indispensable he'd become to his committed Christian employer. By this time The Great Man wouldn't pay much mind to his Cutting Room manager failing to break bread and drink wine.

And the boy? For a fair while he had felt connected to only one group of true believers, the Collingwood congregation, those Magpie faithful. God had finally lost him after Gabbo's stumbling run and goal in the '64 Grand Final put the Pies in front, but no amount of prayer prevented a sneaky Demon back-pocket called Compton creeping forward like a biblical thief to steal a win for his bunch of red and blue heathens. From then on, taking up much of the boy's Sundays, were piscatorial pursuits.

To the faint peel of distant church bells, in the garage the boy rigged up his trout rods. As he did so that 1964 VFL season decider came back to him. More to the point, an aspect to it other than Collingwood's defeat did. This was the contempt one suddenly atheistic son could feel for a father who'd barracked against his demi-god Magpies. Not that his dad had actually cheered-on the Demons per se. Arriving in Australia never having heard of Australian Rules, and continually told he needed to pick a footy side to support, not long after his son's birth one free-thinking tailor decided he simply liked the cut of a young footballer named Ronald Dale Barassi. So alright, instead of a team, he'd just follow 'Basass'. This eventual Sport Australia Hall of Famer's success as both player and coach meant that in his lifetime the father would enjoy ten winning Flags featuring Barassi's direct involvement. The boy could well have taken note of, perhaps even admired, his old man's prescience. He didn't... true Magpie supporters, sons or otherwise, are never renowned for their magnanimity toward those who oppose them.

Bike bearing pair of light tightly tied-on trout rods, riding into the north-west countryside the boy found himself reflecting on this sunny day-of-rest morning. Although always he'd prefer winding in fish, he did occasionally miss that Presbyterian palace's sumptuous stained-glass windows and the ecstatic playing of old Arnold Westgarth the organist who rejoiced in going apeshit on the ivory keys at sermon's end. Yet regret not hearing their banging-on clergyman, his batshit boredom preaching...? Oh no, never!

Generally slow though, are country Sundays. Along they go at the sedate flow rate of a deepish stream unaffected by flood. The boy too pedalled at a leisurely pace. Imposition of paying homage to a Nazarene carpenter crudely nailed to substandard Roman joiner's handiwork may no longer have curtailed him, but he was nursing his own bruising and wounds. Saturday's Under-17 game had been a willing affair.

From crest of road rise above gentle secondary river, the boy freewheeled downhill into a farmlands-surrounded hamlet, crossed a stone bridge spanning that stream's upper willow-edged reaches, and after this took an unmade lane which led a little way back downstream. Dismounting at a post-and-rail fence which then doubled as a bike rack, trout rods in hand he started a short riverside hike. At a narrow flat of hard mud by water's edge, and backed by a rising bankside overgrown with blossoming sweet-scented hawthorn, he deposited his gear, while behind him blissed-out bees buzzed in their hundreds. After this, well concealed by the vegetation, a flick of rod-tip and out went a first squirming red flat-tail worm. On an unweighted hook this landed just short of a willow tree opposite, its strands trailing in the mild current. Out went bait number two, and a laidback wait began.

Reclining, hands behind head, the boy kept a casual eye on those finest variegated lines lying across the reeds. Rising off bottom close-in these were bent flat by the gentle flow to make a green mat on the surface. Even with nothing doing, or more because of it, a halcyon pleasure this situation provided. What it offered too, future generations of anglers would never know because of some environmental department's dictate during the 1980's that the whole embarkment be fenced off for 'ecologically sustainable reasons', thereby allowing the bankside vegetation grow uncontrollably. Yep, bugger a few fishos' enjoyment, far better to create an unusable weed-choked fire hazard.

But here and now, yeah and heh, this current Sunday fishing, oh Huey how the boy placed total faith in his special squirming baits, those ripper red flat-tail worms! Crimson really, with a thick collar which held a hook well. Livelier than other types, they oozed juice, attracting brown and rainbow trout the way a Mister Whippy van enticed ice-cream addicted toddlers. Even better, red flat-tails were easily obtained... well alright, so long as the worm digger wished to risk ptomaine poisoning or other dastardly diseases.

As that week the boy had done, red flat-tail getting entailed shovelling behind their town's train station. The wormer scrambled down embankment to where, from a tunnel under rail-lines, seeped a polluted runoff, the 'Hospital Drain'. Accurately named. This smelly ooze went on to enter a brackish lake separated from the sea by a long sandy stretch of low dunes and inside which on a short-grassed foreshore patch stood a lifesavers' clubhouse, bathing sheds and a big gaily painted wooden kiosk. In summer this area also supported a carnival featuring amusement rides and galleries. Holidaying families camped along this beachside too. However, swim in that crappy lake across the way from their tents and caravans? Not a bloody chance!

Cripes, that Hospital Drain, how it stank! Bangkok gully traps and Calcutta gutters were frangipani fragrant in comparison. Built-up silt to either side of this trickle contained bloodied Bandaids, used sanitary napkins, filthy surgical dressings, spent syringes, and other putrid medical paraphernalia, all of it washed down from the local infirmary whenever heavy rainfall happened. Beneath these dodgy decorations though, lived red flat-tail worms by the billion. Couple of digs, an angler had bait enough for a week, plus an impetus to hasten across tracks into rail station restroom and use its soap-dispenser to decontaminate ponging hands.

Such effective bait however, the red flat-tails, so well worth the risk of contracting some contagious lurgy. By his side today the resting boy had a large jar of them, wriggling and entwining and slimily fornicating, totally unfazed by their capture. Although, okay, their rapture did diminish once a hook went into them. But in using these worms it wasn't if, but when, that monofilament lying inert across the surface reeds would twitch, and then gradually start to snake outward.

Old Ron's, 'Always give your trout enough slack to hang himself,' spoke to the boy. He peeled off another foot of five-pound breaking strain line. That made six feet of it lying loose-looped on the smooth mud. 'Fine,' he thought, 'that's me properly set.' Meantime, the sedate almost motionless waiting brought a bonus, the appearance of that strangest native mammal of all. Colour of dark bark, up it popped, silent as a waterlogged lump of wood risen from the bottom, which, but for its eyes, the floating platypus closely resembled. Experts reckoned these creatures were endangered and rare. Elsewhere maybe. In this short but healthy feed-rich river they thrived.

After a while of more or less immobile youthful human and inquisitive platypus observing one another, the furry monotreme dived soundlessly. These oddest of animals seemed never to spook the fish. As if to verify this, twitch, twitch... and then outwards moved the line until it tightened, rod slow-bowed, and grasping this, with a deft delicate lift, the boy set his hook.

Straight out above surface the day's first trout leapt, revealing itself as a splendid rainbow. Now, showering golden droplets in the sunlight, back in it splashed: a marvellous moment, a snapshot in time. Had the boy but known it, this thrilling snatch of action also marked the start of successive significant occurrences. In playing that beautiful fighting fish he wasn't to guess that, among other developments, scholastically his year would come to an abrupt close, and that inevitable life shifts thereafter were destined to disrupt, and for far too long almost prevent pursuit of his purest passion, angling.

Too true it was that the boy abhorred authority. Not a huge anomaly though this. In Downunder society, meek acceptance of discipline almost amounts to un-Australianness. Alright, for practical purposes he accepted his father's rules, free food and lodging two of several good reasons to do this. Nor, even if now more muscled-up and standing a head taller than his dad, would he have risked a full-on challenge anyway. Despite tailoring's light physical demands leaving this essentially passive Scotsman with softening hands and slackening biceps, inside still lay the slum kid who had every dirty trick in Glasgow's dog-eared street-fighting book up his well-cut sleeve. And as for his mother, long ago he'd learned not to cross her.

With tyrannical teachers however, came a refusal to toe the line. Into school's second term, events were about to take a twist that would put him on a collision course with his Tech's most authoritarian educational figure. Russ Mac had moved on to take up a position in Melbourne. His replacement as deputy-head had been a character with a sneering veneer who, astoundingly soon, had been steered into full headmastership. This did not happen though before he'd already acquired an apt cracker of a nickname.

'Myxo' Davidson was the kind of jerk anyone could get off-side with, a mean-spirited berk capable of tipping over any student's cruisy schooldays applecart. An uptight stiff-backed chain-smoking dictator, in this Monday he had barged to address Schmoo Schmidt's class. Following a short threatening pep-talk, who should his bony nicotine-ed finger then point to but the boy. 'And you there, mister paying-no-attention-to-me, what would you say our excellent school system is preparing a wasted space such as yourself for?'

Thus provoked, the boy's jokey, 'Probably collecting shit-cans on the night-cart, sir,' may nevertheless not have been the wisest of replies.

The classmates laughed. Schmoo quietly too. But alas, Myxo had an allergy to all humour, toilet or otherwise. 'Oh, so, class smart-arse are we? I will see you in my office.'

Six savage cuts from one narrow but thick black strap, were not the only outcome. Into this unsavoury educator's black book went the boy's name. Thereafter, he found himself accused by Myxo of peccadillos which, usually, he had nothing to do with.

Inevitably, these brought further punishments and penalties. So far as the boy's already unenthusiastic attitude to general schooling went, he'd stepped onto an ever-steepening downslope.

Some school-associated mischief however, the boy definitely did get up to. How acute would that down-tilt of his cobbly academic path have become had he and a few of his other classmates got sprung in this next caper they put into practice? Two kids, Cue Stick and Churchie, had dads who'd taught them to drive. Having saved thirty quid delivering newspapers, they'd somehow bought the sort of vintage Jaguar that required side-pipes hanging out of its engine. What this enterprising pair proposed was that if others would kick-in for petrol, they could all wag school on a Friday and drive a hundred miles up the highway to Geelong and watch the Cats play the Magpies. With sufficient pocket-money put away, and almost since he could walk bleeding black and white, the boy declared, 'I'm in!'

Driven in turns by one or other fifteen-year-old Fangio, and otherwise holding six more boisterous youths – of whom a couple were inclined to flash brown-eyes at passing autos – and all of them still in school uniform, how slim were the chances of an unroadworthy classic car not attracting, during this six- hour round-trip, the attention of a Victoria Police highway patrol? It did not enter the woolly mid-teens heads.

Yet, sans cop interference, make it to Geelong and almost back they did. Not until twenty miles from home did the Jag's lagging donk totally crap itself, leaving the odyssey to be completed via hitch-hiking. The escapade went undetected by the school too, a minor miracle considering eight garrulous lads were involved. Sadly though, no miraculous twist had saved Collingwood from a one-point loss.  Yet another appalling umpiring decision had cost them a win, something the boy just took on the chin. He'd long since become aware of what price any person paid to be a constantly robbed Magpies supporter.

Onward that academic 1966 year crawled, all pretty ordinary week by week, no more stimulating underage jaunts in jalopies, only continued persecution by Myxo. Yeah, and the irksome substandard education itself. Not only were reading and writing far from advanced, external to classroom learning, matters concerning any adventuring down the twisty pathway occupied by the opposite sex continued to be opaque. Desperate the boy was, to know even half as much regarding this territory as he did about angling. Over dividing fence, he got to again jawing regularly with Snappa and Titch, eagerly absorbing their assessments of certain high school girls visible in the background who apparently had advanced attitudes to activities amorous. This pair's more confident chatter suggested they were, theoretically anyhow, now a fair way further down lover's lane, albeit still as yet short of a parking spot.

Therefore, sure, strong was the temptation to once more get involved with Snappa and Titch in pursuit of that magical mistily mystical sought-after outcome. Yet restrained by his uncertainties re the full procedure required, the boy figured it best to still confine aspirations about scoring to footy games or via a cricket bat or in counting the number of fish caught. This decision he felt okay with too, until one day into the boy's class at Tech swaggered fearsome behemoth Mikey Mathers.

A.k.a 'Mugger', by his own loud accounts sexually switched-on, this blob of youthful yobbo-ness had been newly released from a different form of education, at reform school. Like many dinosaurs he'd a tiny mind, but his brontosaurus body was vastly larger than any of his younger schoolmates. In a finger-snap Mugger assumed Fuhrer status, and ruled by intimidation. Even the teachers waxed wary. His broken teeth made for a smile of pure evil.

Despite the boy's at-first-sight dislike of this brute, he did listen when Mugger shot his mouth off. For, command an audience, this delinquent did due to the content of his boastings. When these weren't about bloodily bashing people half to death, they usually involved what he'd been able to do with that hyperactive organ inside his trousers. Never, when hanging on these extravagant rants, did it occur to the boy or his rapt classmates that this delinquent bragger's reformatory had been even more all-male than their Tech schooling. Nor were any of them blessed with the practically acquired nous to be able to call out fornication fabrication when they heard it. Not that, even had any kid been sufficiently savvy, he'd have been game to suggest Mugger might be a bullshit artist.

Winter proper had passed, and with this too had those shortest days, longest nights, persistent rains on roof, near ceaseless strong-cold winds, and footy grounds ankle-deep in mud. Now buds were forming on fruit trees, daylight hours warming. Soon football finals would begin, and not long after those the boy's sixteenth birthday occur.

A tough season it had been in the Under-17's however. Too much rain made for heavy playing conditions. Yet this had favoured the boy. To his increasing tallness had been added, through thudding into muddied packs and battling the pressure of other bodies, true fitness and toughness. From the undersized beanpole who'd first joined the Tech side, and aided as well by weight-training, he'd developed into a robust player who revelled in congested situations. Regularly he'd featured in his side's best performers.

But that happened on Saturdays. Most Sundays still found the boy cycling down to the river where, relaxing by a couple of rods, he could nurse a stops-gashed back or bruised shin copped during the previous day's game. Today, taking it easy on his favourite jetty, he was casting out 'shellbacks', those voracious big brown snails which assailed everyone's vegies. Stream in minor flood from continuous Grampians rainfall, a tip from Old Ron had been recalled. 'When it's a discoloured flow,' claimed he, 'these large snails, you crack 'em out of their shells and they're great bream bait.' This they were proving to be.

Half a dozen good fish the boy had in his bag when, after hard riding uphill back toward home, and hardly any less knackered and sore from Saturday's play, he dismounted from his bike halfway up that last hill. In beginning to push-walk Malvern Star, he thought about what a wasted season all this had been for their Under-17's, how they'd fallen short of making the finals. A struggle alright. In fact, that year the only game he'd really loved playing in had been the annual Teachers versus Students one, their ruckman Douggie Sproal breaking the nose of despised carpentry teacher 'Termite' Walsh, the highlight, despite the corollary of this being Myxo Davidson banning all such future contests.

Thinking of Termite being helped from the field, bristly ginger moustache all the redder from blood, as he pushed two-wheeler up that steep gradient the boy noticed a strange car parked on their nature-strip. And soon enough, after entering the family home, he encountered a convivial, if a smidgen strained, atmosphere. Four adults were seated around the kitchen table, the boy's parents and two rugged-looking blokes. One he recognised as a former champion Red Rovers footballer. This joker was legendary. Bound for VFL stardom, he'd lost his hand above the wrist in a farming auger accident. Two days later, blood seeping from bandaged forearm, and taking the field in that year's local Grand Final, he'd marked one-handed, kicked the winning goal, got reported for jobbing an opponent in the eye by using his bleeding stump like a bayonet, and then announced his retirement. The other chap turned out to be the footy club's president, Barney Hill.

Both men had, they said, been following the boy's footballing development. They'd come seeking permission to play him on permit in their team's last two games of the senior season. Reluctant mother deferred to her husband, who without hesitation referred the proposition to the schoolboy player in question: 'Aye, well son, Ah'm of a mind it's actually up tae you. Whit dae ye think?'

Think, the boy did not. 'Yeah, bewdy!' he said.

The maimed footy legend, jumping in quicker than once he'd split packs, promised the mother, 'No worries, missus, he'll be looked after. Guarantee yer, no way'll no harm come ter 'im.'
No harm would, at least, befall the boy from any untoward behind-the-play incident. Red Rovers may have been bottom of the District League's table that year but their team included lethal duo Cement-head Cleary and Bull Turpin. Opponents the ladder leaders Old Collegians, entering their rooms pre-game, Cement-head and Bull promised hospitalization for '... any one-a yiz what king-hits the kid!' They did however, in all fairness, emphasise, 'But go ahead an' shirt-front him fair an' square if yer like, cos that's alright yair?'

Save for shaking knees and a thousand butterflies fluttering in stomach, running onto the ground with these new he-men teammates, accompanied by routine sounds of surrounding cars tooting and spectators' cheers, the boy felt pumped to perform. As adventures went, this maybe even exceeded landing that first mulloway. His opponent would be three hundred game veteran Tank O'Grady, a spud cocky off the volcanic lands to westward. An ambulatory brick shithouse, Tank crushingly shook hands, his grip resin coated. 'Good luck, son,' he growled, 'you'll bloody-well need it.'

Luck though, had little to do with getting that first kick as a half-forward flanker. Nor did skill. Not the boy's anyway. Red Rover's captain-coach 'Soda' Fountain, ex-St Kilda winger and once the smallest man playing VFL, had slowed but not lost his ability to blind-turn out of packs and deliver sizzling stab-passes. First bounce, straight after... *Whack!* Fair and square into the boy's bread-basket sank the Sherrin. Un-droppable! Cheering erupted. Just for him, the kid. What a heady sensation! All residual fear vanished. At full-bore, out led their full-forward. Cripes and crikey, the roar when the boy emulated Soda and drilled pill onto this bloke's chest! Pats from teammates spattered upon the boy's back. He didn't feel his scone swelling but ought to have. He should also have noticed the thunderstorm brewing inside Tank O'Grady's skull.

How seamlessly too, powered by adrenaline, and legs twenty-five years younger than some stumblebum veteran, the boy continued running rings around Tank. Several times he did it, collecting further possessions, until... a fumble. All it took, that hesitation. Runaway trains crash into stations with less impact than steaming humungously pissed-off seventeen stone half-back flankers. Yet, a hip and shoulder hit, nothing dirty, legitimate bump. Nevertheless, boos broke out, players scuffled, haymakers were thrown. Meantime, winded, the boy lay on the ground while out at a trot came club trainer Gus Gray.

Gus's perpetual smile featured the single crooked tooth left in his head. He never bore more than smelling salts and a putrid wet towel. When those filthy jogging pongy sandshoes reached the boy however, struggling to his feet he waved their trainer away. More applause. Supporters later lauded such gameness. What actually brought about his revival however, had been teammates' warnings you could recover from a shirt-front but from Gus Gray's contaminated ministrations, perhaps never!

At the final siren Red Rovers were two points down, so they'd lost. It lessened none the boy's sense of achievement. A nice touch too came from Tank O'Grady, gracious enough to say, 'Well played, ya young prick... yer might even 'ave a future in this game.' Further plaudits came inside the change-room, although a pride-filled father's embarrassing public hug could have been done without.

Then, better still, the parents went home, allowing their boy to stay on at the club's post game function and bask in the limelight from acquitting himself with distinction in his first senior game. Young footy stars receive all sorts of awards, and rewards too. A couple of fivers were pressed into the boy's hand. But right on night-time manifested the best one. Outside of the clubrooms came another hug. This one he'd no urge to resist. Nor would he baulk at the whispered offer which came with it. Finally, the dreamed of golden opportunity had arrived!

Guide to his hometown Tunnel of Love was Sally, amply endowed daughter of Barney Hill. Hastening through carpark shadows cast by pavilion's external lighting, into back seat of the Hill family's Holden HD Special the boy found himself bundled. Already sixteen, a charming cuddly dumpling umpteen oodles more advanced in the ways of amorous forays than he, Sally's fleshy arms enwrapped like the tentacles of a soft tenacious but well-fed octopus. Thrillingly trapped, the boy found his lips half kissed, half bitten. An angling analogy might have been she'd hit him harder than a voracious mackerel latching onto a lure! But fishing could not have been further from his mind.

Sally's sudden down throat tongue-thrust about choking him, and near anaesthetized by her *Pretty Peach* perfume, a mix of alarm and blood-rush excitement overcame the boy. He realized too that his belt had been undone. Sharp-nailed fingers were delving dangerously southwards toward a specific appurtenance which, although virginal, on evidence did not seem at all disconcerted!

This then, was it! Here exactly was what school scuttlebutt calculated football stardom amounted to, some blonde footie groupie who threw herself at you. On, indeed... oooh, indeed! Inside pavilion Sally had taken total initiative, spiriting the boy outside the instant her dad's customary post-match speech ended. And now, she so clearly familiar with the modus operandi of extreme courtship, here, hotly, they lay across Holden's cold rear vinyl upholstery, with him all set to, as school chat had it, 'slip in and shag away.'

Well, okay, but what exactly to do? The boy knew he couldn't remain a passive party here. Um, alright, how about for a start…? Uncertain hand slid under Sally's skirt. As if with a mind of its own it stroked up her stockinged leg. Confidence grew. Oooh, the thrill of locating a suspender, followed by feeling plump naked high-up thigh! Not unlike slipping fingers under submerged bark in a creek to grip a fat soft-shelled yabbie, albeit even the risk of getting nipped didn't set his pulse so radically racing like this. Next, faster and fumblier, came the real breathless advancement to feeling elasticized nylon and lace knickers and…

'Sal? Sally? Where the hell are you?!'

Shit, it's me dad!'

What a time too, for a lad to be seized by cramp. And in both hamstrings! Jeans falling to his knees, stifling a scream, backwards out of HD Holden tumbled the boy.

Sally followed, fast. 'Quick,' she hissed, 'go back inside! I'll head this way an' tell dad I was having a piss.'

In language as well as activity, romance had abruptly gone missing. Somehow afflicted footy fatigued legs were straightened, strides hauled up. Bent low and suffering agony in not just both hammies but also a lower abdominal ache, off the boy hobbled. Sufficiently hidden by other empty cars, and making it back to the pavilion, he hobbled inside. Crikey, what a smorgasbord of smirks to be met with! How awfully well all players and supporters knew their humping hyperactive Sally.

Across came Bull Turpin. Shepherding the boy over to club's bar, he adived, 'Come on, Romeo, I'll shout yer a beer. But then I reckon me an' a few a them other fellas better getcha outa here quick smart.'

How the boy made it home he knew not, nor, post pavilion piss-up, exactly what he had got up to. Too unwell and confused to think, one strong clue covered half his pillow. Not only had he drunk copious beers, apparently at some stage he'd eaten fish and chips. In jig-saw puzzle mind scattered pieces began to fit. Several Red Rovers players had bought three slabs of beer. Then, zooming to Seafoods in the main street to give George and Helen Politis good business, after this their souped-up jalopy had careered off in top gear to Thunder Point. There they'd parked, and all occupants, including one under-age half-forward flanker, had got blitzed on Victoria Bitter.

Bitter did not begin to describe the boy's mother. Pained disdain accompanied her dropping of soiled spewed-upon bedding into washing machine. Her dreaded silence would for some days dominate existence. His father however, reacted not too badly. He accepted that experiences positive and poor and downright abject were all part of an adolescent's journey to adulthood. Yet dad would have been in mum's bad books too had he not kiboshed any further playing of footy on permit with grown men who still behaved like immature teenagers.

What a severe blow though, this banning from more senior footy participation. Dampened massively was immediate dream of being a rising fifteen-year-old talent invited for a run with Collingwood. A far greater disaster however, came in finding there'd be no re-run with Sally. In making a furtive nervy call to the Hill's home phone that afternoon, he discovered he'd done his dash. No interest whatsoever did amour insatiable Sally have in delivering an astronomical boost to the Casanova status of any male who didn't roost a football for her adored Red Rovers.

A missed double-chance – of a VFL signing, together with ultimate intimate sporty participation. Could there be a worse outcome? Unfortunately, yes. It awaited the boy at Tech on the following Monday. That morning's local paper bore a story about the schoolboy star who'd helped his lowly side almost beat the top team. Fair enough, this guaranteed a minor celebrity's reception upon arrival at the school bike shed. So far, all good. A terrific ego feed. Too bad the boy then decided to go take a pre-class leak at the nearby toilet block...

Inside smelly grey Besser Brick structure awaited ox-bodied meathead Mugger Mathers. The cold bovine eyes narrowed even more than usual. Twisted lips pursed. Otherwise, the former reform school brawler stood silent. Not that, unless about himself, articulate speech was his strongpoint in any case. Yet clear enough his message: 'Listen you dingo, this school's got room for only one top dog, and that mongrel is me!'

'G'day, Mugger,' tried the boy nervously as he stepped up to the urinal.

'Fuggin' fairy!' snarled Mugger, 'Think ya dick's fa pissin' outa dontcha.'

Well, first and foremost, yes... although okay, Sally sure had revised the boy's appreciation of its potential.

Some small credit to Mugger at least. The thug did choose to wait until urination's termination before launching his assault. The boy sussed exactly what was coming. In stepping back from urinal, he readied himself. He'd seen Mugger beat up other kids. No way would he be able to withstand the man-sized moron. To mind however, came some further fatherly advice given during the boxing lessons all those years ago... 'But dinnae forget, son, if ye ever get intae a street-fight, the first thing ye do is ditch these Marquis o' Queensbury rules Ah'm teaching ye here, okay?'

Another Glasgow Kiss situation then? That's an extremely difficult action to accomplish, alas, by someone who is flat on his back. It's even impossible when a monster attacker has their fair hair hard-held as he bashes victim's head onto a disinfectant-pongy toilet block concrete floor. Not that, prior to getting felled, the boy hadn't managed retaliation. Mugger's left eye was reddened and weepy and far narrower than even originally it had been. His hooter too, damaged by a classic straight-left, trickled blood. But yep, standard Marquis of Queensbury defence is pretty much ineffective in repulsing a homicidal Neanderthal, and the boy simply hadn't been quick enough to act on his dad's long-ago suggestion to, in such a circumstance, abandon a boxing stance.

But alright, would it have made a significant difference had he done so? A battering the boy sure was now undergoing. Of course, the two combatants weren't, in that urine perfumed space, on their Pat Malones. Any schoolyard stoush – 'Fight! – will bring, like blowflies to fresh poo, a delighted student stampede to spectate the violence, and to barrack. Luckily, such a racket will attract too, some conscientious chalkie. No doubts about who was well behind on points would solid Schmoo Schmidt have had when he broke through the yelling throng to separate both bluers. Dragging them apart, most of the blood that came to stain his suit definitely did not belong to Mugger Mathers.

Such a good man, Schmoo. Obliged by school law to escort all students involved in physical altercations to Myxo Davidson's office, first he let the moderately worse-for-wear aggressor and his far more badly damaged opponent clean up some. Once enough blood had been washed down the drinking taps trough, to the headmaster's den he then accompanied them. But once there, Schmoo found himself instructed to leave.

In Schmoo's absence, to Mugger Mathers a concerned-looking Myxo then commiserated, 'Michael, I fully appreciate the unfortunate circumstances of a broken home from which you have come, and that this is why obnoxious antagonists such as...' and he glared at the boy, '*this* individual, will pick on you, thereby obliging you to defend yourself.' Following this astonishing statement, the bland hand gesture of an understanding uncle signalled Mugger should depart. 'You are therefore,' said Myxo gently, 'excused.'

Could the boy believe his ears here? Flabbergasted as much as battered, he dully heard the headmaster's now harsh voice say, 'As for you, vicious young sir, you will not be strapped.'

Well, that was a relief anyhow, pain enough already suffered.

'Instead,' said Myxo, suddenly smiling as might a well-satisfied snake, 'you are going to be expelled.'

Both parents were aware their son had issues with Myxo Davidson. They were prepared to accept too, that some people have almost automatic animosity toward one another, and that irrespective of age difference, personality clashes do happen. Here however, the unjustness drew a severe reaction. With the father, prone to careful consideration, not quite so much. The boy's mother though... shit, did this ever kibosh that silence she'd kept these past days since his after-game overindulgence! Raised in Scotlad, yes, but volatile Irish to the core, she swore Myxo's eyes were going to be in far worse shape than any infected rabbit's once she'd torn into them. It took the combined intervention of father and son to settle her down.

Once calm returned, the father, experienced in treating battlefield wounds albeit he'd never said as much, bathed the boy's abrasions with Dettol. In applying Elastoplast dressings, he then asked, 'Listen son, rather than me seeing tae it that ye'r reinstated at school, how would ye feel aboot actually leaving?'

Now, no worries, aside from sport participation and one or two admirable teachers such as Schmoo, the boy gave not a monkey's fornication about attending that Tech. Then again, the obvious alternative...? Dread rising, tentatively he replied, 'Dad, don't take this the wrong way, but I really don't want to work in the factory.'

Not a hint of disgruntlement though, did the father show. Simply he drew the boy's attention to their local paper. On page preceding that match report extolling the boy's footballing prowess, red pen had circled a jobs vacant ad: *Proof-reader/cadet reporter required...* A position with that same rag. Now, Fleet Street this was not. In fact, townsfolk routinely referred to their humble broadsheet as 'the three-minute silence'. Your beggar cannot afford however, to be the choosy one.

'Whit dae ye think?' pressed the father, 'Ye *are* quite good at English?'

'Tech school English, dad,' emphasised the boy. 'Last time I used a verb of over four letters they talked about transferring me to La Trobe uni.'

Humour, the father was in no mood for. 'Ah am saying, son o' mine, for ye tae gie' landing this job a try. Otherwise, aye, it will indeed be a factory future ye'll be considering.'

Wholly the parent here and no trying to be a mate. The boy detected the deliberate distancing. For them to become close cobbers, no matter how much both might – the father greatly, the son covertly – covet such a relationship, in this moment to the boy it seemed this would always be a bridge too far. Contrasting personalities, vastly different attitudes... never mind a nearly forty years, almost two generations, age gap. Yeah, between them an apparently unbridgeable space. Just the same, the boy did appreciate the couple of feet of slack his old man had fed him here... even if it did have a hook attached.

Ahhh, and if the father had implied a pressganging into factory drudgery might well lie ahead, how about where he had said it. As happened after that touchy time Sir Fuckface's clinkers were set adrift, again his father had spoken in the dining-room, with behind him above its door into their kitchen, that wall-mounted instrument for ritual and summary murder, the samurai sword.

By design or just coincidence, the father's positioning? To the boy, still, not a word had been uttered to even infer that the weapon might mean more than just a war souvenir. Nor, of course, a decade since its first appearance, had he experienced any real inclination to make a related enquiry. Undeniably however, its presence lent substantial gravitas to the father's pronouncement of a probable career path.

Getting the arse from school did anyhow, allow some mid-week fishing time. Due to the requirement to provide 'three character references', the newspaper job interview had been scheduled for the following Monday. No worries, those attestations of inherent qualities could be rounded up at leisure during the days ahead. Therefore, first freed-from-school morning, to the bridge the boy cycled. Bait out, leaning on top rail by the splendid arch, he toyed with cane rod. Only one brought. Really, not there with any intense purpose to catch something. He'd come more for a little deliberation.

This newspaper position, did he actually want it? Not particularly. Gazing down at the surface ripples plip-plip-plipping against bridge pilings brought however, more focused thought. This potential job in the print media, truly, it had to be properly gone for. 'Yeah, I've got to have a fair dinkum crack!' resolved the boy. The alternative, daily factory work, loomed too gloomily large. Repetitious production-line garment-making? Christ, no, no, no... if at all avoidable, no way!

Hmmm, then again, did fifteen-year-olds still run away to join a circus? Heh, maybe a bloke could land himself a gipsy-like vocation feeding 'big chooks'? Reeling in, the boy readied to return home. Best to get the ball rolling right now. He'd get respectably dressed, and after that set off in search of obtaining those suitable, if spurious, testimonies as to his reliability, charming personality and glittering abilities.

Those three references for the proof-reader/cadet reporter job... in examining the criteria, oh shit, one needed to be from the school last attended! 'But hang on,' figured the boy, 'Schmoo Schmidt will write me a ripper recommendation.' As for two other affirmations re his sterling character, The Great Man always supplied such to all employees' offspring, even for kids determined never to work in his factory. Which left reference number three. Yet no worries there either, already pretty much taken care of. Although seldom anymore a church-goer, the father remained in their Presbyterian minister's good books, and for his son the reverend had promised to scrawl something appropriate.

They're awfully good, God-botherers, at writing such required fiction, even for borderline pagans such as the boy. Then again, the well-meaning reverend was also an optimist. He believed such simple kindnesses as lying about people's virtues often brought his flock's strays back into the holy fold. Well, perhaps...? In the boy's case, only if fish had gone off the bite and he reckoned a prayer to improve their appetite might be answered, or in hooking a huge 'un and seeing it was only lip-hooked, and desperate for divine assistance to ensure it didn't flip free. As for praying that other special, though still inadequately understood, shared physical opportunity might arise? Come on, God had no interest at all in sex anyhow.

Facial fuzz buzzed off via Philips electric razor, the boy then showered, scrubbed, brushed, and then neatly attired, away from home he pedalled, sure his quest to collect three references would be a shoo-in, perhaps even achieved in that single afternoon? Thanks to his father the initial couple were indeed got seamlessly too. Aside from arranging things with their Presbyterian clergyman his dad had also smoothed the way at the factory. Called there first, straightaway over her desk The Great Man's secretary passed one glowingly positive appraisal of his valued employee's lad. After this, another mile biked to reach church, and witnessed by adoring phantasmagorical Saints staring down from spectacular stained-glass windows, sanitized hand of their fine reverend himself released into the boy's that second splendid summing-up of his virtues.

Gee, too easy, eh? Well, in fact, it was. The onward and upward Malvern Star-borne third leg to the Tech school completed, followed by creeping along corridor passing of in-session classrooms and a furtive skirting by headmaster's door, Schmoo Schmidt was located. Uh, but... *The best laid schemes o' mice an' men gang aft a-gley.* Although Schmoo, that choicest of all chalkies, wished to assist, he explained that pain-in-the-freckle Myxo Davidson had a new policy: 'References for students will be written exclusively by me.'

Shit and accumulated sewage! Yet, 'Alright,' decided the boy, 'I'm here, so what have I got to lose?' Certainly not his self-respect, for be buggered if he'd grovel. If Myxo pulled his Mister Nasty Bastard act again, that dead-set martinet might find this time it wasn't him meting out the corporal punishment.

Except, surprise, surprise, one otherwise horrible headmaster could not have been nicer. 'Go for a little walk,' advised Myxo with the warmest smile, 'then come back in fifteen and I will have ready what you require.'

Out of office and once more along main corridor went the boy. In fact, he strolled jauntily, almost rolling in confidence. Imagine Myxo turning so cooperative? Glancing in at those studious inmates, could his gladness be greater that school days were over? More than four years of technical education, and what an impoverished learning experience it sure seemed to have been. Yep, the worth of those practical skills in carpentry, metal work and drafting he'd acquired, would only to be revealed years later in designing, and then with hand tools, constructing his first remote home.

Re-entry to boss cocky chalkie's domain found the man still smiling with as much warmth. A long brown business envelope was placed face-down on desktop before the boy. Hey, Myxo had even put a fancy red wax seal on it! 'And,' beamed the headmaster, 'despite our past differences, I have given you a most excellent reference.'

'This reference from Mister Davidson is the most damning I have ever read,' said the paper's Managing Director. The boy, seated opposite, felt a dying-in-arse emotion overcome him. He glanced at some framed headlines adorning a wall before gazing back across his prospective boss's expansive desk. Mister Charles had such *oldness*. Beside him some Stone Age artifact would have appeared almost new. His melon mush's mass of creases and cracks made the poet W.H. Auden's craggy physiognomy baby-smooth in comparison. The bloke probably wasn't even sixty either.

Oh dear, how his cycloidal facial catastrophe made the apparently fatal statement which had issued from it even more devastating too! A frown now further creased that full fissured moon with its imposed bulbous nose, as onto desk got dropped the typed sheet of headmasterly condemnation. But then, upon this cruel composition, Mister Charles planted an emphatic hand. 'How-ev-er...' he said, 'according to... ', and came the names of The Great Man along with their optimistic Presbyterian God-botherer, '...whose effusive attestations as to your attributes contradict headmaster Davidson's opinion, I am, young man, going to give you a chance.'

From where it had been residing in the boy's bum, hope sprang back into his heart.

'But, be assured,' went on the prematurely ancient Managing Director, and now one job-seeker boy's employer, 'I will most certainly be keeping the closest of eyes on you.'

He could also have told the boy that in this epoch of abundant vocational opportunities, there had been but one other applicant, a

Christian Brothers College kid. And well, like all that newspaper's managing directors before him, Mister Charles also happened to belong to the Presbyterian Church, never mind his membership in the Masonic Lodge. Throughout a so-slowly enlightening Australia religious biases remained rife, and they cut both ways.

In truth, within that town, only at the clothing factory did a level playing field appear to exist – The Great Man's policy an adamant, 'We hire anyone regardless of colour or creed,' and his take on IQ a not dissimilar, 'Second-class brains and first-class attitude tops the reverse every time.' A pity that he would never run for Prime Minister. Although okay, his hell-sent speech impediment would have made pitching to voters dreadfully problematic.

Considering the district's healthy population though, was it odd only two aspirants went for this job the boy had landed? Not at all. Proofreading involved nightshift, along with a starting salary lower than a taipan's tum. Economy booming, better qualified juvenile job-seekers had more attractive and lucrative professions to aim for – and even higher prospects if able to provide three references each as excellent as the other. Yeah, bloody right, so why would Myxo Davidson, mature man in a responsible position, besmirch some kid who, occasional unruliness aside, had given him no truly valid reason to do this? Worse, to lie to the boy that he'd done otherwise…? What a lousy bastard!

No surprise that, 'Up you, Myxo, you dirty prick!' came to the boy's mind, together with a few choicer expletives, as he departed the newspaper offices. Yet otherwise, a feeling of stepping onto a magic carpet. Employment obtained – ripper! Almost as pleasing, this meant avoiding dole application and interrogation by the Social Services Gestapo. Relieved indeed, he hastened home on his treadly.

Once inside house around 3 pm, and this a work day Monday? Yeah, neither parent there with whom to share the glad tidings. 'Right, let's head to the jetties,' he urged his workforce-bound self, for how severely might his leisure time soon be lessened? A couple of rods grabbed and strapped bike, remounted this got. For like, how good to be dining that evening on fresh-caught bream as he promised his folks what ripping reportage he would produce in the newspaper game once he progressed from being a humble proof-reader? Nor would this boast be unrealistic. Once placement within true journalism was gained, any cadet worth his or her salt could aim for a posting to some exotic locale and rake-in big bucks as a foreign correspondent. And hey, even investigative reporting on home soil would be pretty neat.

Malvern Star parked riverside and favourite jetty strode onto, out flew hooks baited with green shrimp. Soon one rod bent. In came the first fat bream. Life was terrific, and only getting better. Ahhh, bewdy, you bloody bewdy!

Newspaper nightshift, what a different world! In expansive high-ceilinged Composing Room preparation for next morning's edition was well underway. A misnomer really, 'composing room', this space where compositors set the solidified type. The actual composing got done by journalists. Yet the name had been there for as long as newspapers existed.

Navigating the boy through all this fuss and bustle forged foreman Hal, displaying a stiffness of manner born of his former army major service. Another Free Mason too, like Mr Charles, and many of these other staff also. As for the newspaper itself, although townsfolk often disparaged it, no throwaway read: circulation went beyond main coastal hub into farming areas and communities for fifty miles around. Reportage concentrated on all district sports no matter how obscure, plus social happenings, local politics, do-gooder ladies' fundraisers, and so on. Mentioning every participant in these events ensured substantial sales.

Already Hal had explained to the boy that in producing their small broadsheet about fifty people were involved. Most appeared to be working in this astonishing open high-raftered space. On raised parallel benches were the galleys. In these, small lead blocks were manually arranged into squares that became the letters, words and sentences of each complete page. Such noise: talk, shouting, laughter, the clatter from a row of six massive and ultra-mechanical linotype machines... In these contraptions, out of pots holding molten metal, drifted a mild stink of the lead-zinc alloy which solidified into wordage.

For the boy, all so strange and stimulating. He felt relieved as well, for the exclusively male workforce seemed too busy to take much notice of a self-conscious newcomer. Because of this, introduction to this new newspaper caper was much less embarrassing than it might have been.

Hal carried on towards the far-end Proofreading Room. A separate cubbyhouse, this was where rough-inked paper sheets went to be checked for errors prior to the set type reaching printing press – after which came all those finished pages which might occasionally be preserved for posterity but more often wrapped next week's fish and chips, lit a wood fire, or, if scissored into squares, wiped someone's bum.

As their progress continued, the boy noted that though the compositors ignored him, an acute awareness of Hal existed. A straightlaced fellow for sure, the foreman, reserved and strict. Nevertheless, the boy knew he belonged to the Anglers Club. He'd someone here then with whom fishing might sometimes be talked... a favourable omen surely?

Less welcome was an abrupt realization by the boy when they reached the proof-readers' door. Shit and little fishes, just what had he got himself into?! An instinct for correct spelling he did have, but Tech English as preparation for distinguishing a pronoun from a past-participle, never mind a simple verb...? Not a hope! Of punctuation too he hadn't many clues. In fact, with such a shaky grasp of rudimentary syntax, how were complex grammatical errors to be rectified?

Hal's mitt making contact with Proofreading Room's door handle saw therefore severe doubt clout the boy. That the rectifying of journos' shite writing fell largely to sub-editors would be a later discovery, one of many newspapering aspects he'd learn along the way. Yet under-schooled and oft lacking in focus though he may have been, a moron he wasn't. To himself he insisted, 'Take it easy, it'll work out.' Which it would. In looking back on this portion of his life he'd find a compact goldmine from which to extract many valuable nuggets.

In-pushed Proofreading Room's door revealed a right-way-up vampire. Wearing a black suit and collar and tie, an oldish bloke hung from a rafter by his hands and arms. So, alright, not your inverted bona fide fanged blood-sucker, 'Quick, quick' gasped this florid silver-maned fellow, 'put that chair back under my feet!' Swiftly done by Hal. The elderly chap got down and, massaging his chronic crook lower back, gulped, 'Thank goodness. I accidentally kicked it away.' He went on, in a flustered way, to explain that his lumbar region supposedly benefitted from such suspension.

Introductions were then made, the boy, in jeans and pullover and open-neck shirt a bit underdressed compared to chief reader Alby. The principal scanner of incoming proofs, these he then passed across desk for that individual seated opposite him to re-check. If corrections to some metal type in the grand room outside were required, until this occurred no go-ahead to print the relevant page would be given. Task a junior proof-reader was asked to perform then, amounted to a straightforward, if unexciting, one. Alby had outlined all this after Hal's departure. Taking it in, the boy anticipated that so long as his cock-ups were few, soon enough he'd be promoted out of this stuffy room and into the glamourous world of reporting.

A nervy pedantic fuss-about was Alby. Behind his back the Composing Room complement called him 'Our Old Woman'. Some said a horribly hen-pecked one too. It seemed a single chance to escape his shrew missus had come during World War Two when, already of mature-age, he volunteered to join the AIF. Fair play to him there then, for that took a bit of bottle. But maybe at the time, death seemed preferable to cohabiting with a scary spouse? Rather than shoot a gun however, as a clerk at Army headquarters Port Moresby, Alby had fired off missives about troop movements and supplies.

Of this overseas service, Alby blissfully reminisced that first night as he and the boy sat idle between incoming proofs. Albeit steadfastly eschewing crudity, most of his prattle concerned extra-marital escapades. Across desk would drift wistful disclosures such as, 'I kid you not, in Papua New Guinea those lovely dusky maidens can be relied upon to welcome a man with more than just open arms!' Which left the boy's still limited imagination tested. Thus distracted, this would result in some elementary spelling mistakes entering the following day's edition.

At supper room break around midnight, a couple of the compositors confidentially explained to the boy that Alby, when at war's end offered the chance to stay in the army up among Australia's amorous northern neighbours, he had instead 'done the gentlemanly thing' and returned to his misbegotten missus to spend every day since verbally beaten-up. What the boy also discovered while heating and then tucking into an alfoil covered chicken curry pre-prepared by his mum, was that at this long table occupied by munching and yacking full-grown males, that although sports such as footy, cricket, and even fishing got mentioned, sex featured as the most popular subject. From some of the more voluble, what bewildering and astounding declarations he heard too!

Also learned through the chit-chat was that besides Alby and Hal, the Composing Room's workforce comprised several other ex-servicemen, of whom one had experienced horrific D-Day action. Chuck Harvey operated the nearest linotype to the Proofreading Room. Of imposing height and bulk, he had been a rifleman with the first wave of Canadians who hit Juno Beach at Normandy on June 6th 1944. They'd been cut to pieces, a documentary about which the boy had once seen screened at the Liberty.

Later that first work week, taking a corrected proof over to Chuck at his linotype, the boy naively brought up the topic of D-Day. Chuck's response? A slight shake of head. The boy tried again, 'My dad was in the war as well, but y'know, he didn't do anything really dangerous like you.'

The big Canuk just kept studying which minor revisions he needed to make.

'He was in Burma,' the boy went on, 'Ever hear of that place?'

'Uh-huh,' responded Chuck. Without looking up from his keyboard, he went on typing out imprinted-in-lead sentences.

This wondrous newspaper environment, all such a learning experience... and yes, many memorable people earned a living within that large high white stonewalled structure. True characters occupied management, editing, advertising, reception, reporting and night-owl compositing sections. Also, in the building's bowels where the actual print press thundered.

And then there was Percy the photographer. Within his special den, in dark secrecy, this furtive fellow developed softcore pornographic sporting snaps – young ladies doing the splits in netball, or taking tennis tumbles which revealed more than just frilly knickers. Ordinarily their deviant shutterbug sold these pics as a side-income, yet as he did with the boy one evening, now and again he'd show younger employees some shots to widen their horizons.

Indeed though, an interesting and varied workforce produced that paper, no question. Among the compositors for example was a bloke who, as an apprentice printer, had been maimed by the juggernaut printing press itself. That plastic hand which resulted now enabled him to, with impunity, carry the hottest smoking blocks of lead-zinc sentences from linotypes over to galley.

As for the six linotype operators, aside from Chuck, three others were of note: length-of-spaghetti Lester trained a few borderline successful racehorses, Des, a diminutive forever-dying hypochondriac, consumed a hundred pharmaceutical pills every suppertime and yet as a footy umpire would go on to officiate in over five hundred games and not die until he'd turned ninety-nine… And then there was Andy.

Referred to by some as 'The Seal', a part-time abalone diver, Andy would influence the boy in crucial ways. At first however, the boy only knew him by reputation. Short and bald, a muscly bowling ball – several balls really considering his scone's roundness and a roundish rock-hard torso of bulging biceps and cantaloup calves – he otherwise had the cherubic appearance of a cheerful Buddha. This, stressed his workmates, was deceptive. A delightful fella, they agreed, except don't cross him, or worse, double-cross. Moreover, as one malevolent dingo who threatened his adored wife had found out, such behaviour might see someone go very close to dying.

Sure enough, promised those fellow workers, operate a linotype and work with words Andy might but, when necessary, his fists spoke volumes. A former professional boxer, fight, and frighteningly, he could. Therefore, to begin with, the boy waxed very wary of Andy.

The one workmate quickly and properly palled-up with was Snelly. An apprentice compositor, his large hooked hooter and

Beatles' haircut lent a resemblance to Ringo Starr. At seventeen, Snelly ranked as the paper's next youngest employee. A wild spirit of highest hyperactive crazy-mischievous spirits, no nastiness attached to him. Consequently, to find the boy increasingly in his space and attaching himself, Snelly did not treat this as an imposition. Besides, with nightshift came idle afternoons. Having a younger companion to whom he could introduce the pleasures of playing snooker in stale tobacco-stinky poolrooms, or at a similar-smelling TAB place bets when under-age, this sat right up Snelly's alley.

In the boy's otherwise awed opinion, Snelly's single negative was his complete disinterest in fishing. Nevertheless, as fishing for information and insights and new activities were the boy's priorities in these initial newspaper days, for the time being wetting a line had been substantially sidelined. And instead, whenever possible his revelatory questing especially saw him hanging around the Reporters Room. How fascinating these journos were!

To begin with the senior pair, sole female reporter the breastily impressive social columnist Irene 'Razor' Horne, and gruff blaspheming sports doyen Dorsal Burnett, were, accurately or not, rumoured outside their respective marriages to be 'an item'. Then there was rough Robbo Robertson, general news roundsman, whose other love involved catching and milking snakes of their venom for the CSIRO – a sideline to eventually see both his careers end when years later in far west Queensland he'd get snuffed out by a flighty king brown. Next place beside Robbo in the journo space belonged to effete enigma Mark 'Maggie' O'Duffy. Whilst nonchalantly via a long cigarette holder smoking Gauloises while he surveyed his completed copy, Maggie liked to give crocheting displays. His contrary overlay of being married with nine children did though, pretty much confuse everyone, and not just the paper's junior proof-reader.

Yet it was their rag's fifth reporter, 'Rooter' Randall, who most captured the boy's imagination. Rooter covered all police and court doings, and through this reputedly knew every local lady inclined to share her favours. Town tattle endowed him and his hood-down British racing-green MG with considerable renown as an inseparable copulation team. Controversial too however, he had over two hundred small red swastikas painted in neat rows on the MG's chassis. Zilch to do with anti-Semitism or Nazi-ism, of course, simply an ace fighter pilot's approach to tallying those conquests consummated in cramped sportscar cockpit.

Courtesy of that brief rear-seat entanglement with Sally Hill, the still amorously earthbound boy reckoned he could identify with Rooter. Sure, only just, but how about the chance to sit behind a typewriter at that expansive reporters' table and hear instructive first-hand coverage of this suave news-scribe's fabled parking bay successes? The boy began to crave elevation to cadet journalism. Initially his attitude to proofreading had been one of contentment. But sure enough, all that sizzling saucy conversation overheard within the confines of both reportage and composing sections was undermining this.

Oh yeah and oh dear, here he was, now so near to turning sixteen, and it seemed almost everyone around this workplace, not only Rooter Randall, had experienced horizontal adventuring except him. Acute the infiltration of frustration. How desperately he wished for some senior work colleague, be it linotype operator, compositor, printer, journo, even one of the cleaners, to impart accurate information on that specific activity, and even more importantly, suggest an effective strategy to ensure his participation.

As for the less complicated and gently convoluted pastime of angling, that he did know plenty about, yet rarely now ventured to his river. After a sleep following work nights, the boy had taken to attending afternoon snooker with Snelly. And then at weekends, cricket season again just underway, even if not as keenly he'd gone back to playing that. Nevertheless, when he did manage to get a line in the water, the familiar fulfilment returned. Contributing to this, if he'd given it any thought, might have been that fishing offered a respite from concupiscent chatter: nobody nearby casting out a baited monofilament ever seemed to speak about 'scoring', 'roaring horniness', 'boring one in', 'whoring', nor even of 'catching the clap'. They only talked about catching fish.

A scorching January 1967 day it had been. Now night, Composing Room's temperature not dropping, all windows in the north side of its great space had been raised wide-open. This however altered but infinitesimally the oven-like interior, linotypes' pots of melted metal contributing much to a popping thermometer. Meanwhile compositors placing hot type into paragraphs dripped their perspiration onto the galleys, and the Proofreading Room had long since turned into a sauna.

Small electric fan that Alby had thought to bring in only circulated the stifling atmosphere whilst blowing unsecured proofs onto the floor. Both proof-readers worked in just trousers and singlets. At last, just past two a.m. Hal threw open their door. Brandishing a single inked sheet, he uttered that sweetest, 'Right you are, chaps, that's the last one!'

Announced loud enough for all compositors outside to hear, from a sweating Snelly erupted, 'Huzzah!', a pet exultation picked up from some TV cartoon. Cats throw such maddies: off he tore along ink-stained wooden floor down aisle between galleys, right for an open window, and without hesitating, dived straight through it!

Now, that building had been erected in a former sandstone quarry. Its rear had a thirty-foot drop onto concrete carpark. Over Composing Room's always boisterous interior fell a hush.

Then a yelling bunch of workers, the boy included, rushed for the window. Down they stared, only to hear from above a cackled, 'I fooled youz, I fooled youz…' On roof, legs dangling over guttering, perched the manic grinning gymnastic Snelly. As he had secretly rehearsed, on outward leap a hand hooked behind guttering downpipe caused his body to swing in an arc and into a controlled collision with the wall. After which, up the pipe he'd shimmied.

Chuck spoke for just about everyone when, swivelling his neck to look upward, he hollered, 'Snelly, you're a goddamn fucking idiot!'

A certain linotyping diver most definitely agreed with Chuck's sentiments. As that final proof underwent its checking, into the small sweltering reading room came Andy with a proposition for the boy. 'Got a question for ya… How'd you like to start a part-time job tomorrow?' He meant as a sheller, shucking abalone for him. This was a task that Snelly had been performing whenever the sea turned suitable for diving, which the following day's forecast said it would be. 'Snelly's too erratic,' continued Andy, 'If something ever went wrong when I'm underwater, I can't rely on him.'

Okay, with accuracy this bald pocket-battleship of a bloke was regarded by his newspaper workmates as an ironman. Whenever ocean flattened, once his linotype shift finished, home Andy would go, grab three hours' sleep, and then spend most of the following day free-diving for mono-shelled abalone, before selling the meat to a local fishermen's co-op prior to showering away all sea salt and resuming his night-time toil.

As for Andy's sheller, their monetary reward? Pre value of abalone soaring, even the diver's earnings for arduous harvesting equated to peanuts. His sheller then, made little more than peanut shells. Previous year's introduced metric system decimal currency meant Andy's off-sider therefore got just five dollars for filling a king-size plastic garbage bin with shucked shellfish. Nevertheless, considering a junior proof-reader's dismal pay snuck in at fifty cents under twenty bucks, the boy jumped at this chance.

Although... what now about the out-of-window jumping Snelly? Wouldn't he, at the very least, be miffed re losing his extra income? To the boy's wary enquiry, Snelly only laughed, 'Bewdy, tomorrow I'm just gunna sleep an' sleep an' sleep,' before adding a sly, 'And you'll see, it ain't bloody easy.'

At first though, any easier this abalone caper could not have been. In his Kombi, arriving outside the boy's home at 9.30 a.m. sharp, Andy had collected still half-asleep junior proof-reader colleague, prior to motoring across town and continuing on down beyond town's close-to-coast golf club and onto lush grazing land lying in behind high sandy sandstone hills. There, parking between lesser river's lower reaches and those substantial tea-tree covered dunelike rises, Andy hauled on his thick wetsuit. After this, encumbered by heavy weight-belt and a packed rucksack containing mask, snorkel, fins, gloves, dive-knife, abalone iron and catch-bag, as well as snacks and drinks, he hiked away up a narrow loose-sanded and scrub-overgrown track. The boy followed, required to carry only one empty king-size plastic garbage bin. However, he too wore a small backpack holding his own basic dive gear, for until the first abalone were brought in, he was free to snorkel.

Over a broad elevated expanse of sand and broken sandstone they continued towards the seashore. Another day of extreme heat pending, the mercury had yet to soar. Highest point reached, southward from here stretched a panorama of flat ocean sapphire to horizon, and inshore a glorious mosaic of kelpy reefs. Marvellous, just marvellous! What luck to live in such a country! Or perhaps being lucky enough to have parents with the foresight to take a chance on coming here? The scene could be admired all the more because there'd hardly been a drop of sweat lost nor a laboured breath taken getting to this vantage point. As for Snelly's '…it ain't bloody easy,' the boy thought, 'What a lotta shit!' This was dead simple.

Once at shoreline's beach of coarse grains and shell fragments, outward they strode onto a dry sandstone shelf, its surface jaggy with sharp rock and pointed limpets. Referring to a series of washed-over rock shelves, Andy assured the boy, 'All those are thick with abalone.' But he wasn't there to mull such things over. Minutes meant money. Most of full kit fitted, over to shelf's edge the diver shifted. Seated there, he pulled on his fins, before, legs in water, shiny silver iron for levering-off the abalone gripped in one glove, mesh catch-bag held by other, he hesitated. 'You're gunna go for a snorkel before I bring in the first bag, right?' he said to the observing boy. Ab iron indicated a stretch of open water made inviting by an absence of ensnaring kelp. 'Well don't go near that section, cos there's a bad rip and its full of bloody big wobbegongs!' Mask spat into, Andy gave it a rinse, before asking, 'You do know how to snorkel properly, yeah?'

'I've done a bit,' admitted the boy.

'So, you're aware of the main do's and do nots…?'

The boy's uncertainty about diving in more turbulent blue water than he'd known previously must have shown. Though primed to get going and make moolah, Andy took time to deliver a condensed lecture on common-sense free-diving: don't hyperventilate and risk blacking-out, never fin under a ledge without first grasping its top and peering under to ascertain what awaits, refrain from stirring-up wobbegongs by encroaching on their territory, if bull-kelp wraps and entraps just relax and float out of it, 'And here's the best way to clear your ears and sinuses from pressure…'

Now sure, from going with Snappa and Titch the boy already had some dive nous. Also, he'd done a bit on his own. But this sound and concise advice from Andy he'd retain with tropical sea clarity and forever value. Finally, the dive veteran said, 'See that piece of reef over there? Ledge under it's usually got a big cray.' And then away he fast-finned, a muscle-torpedo surging straight outward and into a broad spread of kelp, where he jack-knifed, submerged, and began harvesting those mono-shelled black-lipped suction padded molluscs which in time he'd come to call 'slimy gold'.

If a fun dive was to be had, the boy needed to extract his digit. Andy would take no more than a half-hour to fill his first bag. Mask, fins and gloves on, in just shorts and T-shirt the boy slipped into the water. Yoooof! Some contrast to that now rising heat, sea an icy cocoon. Enough abalone shucking bucks saved, and, 'I'll be buying a wetsuit,' he promised himself, before snorkelling across to that spot Andy had suggested. A duck-dive revealed, sure enough... under a shallow ledge lay a large cray. Easily grabbed too. Ripper, be finest dining in the family home that evening! Crayfish or lobster, whatever people wished to call them, never did such delicacies appear on the plates of Glasgow's impoverished. His parents sure did love what a by now Australianised father described in Scottish Strine as, 'Och, braw luxury tucker!'

Yet as a prize, the crustacean came a poor second to what, much later in the day lay glistening and round on the flat surface of that modified paint-scraper used to shuck each abalone. A mass of high rock occupied one side of the reef shelf, and in its shade the boy had by now shelled hundreds of molluscs. Until this moment though, none had held a pearl. Not just that, but a *pink* one. What an overwhelming thrill!

Andy had just swum in too, dragging a last loaded catch-bag with him. Holding the pea-sized pearl in one sea-washed palm, 'They are really, really rare,' he responded, 'First one that's ever come out of any of my abalone, I'll tell ya that... Ha-ha, you're a bit of an arsey young bastard.'

Ahhh, as already the boy had been told. Sequestering pink pearl inside a squelchy glove, the boy put it away inside his backpack, decades distant yet that day when he'd have a dolphin brooch made featuring this pearl as its eye, a twenty-first birthday gift for a special daughter.

Diver and sheller now got stuck into shucking that final catch. Filled to brim garbage bin then had excess juice exuded from the abalone meat drained out and its lid clipped on. After this, packs swung onto backs, black wetsuited Andy one side and the boy the other, bin handles were gripped. 'Lift!' the diver man's command. Done. Jesus, the weight! Short years since his balls had properly dropped, the boy feared they'd just plummeted further, onto that flat spiky sandstone on which he stood. Any chance he'd get to dwell on this though? Nil. 'March!' came the follow-up order.

Off they moved, laboriously, stumblingly, late afternoon temperature still scorching, bearing between them a slopping almost ninety-kilogram load which sure wasn't going to lighten any during ascent of that shifting sand ahead tilting steep-upwards from brief narrow shell-gritty beach which abutted the reef. Only more torture could follow. Hollowly now in the boy's head echoed Snelly's '…you'll see, it ain't bloody easy,'.

Not only did the boy have to agree, he reckoned it quite some understatement. Finally, fin-al-leeeee, at towering unstable dune's apex one ligament-straining fifteen minutes later, 'Down!' commanded Andy, by now every drop of seawater on skin under his neoprene covering transformed to sweat. Rest, a brief one, taken. Knackered young sheller studied phlegmatic diver. That baldness, the moonlike mush, the short stature… Andy sure did resemble a nuggety Buddha. Even more to the fore this comparison, when came the counsel, 'You've gotta treat this as a Zen exercise, lad. Pain, you ignore. You store it in the back of your brain. Concentrate only on the end-gain.' Those immense capacity free-diver's lungs then drew in huge breath. 'Now, once more, let's go. Lift!… March!'…

That night, fresher than if he'd lain all day on a couch, Andy tapped away on his linotype. In Proofreading Room, fatigue saw the boy falling asleep over stories and advertisements he ought to have been checking for flaws. An exasperated Alby admonished him that such behaviour could lead to dismissal. Yet the crisp fiver in his young colleague's hip pocket served as an assurance no heed needed to be taken of elderly fusspots. Advice the boy really ought to have absorbed however, had been Andy's as they travelled homeward: 'Listen, young fella, buy an abalone licence. There'll be real money in this one day.'

During supper break that night, observing Andy, something occurred to the boy. During all the usual prurient patter bandied about in those near to midnight meal breaks, although customarily garrulous, whenever the blokey talk turned risqué, he quietened. A conscientious family man with two kids and devoted to his wife, boudoir banter did not interest him. Such matters he considered to be private. Never therefore, would Andy further the boy's ever keener quest for useful revelations about society's oldest entertainment. That first abalone getting day, the only remotely sexual sentence the super-diver had uttered was when urging the buying of an ab licence. He had added that Asians regarded the shellfish as an extremely delicious aphrodisiac, which guaranteed their market value would inevitably explode.

Back in the Proofreading Room, making no effort to stifle a huge yawn as the eyes of a frowning Alby were drawn towards him, 'What if Andy's right?' thought the boy. Ought he to, if decent bucks really were one day to be had from ab diving, get a licence? Zombie-like, onto their lead-based spike he plonked the latest perused proof. Nah, geez, so little dough in abalone currently, and a proof-reader underling's pay so meagre, how dumb to blow those same five bucks earned that day shucking, and in such gut-busting haulage, on a virtually worthless permit to gather what on the Australian seafood market had the reputation of being almost inedible.

My, my, my, yes-oh-yes, five chickenshit dollars only licences to dive for abalone cost in 1967. Not even Andy though, could have foreseen exactly how sky-high prices for this precious wild catch would go, or the cost of fees to legally harvest these then shoot to almost unaffordable levels, nor that as a consequence he and his financially shrewd, extraordinarily savvy wife, would some years later shift from their modest suburban home into a swankiest of penthouse apartments overlooking the boy's revered river and its bridge.

Another different aspect to Andy, along with his not being interested in risqué repartee, was being another of those odd people not at all into fishing. It seemed he'd just never picked up a rod and line. Perhaps as a diver however, and long before the boy did, he had discovered how matey fish became when unthreatened, and thereby preferred to be as one with the sea's creatures rather than killing them... abalone excepted.

Canny with a quid though, was Andy, no doubting that. Never did he join others from the Composing Room when, duties done early, they'd kick off one of those euchre schools in the supper space. Yes, the very moment in building's bowels that the newspaper's actual print-run started up, often out would come a deck of playing cards. Not that had he stayed Andy would have risked losing much moolah. Always small stakes only were played for, thus ensuring cool tempers and humorous banter prevailed during all games.

Snelly however, was Andy's polar opposite. Their apprentice compositor loved any sort of punt. Nor did Snelly have much trouble convincing the boy to participate in a euchre game whenever heavy swells would, as normally they did, prevent Andy diving the next day. Just the same, delays to anticipated card games sometimes came without warning.

Main disrupter of planned euchre get-togethers was the arrival of jovial Jack Guyett when some inconsiderate local punter had chosen to cark post-midnight. The town's preeminent undertaker, Jack always required that parking space be found in the paper for his late death notices. A warm personality, the only cold aspect to anything associated with Jack was the blue light he burned at night on the streetfront of his nearby premises, which sent a chill up the boy's spine whenever in frigid wet darkness he'd happened to cycle past it.

Otherwise, forever good for a joke or a humorous yarn, Jack was the bloke most citizens wished to be planted by. He fitted neatly in with something the boy's father had once said he admired about the Australian character: 'Aussies aye know how tae bury their dead,' which at the time his old man made this remark, and for too long after, the son didn't realize how many good mates his father also had helped bury in Burmese jungle soil. As for that all-Aussie approach of 'bury 'em, booze up, and then bloody-well get on with life', the father saw this stemming from the high mortality rate of pioneering days. If so, if would be a practical attitude that later generations of Australians, almost obsessed with endless maudlin remembrances, would lose.

Jack Guyett however, he was old school... albeit hardly throwing a knees-up either in arranging his grave-bound corteges. On interment day, like all accomplished funeral directors, Jack could stage a performance of such sombreness he'd have cracked a Hollywood Best Supporting Actor Oscar. Oh, but that street-fronting funeral home of his and its death-blue light...? If cycling homeward in 4 a.m. darkness from an after-work euchre school, how diligently the boy learned to avoid riding by it. The visual chill didn't just reduce his residual card games enjoyment, it dramatically diluted too, another unique pleasure. Yeah, breathing air redolent from the central bakery's fresh loaves! As delicious as hits to the senses go is smelling crispy oven-new bread in a dewy pre-sunrise atmosphere.

Those post-work euchre get-togethers though, under Snelly's influence a keen interest in gambling was slowly growing. Dealer's deft shuffling of deck, the slick flicking of cards casually accurate as Old Ron casting a lure, ever more stimulating the boy found this. The main attraction lay in gaining extra income. Stakes low, okay, not a lot to be got. Aiding his monetary accumulation however, the boy tended to be lucky. And, whenever dealt a jacks-full hand, he'd again hear a chuckled, 'Arsey young bastard.'

In regard to this, the boy couldn't but agree some truth applied. Drawing your first breath in a peaceful picturesque town surrounded by stream and sea wasn't a bad start. Then there were scant health issues, those big fish he'd bagged, the finding of that pink pearl, landing a job correcting grammar and spelling when lacking the qualifications normally required to make this obtainable... He might too have seen that having loving parents who mostly treated him like the sun shone out of that very arse of his, also amounted to great good fortune. But definitely, in general, how firm his luckiness stuck. So much for being born on a Friday the Thirteenth, eh?

One problem: regardless of birth dates, few who believe they are indeed blessed with arsey luck aren't poised to come a harsh cropper. Therefore, even when ambling along an apparently innocuous trail such as playing ten-cent euchre, upon it awaits that virulent bug ever-ready to deliver its infectious bite to the potential gambling addict.

Nothing contributes more to nightshift workers getting hooked on punting than dismal afternoons of persistent drizzle. The Scots call such damp days 'dreich'. On this particular one, although inclined to wet a line off jetty or bridge, the boy found himself drawn, as often he now was, to Snelly's house.

2 a.m. beginning-of-winter finish at work had been followed until 3.30 a.m. by euchre. This meant, once home, the boy had slept until midday. A good kip therefore enjoyed, followed by consumption of sandwiches left for him by one continuing-in-receptionist-employment mum, daisy-fresh he then donned a waterproof jacket, jumped aboard treadly, and spray issuing from tyres, speeded towards Snelly's abode.

Snelly's war widow mum rented his indoor bedrooms to boarders. This caused her exuberant son to inhabit a musty backyard bungalow. But cosy and quiet, it suited an apprentice worker who might not get home until dawn. Loved his dreamland too, did Snelly. As often before, the boy arrived to find him snoring. No hassle. While his damp clothes steamed dryish, the boy sat silent in funky bungalow's dim dank interior, and waited. Surrounding him were tacked-up posters of rock bands and, rather than those Playboy centrespreads featuring in most young bachelors' rooms, pin-ups of sexy racehorses.

Soon enough, the boy knew, there'd be a sharp fart, a throwing back of bedclothes, and Snelly would leap upright like a galloper after an amphetamine injection. A natural drug propelled Snelly though, the gambling bug's toxin. Impetus to arise usually had association with an urgency to reach Totalizator Agency Board building before betting on a chosen race closed. Inevitably, influenced by Snelly, the boy had begun to dabble in such punting too. Only fifty cents here however, fifty there... yeah-yeah, merely an interest.

Today's smelly Snelly fart came loud as ever but the wait in ejecting himself from cot was even briefer than usual. While rain plapped on upon bungalow's rusty tin roof, he dressed fast. After this, briskly on foot, the pair of lads set off for their TAB. A line of cloud-nudging Norfolk Island pines occupied both sides of this particular street. Beneath these dripping giants the two newspaper night-shifters now broke into a jog, anxious to reach the town's legal gambling den in time to wager. Lean Lester their small-time racehorse trainer linotyper had tipped one of his hayburners in that afternoon's bush race meeting. Snelly, holding tight in hand tan-coloured envelope containing his weekly pay collected only the day before, had resolved to place every cent of it on this one horserace.

Like cantering thoroughbreds, the pair of them rounded corner at main thoroughfare's bottom-end pub, and in the unabating rain paced even hastier. Uphill they ran until veranda protection allowed them to slow, but only a bit. They passed a café, its wily proprietor frying onions to entice drunks whose alcohol enhanced appetites might urge them in, as if drawn on an unbreakable game-fishing line by the hotplate aroma which hit them that moment they left any one of the long principal street's four hotels.

No hesitation for the two young jogging cobbers though. On, they progressed, going by an army disposals store, then fashion and butcher and cosmetic and chemist shops, and also one specializing in assorted sports equipment run by ex-army commando Stan McPhee. Highly eccentric and incredibly fit, Stan was a man before his time, eating seaweed extracts, wearing his grey hair in a long, plaited pigtail. As a lone-wolf scuba enthusiast he had dived dangerous deep cliff-side waters to find the remains of the Shipwreck Coast's most famous clipper, and would go on living riskily until, decades later, at the age of eighty-three, he'd be knocked off his racing bike and killed whilst training for a triathlon.

Speeding along too, continued Snelly and the boy. Pace once more increased, conversation came in broken breaths. Almost before he knew it the lad had agreed that he also would place his whole wage packet on linotyping Lester's thoroughbred, convinced as he'd been by Snelly's insistence that the animal's history of lameness meant they would get '...mate, just fantastic odds!'

Warnings against gambling excess were hardly needed within the TAB. As a deterrent, intending punters had only to note those seedy-looking types who hung around this establishment. Damp fag in one mitt, crumpled red-pen defaced racing form in other, they'd mooch around with bums out of trousers which in the clothing factory many years before had been proudly scissored to measure in the Cutting Room by the boy's dad and his skilled tailors.

Perhaps those prideless punters in their threadbare once-swish strides registered with the boy. Otherwise, why else did he hedge his bet? Blindly going to the same betting window where Snelly had placed his total pay on the nose of Lester's nag, self-assurance that his arsey luck would once more deliver, flagged. What spilled from one suddenly clear-eyed boy was, 'Twenty bucks for a... um, no, make that a place please, on...' and he gave the scrawny cashmere sweatered hair-in-curlers lady behind her grill the horse's name.

What mocking too, he copped from Snelly. 'Bloody idiot, you're gunna win bugger-all now!' But done, and so, wagering on the race closed, no again changing bet. Therefore, what horror when caller Bill Collins had Lester's hayburner five lengths in front at the home turn. Snelly, simmering with evil mirth, settled his gaze on the boy... for a further one, two, three, four, hoof pounding seconds, when linotyping Lester's horse broke down and by a short half-head limped, and only just, into third place.

Snelly would be broke for a week. As for the boy's place-bet? Those days TAB's displayed no odds. Not until collecting his winnings did the fact smack that he'd risked his entire week's wage to pocket a princely fifty cents. It cured the boy for life of ever again placing a hefty bet. Not Snelly though, not a hope. He only laughed, 'Ha-ha, what a bastard, ay!... Come on, you're the one with the money, your shout for a game of pool.'

Freddy Thompson's dusty downtown mildew-spotted nine-table billiard parlour attracted within its stained walls many of those types who frequented the TAB. However, a mix of others – truckies, lawyers, teachers, tradies, coppers, and such like – also fronted its barnlike interior to play on the knocked-about green felt tables. Also, occasionally, came the same two sassy sexy chicks of eighteen or nineteen. Sauntering in for a game, always caked with more makeup than a corpse in an open coffin, lower clothing the tightest jeans or shortest skirts, pouting provocatively after chalking cues, lining up shots they'd bend over table far longer than any male player ever did. Oh yes, on razzle-dazzle display alright!

Hoo, and those bug-eyed middle-aged players standing around... had their engorged thoughts been Four n' Twenty pies they'd have choked gnawing on them! Not that, in the boy, the sporadic appearances of these tantalizing vamps brought forth a markedly different reaction to the older attendees. It also reminded him that since his fleeting post-footy fumble with Sally Hill, no opportunity to engage in that longed-for contact of the closest kind had materialized.

Ouch, ultra-pally Sally, and what might have been...? Sometimes, bedded down after nightshift, drifting dreams still featured softest warmest flesh and coldest hardest HD Holden back seat vinyl... and *Pretty Peach* perfume! At first, he'd wake almost replete with a compulsion to, as a psychological purgative, go fishing. And fast! The difference now was that rather than angling offering a solid diversion, the company of Snelly could be sought.

Almost ultimate distraction the apprentice compositor provided too, through his jaunty mannerisms and ecstatic good-humour. Just like as at this moment, chuckling away while he extracted overused cues from stacked rack and, rolling them on a felted table, checked their straightness. Infectious, was Snelly's ebullience. The boy reckoned himself mightily fortunate to have such a blithe older brother type to knock around with. A year nearer in age, and here might have been that closest of mates he'd always wanted. Then again, sometimes Snelly acted more like the younger one, despite being only a month off eighteen.

Another odd thing about Snelly, despite at an age where the average male's mind-stage is thick with foxy chicks... sure, he'd show interest in some passing girl, perhaps even grin a, 'Geez, she was pretty,' once the feminine figure carried on out of earshot. But pumping red-blooded passion? That, Snelly reserved for punting. And in the poolroom, should there be money on a game, the presence of those two dollybird teasers would never distract him. Importantly, this day too, for on one of such inclemency, pool games involving proper moolah might well be got going.

Not that Snelly exhibited lots of skill with a cue. Exuberant manic energy carried his play. Simply, he provided a wonderful entertaining spectacle, although if getting on a roll, he did have the capability to pot ball after consecutive ball. Yet okay, mostly erraticism ruled. So much so that a suspended ban hung over Snelly's head. Ever again rip his cue tip through one of the precious green-felt table coverings and Freddy Thompson's chucker-out would do just that with a well-placed toecap up one young compositor's clacker.

How much heavier, the rain, in the half-hour since they'd left that TAB. Outside it now bucketed. Best possible place in town then, to while away an afternoon, was this poolroom. In such weather too, those two tightly and lightly attired young ladies would be a no-show. All participants could concentrate on purely playing. And alright, in some respects the absence of that pair of pets being regrettable to him, the boy reckoned this did bode well for his snooker application. Even a few trickiest of shots leading up to potting black might be managed... if he could also shut out the jocular stirring which would surely be coming from sources other than Snelly. Some other familiar faces had begun to turn up.

Many fellow newspaper night toilers were lawn bowls devotees. Workhours, always there'd be someone in an aisle twixt galleys demonstrating a draw-shot or some similar finessing play. Today many of these blokes, their afternoon greens competition washed-out, were trickling into the billiard parlour. Indeed, more and more arrived, shaking droplets from umbrellas and overcoats – almost a man flood. So many, it all but ensured that Snelly and the boy could ditch all notion of playing snooker.

'Righto-righto, who's game for a game of Kelly?' came the cry from parlour proprietor Freddy Thompson. Striding to main pocketed table he vigorously shook a leather bottle in which rattled marbles of different numbers. Not strictly legal, but money sure got played for in that poolroom. 'C'mon all youz poor half-drowned bowls buggers,' he shouted, 'whaddaya reckon, ay-eeee? Let's start us a proper ripper ring-a-ding game going!' An obnoxious little shite shaped a bit like a lumpy spud, Freddy was a loud-mouthed one-time carnival spruiker. An antagonizer, his misaligned noggin would have got punched-in on a regular basis had he not employed that hulking standover heavy whose bulk now occupied, the boy observed, the room's dripping doorway.

Due to Kelly Pool schools always involving dollars, only Freddy organized them. Stakes weren't all that high, but by staging numerous games and taking fifty percent of the kitty – at a few bucks entry per participant, and fifteen players involved – he did quite well. That nasty-arse bouncer ensured no would-be Welcher stole away without payment, and that disagreements over cheating... well, they just weren't going to happen.

As around chosen table gathered the newspaper nightshift mob, Freddy readied to dole out starting order marbles. The boy, although able to play with more consistency than Snelly, paid for his older mate's participation. Better to let him take up a cue for the two of them. An impetuous banger of balls Snelly certainly was, but if, *if* he got into a groove, he seldom missed. Therefore, fair enough, good forward thinking. It just had one flaw.

Those newspaper staff assembled included Chuck Harvey the linotyping Canuk. Playing order drawn via Freddy's out-tossed marbles, who drew first whack at those multi-coloured balls but their lumberjack-like former World War Two footslogger workmate. Chalking-up and then cracking in, look back Chuck did not. Entire table cleared with dead-eye dexterity, no-one else got a look-in.

Snelly, aware the boy wasn't about to shout him another go, declared, 'Stuff it, I'm goin' home to get some more sleep.'

The boy however, awed by Chuck's sharp-shooting, lingered. Twice more the big Canadian won before stepping away to let others play. Over to the grizzly bear dimensioned linotyper went the boy to, too familiarly, slap his back, and enthuse, 'That was brilliant, Chuck. Mate, you must've been a fantastic shot in the army!'

Response a Rockies-hard look, 'Get this straight, sonny,' growled Chuck, 'until you graduate from wet-behind-the-ears university, to you I am Mister Harvey. Ya got that?'

'Er, sure Mister uh... Harvey,' replied the boy, now appreciative that between some humans there did exist a great gulf to them being equals.

'As for my ability as a marksman?' Chuck gave off a sort of gravelly gargle, 'We were well trained.' Replacing cue in rack, back over his shoulder he then said, 'Told me one time your dad was a soldier too, right?'

'I...? I might have, yeah.'

'So, what sorta shot is he?'

'Alright I suppose.' The boy thought for a second, remembered the tiger snake incident, but decided not to mention it. 'Like, at shooting rabbits I mean... I reckon he never got involved in any real hairy stuff like you did.'

'I did, did I?'

'Um, these blokes say so,' said the boy, directing his thumb to the Kelly Pooling others from the Composing Room and Print Press section.

'They do, huh?' Chuck jingled those winnings filling his pocket. 'You mighta also mentioned your dad served in Burma, yuh?'

The boy couldn't exactly recall saying this either, but confirmed it.

'Mmn, so okay young feller, you and me we're outa here, and we are going up to the pub, where I will buy you a shandy, and we will have ourselves a serious talk.'

In their passing through doorway and out into a wet mucky lane, the boy detected the bouncer's respectful regard for Chuck. Once on street proper, a hastening along rain-spattered pavement took them by the Capitol Theatre to that nearest hotel. Once inside, over a couple of jars at its classical bar's far end, one very serious one-way talk took place. Nor was Chuck a man anyone, let alone a still very unworldly teenager, could refuse to listen to. Heavy raindrops went on pelting down as the boy collected his bike from beside Snelly's bungalow. Inside lay one re-zonked out mate, but he had no mind to disturb him anyhow. Wow, that been quite a talking-to from Chuck! Mounting Malvern Star and pedalling out onto wet tar, the boy was still trying to process what he'd been told. Aiming front wheel east, he peered along the puddled and rain-pocked Norfolk Island pines lined road. A stiff following wind on this sodden cycle home would be a small consolation. He still felt somewhat shaken by Chuck's uncompromising lecture.

Soon enough the boy entered a cold empty late afternoon house. Another hour before any work-weary parental company would arrive, he ditched wet apparel before switching on electric fire – upon arriving home his fatigued folks would appreciate a little heat. He then took a hot shower, got himself changed into warm clothes for that night's proofreading, and only after this went to the lounge bookshelf. Out from a swag of close-packed tomes he coaxed that battered bug-chewed Bawley Guesthouse book Reg had slipped his way, *Burma 1941-45.*

Could it be those previous months of reading proofs had made for a more trained eye? This time, absorb the reportage on those frayed pages the boy most certainly did. No less pedestrian the writing, but mid-teens lad now reached a man's understanding. A bayonet thrust of appreciation entered as to what appalling conditions that Fourteenth Army of mixed British and Commonwealth forces had fought in. Also, to a decent degree, an understanding re the sheer savagery of the fighting. Yet when ex-soldier father arrived home and asked, 'Aye son, and so how was ye'r day?', all the boy could find to reply was, 'Dunno, dad, pretty ordinary I suppose.'

And as at kitchen stove the mother prepared her husband and son their evening meal, in the lounge the boy found himself unable to even allude to what he so wanted to say. The expectation, as he re-read the Burma book, that he'd now see his father as a battle-hardened emotionally damaged frontline veteran and be able to speak with him about all that, had come to nothing. Instead, over from him sat this same passive Scottish accented, hopeless-at-Aussie-sports, soft-cloth tailor. Would the appropriate moment ever come when, rather than his son instigating it, this dad might himself open up about Burma, and thus bring on a bonding response, swinging wide that door almost always closed between them?

Was it fully strange that despite removal of some scales from the boy's seeing, empathy between he and his father should continue every bit as awkward – a still looking sideways by one in wondering about the other? Or are such situations just part of the underexplored ocean that too often separates fathers and sons? Had the boy but realized it would take three more decades for his old man, by then genuinely elderly, to finally speak of his traumatic war, might the sixteen-year-old have, on that dreich southern coastal day, indulged in some verbal fishing, and at the very least jagged a few telling disclosures? Perhaps, but unlikely. Some things in life are like special wines, better left, beneficially or otherwise, a long time untouched.

Too many more years of uneasy and uneven affection will pass between father and son before that wartime bottle is opened. Except maybe in determination, they are one pair of very different individuals. Always closer to his mother in temperament, the boy, mutual their understanding, seldom uncomfortable together, reinforcement of loving feelings unnecessary. Of the three of them though, the one real distinction is probably that, when moved to do something, the mum is even more resolute than both of her males.

The parents' Gold Coast retirement apartment it will be, same location where a year earlier the father had thrown full light on the beginnings of his tailoring apprenticeship, when finally, circumstances combine to extract that Burmese cork...

It is an early Queensland morning. The boy, now a tall robust man, and his age-diminished father, have set out to fish. Then, as they stand side by side casting for bream off Currumbin bridge, the old bloke is hit with a massive coronary. Should kill him. Doesn't – that residual Glasgow slum upbringing and Burma battlefield toughness. The son, foot flat to the floor as he speeds toward Tweed Hospital, listens to strangled sounds the father makes lying slumped across the back seat of his first ever new vehicle. Of all makes, a Datsun, after a lifetime adamant he'd never buy anything Japanese.

Faster than the once famous Fangio drives the grown son. From that space behind him comes a whine of automatic window's descent. On an in-rush of air to aid failing heart, there follows too, a sucking of oxygen into the ageing Scottish lungs. Fighting-for-life father has started to take those same deep existence-affirming breaths he'd draw on misty bushland mornings when they all camped by a Grampians mountain-top lake. Scrambled thoughts come to the son. There is so much he ought to have, but hadn't, asked his father, never mind the most important thing of all he'd failed to tell him.

After hospitalization however, months later, a miraculous recovery. There is even amusement in this upstanding elderly father cutting out a lifetime's self- censorship to drop occasional expletives: he has concluded that as appreciation of gentlemanly behaviour no longer exists, and all of society seems to be blaspheming, 'Christ, Ah may as effing-well dae it tae.' Albeit yeah, sometimes he still hedges at saying that magic word out aloud.

And the boy as man, what joy he gets as well in seeing his old dad's unbridled glee after the doctor's nod that a wee single-malt or three may be gargled. Thereafter, Scotch whisky will also act as a lever to release lived-through battlefield horrors from the jungles of Burma and north-eastern India.

One pink cloud evening, picture window's outlook the Palm Beach sands and distant Surfers Paradise beachside glitter strip, in bright white-walled retirement apartment's kitchen the mother is engaging in her usual magnificent meal preparation, whilst out in the living room father and son are jawing away. They have been getting along well, some beach walks, fishing again, this closeness maybe aided by an absent sister's distance. Always so precious to the father, but now estranged from them all, that his daughter could not bring herself to visit him in Intensive Care has caused deep hurt.

Regardless of whatever is contributing to it however, in this seaside setting the elder and younger male pair are getting along swimmingly. Yet those standard frictions are once more set to surface...

Oh, och aye, deny the cathartic but often hair-trigger effects of imbibing Scotland's peaty truth serum no-one should. Drams comfortably clutched, father seated in his favourite armchair and son standing, the Datsun's effectiveness as an ambulance for conveying the old bloke to Gold Coast Emergency is mentioned. '...But y'know dad,' says its driver of that dramatic day, 'why after decades of refusing to have anything to do with Japanese stuff, did you finally go and buy a Japanese car?'

Scant thought the father gives. 'Ah jist decided the time had come tae bury the hatchet,' he says, adding with the most Scottish of smiles, 'And besides, the price... it was an awfi good deal.'

From his laughing lad the father now hears, 'Aw, you silly old bastard. You could have been getting bargains like that for the last forty fucking years!'

Jocularly said, but unfortunately the aged individual, a smidgen effected by Highland firewater and therefore interpreting disrespect, takes exception. Glassy glare precedes careful placement of tumbler on upholstered chair's arm. The creaky Glasgow frame rises upright, and smaller much older man approaches towering broad-shouldered son. Once close, he stops, glances upward, shuffle-sets his feet, slightly dips one shoulder...

'Jesus,' realizes the son, 'he's going to chuck a left-hook at me!' Bearhug implemented is immediate and maintained. Into the ageing lug is whispered, 'Stop it, you old bugger, you took that all the wrong way...' Which is when at last the father hears his boy declare, 'I love you, dad! I love you, mate!'

An arrow of overwhelming affection enters two hearts. The father had many times indicated as much to his boy, but without really saying it either. They separate. 'Aye, me too, son,' he replies. Tears fill both sets of eyes.

After returning to the southern coast the boy will relate this close-to-disastrous confrontation to a friend, and in response receive a horrified, 'Your own father was going to punch you? That's awful!' Yet he'll tell her, more chuffed he could not be, reckoning his dad's reaction an absolute corker, the Scotch-misted misinterpretation understandable. 'Don't you see,' he'll say, 'at his age, having the balls to take a crack at a disrespectful son who's forty years younger and twice his size...? Meg, that's brilliant!'

Meanwhile, the half-a-lifetime-overdue bonding results in more than simply an overwhelming gladdening for both. Also, into that part of the father wherein secrets are secured, a key has been inserted. What the unlocking needs is no more than the pouring of two further drams, before the boy, this the now grown into middle-age visitor son, ventures, 'Look dad, something's always puzzled me. Why stay so bitter about the Japs? After all, you were trying to kill them as much as they were trying to kill you?'

Two solid sips of Caledonia's finest it takes, after which the father says quietly, 'Ye see, we... at one stage, aye, we'd... we had tae retreat, so fast we needed tae leave oor wounded behind in a field hospital. Then when we counter-attacked...' A brief clearing of throat. 'All thae fellas...? We found all those fellas had been bayoneted tae death in their beds.' Another pensive tasting, and a solid swallowing. 'Aye son, there are some things ye cannae forget, and that ye jist cannae forgive.'

Opened now though, are the flood-gates to a disclosive gush, albeit speed and quantity of words issuing have almost as much to do with the certainty that at any moment the mother will call, 'Hie you pair in there, stop ye'r blethering and come and eat!' But definitely, a psychological dam wall of fifty years has broken. In the father's retelling of certain horrific events there is no bravura, only a reconstruction of physically and mentally destructive encounters. All these however, lead to one specific incident.

At times, says the father, masses of fanatical attackers had been faced, but none of these battles ever left the scar of a single isolated ambush. Jungle track, just him and another bloke, the father armed on this occasion with only a Lee-Enfield .303, his pal gripping a Sten. Three infiltrating Japanese infantry approach... Sten gun takes out the right-hand pair of soldiers, the father's rifle that Nippon officer to the left. When searched, as had to be done, the dead young officer's pockets hold only a photo – of a wife with a baby in her arms, '...aboot the same age as ye'r sister then was. Ah was never sae devastated in mah life...' A handkerchief produced, eyes dabbed, nose emphatically blown. 'As ye can see, son, Ah still am.'

What it can take to make a full understanding. Here had been a civilian tailor turned soldier, thrown into jungle warfare's steaming chaos and killings. So many things he had been compelled to endure and to do when all he'd known previously was the neat concrete and soot-stained stone of a tough enough, but orderly, peacetime Scottish city. And then too, the grown boy had his explanation as to the significance of that war souvenir which now rested, mounted on a carved teak base, upon Palm Beach apartment's immaculately clean mantlepiece: not a 'samurai' sword but a standard military issue *shingunto* which once belonged to one young Japanese officer.

When snake catching senior journalist Robbo scored a position to cover sport for the Melbourne Sun, open for one young proof-reader swung that Reporters Room portal. Through it walked the boy. 'Just in time, too,' he keenly appreciated, settling into his allotted spot behind a too-used unfamiliar cast-iron typewriter. But proofreading had become boring, a repetitive chore. Although unsure of what other work may have been available for inadequately educated youths of sixteen, he'd nonetheless been set to jack-in his stalled newspaper career. Now, bewdy, enthusiasm again reigned! Engrained in his B-movie influenced brain were those actors portraying wise-cracking action-man hacks on the Liberty and Capitol theatre screens. He'd attended matinees primarily to swap comics, but no worries, Hollywood's flickering hard-bitten journo jocks had also, like limpets to a sea-washed rock, stuck in his psyche.

Still, the road of the boy's transition to journalism was not to be all smooth. Corrugations included exclusion from Composing Room camaraderie. When raised with foreman Hal, the ex-AIF major explained, 'It's like us in the Army, we didn't mix with the Airforce or Navy. Nothing personal, you're just no longer one of our mob.' Yet in saying this, oddly Hal waxed friendlier than when he'd been an immediate boss.

Less so those Composing Room others though. Not unfriendly, yet plainly the newest reporter no longer belonged to their specialized throng, the nightshift team. Regrettably too, the only one whose attitude probably wouldn't have altered was gone. Snelly had scored a job with the daily NT News in Darwin. Soon to marry, he'd have a couple of kids, and then an off-road mishap involving a hoon driver, and perhaps his own irrepressible irresponsibility, would see their paper's loveable larrikin die leaving behind those two children and a wife pregnant with twins.

That roughish reporters' road however... for the boy a further wee pothole appeared when summoned to the editorial den of his new superior. In nearly unbreathable air, cigar-puffing Clarrie Cruikshank sat behind an ink-stained desk covered in scattered pens and paperclips and spiked proofs. To one side a wastebasket overspilled with discarded copy, snotty tissues, soppy stogies, burnt matches, and an empty port bottle. Clarrie's famously gravel larynx clarified the cadet reporter's duties: 'Our amoeba must earn his stripes, yer get me...?'

Clarrie went on to instruct the boy he could forget court reporting and sport, never mind any chance to do crusading or investigative journalism. In short, no earth-shattering stories would he break. As amoebas, cadets covered, he said, congenial Country Women's Association tea parties, carpet bowls contests, town council sewerage improvements, cattle prices at the saleyards, and other ho-hummery. All up, a tarnishing and trashing here of one journalistic dream. Rather than a brimful of fun future, the boy once more perceived his foreseeable employment shaping as dim-to-grim. Clarrie's dismissal of him carried with it a solitary instruction on reportage, the only one he'd ever get. 'Keep your sentences short!'

Dinkum learning on the job was rural journalism. Along with this came an expectation that shorthand and typing too were to be self-taught. At one time the paper had paid for these skills to be picked up at night-school, thereby also offering its amoebas opportunities of close proximity to winsome trainee secretaries. However, a requirement to cut costs had arisen. Regarding this, senior reporters reckoned the buck stopped squarely at Mister Charles.

Indeed, undeniably baboon's arse ugly, their vintage Managing Director. But his position bestowed massive influence in that town. Therefore, like many repulsive men able to exercise power, according to reliable Reporters Room scuttlebutt this had attracted an attractive mistress. Not a young one though. 'Mature,' Mark Maggie O'Duffy assured, 'An astoundingly well-preserved pensioner.' But high-maintenance, and the news-rag's economy drive was all about their mangle-mushed boss striving to keep his not-so-secret love entanglement extant.

The boy, now not too far himself from the adult world's cusp, figured that was how things went in it. He shuddered however at the thought of their gargoyle-like boss-cocky participating in any boudoir business, shadowy though to him the specific moves therein continued to be. Certainly, he had no wish to contemplate even a foggy template of Mister Charles 'on the job'. He did concede however, 'Good luck to the old ram, he's scoring heaps more than I bloody am.' Not that the randy old bugger would have needed to be getting much of whatever the boy reckoned it all entailed. Indeed, and oh dear, if tyro journo here's newspaper journey wasn't exactly waxing rosy, in the would-be Romeo stakes he was faring far worse: *Here lies a cadet reporter, died a sinless virgin* not the epitaph desired. Yet accurate should his life-chips be cashed-in at present.

Such concerns aside, the boy did accept he needed to give journalism a fair dinkum go. In the first place, a focus on actual reportage process would be required, regardless of how mundane the subject for coverage. Essential then, that there be a shift of mindset from his desire to jump straight into dapper Rooter Randall's stylish shoes simply as a segue to activities vastly different from news gathering. Yeah, and he could erase also that amusing notion of fast-tracking advancement to those racier assignments. Not that slipping strychnine into their bedroom bandicoot crime roundsman's cuppa of locally manufactured instant was actually on. Besides which, as their mellow fellow scribe Maggie O'Duffy had cautioned Rooter, 'You're too greedy, darling, and some day you'll impregnate one. There's many a slip when dipping it in.'

The boy guessed that Maggie, comprehensively confusing but nevertheless the father of nine nippers, had to know what he was talking about. So, should their virile newshound put a bun in one of his too many girlfriends' ovens...? Yep, a quick elopement in British racing-green MG, and yippee, vacancy on the crime beat! And who to fill it? Only one able overheated cadet, chomping at the bit to meet all those shady ladies who came with that same journalistic territory. Oh, to be fully cognisant though, as to what all that shadiness entailed.

Uh, but hang on, hang on... he'd promised in himself to shelve focus on that smutty stuff? Workday energies were to be directed at becoming a conscientious cadet, right? Bloody right! Dedication, dinkum dedication, young sport. The trouble was, the boy simply idolized Rooter Randall. Eject this journo jock from his amoeba consciousness? Impossible.

Chatting with the bloke whenever opportunity arose had quickly become a habit. In one instance, as a means to properly pick the senior reporter's brain re naughty nitty-gritty, the boy proposed that they might go fishing together. But this only ascertained the senior journo's aversion to any association with angling. For Rooter, ever going near the main river only meant conveying a lady passenger over the bridge in his MG late at night, parking in the hidden tea-treed lovers' lane of that sandy dune and midden country behind the Blue Hole his aim.

Cunning angling angle a dud then, so far as gathering those elusive bona fide facts of life and involvement therein, the boy reassessed his best journalistic approach to obtaining these leads. Yes, smarter to, while in those Reporters Room confines compiling copy about the town's mundanities, chill-out a bit and bide his time. Their hyperactive senior newshound's nous re the pastime of passion could be absorbed by diligent eavesdropping. Besides, opportunities to directly fish for such info would arise naturally... such as this particular arvo, Rooter banging away on his Remington as he covered the latest carnal knowledge hearing before their County Court, but then taking a Nescafé and cigarette break.

At the speed of Superman as a cub reporter leaping on a lead, in beside Rooter the boy jumped, pumping him with questions on the racier aspects of his current courtroom case. As well, he fast ran past his distracted smoking and sipping senior colleague, lubricious revelations acquired via Tech school tattle and salacious anecdotes acquired in the Composing Room's euchre playing supper space.

All a fishing to try and hook hard facts. The boy understood most of his bonking related babble contained uncountable inaccuracies. His main hope was this man-of-the-world might just be of a mind this time, to put him straight about misconceptions and deliver concrete information about the path to grasping that paramount holy grail – what this specifically entailed, and more importantly, what to do once one's hands were on it. Yet what came back, after the retelling of some compositor's outrageous cocksmanship, was the single tart remark, 'Not even a professional contortionist could do that, kid.'

What, in fact, the boy failed to appreciate was this: his A-grade journo idol was a serious reporter first, a leisure-time lothario second. Rooter had a true passion for concise writing. He took his craft very, very seriously. In hammering out his copy he desired not to be hounded by some probing puppy desperate to put that richest of icing on an incipient manhood. Essentially though, a polite fellow, Rooter tried by ever-longer lapses in responding, to deliver one clear message – that an amoeba's newsroom place played out as two-fingered tapping away relaying onto a carbon-copy backed page the most boring local happenings, and not to sit yapping at his senior colleagues.

Some adolescents though, too desperate for knowledge about the aesthetics of athletic entwinement, will just drop the ball when handpassed a hint. Following early Friday evening, the boy grabbed what he saw as another chance to pester Rooter. But this time, their ace amorously accomplished journo, a long and trying day in court behind him, lost patience. 'Listen, kid,' he snapped, 'stop with the shagging interrogation. Piss off and find out for yourself just like I had to, okay?' Punching out a report on saucy divorce court proceedings, but diverted by the boy's chatter, Rooter had stuffed up his last paragraph. Ripping typed sheet from Remington and scrunching it into a ball, he pinged this at the boy's scone.

Now, although aggravated, Rooter's chucking of his crumpled copy had been playful. The boy was crestfallen however, at their hotshot reporter's rebuff. More so too, because this apparent shining avenue to achieving the ultimate had ended up as a dull cul-de-sac. Yet as he returned to his own typewriter, he did appreciate that valuable titbits had indeed been picked up via the guy, and by inserting these into other salacious assertions, accurate or not, he had got a slightly better handle on how to bring to fruition his aspiration of indulging in that magical panting passionate tussle-for-two.

Aiding in such understanding of late had also been, outside of work, picking up not fishing rods but steamy novels. Penned by notorious smut scribes, far from finest writing and definitely no aid to his journalism, but as further learning... oh yes! Up for that apex challenge the boy at last pretty much felt. Ho-ho, bloody oath, his kingdom for another Holden HD Special backseat chance! But one, two, three, such chances do quickly pass. Even if next footy season he joined Red Rovers fulltime, alas and alack, how slack even apparently firm certainties can become. A recent 'shotgun wedding' to Red Rover's ruck-rover had seen an end to Sally's dalliances.

Disheartening, all so disheartening to a continuing non-starter... The boy resumed his task of tapping out a few paragraphs on the pennant bowls competition that Clarrie Cruikshank expected him to somehow make entertaining. Not helping was his mind being elsewhere. In truth, when it came to sex, all rural Australian youth were in those days occupying the same upright uptight boat. Opportunities for mattress pressing adventures were painfully thin – emphasis on painful, in the most sensitive bodily region. Or anyway, so the status quo appeared to the boy and most of his local age group. What they remained unaware of was a strain of change had begun to build in their town's salty mid-1960's air. In, on a fresh zephyr, was drifting the sexual revolution.

7 pm, and the hero-worshipped Rooter had driven home in his MG, to spruce up before picking up Peggy Sue, Lindy Lou, or whichever other quick-peeler sheila he had his sights on that night. This being week's end, and their contributions for Saturday edition done, all other journalistic staff had shot through too. Only the boy occupied the typewriters and butts-filled ashtrays adorned table, expected for another hour to field incoming calls... such as this one. Shifting to stale cigarette scented space's far end, he answered ringing wall phone, 'Hello, Reporters Room...'

As he did, foreman Hal, in to start that night's Composing Room stint, poked his noodle through the door. The boy had been barking up a wrong tree about Rooter becoming his grand font for acquiring carnal knowledge, but he'd been correct to detect that since his proofreading period ended, Hal's attitude had altered to one of amiability. Despite this ex-boss's proclivity for angling, he had been unapproachable on subjects piscatorial. Now however, as the boy's journo duties finished and Hal's nightshift ones began, the foreman would pop in to deliver a daily river report... which this he would again, once the boy finished with his phone call.

Yet until that chat with Hal could happen, a listening, listening, listening exercise this was, along with an untidy jotting, jotting, jotting down of details. Finally the boy sighed an impatient, 'Yes, yes, alright, alright...' Yet every time he offered assurance into the Bakelite mouthpiece, he'd once more be interrupted by this insistent aggravating caller. In the end, 'Hang on, wait, look lady... um yes, madam, I promise you, it will definitely be in tomorrow's paper, okay, yep, good? Fine!' Without suffering any additional adamant instruction from this tedious woman, back on wall fixture went the phone. Unbelievable! Imagine insisting her Red Cross stall fundraiser had precedence over all other events that weekend? Just bloody ridiculous! Shaking his head, the boy grinned at his former Composing Room superior, 'How's it going, Hal?'

'Mulloway!' exclaimed the foreman.

'Eh? Where?'

'Shoal's in. Caught two off the bridge this arvo.'

'Jesus, how big?'

'Twelve pounder and a ten pounder.' Sure enough, metric had replaced imperial, but how much bigger fish sounded in poundage. 'Going to have a go?' asked Hal.

'You better bloody know I am!' responded the boy. And, forgetting all about Red Cross fundraisers run by annoying blue-rinse matrons, aside his writing pad and pen were pushed.

On was a Hubert Opperman flat-chat towards hillside home, goal to grab cane rods along with those cut-mullet baits which happened to be keeping company with the bacon in kitchen's fridge-freezer, and then shoot off to the bridge. Just the same, for a junior reporter to have promised a particular caller prime coverage for her charitable project yet fail to write a syllable about it? Ooooh, not very professional! When too, what sounded on the dog and bone to be just some nagging old boiler is actually the volatile paramour of one mangle-mushed Managing Director, that is no way to gain journalistic promotion either, or indeed, to guarantee continued employment in the newspaper caper.

Hal's mulloway tip-off had fallen at September's start, and not in the heart of March, that month Julius Caesar copped his whack. Yet the ancient Romans did have *Ides* in September too. Fair enough though, those oldie Italians didn't have telephones on which promises made to amorously energetic elderly sheilas could go unwisely undelivered. However, like Nino Culotta, they did go fishing. Might skiving off to do so have jeopardized the jobs of a few who did? And what about being beware of overconfidence that they'd catch a bagful?

Past 11 pm, and one soon-to-be-sacked cadet reporter angler had been three hours now without a bite. An element of change, if perhaps not exactly portent, did lie somewhere in the new spring night air, no argument about that. In following a run of baitfish, entry into main river of these mulloway had been unusually early. Whenever such a shoal showed up, they either hung around the estuary zone a fair while, or else rapidly roamed on up into the furthest salt infused reaches and stayed there for months feeding and fattening. The boy had begun to reckon that shoot straight on through upriver this current mob of mulloway must have done. The darkness concealed many other disappointed fishos lining the bridge railing, none of whom had got a touch either. Fisher numbers were beginning to thin.

By that Friday's midnight, stationed in customary spot east of archway, the boy had his beloved bridge and river all to himself. Even honking hoon Holdens had ceased to hammer across. Nor did any likelihood exist his father might cruise through for a bit of boozy post-pub banter. Mother had put her foot down about end-of-factory-week wassailing. And fair play to the old man. He'd pulled on the handbrake, taking now just a couple of beers with his Cutting Room cobbers before going home to an assuredly peaceful atmosphere. And yeah, these days what a truly comfortable affectionate relationship the pair of them shared.

Standing between his two canes, elbows in place upon top railing, the boy occupied himself by thinking about footy. 'Bloody right, an ounce of luck, and instead of wasting my night here fishing...' Yep, he might have been sleeping in preparation for tomorrow's Under-17's semi-final. Despite leaving school he'd been eligible to keep playing with the Tech side. Percentage-wise, one more goal kicked during the season and they'd have made the finals. A good season personally though. Red Rovers had made a tempting offer for him to join them next year. Uh-huh, earning extra dollars on the sporting field? Even with cute close-to-carnivorous Sally wedded and no longer in circulation, how enthralling the attraction to boot footballs as a professional!

Had the boy appreciated the imminence of a 'former cadet journalist' tag he'd have appreciated this massively more. Flame of kero lantern adjusted lower, his thinking shifted back to fishing. Despite dearth of bites, an upbeat attitude arose. Not another soul left on bridge, 'Perfect,' he told himself, 'stray mulloway around, only one bloke's going to catch it.' And if not that, a huge blue-nosed black bream might venture out from under the coral-caked piles to, overcome with hunger, swallow a sumptuous slice of mullet on a big long-shank Mustad hook.

His father's infinite patience when angling the boy did not have. Yet he too could quite contentedly go fishless for hours. Tonight, if encouraged by even one touch, possibly he'd stay on until Saturday daybreak. Not only didn't he have a footy game tomorrow, and no Sunday paper, not a workday either, he'd plenty enough eats to keep him going. As could be relied upon, and which until her dying day always would apply, his mum had seen to it that her 'big son' wasn't likely to go hungry. Cheese and ham and lettuce sangers large enough to choke a groper had been packed. And yeah, ever since he joined the adult workforce, she'd taken to referring to him as, 'Mah big son.'

The boy checked his slack line. Still unshifted. Catching or no though, sure, why not stay on till dawn? Glorious mild bright night, Milky Way aglow, only slightest northerly blowing... discomfort nil. More hours of just wishing for a passing fish not an issue. Too easy this, simply leaning on top railing assailed by no concerns other than maybe of uninspiring journalism's grind. Oh alright, and an inability to find some elusive audacious uninhibited girlfriend... But staring up, gee, just look at those unfathomable stars!

Ahhh, the universe? Too much to comprehend for the minor mind of a young angler or even the brightest one of some astrophysicist. Even Einstein. All he could do too, really, was marvel. But alright, 'Yeah, be nice to get a bite,' decided the boy. Then again, really, did he care, for how grouse was this! Uh-huh, and occasional skreeking of disturbed plover aside, the finest aspect to it was this starry canopied river world's quietude, the sheer reassuring peace of...

*CLUNK!*

The dull heavy sound rose from below bridge's road level. A series of muffled human mutterings followed. Then louder declarations, all obscene. Raising lantern and turning wick up, the boy peered downward. Upon the rippling inky water, a rocky rowboat contained two shadowy and stumbling figures. Light breeze had served to bring hired clinker drifting downstream to bash against the coral-corseted ironwood pilings. A powerful torch beam flashed upward into the boy's face. A familiar voice said his name.

'Uh, Snappa?' half-guessed the boy.

'Yeah-yeah-yeah, it's me an' Titch,' came the thick throaty confirmation.

'Yeah, shit, fuck mate, Jeeeesus, we're totally pissed,' announced Titch.

'Yair, pissed as fuckin' farts.'

'We musta flaked.'

'Pretty awake now but ay?... Geez, I'm so-o-o-o pissed!'

'Hang on a minnie, we'll row into the bank an' come on up.'

The boy wanted to say, 'No, no, don't bother!' But too late. Bugger it, the last development required or desired this night was these two never quite really close mates, unmet again since that final school day, arriving at his bridge in a rented rowboat. Not only did this now mean putting up with drunken antics, the noise already generated would have scared away any lingering mulloway.

Boat one of Sir Fuckface's clinker fleet, Snappa's torch staying on allowed its uncoordinated progress to be followed. Seated side-by-side, each on an oar, its occupants were sculling with absolute ineptitude. Not unlike a nervy brown trout's tail, bow of clinker jerked one way and then the other, while its stern behaved in an opposite manner. Out over that weaving transom poked two game-rods fitted with huge geared reels more suitable for marlin than mulloway.

A violent rocking sent several empty mega-size Fosters Lager oilcans rolling about abruptly tilting deck-boards. Across the water came a roared, 'Sit still, ya silly bastard!' from Snappa.

'Me? *Me…*?' laughed the always unperturbable Titch, 'you're the bloody twit that keeps friggin' shifting!'

Cackles issued from both. Rollicking rowing resumed. The rolling oilcan empties continued to clank about, whilst thrown torchlight spotlit a large esky filled with still more big Fosters tinnies, all uncracked. Since getting plastered and chundering post his Red Rovers game, the boy had sometimes again imbibed, but moderately. Despite opportunities nowadays to participate in that finest of journalistic traditions, the liquid lunch, he'd held to such moderation. Yet so much undrunk grog there in that clinker up for grabs…? Licking lips, attitude toward these intruding cobbers underwent abrupt improvement. 'Yeah,' he said to himself, 'I wouldn't say no to a beer.'

And here they came, these underage larrikins, and those beers. Fishing gear left behind in beached rowboat, on weaving approach along bridge, cheerily chiacking and bawling friendly blasphemies in the boy's direction, they bore between them the refreshments-loaded esky. Deposited on roadway upon arrival at archway… *cracko!-cracko!-cracko!*… three royal blue gold-lettered oilcans of liquid amber got opened.

After this, Snappa and Titch began to really talk. Aiming to become teachers, both were continuing their high schooling. There, where fishing had been seen as uncool in the extreme, attitudes, they said, had changed after some paparazzi sprung

Mick Jagger fly-casting for salmon. 'Now every dude at school is into it,' averred Snappa with a mild slur. Making a big show of bringing up an oesophagus oyster, he spat over the railing.

Titch followed suit. 'Yeah, now nothing's cooler than fishing,' he agreed, wiping lips on his sleeve.

Presumably the Rolling Stones were pretty adept at launching green gobbies too.

The boy took another guzzle of lager. No way he'd look this gift horse in its north and south, and yet, these two cobbers still being students...? 'All this grog must've set you back a bit?' he wondered.

'Aaah well see, me brother's working in the bottle shop at the Cally,' Titch, less booze tolerant than Snappa, slurred thickly, going on to guarantee any time the boy wanted to join them for a piss-up, free Fosters would always be available. '...least till me dopey brother gets the sack or whacked in jail,' he chortled.

By second oilcan's emptying, bites or no bites, the boy reckoned fishing had hardly ever felt better. What really hooked him however, wasn't rising intoxication but Snappa and Titch's jocular talk of debauchery. It drew him in like...? A perch enticed by a tasty bait? More your bloke beckoned to by some languorous lover folding back her black satin sheets... even if that invitee continued to be less than one hundred percent sure of what to do next. The high schooler pair's casual boasting made one thing clear though: since last seen, their girls-associated questing had involved comprehensive exploration. Suddenly, the last thing on the boy's mind were mulloway.

'Like y'know, last Friday night,' bragged Snappa, nonchalantly pulling out a packet of Rothmans, 'we were at this disco, see, and you wouldn't believe all these stunner chicks... Knockouts, man. Knockouts!' Pinching filter-tipped fag from flip-top box and flicking it between his lips, he then offered another to Titch, who with alacrity picked one out. The boy also selected a filtered coffin nail, albeit less eagerly. A non-smoker, and due to sporting pursuits never to get hooked on the habit, circumstances here meant he couldn't be a piker.

Snappa, in bringing lighter flame to all three ciggies, explained the discotheque he'd mentioned had been a fortnightly rage staged riverside in that grand hangar-like boatshed once owned by Bill's family, the tough little dad's dodgy heart causing a shift up onto the Murray to run a less strenuous houseboat business. Yet, those current boatshed disco nights...? On-shore night winds wafting in through the boy's bedroom window carried their blaring rock music. However, temptation to, under darkness's cover, sneak down for a peek at the shimmying and twisting pelvis-to-pelvis action had never been acted on.

'Heapsa chicks going there you'd know too,' prompted Titch, 'Remember Dinger and Popsy?'

Impossible not to. Fishing fully forgotten, the only casting by the boy that of his mind back to riveting tall and short duo in mini-est of mini-skirts.

'On The Pill now, see,' continued a Cheshire Cat grinning Titch, 'and mate, they're doing it with everyone!'

'Yair, oodles of other chicks're into it as well,' enthused Snappa. 'Like, half the sheilas in our class've gone all-the-way this year!'

The gobsmacked boy could only listen, cough carcinogens, and in rising excitement, more tightly grip his oilcan. Needless to ask either Snappa or Titch if they'd actually 'done the deed'. The salivating way both spoke said it all. Geez, what a bastard to have been instead, a Tech attendee! Proficiency in technical drawing? High school studies would've progressed to practical application in a subject immeasurably more interesting than that.

'So hey,' jumped in Titch, 'whatcha doing next Friday when it's on again?'

'You mean the boatshed disco?' understood the boy.

'Yair, yair, it's every fortnight, right?' reminded Snappa. 'Like, come with us, an' no way you'll miss out. Jesus, ya can't!' After thus insisting, he down-throated the dregs from another tinny before nonchalantly tossing it into the river, flicking ciggy butt after it, and then picking up and cracking a fresh oilcan.

Now, hyper-excited though the boy had at this juncture become, something punctured his focusing on those ultimate fleshly pleasures. This was none other than his rudimentary – and soon to be redundant – journalistic instinct. Pushing aside all this promised highschooler promiscuity, he probed, 'So um, y'know like, The Pill, how come it's so available all of a sudden?' Ha, well, explained Snappa, this relatively revolutionary yet hard-for-rural-teen-set-to-get medicinal had become available via an enlightened GP whose three frisky daughters attended the High. This clear-sighted physician wished, said Titch, to prevent not just unwanted pregnancies in his own offspring but to also stop their girlfriends becoming mothers too-young.

Wow, if ever one grass-green hack had a golden opportunity! For a briefest moment the boy saw himself writing that scandalous break-through exposé, entrée to a future career with the Melbourne *Truth*! But no, the notion swamped in an ocean of doubt. A couple of newsman traits he may have acquired, but never would he possess the cold carotids of a true investigative journo. Therefore, no impediment to that most decent GP sensibly providing those essential prescriptions would appear in print... even when such a story might have prevented his sacking. Inevitably, the town's conservative anti-contraceptives element would hound the good doctor out of their district. Until they did though, he'd be free to continue with his exemplary deeds.

By three a.m. every Fosters oilcan had been gargled dry. Fish remained uncaught of course, but at least the boy had finally got his irrepressible but imprudent pals to stop tossing their empties into his river. They on the other hand easily convinced him to accompany them to that next waterfront disco. Mightily slurred and blurry farewells taking place, arrangements for the following Friday were locked-in. They'd meet behind the Caledonian Hotel for a few freebie beers courtesy of Titch's brother, before, suitably fortified, grabbing a cab to the riverside dance scene and its sizzling high school teeners.

Shoulder hard against archway, the leaning boy watched his two now closest and best-est, if *unsteadiest*, cobbers depart, esky of rattling empties grasped between discombobulated bodies, swaying away along the bridge roadway. Far-end streetlight's low glow then bestowed a dim illumination of the pair stumbling, prior to tumbling down embankment and falling into a cackling clanging river's edge heap. Next, rising to feet, and loose cans kicked around, beached rowboat got shoved afloat before they clambered in, and with flailing oars, and leaving a weaving phosphorescent trail, one precarious return voyage to Sir Fuckface's boatshed commenced.

Baited lines still in the water, the boy saw no reason for not seeing-in the sunrise. Resumption of some peace might still see one lonesome mulloway come his way. Straightening and leaning elbows on top railing, he struck a familiar pose to further observe his mates' radical meanders. They'd had a head-start in the drunkenness stakes, but he sure had caught them up. Yeah, he felt rinsed alright. Bike ride homeward would be anything but straight. Glowing though, his mood. In pit of stomach alcohol reservoir fuelled exhilarated anticipation similar to, inch by inch, monofilament slipping through the fingers as a big fish took up slack. Delicious nervousness about described it.

Before Snappa and Titch had left, all of them taking a final leak through railings into river, the pair had promised they would personally see to it that the boy scored at that boatshed disco, practically harmonizing, 'Mate, aaaw mate, no worries, we'll make it a dead cert, man. No way you ain't gunna get your end away!'

Crikey, next Friday's arrival, yeah, forget about chasing fish. A bloke was set to become hooked on that greatest natural drug of them all, and to cast away forever further innocence about this intoxicating practice so intensely associated with procreativity!

Clinker returned to its moorings, those wayward mates had long since been two distant black dots departing from a riverside effected by reflected cemetery lights dapple-dancing on the water. Alcohol impaired uncoordinated boy reeled in. Clumsily he de-baited. Yet, in preparing to walk off down along the bridge for a maladroit mounting of his two-wheeled steed, his brain cleared sufficiently to further appreciate the profundity of this pending change. About a week from now, if all went smoothly, it would not be a Malvern Star he'd be throwing his leg over but a warm body. Or, to employ a euphemistic analogy one tailoring dad may have used, transition from wearing shorts to climbing into a pair of long trousers would be on.

Meantime, home-time, and no waiting to see the sun rise, for there'd be none. During the wee a.m. hours cloud in the west had crept across to blanket the heavens. Eastern sky turning light grey, picking up all his gear and then skirting bridge's trail of railings, the boy arrived at his bike. Tying trusty canes to its crossbar he thought about how much this going from youth to more or less manhood might alter him. First and main difference, he guessed, would concern fishing. To waste hours and energy gathering baits and awaiting a strike when another enthralling activity could be pursued with barely more preparation than a shower, shave, and a splash of Brut? Yep, he reckoned his days as a fisher on this river were pretty much done!

As first sparrow fart starter angler's car approached, unsteadily readying to mount bike frame and settle upon saddle, the boy's attention went to the rippled waters extending upriver. Past the jetties and boathouses to that first bend he gazed. Around this and out of sight lay the pumping station, beyond it the Mile Post, Bay of Biscay, The Place, then The Hole from which his father pulled that ripper perch. Further on still were those runs fished with Old Ron. 'But,' he thought, 'yeah, this really is me finished with all that.' How primed he felt, emphatically, to accomplish what all creatures, from amoebas to fish to human beings, do that first time in their lives, and to hook into its pleasures and wonders. Fair enough it was therefore, to harbour more than a strongest suspicion that a passion for angling would slip into massive decline, if not vanish forever.

And all but end, the boy's fishing outings did. Yet just now and again, somewhere in the world, out would go his bait or lure or far more rarely, even a dry or wet fly. Decades were to pass however before one day, after half a lifetime of long absences from his home town, the bridge would be once more experiencing the tread of an elderly angler as, slowly, he walked to its centre arch. Holding a single cane rod with centrepin reel attached, he cast out, and then, elbows now a little more brittle, but as familiarly as ever, he settled them on the top railing.

Returned to the district to live out his retirement, by this time a few far-flung adult children bore his genes. One daughter in particular precious, no surprise though, even she and he weren't as close as either might have desired. Otherwise, most of those folk this grey-haired man had loved existed only as memories. His parents were long dead, their combined ashes, as asked of him, scattered half in Australia and half upon Loch Lomond. Gone as well were the grandmas and family friends he'd been close to such as Franz and Elsa and Old Ron and Reg. A couple of truly good women smart enough to give him the slip had also tripped on that eternal rainbow. And then there were those special blokes from the footy field who'd snuck away to their celestial MCG, cobbers that, if finding himself trapped in a vicious hacking pack, always protected his back.

Over sixty years since he could accurately have been called a boy, peering upstream from bridge middle the ageing man's mind meandered. Yes, there'd been great mates, along with special people who had loved him unconditionally, perhaps even one or two that still did. Yet after everything, what remained was not someone, but something, a body of water which never had taken and continued to give. Until he'd no longer be able to stand here with fishing rod in hand, his cherished river would do just this. That alone was enough reason to hear himself say, 'Why did I ever leave you?'